RISING PASSION

"Aren't you carrying this macho Tarzan and Jane routine a little too far?" she hissed.

"Under normal circumstances, I wouldn't be reacting this way. But these aren't ordinary circumstances, Kelly. As long as we're stranded on this island, we're back to survival of the fittest. And I'm damn well going to survive. If you'll let me, I'll see that you do, too."

"Said the spider to the fly. Why me?"

He chuckled softly. "You're beautiful, and you know it. But I also want to protect you, Kelly. There's just something about you . . . something infinitely feminine, soft, warm. And those green eyes combined with that tail of copper hair—you remind me of a long, lean marmalade cat. I want to stroke you and hear you purr."

Kelly swallowed. Hard. Her tongue crept out to wet lips gone dry. "If anyone could do it, you could," she allowed.

His sharp golden eyes zeroed in on her mouth. "Not just anyone, Kelly. I want it to be me. Only me . . ."

She met his mouth halfway, her hands delving into his dark hair to hold his head to hers. Fire leapt between them. . . .

Praise for Catherine Hart's *Charmed:*

"Takes lucky readers on a wondrous journey. *Charmed* combines magic, history, and romance into a most enthralling read."—*Romantic Times*

"A good story . . . bold and audacious."

—*Publishers Weekly*

ROMANCE FROM ROSANNE BITTNER

CARESS   (0-8217-3791-0, $5.99)

FULL CIRCLE   (0-8217-4711-8, $5.99)

SHAMELESS   (0-8217-4056-3, $5.99)

SIOUX SPLENDOR   (0-8217-5157-3, $4.99)

UNFORGETTABLE   (0-8217-4423-2, $5.50)

TEXAS EMBRACE   (0-8217-5625-7, $5.99)

UNTIL TOMORROW   (0-8217-5064-X, $5.99)

HORIZONS

Catherine Hart

Zebra Books
Kensington Publishing Corp.

http://www.zebrabooks.com

ZEBRA BOOKS are published by

Kensington Publishing Corp.
850 Third Avenue
New York, NY 10022

First Printing: September, 1997
10 9 8 7 6 5 4 3 2 1

Printed in the United States of America

*I dedicate this book to all the faithful fans who
followed me from historical romance to contemporary.
Thanks for being so loyal!*

*And to Bob, with love and gratitude for being such
a wonderful sweetheart. And to my friends and family,
who helped out, if only by honoring my crazy schedule.*

Chapter 1

Kelly Kennedy stashed her carry-on in the overhead compartment and settled into her seat with a sigh. It was going to be a long flight from New Zealand back to the U.S., and hopefully a quiet one. With any luck she'd sleep most of the way.

She was exhausted—physically, emotionally, and mentally drained. The past few months had been a hell she never wanted to relive, fraught with one traumatic event after another. In the midst of trying to launch her newest beauty-and-fitness boutique in Australia, the third in a fledgling chain, she'd been forced to deal with a messy divorce. Three weeks ago, with the ink not yet dry on the divorce petition, she'd flown from Phoenix to Sydney, leaving the smoldering ashes of her marriage behind her, hoping to find some sort of relief from all the heartache and anger.

It hadn't worked out that way. Simply fleeing the scene of the disaster hadn't been enough. Even with all that distance, and the rigors of getting the new store ready to open, of ironing out last-minute problems, she'd kept bumping up against the residue of her failed marriage. The wounds were too fresh yet, and would take time to heal. Mentally, rationally, she knew that. Emotionally, she kept hoping for a miracle cure, some type of super-injection that would jerk her off of this endless, energy-robbing treadmill of misery and rage, recriminations and tears.

But for now, it was back to Phoenix, via Auckland, Hawaii, and San Francisco—back to sorting out the strange mix of his-and-her friends, relatives, and acquaintances that were arising in the wake of the impending divorce. Back to listening to well-intentioned advice she didn't want to hear. Back to attempting to adjust to the role of the single female after five years of playing doubles. God! It was simply too wearisome to contemplate!

She was staring out the small, dingy window, trying to muster the energy to buckle her seatbelt, when a strident voice at her elbow claimed her attention—and everyone else's.

"Seat four A! That is what my ticket says! This woman is in my seat! I demand that you make her move!"

Kelly looked up, recognized the indignant pain-in-the-ass Mexican starlet, and gave an inward groan. Geez! Once life decided to dump on you, it just wouldn't quit!

"Miss Gomez, please understand," the harried airline attendant said, "when a person doesn't arrive prior to half an hour before boarding, his or her seat is allotted to someone else. Especially in the case of an unconfirmed reservation, such as yours. If you read the instructions with your ticket, you should have been aware of this. There are seats at the rear of the plane. . . ."

"No!" Alita Gomez stamped her spike heel in demonstration of her ire. "I paid for first class, and that is what I will have! How dare you think you can treat me this way!

Me! I could cause you to lose your measly little job with a mere snap of my fingers! Do you know this?''

Kelly was in a lousy mood at the moment herself, and Miss Hot-to-Trot was the last straw. ''I didn't think it was possible to snap your fingers with nails that long and weighted with that many layers of enamel,'' she piped up, drawing Alita's regard back to her. ''You might not want to chance it. Those claws of yours might break off all the way back to your wrist.''

''Oh, it's you!'' Alita sneered. ''The manager of that hole-in-the-door beauty salon at the hotel. I cannot imagine why such a highly rated hotel would allow you to set up your shabby little shop there.''

Kelly smirked back. ''Probably because it's such a treat to annoy snobbish clientele such as you, and it's not a hole-in-the-*wall* salon.''

''Well, you won't last long,'' Alita predicted airily. ''Whoever heard of combining a fitness center, a beauty salon, and a boutique in one business? Bah!'' Her nose rose in disdain.

''If you gave us a chance, Attila, even you could benefit from our services. For one thing, we could teach you how to apply your make-up without a trowel.''

Just across the aisle, Zach Goldstein didn't even try to hide his grin. What had promised to be just another boring trip was starting off to the contrary. Here he sat, with a ringside seat at a cat fight between two irate beauties. One hot Mexican tamale and one cool, tart-mouthed blonde. He'd never considered himself a womanizer, but the thought crossed his mind that if they started yanking hair and tearing at each other's clothes, it would be almost as good as a female mud-wrestling match!

Personally, he was rooting for the strawberry blonde with the long French braid and big green eyes. She really was quite attractive, with a clean, naturally pretty look about her. Of course, Alita Gomez was no slouch either, but Zach had always been drawn to a less flamboyant type of beauty. More wholesome, less artificial.

Like Rachel. Rachel had been his concept of the ideal woman, the perfect mate. Somewhat shy in public, a little bold in private; more prone to listening than speaking, though she didn't hesitate to take a firm stand on issues important to her. Zach used to tease her about being a closet zealot. He'd give his right arm to be able to do so again.

God, he missed her! Three years since her death, and that soul-deep ache still lingered. There seemed to be no escaping it, especially when, with each passing year, their daughter was maturing into Rachel's mirror image. Same huge brown eyes, same nose, same stubborn chin. Becky was twelve now, teetering on the threshold of womanhood, but still young enough to be Daddy's little girl at least half the time. Mostly when she wanted her own way.

His job as an architectural engineer kept him away from her more than he'd have liked, but his mother and dad and two sisters helped fill the gap so that Becky could remain at home with family and friends. He tried to sched-ule time off from his work to coincide with breaks in her school term, and in summer she'd often join him on site for several weeks. It was rough going, but somehow they were making it work. As soon as he got settled in Las Vegas and got this latest project off the ground, so to speak, he would send for her again. In the meantime, his telephone bill would soar to new heights, and he'd continue to worry that his baby would soon be wearing lipstick and devel-oping a figure, and, God-forbid, dating!

His attention veered back to the matter at hand as the airline hostess tried to reason with the two women passen-gers. "Ladies, please. The plane is nearly ready to debark, and everyone must find his or her seat and get buckled in."

She turned a pleading gaze toward Kelly, who seemed the more amenable of the two. "Ma'am, if you would agree to give up your seat, I promise you a first-class meal and complimentary drinks from here to San Francisco."

"Throw in a free ticket for a future flight, and you've got a bargain," Kelly told her.

"I'll do my best," the stewardess promised. "Thank you."

"What about my manager?" Alita Gomez persisted. She gestured toward the short, rotund man waiting silently behind her. "Eduardo was to have a seat with me. We have much business to discuss."

"I'm sorry, Miss Gomez, but . . ."

"No problem. Make me the same deal that you did for the lovely lady, and Miss Gomez's manager can have my seat," Zach offered.

Alita graced him with a brilliant smile, her eyes quickly assessing and approving his dark good looks. "At last!" she purred. "A man who knows how to be a gentleman! I will have Eduardo reward your generosity by providing you with a free ticket to the concert I will be giving in Hawaii this weekend."

"That's very gracious of you, Miss Gomez. Unfortunately, my layover there will only be for as long as it takes to refuel." His regret was genuine. Though Alita had yet to prove her worth as an actress, she was indisputably one of the best recording artists to come along in the past decade. Her rich alto voice, low and sultry, turned a simple song into a seduction. Zach already owned both her CDs, and was looking forward to the release of the next.

"I wouldn't mind an autograph for my daughter, however," he suggested as an alternative. "Her name is Becky."

"And what is yours?" Alita asked with a come-hither look.

"Zach."

"Do you really have a daughter, or is the autograph for you? "I could sign it, 'To Zach with the sexy gold eyes.'""

"Oh, for heaven's sake!" Kelly groused. "If you want this seat so badly, Lolita, I suggest you postpone the flirtation and let me out of it. You're blocking the aisle."

Alita's smile instantly transformed into a glare, which she turned toward Kelly. "My name is Alita. A–li–ta!" she stressed.

"And mine is Kelly. Kelly," Kelly mimicked. "And you're still in my way. Unless you've changed your mind and want to sit elsewhere."

Though the starlet's glower remained, she stepped back just far enough to allow Kelly to vacate the seat. As Kelly reached for the overhead compartment, the stewardess offered, "I'll be happy to bring your things back to you later, Ma'am."

"No thanks," Kelly told her. "Unlike some people, I'm used to *carrying* my own weight, as opposed to throwing it around."

Collecting his briefcase, Zach relinquished his own seat and followed Kelly down the aisle to the rear of the aircraft. As he settled once more into an empty seat directly opposite hers, the young black serviceman next to him leaned nearer and whispered, "Is the fox with you?"

Zach gave a low chuckle. "No such luck."

Familiar with the phenomenon that frequently compelled travelers to converse with complete strangers—often to the point of revealing intimate details their captive audience had no wish to hear—Zach quickly removed a sheaf of papers from his briefcase, and his reading glasses from the pocket of his sport jacket, and began to study the notes on the hotel complex he was to build in Las Vegas.

Across the aisle, Kelly was biding her time until take-off. White-knuckle flyer that she was, she knew she would not be able to relax until they were airborne. Reminding herself that, statistically, more people were killed on highways than in air disasters, didn't help ease the jitters much. To alleviate her own nervousness, she concentrated on her fellow passengers, wondering with envy how so many of them could seem so calm.

Kelly had always been an inveterate people-watcher. Not that she was particularly nosy; other people and other cultures simply intrigued her. She found the varying customs, modes of dress, languages, foods, and mannerisms fascinating. While someone else might be bored to tears upon observing a Japanese tea ceremony, Kelly would have been totally enthralled. She'd once sat practically mesmerized through a day-long presentation of Native American dances—complete with drums, chanting, and authentic costumes. Afterward, she'd incorporated some of the unique Indian artistry, the colors and patterns, into a special line of clothing for her boutique. At the Olympics in Georgia, a virtual global melting-pot, she'd ecstatically garnered many additional ideas for her business.

Now, she sat observing those around her, her sharp green gaze taking in all the subtle nuances that hinted at the character of the people around her. Coming down the aisle was a Japanese gentleman in a suit undoubtedly custom-tailored, so fine was the material and so perfect the fit, which led Kelly to think he was probably a very precise person. Behind him was a fellow, either a native Australian or a wanna-be Aussie, in a tan bush outfit and hat. Further on, blocking the passageway, was a heavy-set woman dressed in stretch pants and a horizontal-striped blouse which only accentuated her weight problem. Kelly couldn't help but wince at the picture she presented, her fingers literally itching to take the woman in hand. A good diet and exercise program, proper clothing, and a more complimentary hairstyle, all of which were right up Kelly's alley, would make a world of difference.

A few rows up, a young couple was trying to settle their toddler between them. The little girl, complete with toothy grin and dimples and a frilly pink jumpsuit, was absolutely precious! She was also having too much fun waving and babbling at the two elderly people in the seat behind her to want to sit down.

Kelly's heart gave a painful twinge. She'd miscarried two years ago, and hadn't gotten pregnant since, which was probably a blessing now, considering the divorce. Still, she looked at that darling child and felt tears stinging at the back of her eyelids. How she'd wanted a baby! A family all her own, upon which to shower all her love.

Seeing the older couple, their snow-white heads so close together, turn to each other and share an adoring smile, only made Kelly feel worse. From all indications, they had the relationship she wanted, the one she'd thought she'd had. A love so secure that it could only grow stronger through the years. Mutual devotion between life-long mates.

Kelly swiped at an errant tear, angry at herself for letting her ragged feelings get the better of her. Sniffling, she delved into her handbag for a tissue. Failing to find even one among the multitude of items overflowing the purse, she heaved a sigh of disgust.

Suddenly a white cloth appeared before her, suspended by deeply tanned fingers. She glanced to her right, into the topaz eyes of the man who'd given up his first-class seat to Alita Gomez's manager. Zach something-or-other. He was offering her his handkerchief.

She gave a self-conscious smile. "Your mother must be very proud of you. Gentlemen are a rare breed today."

Zach grinned back at her. "Maybe I'm not polite at all. How do you know this isn't a flag of truce, or an offer of outright surrender?"

Kelly laughed. "For one thing, I wasn't aware we were at war." She accepted the handkerchief from him. "Thank you."

"You're very welcome," he replied. With that, he went back to his work, affording her the privacy to properly compose herself.

Finally, everyone had boarded and the plane began to taxi away from the terminal. The steward in charge of the last several rows of passengers, a good-looking young man with red hair and soulful brown eyes, commanded their attention. He welcomed them aboard and commenced the usual speech, citing the rules about smoking, keeping their trays locked into position in front of them, and staying in their seats until the seatbelt sign went off after take-off. He continued with instructions concerning air-sick bags, flotation cushions, oxygen masks, and emergency exits, ending with, "We are here to assist you in any way we can, to make your journey comfortable and pleasant."

In the rearmost seat, which butted up to the galley, a burly passenger grumbled, "Comfortable? Hah! That's a laugh!" He jingled the handcuffs that bound his wrist to that of the detective seated next to him. "I can't even blow my nose without seeing your paw in front of my face."

"So pretend we're Siamese twins and shut up," the law-man advised brusquely. "I don't like it anymore than you do, and I'm not the one who splattered my wife's brains all over a bedroom wall, then skipped out of the country. It's gonna be a long trip back to Tennessee, Roberts, and only slightly better if you're not bitching the entire time."

"So dig out the key and unhook us," Earl Roberts suggested. "It ain't like I can go anywhere. What do you think I'm gonna do? Open a door and throw myself out into the ocean? I didn't see them handin' out parachutes when we got on this over-sized death-trap."

"Relax, Roberts. The 747 has an excellent safety record. And out of about two hundred passengers, as near as I can tell you're the only one whining like a baby."

"Maybe that's 'cause I'm the only one tied to you. And you did some big-time gripin' of your own when they made you turn your gun over to the pilot when we boarded." Earl added that jab with gleeful spite. He eyed the smaller man with a sneer. "You scared, sittin' here without your weapon, knowin' I could strangle you with my bare hands anytime I took the notion?"

The detective met the threat with a challenging glare, not in the least intimidated. "Try it, and you're gonna wish you did have a parachute. Nothin' says I have to bring you back alive."

They'd crossed the International Date Line, thus gaining a day on the calendar, and were somewhere over the Polynesian Islands, when they hit a series of thunderstorms, one after another. Though the pilot came on the intercom several times to assure everyone that there was no cause for alarm, passengers were encouraged to remain in their seats, with their seatbelts fastened. The turbulence became so great that the flight attendants had to secure the carts in the galleys. Contrarily, the rougher the weather became, the more drinks were ordered. The poor attendants were being run ragged serving alcoholic beverages to those passengers who evidently preferred being thoroughly anesthe-tized to being soberly aware of the frightening situation in which they now found themselves.

Many people, seasoned travelers and first-timers alike, resorted to the air-sick bags, as the aircraft lurched and bounced, and pitched through the dark, ominous clouds. The busy, friendly chit-chat that had previously permeated the atmosphere soon dissipated into whispered exchanges, quiet fervent prayers, and an ever-growing silence.

Each time the plane took one of those heart-stopping thirty-foot drops, as if the air beneath it had suddenly been whisked away, Kelly swallowed a screech of pure terror. She was clutching the armrest so hard that her fingers ached from the prolonged pressure.

Witness to her fear, Zach offered, "If it would make you feel better, we could hold hands."

Kelly shook her head and declined the gallant gesture. "I'm afraid to let go that long." A pry-bar couldn't have loosened her hands from the armrest—or wrested her from her seat. Which made Alita's appearance all the more startling as the singer made her way slowly down the tilting aisle toward the rear of the aircraft.

Though her own face was strained, Alita cast a glance at Kelly's white-boned knuckles and laughed. "It appears that you, not I, will be the one with no fingernails left."

Kelly unclenched her jaw and muttered, "Slumming, Miss Gomez?"

"I came to give Zach his autographed photos," the actress said, turning a three hundred-watt-smile on Zach. She handed the pictures to him, and explained in a husky murmur, "The one of me fully dressed is for your daughter. The other one is meant especially for you."

Zach had just thanked her when the beleaguered stew-ard appeared and curtly suggested that Alita return imme-diately to her seat.

True to form, Alita tossed her raven hair and declared loudly, "I do not care what your stupid sign says. I have had to come all the way to the back of the plane in search of a restroom that is not occupied. I am going to file a complaint. For so many people, on a plane this size, there should be more restrooms available." With that, she flounced past him, nearly shoving the man into Kelly's arms, pushed another passenger headed for the facilities out of her path, and promptly claimed the small cubicle for herself.

The door had no sooner clicked shut behind Alita than the entire interior of the aircraft was filled with a blinding white glare, accompanied instantaneously by a loud, deafening crack. Immediately, the plane pitched into a steep dive.

Panic ensued. Screams rent the air, above which the attendants were frantically trying to issue orders. Though he was standing next to her, Kelly could barely hear the steward yelling, "Secure your tray tables. Remove your eyeglasses and any sharp objects from your pockets. If you have a pillow or blanket or jacket, place it in your lap, between your legs. Put your arms over your head, bend over, and put your head between your knees."

There was no time to think, barely time to react. And yet in that same surreal period, everything seemed to be happening in slow-motion. Half-ripping it, Kelly struggled out of her jacket and hunched forward. The woman to the left of her grabbed a partially knit afghan from her bag and did likewise. Across the aisle, Zach tore off his sport coat. Next to him, the soldier tucked his face into a tiny airline pillow. In the rearmost seats, the detective and his prisoner swore at each other as they tried to stretch the lawman's suit coat between them.

In those horrible, stupefying moments, sobs and curses and prayers mingled. The baby was shrieking at the top of her lungs. Above the din, the plane's engines were whining and coughing as the craft lurched dizzily downward.

Half suffocated by her tears and her jacket, Kelly raised her head slightly. Her terrified gaze met Zach's for a split instant before he reached out one large hand and roughly shoved her head down again.

His voice, shouting at her to stay down, was the last thing she heard—just before the tremendous jolt that rendered her blessedly unconscious.

Chapter 2

The initial impact rammed Zach's head against the back of the seat in front of him. Amid the horrendous din of ripping metal and the screams of the other passengers he felt, rather than heard, the bones in his neck crack painfully. His shoulder hit something solid, and his left arm went immediately numb, while his right kneecap felt as if it was on fire.

Contrary to popular belief, Zach's life did not pass before his eyes in those next few seconds. Rather, a dozen thoughts flashed through his mind. His daughter was about to lose her only remaining parent. How would she cope? Had he told her lately how pretty she was? How proud he was of her, and how much he loved her? Would his mom and dad find his will in the filing cabinet? Were his bills paid up? Would death come quickly? He prayed it would. Was Rachel waiting for him on the other side, with Grandad Zeke and Aunt Esther?

"Oh, Becky! I'm so sorry! Be good for Gramma and Grandpa. Be happy, baby."

The plane tilted sharply, throwing Zach's ribs hard into the armrest between him and the soldier, robbing him of his breath while lights flashed inside his head. "This is it," he thought. "I'm coming, Rachel. I'm coming."

But it wasn't over yet. In retrospect, it would almost seem as if it had all happened in slow motion, while in reality it took only seconds. The aircraft rolled, somersaulting onto its back. The movement caught Zach off-guard, slinging him backward in his seat like a sprung coil. His eyes flew open. His arms lost their grip, flinging outward, sending his hands smacking into the overhead panel. The lapbelt gouging into his belly was the only thing holding him in place, as he hung helplessly, upside-down, his knees dangling inches from his nose, witness to a horror beyond his worst nightmare.

Those windows that hadn't popped at first impact did so now, spraying shards of plastic in every direction. Overhead compartments sprang open, the contents flying out like randomly aimed missiles. Next to Zach's head, a large hole was suddenly ripped in the ceiling above the aisle. A few feet forward, with the ease of a beer can being crushed in a man's fist, the roof of the cabin caved inward over the seating area. A woman's scream, cut short, told its own fateful tale.

The tumbling continued, tossing the plane onto its opposite side, then almost upright again. Zach, his teeth clenched tightly together, let loose a muted howl as his shin cracked against a floor bracket and his aching ribs took another battering from the armrest. Then, miraculously, the plane rocked to a shuddering halt, tilted at an acute angle, tail-end down.

For several long seconds, Zach didn't even dare to breathe, let alone move. Truth be told, he didn't know if he was capable of moving at this point. But he was alive, at least for now. His throbbing body was verification of this, as was his pounding heart, which seemed to be permanently lodged in his throat. Finally, when the plane did not resume movement, Zach sucked in several great gulps of air on a fervent prayer of thanksgiving. He was alive!

Fast on the heels of that thought came another. Yes, he'd survived, but how many others had? And why, if they'd gone down in the middle of the Pacific Ocean, wasn't the cabin being flooded with water? His last question was promptly answered, as Zach cast a quick glance around him. Through the tiny portholes, rather than a sea of liquid blue, he saw a dense wall of vivid green. Branches and leaves poked through many of the shattered panes. Zach could only conclude that somehow, either by sheer luck, or perhaps the result of some last-minute navigation by the pilot, they must have crashed on one of the many islands dotting this part of the Pacific.

And he wasn't the sole survivor, either. As his panic subsided, he heard others around him beginning to stir. Cries of pain and hysteria rose, prompting Zach's brain into working order again. Logic, and a strong sense of self-preservation, told him that the next course of action was to get off the plane before something else catastrophic could occur. Only God knew how long it would be before the aircraft caught fire—and the extreme tilt of the plane made him wonder if they were in danger of sliding into the ocean at any given moment.

Following the urgent impulse to flee, Zach released the catch on his lapbelt and pried himself out of his seat. Not a simple task. The rows of seats had been shoved together, compacted like the bellows of an accordion when the plane had crashed. Despite his throbbing ribs, and a shoulder that was surely dislocated, Zach had to literally contort his body and squeeze out into the aisle. He fell panting to the floor, crouched on hands and knees, fighting to remain conscious as pain lanced through him.

Next to him, Kelly moaned and shifted slightly. Zach reached out and shook her arm. "Wake up. C'mon. We've got to get out of here." Not knowing the degree of his own injuries, he could only hope hers were not too extensive.

Kelly's first reaction was one of supreme annoyance. "Buzz off, Brad," she mumbled drowsily. ". . . Gotta headache."

"If that's the worst of it, you can consider yourself fortunate," Zach replied, shaking her again. "Wake up. Now!"

Kelly's lids fluttered open, and she peered at Zach with a frown. "Who . . . what?" Her expressive green eyes reflected the moment her memory returned, as they widened with fear. "Are . . . aren't we dead?" she asked hesitantly.

"Not yet. Can you wriggle loose of your seat? We've got to hurry."

"Why? We're down now, aren't we?"

Zach nodded. "Yeah, but I don't exactly want to be around if this heap of metal decides to explode."

His words were prophetic. No sooner had he uttered them than an enormous blast rocked the plane. The craft slid downward several more feet, tilting at an even more precarious angle. Beyond the thick veil of branches, a bright orange glow appeared, quickly blotted out by thick black smoke.

Screams of terror erupted anew. The explosion sent Zach skidding toward the rear of the cabin on his stomach. When he stopped, he was face to face with the steward.

"The emergency exit," the other man groaned, nodding toward the door a few feet away. "Get it open. Throw out the chute."

"Right." Zach staggered to his feet. It was then he noticed the steward's leg, caught fast between a utility cart and the wall. Most of the partition sectioning off the galley had crumpled. A jumble of trays, cans, and miscellaneous rubble littered the passageway, pinning the cart, and the steward, in place. Zach wrestled with it for several seconds before admitting defeat.

"I'll get help."

"I can do it," a man offered. "Just give me a minute to get rid of these cuffs first."

Zach turned toward the voice. His volunteer was a bear of a man, working a key into the handcuffs that linked him to his limp, blood-soaked seatmate. The cuffs sprang loose, and the giant lurched into the aisle.

"What about him?" Zach motioned toward the remaining fellow, the one instinct told him was the cop.

"Dead. Piece of metal speared through his side."

The prisoner pushed Zach out of his way. "I'll get the steward. You get the door."

Glad for the help, Zach hobbled through the wreckage to the rear-most exit.

Some distance forward, Kelly finally managed to free herself of her lapbelt. On quivering limbs, she had to actually climb out of her seat. She stood quaking in the aisle, her head throbbing and her mind still too muddled to function properly.

"The kid," someone said. "Get the kid." It was the soldier, the man who'd been sitting next to Zach. He was trying to wedge himself out of his own cramped space. Blood trickled from numerous cuts on his dark face, and his right hand dangled crookedly from his wrist.

"The baby," he insisted, jerking Kelly from her stupor.

From somewhere toward the front, the child was wailing loudly. Kelly followed the sound, hauling herself slowly up the steep incline by grasping seatbacks, half crawling through the tumbled luggage clogging the passageway. She found the toddler partially buried beneath a mound of debris, battered but apparently not badly hurt. Bracing herself, Kelly pulled the little girl free, hugging her close. "It's okay, honey. Sssh. Hush now, pumpkin. Where's your mommy?"

The child, still sobbing, pointed a chubby finger. Kelly's gaze followed. Her stomach lurched. The young woman was still hunched over, her head totally immersed in the seatback in front of her. Her neck rested on the horizontal slat of the metal framework which had served as a guillotine. Beside her, her husband slumped half-in, half-out of a large hole in the plane's side.

Kelly gulped. So much blood. Everywhere. "Oh, God! Oh, God!" she whimpered, clutching the child tighter to her. Pivoting away from the grisly sight, Kelly fought the waves of nausea and panic threatening to engulf her.

When she dared to open her eyes again, she encountered the misty blue eyes of the elderly lady seated behind the child's parents. Tears ran unheeded down the woman's face as she held her husband across her lap, stroking his head with gnarled fingers. Her voice was strangely childlike as she murmured. "Wake up, James. We've landed. Wake up, dear. It's not like you to be such a slug-a-bed."

Zach appeared suddenly. He knelt at the old woman's side. Placing his fingers at her husband's neck, he felt for a pulse. His gaze met Kelly's and he shook his head. "I'm sorry, ma'am," he told the older lady. "He's gone."

The woman's head jerked in a gesture of denial. " No. He's just sleeping. He naps a bit these days, you see."

By now, Zach had the woman's belt undone. As gently as possible, he urged her from the seat. "We've got to go now."

She looked from her husband to Zach with confusion. "Isn't James coming, too? I can't leave James, you know. If he wakes to find me gone, he'll be most distraught."

"It's all right," Zach lied, aiming her toward the back

of the cabin. "I'll bring him along later. You just go with Kelly. Be careful not to fall."

On an aside to Kelly, he ordered, "Hurry. Get them to the rear exit. The corporal and I will check the rest of the passengers."

The soldier, his hand now bound up in his necktie and secured to his belt, pushed past her. By the time the two women negotiated the strewn baggage and reached the exit, he and Zach had caught up with them again. Each carried an unconscious passenger. A middle-aged woman hobbled close behind.

The steward had released the emergency chute through the open door. "Sit and slide," he instructed succinctly, motioning toward the old woman. "Ladies and children first."

Zach had been busily counting heads. "Where's the other guy? Our newly liberated felon?" he inquired.

The steward nodded toward the bottom of the chute. "A'ready out and waiting to catch the others. Miss Gomez is down, too. We heard her pounding on the restroom door, or she'd still be stuck in there."

Zach lowered his burden to the floor, then helped the corporal do the same. "You assist the ladies. We're going back to search for any other survivors. I wish we could get past that barrier of trees at the top of the aisle, but they're blocking it solidly."

"That's probably the only thing keeping the smoke at bay," the steward suggested. "A lucky break for us." He indicated the black billows outside the aircraft. "Don't dally, mates. I've got me a bad feelin', like this tail section isn't gonna stay put much longer. And heaven knows what'll happen when she goes."

"Don't forget my James," the old woman called after them, lowering herself gingerly to the floor.

Peering past her, Kelly surveyed the bright yellow chute

with trepidation. It was slanted nearly straight down, with the lower end hidden among the tree limbs. "I can't see the ground from here. Are you certain the others got down safely?" she dared to ask.

"Right as rain, miss" the steward assured her. "That big galoot's holdin' tight to the other end. Not to worry."

Somehow, his words did little to reassure her. Still, anything was better than remaining aboard the plane, waiting to be blown to smithereens with the next explosion. Strain her ears though she might, Kelly could hear no sounds from below which might indicate imminent rescue. No sirens. No squeal of tires. Nothing. Did that mean they were solely responsible for their own rescue? Was help still miles, and perhaps hours, away?

Kelly scanned the small, battered group of passengers around her. Collectively, they sported numerous wounds —everything from deep lacerations to broken bones, and possible internal injuries. If they were to be on their own for a while, they'd need more than the clothes on their backs. They needed cloth for bandages and slings, blankets to ward off shock. Any type of pain medication, even if it was just aspirin, would surely be better than nothing.

"Here. You take her," Kelly said, shoving the whimpering baby into the middle-aged woman's arms. "I'll be right back."

As she searched quickly through the jumble of luggage, and carry-on items at her feet, Kelly cautioned herself not to look too closely at those passengers yet in their seats, so quiet and still—or at the streams of blood pooling on the cabin floor. Within minutes, she'd collected several blankets, jackets, and sweaters. She'd found her own dufflebag, and a couple of purses. These she carted quickly toward the exit, dumping them into a heap near the exit.

She was just starting another round when Zach grabbed her arm. "You're going the wrong way! I thought you were already out with the others! A minute more, and you'd have been left behind! What are you doing?''

''I'm trying to collect some things we might need,'' she explained, pointing to her small cache.

''Damn, woman!'' he bellowed. ''Now is not the time for a scavenger hunt! Get your butt down that chute!''

He shoved her to the exit, pushed her to her knees. ''Sit!'' he commanded.

''I'm not a trained dog!'' she retorted. Shooting him a glare, Kelly made a mad grab for the pile of gear she'd amassed, gathering the corners of the bottom blanket around the items atop it. Scarcely had she wadded the edges in her fists than Zach booted her from behind, and she went sailing down the rubber chute on her back, screeching all the way.

Hands caught her arms, yanking her upright and out of the way. She still hadn't regained her wits when Zach hit the ground beside her.

Again he grabbed her, shoving her away from the plane. ''Go! Quickly! I'm right behind you.''

Though Kelly had no idea why there was such a need for haste at this juncture, she broke into a lope, following close on the heels of the man ahead of her.

They were breaking their own trail through junglelike terrain. Branches swatted at her. Leaves, some as large as pillowcases, slapped her in the face. Underfoot, rocks and vines threatened to trip her at every step. Fortunately, their frantic trek was short-lived. Within a few minutes, they caught up with the forward part of their group, waiting on the slope of a slight rise.

''Here! Over here!'' The soldier waved to them from the rocky incline.

They scrambled up the barren swell, and found themselves on a small plateau. ''Look!'' the corporal said, pointing back the way they'd come.

Kelly took one look, and gasped loudly. Beside her, Zach's low curse was oddly appropriate. From here, above the treetops, they could see the wreckage of their plane. Upon impact, the huge 747 had broken apart like a child's toy. One wing had sheared off. It was lying some distance away, burning. The mangled cockpit had rammed nose-first into the side of a flat-topped mountain. It too, had broken away. The main body of the aircraft, with one wing still attached, was engulfed in fire, burning like a gigantic funeral pyre. Though the storm had passed, clouds still hovered overhead, tainted now by the plumes of black smoke and flame that shot hundreds of feet into the air. Behind the main body, perhaps the length of two football fields away from it, the tail section clung precariously to a steep hillside. From this viewpoint, it appeared the only thing holding it there was the crushed forest of trees beneath it.

As he gazed at the scattered wreckage, Zach realized just how fortunate they'd been. Had they been seated anywhere else on the plane, he and the few people with him would not have survived. If he and Kelly had not given up their seats in the first-class section—if Alita had not chosen that precise time to come back in search of an empty restroom—they, too, would be dead. Call it luck, kismet, fate . . . whatever. A select band of guardian angels had surely worked overtime today.

Chapter 3

Kelly sank to her knees, her whole body trembling violently as she stared at the inferno in wide-eyed dismay. Tears fell unheeded. "There, but for the grace of God," she murmured, echoing everyone else's thoughts.

"We got out," Zach reminded her. "It was a close call, but we made it."

"You don't suppose there's any way. . . ?" Her voice trailed off.

"No," Zach replied gravely. "There nothing we could do for them now, in any case."

"I suppose not, but just the thought that some of them might still . . ." She pulled in a large breath and released it heavily. "Good God! Those poor people! What a dreadful way to die!"

"Try not to think about it," Zach advised.

"Easier said than done," the middle-aged woman with the lank brown hair commented, her voice quivering. "I'll be having nightmares of this for a long, long time."

"We all will," the soldier predicted somberly.

They watched solemnly for some minutes, until one of the unconscious passengers on the ground moaned in pain, drawing their attention away from the burning plane and back to their most immediate problem.

"How long do you thing it will take our rescuers to reach us?" Alita questioned.

"I'd say that depends largely on where we've landed," the steward put in. "If we're lucky enough to have crashed on a populated island, it could be anywhere from minutes to hours, I suppose."

"I take it you've flown this route before," Zach said. "Do you have any idea where we might be?"

The man shook his head. "About halfway between New Zealand and Hawaii, somewhere in the Polynesian chain. But I have to tell you, there are thousands of atolls and islands dotting this part of the Pacific, and as far as I know, less than a third of them are inhabited. Trying to predict which one we're on would be like hitting the lotto twice in a row."

The man on the ground groaned again. Zach frowned. "Off hand, I'd say our best bet would be to get ourselves to lower ground. Maybe we'll meet an emergency unit coming from below. At any rate, it won't do us any good to stay here."

The corporal disagreed. "If they send out a search team, or a plane to look for survivors, wouldn't it be better if we stayed here, where we can be spotted right away?"

"That's assuming anyone knows we've gone down," Zach pointed out. He nodded toward the three most severely injured of their group, those lying unconscious at their feet. "I'm not a doctor, but I'd guess the sooner these folks get some medical attention, the better their chances of survival. If we head down now, we can reach the shore by sunset. Maybe find a village there, and some help. Besides, none of us will last long up here without food and fresh water.''

"Again, assuming there is any on this isle," the steward added. At Kelly's questioning look, he added wryly, "Why do you think so many of these islands haven't been settled? They're nothing but a pile of lava, coral, and tropical jungle."

Any way they looked at it, their situation appeared bleak.

"I vote we go down, while we can see where we're goin'," the big American proposed. "I ain't hankerin' to get tangled up with no wild critters or snakes in the dark."

"Snakes?" Alita screeched. Her naturally tan complexion paled even more as she eyed the dense foliage mere yards away.

"Or worse," someone muttered.

"I'm with Zach and the big guy," Alita decided posthaste. "Get me out of this jungle and onto a nice, safe beach. I want a phone, room service, and a margarita . . . and I want them as soon as possible."

"That's right, Alita," Kelly commented derisively, getting shakily to her feet. "Stay true to form. Think of yourself first and foremost. Don't bother to consider that there are others in worse straits than you. Even if you do look as if you've been dragged backward through a knothole."

Alita's dark eyes narrowed spitefully. "I'd wouldn't talk if I were you. Your hair is a fright, and your clothes look as if you've crawled through the gutter in them."

"At least I wasn't caught in the john with my pantyhose around my ankles," Kelly retorted. "You must have looked real cute, bouncing around in there like a marble in a pinball machine."

Alita sprang at her, claws bared. Kelly lunged from the opposite direction. Zach stepped hastily between them. With one arm, he held Alita at bay until the soldier could corral her. His other arm coiled around Kelly's waist, pulling her back.

"Hey! Stop it right now! We haven't got time for your petty female squabbling."

Kelly squirmed, resisting his hold on her. He gave her a rough shake. "I'm serious, Spike. Simmer down and can the attitude!"

"Spike?" Kelly exclaimed irately. "Who are you calling Spike?"

"You, babe." Zach twisted her in his arms until they were eye to eye, his lit with something akin to wry amusement, despite their dire circumstances. "If that bump on your head rises any higher, you'll look like a blasted unicorn."

Her immediate response was to search for a smart comeback, but her beleaguered brain failed her. Her anger disintegrated as quickly as it had flared, and she wilted in his arms. "I . . . I'm sorry. I don't know why I'm acting this way. Especially right now."

He steadied her before releasing her. "Probably a result of the adrenaline," he said, somber shadows etching his features once more. "Everyone reacts differently to a crisis."

"I . . . I'm okay now," she assured him, though still flustered.

He forced a smile. "Good. Don't want you going off the deep end. All of us are going to need our wits about us, and we've all got to pitch in and help one another."

"So, are we headin' for the beach, or what?" the big man drawled in his thick southern accent. "Time's a-wastin'."

They took a quick vote. Only the soldier held out.

"Tell you what, Corporal," Zach suggested. "You help get the others down. Then, if you want to come back up here and man a signal fire or something, that's your choice. But for now, we all might be better off sticking together."

Three of their number—a man, a woman, and a teenage

boy, all unconscious—were totally incapacitated. Additionally, the steward's left leg was badly broken. With help, he'd managed to hobble this far, in excruciating pain. He certainly couldn't negotiate the rough terrain ahead without aid. Of the men, this left Zach, the corporal, and the newly liberated prisoner with the least serious injuries. Not that they'd escaped unscathed, by any means. The soldier's hand was broken. Zach's shoulder was dislocated and at least a couple of his ribs were fractured. Even the giant had broken his nose and was sporting a goose egg on his forehead the size of a softball. And these were just their most obvious wounds.

The women had fared only a little better. Among a variety of scrapes and bruises, Kelly suspected she had a slight concussion. Her vision kept blurring, off and on, and she wasn't as steady on her feet as she was usually. Alita had a long gash along one leg, and kept holding her left elbow. The older woman, now in a fuzzy state of near-shock, was favoring her ribs. The fourth lady was limping on an ankle swelled three times its normal size. Her face was flecked with tiny nicks, the blood now congealed and dried in little blobs. The toddler, though fretful, appeared to have escaped relatively unharmed.

The corporal agreed, reluctantly.

"Okay, let's take stock," Zach proposed. "We've got three unconscious persons and three semi-able men to carry them. Kelly, you take charge of the old lady. Guide her along. Help her over the rough spots and make sure she doesn't wander off by herself and get lost. You . . ." Zach gestured toward the woman with the toddler.

"Blair," the woman supplied. "Blair Chevalier."

Zach nodded. "Blair, you handle the child. Alita, that leaves you to lend a hand with the steward."

"If you can find me something to use for a crutch, I can hobble along fairly well on my own," the man said.

"Can someone help me with the stuff in my bundle?" Kelly asked. "It weighs more than I thought it would, and I'm sure there are things inside we might need."

"Like what?" the felon inquired, scanning the pile of purses with masculine scorn. "Eye shadow and lipstick?"

Kelly scowled at him. "No, you overgrown sexist. Like aspirin and tweezers and maybe even a few band-aids. Safety pins to secure bandages. Even tampons can be used in place of cotton balls."

At this, the man's face, somewhat ruddy by nature, flushed to a dull shade of red. "Yeah, okay. I get the point."

"I can take some of it," Blair offered. "And if we could fashion one of those jackets or blankets into a sling for the baby, so I could carry her on my back, it would help free up my hands."

"Make another bundle into a backpack for me," the steward suggested.

A short time later, they were ready to depart. As one they turned, taking one last look at the burning plane— all contemplating the fate that could have been theirs, and counting their blessings that they'd somehow miraculously escaped.

"Was it a bomb, do you think?" Alita asked.

"I'd put my money on that bolt of lightning," Zach said.

"That's my bet, too," the steward concurred. "It sounded like a direct hit, which could have fried all the electrical circuits and basically put the craft out of commission."

"If that's the case, what are the chances the pilot got off some sort of SOS?" The soldier voiced the question now uppermost in everyone's mind.

The steward shrugged. "I'd say slim to none. The radio equipment was probably knocked out. But the black box might still be sending out a signal."

"You think so?" Kelly inquired soberly. "Even after a crash and fire of that magnitude?"

Again the man shrugged. "Possibly. To borrow a saying from the Timex people, those things can take a licking and keep on ticking."

"I hope you're right," Blair commented bleakly.

As did they all.

Their trek down the mountain—from the height and size of it, it could be termed nothing less—was difficult and fraught with its own varieties of hazard. Like many of the islands in this part of the world, it had been formed by cooled volcanic flow, and the jagged rocks underfoot were razor-sharp. This, plus having to forge their own path through the dense vegetation, slowed their progress to a snail's pace. Of necessity, the men took the lead, taking turns hacking at the impeding undergrowth with sturdy branches, to which they'd tied their pocket knives. The others followed, single file.

Amid the trees, there was no cooling sea breeze. The humidity was nearly unbearable, making it seem as if they were sucking in water with every labored breath. Their clothing clung limply to their sweat-soaked bodies as they trudged wearily along. The endless tangle of rain-dampened plants only compounded their discomfort, slapping at them with sharp wet leaves that cut like knives and smearing them with dirt and bugs of every imaginable variety. Clouds of mosquitos hovered all around, feasting on every exposed inch of human flesh. Added to their constant buzzing were the raucous cries of island birds, disturbed by this rude intrusion into their habitat.

Vines as thick as a man's wrist latticed across the ground and between tree limbs. Alita minced across them in her spike heels, cursing fluently in Spanish. The third time she tripped, launching herself into the brawny Southerner's back, he stopped. With nary a word he tucked her under his arm like a stray pup, plucked her shoes off, and calmly snapped the three-inch heels from the soles. Then he shoved the shoes back on her feet, set her down, and went on as if nothing untoward had occurred.

Alita came out of her shock-induced stupor and promptly went ballistic. "You imbecile!" she shrieked after him. "You . . . you dumb ox! You just ruined a two hundred dollar pair of shoes!"

"So sue me!" he replied on a terse laugh. "And while I don't mind having your sweet lips bumpin' my backside every three steps, I'm a might busy now, sugar. Try me later, when I'm buck naked."

As she guided the old lady and the hobbling steward around Alita, Kelly couldn't hold back a snicker. "What do you know! Insta-flats! Maybe you'll start a new trend, Gomez!"

"Screw you!" Alita spat. "And that giant ape, too!"

They stopped in a small clearing about halfway down for a brief rest. By this time, Zach would have sold his soul for a machete. His shoulder hurt like all hell. It felt as if someone had taken a two-by-four to it, then set it aflame with a blowtorch. He'd dislocated it once before, playing college football, but he couldn't remember it ever hurting this badly. Though the boy he was toting downhill was about a hundred and forty pounds under normal circumstances, his inert condition added weight to his limp form. That, and thrashing through waist-high weeds with a puny stick, was fast taking its toll. At least it was his left shoulder, and not his right. Still, Zach didn't know how much longer he was going to be able to bear up.

Then again, he didn't have much choice. Nor did the

others. Each of them had injuries of some type. All were suffering varying degrees of pain, physical and emotional.

Across from Zach, Kelly sprawled next to the little old lady. The woman stirred, and murmured fretfully, "Where's James?"

Kelly reached out to pat her age-spotted hand in a gesture of consolation. "He . . . he's gone on ahead, dear." *To heaven, or purgatory, or wherever we go when we die,* she added silently.

The elderly woman nodded, accepting Kelly's statement at face value. "We celebrated our golden wedding anniversary in Australia," the woman added with dreamy smile. "Fifty years together, yet it seems just yesterday we spoke our vows. We're both pastors, you know. Done a lot of traveling and missionary work all over the world. Good deeds never go unrewarded. You remember that, miss . . . what did you say your name was?"

"Kelly. Kelly Kennedy."

"Ah, a good Irish name if ever there was one. I'm Wynne Templeton. British to the tips of my toes, but I never did hold with all that fighting between your folks and mine. People need to learn to get along in this world. Life's too short for all that strife and bickering."

Wynne craned her neck in the direction from which they'd come. "Something's keeping James. It's not like him to dally this way and make me worry. He knows how I fret over his heart condition. I do wish he'd hurry along."

Kelly blinked hard to clear the tears from her eyes. Her gaze, when it finally focused, centered on Zach—just in time to see him wince as he attempted to move his left arm.

"Is it your arm or your shoulder?" she asked.

"Shoulder," he hissed through clenched teeth. "I think it's just out of place, but I swear it hurts worse than if I broke it."

Kelly scooted over to him. "Mind if I take a look?"

He slanted her a wary glance. "I thought you ran some sort of beauty salon. What would you know about treating injuries of this nature?"

"My establishment is a health spa, too, and I'm a duly licensed massage therapist." she informed him. "Besides that, my dad and my older brother are both osteopaths. I know more about bones and muscles than you might think. If its simply dislocated, I might be able to pop it back for you, and relieve a lot of your misery."

"Or cause me more," Zach suggested skeptically.

Kelly shrugged. "It's your call. I only wanted to help."

Zach hesitated. "Okay." He mustered up a roguish wink, and added, "Do you promise to be gentle with me, darling? I don't do this sort of 'massage' thing with just anybody."

Kelly had long since heard all the ribald comments and jokes concerning masseurs, and become fairly inured to them, even those delivered by tall, dark, handsome men with bedroom eyes and come-hither smiles. Now she simply rolled her eyes and answered dryly, "Sure, that's what they all say. It goes hand in hand with 'I'll respect you in the morning.'"

Zach grinned and cocked a brow upward. "You will, won't you? Respect me in the morning?"

She grinned back, shaking her head in amused exasperation. "Yeah. And the check is in the mail, too. Now behave yourself and do as I tell you."

Behind them, the Southerner guffawed. The soldier laughed. Even Blair chuckled and said, "Guess she told you!"

Kelly pressed on the back of his neck, urging his head forward. With lean, strong fingers, she carefully probed and prodded all along his spine, the curve of his shoulder blade, the collarbone and socket. Moving his head back, and to either side, she repeated the procedure. Even that cautious manipulation caused him to moan in pain.

"You're right. It seems to have slipped out of place, rather than broken. Now, I want you to just sit there, neck straight. Bend your back and shoulders forward just a tad. That's right. Now, take a couple of deep breaths. Exhale all the way. Try to relax your muscles as much as possible, and let me do the work."

"Warn me before you pop it back in," Zach told her.

"Will do," she promised blithely. "I'll give you a count of three beforehand."

With one hand cradling his collarbone, and the other on his upper arm, Kelly braced her knee into his shoulder blade. "That's right. Breathe in. Out. Relax. In. Out. Again."

At the bottom of his third deep sigh, with no forewarning whatever, Kelly wrenched his shoulder back into the socket. He gasped a surprised yelp. His face pallid as he fought the resultant waves of pain, he rasped irately,"You were supposed to warn me! You lied!"

His indignation didn't phase her. "It was for your own good. You would have stiffened up otherwise, and made it harder on yourself and me." When he tried to turn toward her, she stalled his motion. "Sit still. Your shoulder needs to be wrapped, to limit the strain on the joint, before you start moving it too much. We certainly don't want you putting it back out, which would necessitate putting it back in again. Do we?"

"My shirt will suffice as a bandage, I suppose," he conceded gruffly.

She helped him shrug out of it. Working efficiently, she tore it into strips, wadded some for padding, and soon had him securely bound—even across his aching ribs. "We'll rewrap this later, and check those ribs more closely. How does it feel?"

"Much better," he allowed.

Her fingers probed lightly up the back of his neck, giving him chills. Just as Zach was wondering if she might be flirting with him, her hands came flat over his ears, her thumbs braced beneath his jaw. Again, with no prior notice, she gave his neck a swift twist to one side. Bones cracked audibly. Quickly, before he could recover from that sly maneuver, she yanked it back the other way. Again, the bones in his neck snapped and popped loudly, reminding him of a Rice Krispies commercial, tuned to high volume.

His howl was more one of surprise than of physical distress. Zach leapt to his feet and whirled on her. "You sneaky little witch! What are you trying to do, twist my head off?"

Her smile was more of a smirk. "Why? You using it for something important?"

Again, the others laughed in appreciation of Kelly's snappy retort. Before Zach had the opportunity to respond in kind, Kelly said, "You'll notice that you can now bob your head up and down and turn it from side to side with ease. Which is more than I can do at this point. I wish someone would do me the same favor I just did you."

"Oh, lady! Just give me the chance!" Zach's hands were flexing at his sides, as if itching to surround her throat. Then, tentatively, he rotated his neck. His eyes widened in astonishment, and his fingers relaxed. "God! I feel like a new man!"

Kelly's eyes twinkled. "Like I told you before—that's what they all say. Even the big, bossy, know-it-alls like you."

Chapter 4

Prior to resuming their descent, the ladies made a necessary trip to the bushes.

"What out for snakes and such," the Southerner warned.

Alita nearly tripped trying to stop in mid-stride.

Blair turned on the speaker with a frown. "If I recall my research correctly, there are no snakes in the Polynesians. Nor are there any wild mammals to speak of."

"Yeah? What are you, some sort of walkin' encyclopedia?" the man jeered.

Blair bristled, drawing herself to her fullest, if still diminutive, height. "Actually, I'm a librarian, and proud of it. So, what valuable contribution have you made to society, Mr . . . ?"

"Roberts," the man filled in, shaking a cigarette from his pack and lighting it. "For most of my life, I was a farmer. I helped keep the rest of you folks fed." He held his cigarette aloft, peering at it. "Had a decent tobacco crop going for a while, too, until the government starting hounding the tobacco companies and poking its nose in where it wasn't wanted.''

"Roberts," Zach repeated thoughtfully. "Weren't you one of the backhoe operators who worked on the cathedral project? Part of Sam Wright's crew?"

Roberts met Zach's look squarely, almost daringly. "Yeah, and you're the bigwig in charge of the whole she-bang. I'm surprised you'd remember one of us lowly peons."

"I try to keep abreast of every aspect of any project I take on," Zach replied. "That includes material and labor. I recall you particularly, because Sam commented on your ability to repair or operate almost any piece of machinery on the construction site."

Roberts shrugged. "Not much different than running a tractor or combine, when it comes down to it."

"Sam was impressed. You know, he's generally a pretty decent judge of character. Runs a clean crew. No drunks. Nobody into hard drugs. Somehow, I get the feeling he missed something vital about you."

"Well, ol' Sam's a good guy, and a fair foreman, but he ain't perfect," Roberts allowed. "Everybody makes a mistake now and ag'in."

"What was yours?" Zach asked more pointedly. "The one that got you arrested?"

Roberts chuckled. "Wondered how long you was gonna dance around the barn b'fore you got to the door, Goldstein."

"So enlighten us," Zach persisted. "What crime did you commit that was serious enough to haul you all the way back to the U.S. in handcuffs? What was it, Roberts? Robbery? Tax evasion? Hit and run?"

The man smirked. "Yeah, I reckon you could call it hit and run. I hit my whorin' wife in the head with a bullet and ran like hell."

The others stared at him, aghast.

The corporal let loose a low whistle. "Holy crap, man! You killed her?"

"Deader than a doorknob," Roberts declared. His face was defiant, as if he were proud of the dastardly deed.

"You . . . you murdered your wife?" Kelly stammered.

"Because she cheated on you?" Alita exclaimed in disbelief.

"What kind of low-life swamp rat are you?" the steward speculated with disgust.

"You're insane!" Blair added, her expression one of fear and revulsion. "They need to lock you up and throw away the key!"

Roberts glared at her, his beefy hands forming hard fists. "Hey! You didn't have to live with the bitch! I reckon by killin' her, I did myself and the world one huge favor."

While Roberts's attention had been focused on the others, Zach had quietly approached the big farmer from the rear. Now, he reached out and grabbed the man around the neck in a choke hold. "Corporal! Get the handcuffs out of my pocket!" he yelled.

Roberts went wild. With an enraged roar, he rose up, his hands tearing at Zach's arms as he tried to buck the smaller man off him. But Zach hung on, tightening his hold until Roberts' face was a dull red. The soldier, having retrieved the cuffs, had to dodge and weave around them, but he finally managed to fasten the shackles. Then he added his own weight to Zach's and between them they finally subdued their captive.

"You . . . you ain't cops!" Roberts wheezed furiously. "You got no right to do this!"

Zach pressed his knee more firmly between Roberts's shoulder blades. "Shut up! We have every right to protect ourselves against a madman in our midst."

With the soldier's help, Zach re-adjusted the cuffs, securing Roberts' hands firmly behind him, in a manner designed to render him more powerless than if they'd left them to the fore. "Now, this is the way it's going to be, Roberts. We're taking you down with us, and we're going to turn you over to the law. Until then, you're going to behave yourself, or I'm going to stomp a mudhole in you ass."

"And I'll help him," the corporal supplied.

"I will, too," the steward piped up.

"Count me in on that," Kelly added for good measure.

"Mighty brave of y'all, with me trussed up like a Thanksgivin' turkey," Roberts sneered. "Look, just 'cause I done my old lady in, don't make me crazy or mean I aim to kill anyone else."

"Maybe not, but we can't take that chance, which makes me glad I took those cuffs you left behind," Zach told him. He held the key in plain view before putting it back into his pocket. "Don't even think about trying anything, Roberts, or I'll personally push you over the first cliff we come to."

"You need me to help carry that wounded guy," Roberts protested. "I can't do that tied up like this."

"Nice try, no cigar. We'll manage somehow, even if we have to strap the man to your back."

As it turned out, they didn't need Roberts's assistance in that area after all. Upon checking their wounded, they discovered that the unfortunate fellow had succumbed to his injuries. After conferring for a moment, the men determined that it would be best just to leave the body where it lay, and to mark the spot with a bright piece of cloth so a search team could find it later.

Kelly disputed their decision. "We can't just leave the poor man here, where birds and animals might get him! It's . . . indecent! Can't we at least bury him?"

"How? With what?" Zach argued. "The ground is harder than cement, and we have no tools for digging."

"A cairn," Blair suggested. "If nothing else, we could pile rocks on the body. It would better mark the site as well."

"We're rather pressed for time here, ladies," the steward reminded them. "And we have two other injured people whose medical attention should not be delayed."

"If you won't do it, I will," Kelly insisted stubbornly.

Zach raked his fingers through his hair and heaved an exasperated breath. "Okay, we'll do it. Then we're on our way, with no further delay. I don't mean to sound harsh or unfeeling, but those of us who are presently alive are not out of the woods yet ourselves, and I mean that both figuratively and literally. We can't jeopardize our own lives for those who are beyond help."

While the men, all but Roberts, assembled the rocks, Kelly bound Wynne's ribs, using strips of the lining from one of the jackets she'd collected. She also wrapped Blair's swollen ankle, doing as best she could without removing the woman's shoe.

"I think we'd better leave the shoe on for the time being," she advised, noting how far the bruised flesh was puffed out over the edge of Blair's low-top sneaker. "Otherwise, you may never get it back on again."

Blair agreed. "This business of trail blazing is hard enough without trying it in bare feet. The only thing keeping me going is the thought of reaching the beach, and soaking my ankle."

"Do you want me to look at your elbow?" Kelly offered, turning to Alita.

"After the way you yanked at Zach's shoulder and head?" the singer said with haughty disdain. "I think not. I will wait until I can get proper medical attention from someone who knows what he is doing."

"Suits me," Kelly replied readily. "That way, if you decide to sue someone, it won't be my butt on the line."

It took them the rest of the afternoon to complete their laborious descent—skirting around steep drop-offs, encountering sheer cliffs hidden by jungle growth and having to backtrack to find an easier route, working their way carefully down and around the hazardous slopes. At last they found themselves on fairly even, less-rocky ground, though still amidst the dense growth of towering trees and knee-high brush.

"Which way now?" the corporal, who had told them his name was Gavin Daniels, asked.

"Might just as well flip a coin," Frazer Benson, the steward said, leaning heavily on the limb he was using as a crutch.

Zach eyed the sky, noting the slant of the sun. "There's no way to tell which is the shortest distance to the coast, but if we head west, we might have more daylight. I'd guess the trees will start to thin when we near the shore."

They turned west, trudging wearily along in Zach's wake.

Early on, almost as a matter of course, Zach had assumed the role of leader, the others deferring to his decisive manner, his natural air of authority. On the job, he was used to being in command. Now it was reflexive. That no one questioned his doing so was of no particular significance to him. At this point, his primary goal was to find a way out of this tropical tangle, to gain the shore and whatever aid and safety was to be found there.

It was an hour before the trees began to thin, as Zach had predicted they would, and another ten minutes before they spotted traces of blue water through the verdant foliage and heard the muted rumble of the surf. The soil grew looser, sandier. Then the beach loomed before them, pristine and beckoning. The vast, empty ocean beyond, with a red sun hovering slightly over the horizon, served as a deceptively serene backdrop.

One by one, the survivors set down their burdens and sank onto the sun-warmed sand.

"I'll never go camping again," Blair swore on a groan. "I ache in places I'd forgotten I had."

"So do I," Kelly commiserated. "And to think I prided myself on being physically fit." She blew her bangs off her forehead and sighed. "Oh, but doesn't that breeze feel heavenly? God, but it's good to be out of that jungle!"

A few feet away, Alita sat examining the remains of her spike heels, and the huge broken blisters on her feet. "My poor feet will never be the same again!" she lamented. "And just look what those rocks did to my shoes! They're in shreds!"

"Better your shoes than your feet," Zach pointed out. He looked past her, down the long stretch of barren beach. "Damn! Not a building in sight. Not so much as a thatched hut!"

"No piers, no boats, no sign of civilization," Frazer added morosely. "There's not even any litter, though I never thought I'd hear myself complain of that."

"Maybe all the activity, the ports and villages, are on another part of the island," Gavin Daniels suggested.

"Possibly," Zach concurred with a worried frown. "Could be there are too many reefs on this side, making this section inaccessible to ships and large craft. Still, you'd think there would be some tangible evidence of human habitation, if only a gum wrapper or a discarded beer can."

"Yeah, I could really go for an ice cold beer right about now," Roberts muttered, his tone surly. "On second thought, it could be piss-warm, and I wouldn't care, long as it was wet. My mouth's 'bout as dry as an old maid's twat."

"Sir!" Wynne Templeton spoke up for the first time in hours. "There is no call for such vulgarity. There are ladies present, and a gentleman would monitor his language."

"Well, la-de-da!" Roberts grumbled. "Didn't know I was travelin' with the Queen's grandma."

"It certainly beats traveling with a murderer," Blair announced bravely.

Roberts's eyes narrowed. "Look, you little . . ."

"Oh, *por Dios!*" Alita butted in. "The old woman just lost her husband. Have a little consideration."

"James is lost?" Wynne asked confusedly. "Oh, my! Someone must find him."

Kelly heaved a sigh. "Great! Now see what you've done? Thanks a heap!"

Zach pushed to his feet. "I'll go look for him in a little while, Mrs. Templeton," he fibbed. "First we have to see to our prisoner and get a fire going. It's going to be dark soon."

Zach led Roberts toward a sturdy palm tree. "We'll anchor him to this. Daniels, lend me a hand here."

"Hey, wait a minute!" Roberts protested loudly. "Least you can do is give a man the chance to take a whiz!"

Zach altered his course, steering Roberts toward the bushes. As they passed Kelly, Roberts leered at her. "Yo! Sweet cheeks! You want to come hold it for me?"

She leveled him a cool look of contempt. "I can see why your wife went man-hunting elsewhere. No doubt, it had something to do with your enchanting attitude, your wonderful manners, and your refined speech."

"You don't know jack shit," he retorted. He nodded toward Alita. "What about you, princess? The offer's still open."

"In your dreams, *hombre.*"

With Roberts secured to the tree, they located enough dry driftwood to start a fire. In the course of their search they discovered a banana palm, and several coconuts which they cracked open on a nearby rock. The milk tasted like nectar to their parched pallets.

Sufficiently revived, at least temporarily, Zach announced, "I'm going to walk down the beach and see if I can find a road, or a house, or any indication of civilization." He pointed toward the south. "I'll go this way. Daniels, you try north. We'll meet back here. Benson, you watch over the others until we get back. Keep a particularly sharp eye on our prisoner."

"Won't you need light? A torch or something?" Kelly asked.

Zach looked skyward. "We should be able to see fairly well if we stay out in the open. The clouds have passed over, and there's supposed to be a full moon tonight."

Blair grimaced. "I should have known better than to fly during a full moon. Nothing good ever happens to me during a full moon."

"I love a full moon," Alita intoned with a smirk. "It makes everything so *romántico,* so much more exciting."

"The better to ride your broom, my dear?" Benson inquired mockingly.

Alita rounded on him. "You shut up, you little wimp!" She threw the remnants of one shoe at him, narrowly missing his head. "In truth, you are probably just jealous. But I am used to that. Everyone is envious of me."

Kelly rolled her eyes. "You're really going to have to work on that inferiority complex of yours."

"I'll be back as soon as possible," Zach said with a parting wave. "Hopefully, with help."

"And food."

"And water."

"Wait!" Alita hopped to her feet, flinging her other shoe aside. "I'm coming with you."

Zach was already several paces away. "You'd do better

to stay with the others," he tossed back over his shoulder, not bothering to turn around. "This isn't an evening stroll. I'm not going to slow my pace for you."

"I'll keep up," Alita assured him, huffing to catch up.

"Probably afraid she'll miss happy hour," Blair grumbled.

On hearing this, Roberts called out. "Hey! Send a six-pack back for me!"

"All they're gonna send for you is the local constable, or whatever passes for the law around here, to arrest you again. I know I will," Daniels said as he set off down the beach in the opposite direction.

"Now, where's the Ku Klux Klan, when ya really need 'em?" Roberts shot back.

"Under the sheets?" The words just popped out of Kelly's mouth before she could help it.

Roberts glared at her for a moment. Then, to everyone's surprise, he started to chuckle. Blair joined in. Soon all of them were laughing, except Wynne. After all that had happened to them, the laughter, even intermingled with fear and anger and anguish, felt so good.

It seemed indecent, after such tremendous disaster, that the sunset over the ocean that evening should be so spectacularly beautiful, painting the tropical landscape in bright hues of orange and crimson. The sun, a huge red ball, seemed literally to sink into the sea—and as suddenly as if someone had lowered a curtain on a stage, it was as dark as midnight.

Fortunately, they had the fire and the fruit, though they had yet to locate any source of fresh water nearby. The baby was fussing again, though she'd been extremely good most of the day. Blair was holding the toddler, trying to get her to eat a banana.

"Poor tyke, she's almost too tired to eat," Blair commented. She glanced toward the tree where Roberts was tied and whispered to Kelly, "Has it occurred to you that our fearless leader has left us alone here with a murderer, with only Mr. Benson and his broken leg to protect us? What if that maniac manages to break loose and attack us?"

"Right now, I'm too tired and too busy to care," Kelly admitted. "In fact, if someone offered to strangle me this minute, I'd almost be grateful."

"Yes, but he could beat us, or rape us, or anything!" Blair went on, her eyes wide with worry.

"If he's got enough energy left for that, more power to him," Kelly replied grumpily. "Personally, I'm too pooped to pop. Don't work yourself up over it. The man is effectively out of commission."

Kelly was currently more concerned about her "patients" than any threat from Roberts. She squatted down beside the unconscious woman, who was laboring with every breath she drew. Every now and then, the woman would go into a spasm of coughing, spewing fresh blood. "I know she must have internal injuries, maybe a pierced lung. I wish Zach would hurry back with some help, preferably an entire medical team. I feel so helpless, just sitting here unable to do anything for her . . . for them."

She adjusted the blanket over the shivering woman and crawled to the teenager. "This kid will be lucky if he makes it. He took a real whollop to the head, and hasn't shown any sign of regaining consciousness all day. And if the needle marks on his arms are any indication, he's either into drugs or diabetic."

"Have you checked for a wallet? Or a medical alert tag?" Wynne inquired in another rare burst of lucid speech.

"Good idea." There was no tag, but among other I.D. in his wallet, Kelly found a medical alert card. "Damn! He is diabetic! God only knows when he had his last shot of insulin! No wonder he's in shock. For all I know, he could already be in a coma."

"Probably better off that way than awake and in agony," Frazer Benson remarked, not without sympathy. He handed Kelly another portion of coconut, advising her, "Do what you can for yourself. Eat. Drink. You need the fluid."

The coconut milk was delicious and thirst-quenching. But getting the meat out was another matter. "Do you have a pocket knife, Frazer?" Kelly inquired.

He nodded. "Over there, tied to that stick we were using to hack weeds with," he reminded her. He started to struggle to his feet, but Kelly gestured for him to stay put. "I'll get it. You rest that leg."

She got the knife, and began stabbing the coconut meat. "Let me get mine sliced up, and I'll pass the 'cutlery' on."

"You could check the boy's pocket for another one," Frazer suggested.

Kelly grimaced, but taking the steward's advice, she did so as quickly and gently as she could. "God! I hate this! I feel like a blasted grave-robber!"

Without disturbing him unduly, she came up with another small pen knife. She tossed it to Blair, and kept the other. "You share with Wynne. I'll take turns with Frazer."

"What about me?" Roberts called out. "You just gonna let me sit here and starve?"

"You had some earlier, so don't play on my sympathy," Kelly responded callously. "You can have more when Zach and Gavin get back, because I'm not about to get that close to you, buster. Besides, you're not going to starve. You could live for a week on the fat stored in that beer gut of yours."

After she'd finished eating, Kelly offered to rebind

Blair's ankle and Wynne's ribs. Blair had previously removed her tennis shoes, and was feeling some relief already. Wynne, modest as she was, was reluctant to unbutton her blouse in front of the men.

Roberts was now asleep, or feigning it. Either way, it was only a matter of shifting out of his limited field of view. Frazer was another concern entirely, at least to Wynne's mind.

"I'll close my eyes," he promised.

"How do I know you won't peek?" the elderly lady countered warily.

Benson grinned. "No offense ma'am, but you're not at all my type."

"Look, you young whippersnapper!" she shot back, showing her first real display of animation. "Just because there's snow on the roof, doesn't mean there's no fire in the furnace! Nonetheless, in fifty years of marriage, I've never wanted anyone but my James. So there! You're not my type either, sonny!"

Kelly bit back a laugh. Unless she missed her guess, Frazer Benson was gay. Evidently, Wynne hadn't caught those subtle signals, however. She'd bet a month's income Alita had, though. And most everyone else in their small party.

She bound Wynne's ribs, then turned to Benson. "You're next. Let's have a look at that leg."

He shook his head. "No. It's okay. It'll wait until I can get to a hospital."

"The least I can do is replace that dirty cloth you've wound around it, so you don't risk infection any more than you have already." She reached forward. "I know it hurts. I'll be as gentle as possible. I promise."

"I said no!" Benson shouted, scooting hastily backward. "Don't touch it! If anything needs done to it outside an emergency room, I'll tend to it myself."

His scowl reminded Kelly of a wounded animal, one which could turn on her at any time. She held her hands up in a gesture of compliance. "Okay. Okay. Have it your way."

He seemed to wilt in relief. "I'm sorry. I didn't mean to snap at you. It's just that . . . well, I can't let you do that."

Now Kelly was reading something else in his expression. Something beyond pain. More like a woeful warning. Suddenly it came to her. "Oh, no! Frazer, no!" she murmured.

She saw him swallow hard, and nod. "This was going to be my last flight. I was going to ground myself and take a desk job, where there was less contact with other people."

Kelly dredged up a wan smile, and replied just as quietly. "Hey! Magic Johnson is HIV positive, and he's still doing all right. Maybe it won't escalate any further. Maybe with the right diet and medication it won't become a full-blown case."

"And maybe it will." He held her gaze steadily, sadly.

"You've got to think positively," she rebutted.

"And you, and everyone without rubber gloves, have got to keep their hands to themselves," he stated firmly. "I don't want that on my conscience. If I'm going to die, I don't want to take anyone else with me." He paused, then gave a rueful laugh. "So many perfectly healthy people died in that crash today, yet I lived. Ironic, isn't it?"

Kelly just stared back at him, her face full of pity, not knowing what to say.

Chapter 5

Gavin Daniels returned to camp a short time later. Blair, the baby, and Wynne had fallen asleep. Only Kelly and Frazer were awake to welcome him with tense expressions.

"No," he said to their unvoiced question. He flopped onto the sand by the fire. "Not a soul, not a sound, no lights, cottages, or paths, or boats. Nothing. It was like walking on the moon, it was so deserted out there."

"How far did you go?" Frazer asked.

"Three, maybe four miles I'd guess. As far as I could before I ran into a barricade of rocks where the mountain seems to jut right out into the sea. I couldn't skirt around it, and I didn't want to chance climbing over it in the dark. If I'd fallen, the surf is pounding so hard on those rocks I'd have been hammered to a pulp."

He glanced around. "I suppose Zach and Alita are still out there?"

"Yes."

There was little else to say, and they fell into contemplative silence, listening to the crackle of the flames, the waves slapping rhythmically on the shore. Watching. Waiting. Wondering where Zach and Alita were, and if they were having better success. Trying not to think about the crash, but thinking about it anyway. Wondering if anyone besides themselves knew the plane had gone down—if their loved ones had been informed, if they were anxiously awaiting news, just as these few survivors were anxiously awaiting rescue.

They heard Alita long before she came into view. She was alternately cursing in Spanish and singing a song about washing some man out of her hair. She staggered the last few feet, and dropped to the ground like a limp doll.

"So, where's Zach?" Gavin prompted when Alita didn't volunteer any information.

"In hell, I hope," Alita rasped irritably. "Caramba! I sound like a frog! I need something to drink."

Kelly passed her a section of coconut.

Alita made a face. "I hate coconut! Give me some water."

"The only water available is right behind you," Kelly told her. "A whole ocean full of it. This isn't the Hilton. It's either coconut milk or nothing. Unless you'd prefer to suck on a banana."

"Suck one yourself," Alita retorted smartly. "Better yet, go suck a rotten egg." Despite her aversion for it, Alita accepted the coconut. "Agh! This is awful!"

"Try pretending it's a piña colada," Frazer suggested.

"Try pretending you're an invisible mime," she snapped back.

"Look, snipe all you want, but tell us what happened. Did you and Zach find anything? Is he coming back?" This from Gavin, whose patience was at its end.

"He'll be here when he gets damn good and ready, I suppose. And no, we didn't find anything but sand and rocks and trees. That is why he went on, and I turned back.

That man! He doesn't walk. He trots. He jogs. He just keeps going and going and going, like that stupid bunny in those commercials. I told him to slow down. I told him I was tired, and hungry and dying of thirst. And what does he say? He tells me he warned me not to come along with him. And he just keeps walking!"

"How far did you go before you started back?"

"Clear to the end of the island, I think. The shoreline took a big curve to the left, and I couldn't see any more land straight ahead."

"How many miles?" Gavin pressed.

Alita scowled at him. "How the devil should I know?" She shook her wrist at him. It was adorned with a gold, diamond-encrusted watch. "Does this look like one of those things people wear when they run? No. It is a watch, not a . . . a . . ."

"Odometer," he supplied.

"Whatever. It tells time, not kilometers."

"You didn't see any lights? Any utility poles or wires? No footprints? Nothing?" Kelly asked despondently.

"Nada," Alita repeated succinctly. "Not a blasted, blessed thing."

"Did you and Zach find any fresh water anywhere?" Frazer wanted to know.

Alita shook her head, setting her long earrings jangling against her tangled raven hair. "If we had, I would still be there, drowning my thirst and soaking my poor, aching body."

At first, Kelly wasn't sure what had awakened her. As she looked around, nothing seemed different, except that the fire had burned down and could use another piece of wood. She rose quietly, not wanting to disturb the others, suppressing a groan as her sore muscles protested the movement. She was reaching for a chunk of driftwood when it occurred to her that it was too quiet. Even with the waves still hissing onto the shore, Earl mumbling in his sleep, and Gavin snoring lightly, there was something missing. Some essential sound.

Then it hit her. The woman. She wasn't gasping anymore. The wheezing and rattling she'd made with every breath was gone. With trepidation, Kelly went to her and knelt at her side. The woman's face was peaceful, not longer twisted with pain. Even as she took hold of her wrist to feel for a pulse, Kelly knew what she would find. She was dead.

"If you're considering CPR, don't bother, dearie. She passed on about half an hour ago."

Startled, Kelly spun around to find Wynne propped up on one elbow, watching her. "Did she . . . ? Was it . . . ?"

Wynne offered a gentle smile. "No, she didn't wake. She went in her sleep, the way we'd all prefer to go, if that's any comfort. I said a prayer for her."

Kelly swiped at the tears rolling down her cheeks. "I don't know why I'm crying. I didn't even know her. It's just so sad. We . . . we don't even know her name. At least the man and the boy have their wallets on them, but there's nothing to tell us who she was—if she was someone's wife or mother. She died alone."

"Not at all. We were here with her. God was here."

"Was He?" Kelly countered caustically. "Was He there when the plane crashed and killed so many unsuspecting, innocent people?"

"Now, Kelly," Wynne admonished softly. "Don't be bitter. You know He was there, watching over you, making sure you and I and the others got out."

"Why us? Why them?" Kelly held her hands out, palms up, in a gesture of confusion.

"It's not for us to question the Lord's decisions, my girl.

He alone knows who and why and when." Wynne's eyes clouded. "He took my James. I realize that now, though my mind has tried to deny it all day. I, too, want to question God's authority, but what good would that serve? No, better to accept the Lord's will as gracefully as possible and wait for him to call us in turn."

Kelly heaved a sodden sigh. "Easier said than done."

"I know," Wynne concurred softly. "Just now, I'm feeling very sorry for myself, with James gone. We've been together for so long. I just don't know how I'm going to be able to live without him. I hope our Heavenly Father, in His mercy, lets me join James soon. Somehow, I feel certain He will."

Kelly crawled over to the older woman, took her wrinkled hand, and tenderly stroked the paper-thin skin. "I'm sorry, Wynne. If there is anything I can do to make it easier for you, all you have to do is ask."

"Thank you, dearie, but I think only God can help me now."

Dawn was tinting the sky in shades of pink and pearl gray as Zach limped down the final stretch of beach toward the camp. He felt like warmed-over death, and knew he must look the part, too. He'd walked most of the night, allowing himself only brief rest periods and one short nap. His ankle throbbed, his ribs and shoulder ached. His head felt as if an army of contractors were holding a nail-hammering contest on his skull. His eyes were scratchy with grit and lack of sleep. And every muscle and tendon in his body was in revolt. He could barely place one foot in front of the other.

Worst of all, he was returning with bad news. In the course of his all-night marathon, he had traversed the entire circumference of the island, with the exception of one section on the north side, where the rocks had formed an impassible barrier. Of necessity, he'd had to turn back the way he'd come, and walk the whole perimeter in reverse, thus doubling the distance. Roughly, he estimated he'd walked more than thirty miles, fifteen-plus miles each way. His best calculation was that the island was eight miles long, north to south, and about four miles wide, west to east, with a shape similar to an irregularly curved, knobby kidney bean.

And for all his searching, his efforts had been for naught. He hadn't met one other person, hadn't come across a single building, abandoned or otherwise, let alone a town or village. Not even a rotting boat dock or an old campfire. The only sign of life he'd encountered, other than a few birds he'd disturbed from their slumber in the trees, had been a sand crab that had tried to nip his toe.

Unless there was a village nestled further inland, it appeared the island was totally uninhabited. Deserted. And Zach didn't have to think very hard to determine why. He hadn't discovered any water, either. Again, unless there was a stream or pond concealed in the interior, beyond sight of the beach, there didn't appear to be a source of fresh water—which meant he and his fellow survivors were in extremely desperate straits.

His only remaining hope was that Daniels had had better luck locating help, that rescue was already underway. They had to get off this island quickly. *He* had to, as soon as possible, for a number of personal reasons that had nothing at all to do with his next building contract. It was a toss-up as to whom he was most worried about—his daughter or his father. Knowing his family, they would all take the news of the crash hard. They would surely assume the worst. After losing her mother at such a young age, Becky would be devastated. His mother would wail and pray and cling to the slimmest thread of hope. His sisters would pester the airline officials to no end for the smallest details. But it was his father, and his reaction, that Zach feared for most.

Ike Goldstein was a lovable, stubborn old goat, and lately he'd been displaying that last trait distressingly well, driving his entire family to distraction. Recently, he'd been having recurring chest pains, shortness of breath, and dizzy spells—and adamantly refusing to see a doctor, despite pleas from everyone. Zach's mother, Sarah, had tried everything from nagging to outright threats, employing every guilt tactic known to Jewish wives and mothers the world over, and all to no avail. Ike insisted it was only indigestion, or maybe a touch of angina, nothing serious enough to necessitate a visit to that "quack," who knew next to nothing and charged the earth for a lot of worthless advice.

It had taken a two-hour phone conversation/argument with Zach to get the elder Goldstein to finally relent, under certain staunch conditions. Ike would only consent to tests, which the doctor had already recommended simply on the strength of Sarah's description of his symptoms, if Zach would go with him. Zach had agreed with alacrity, instructing his parents to set up an appointment for the first Monday after his arrival back in the U.S. This would give Zach a few days to get his construction team lined up and put someone reliable in temporary charge of the hotel project.

Zach intended to fly from Las Vegas to Seattle, to stay for as long as it took, to direct construction via fax, or to commute back and forth if necessary—anything to get his father those tests, to determine what ailed him, and to implement proper treatment. Whether it entailed medication for high blood pressure or something as complicated as heart surgery, Zach needed to be there. His father, his brave beloved idol, not only hated hospitals, he held a deep-seated fear of them, feeling that once a person went in they were more likely to come out feet first, especially if surgery was required.

"I watch television. I've heard all the stories," Ike had said time and time again. "They give you tainted blood, they use instruments that aren't sterile, they leave sponges inside when they sew you back up. You're at the mercy of incompetent fools. Once they cut you open, odds are you're a dead man."

To add to this lop-sided equation, Ike had a rare blood type, and Zach was the only member of the family whose blood type matched. Naturally, Zach had already promised to donate as much as need be, if such a demand arose. Ike was adamant about not being infused with a stranger's blood. And if his mother's dire predictions, in addition to the doctor's peripheral assessment, was accurate, there was every chance Zach would be required to do just that.

Zach, too, had a bad feeling about his father's symptoms. He could only hope news of the crash hadn't sent his dad straight into a heart attack or stroke. He had to get home. It was imperative that he reach Seattle as soon as humanly possible. But as things stood now, he was stranded on a deserted island in the middle of nowhere, helpless to do anything but wait to be rescued.

As he finally came within sight of the camp, Zach's heart sank to his toes. There they were, his hapless companions, just as he'd left them—a ragged band of unwitting, undelivered castaways. It looked as if they were all still asleep. "The Devil's Dozen, minus one," he thought irreverently, including himself in their number. "The Luckless Wonders."

If he'd had ten more steps to go, Zach wouldn't have made it. Not under his own steam. He fell to his knees and sat, head down, panting heavily, hoping he wouldn't wake the others. He didn't want to have to give them the bad tidings yet. To see the fear and disappointment on their faces. In fact, he wished he could put it off forever. But this wasn't something he could hide, like a child who'd broken a toy and didn't want to confess. This was a matter of life and death.

He was still hunched there, weaving with weariness, when something lightly bumped his shoulder. He opened bleary eyes to see a brown hand holding forth half a coconut.

"Here, man, take a drink of this," Daniels told him quietly. "Wish I had something stronger to offer you, but things being what they are. . . ."

Zach drank greedily. The milk felt wonderful going down his parched throat. "At least we have this," he croaked gratefully. "Maybe we won't die of thirst after all."

Gavin sat next to him. "Guess you didn't find any more than I did."

Zach shook his head. "Nothing. No one. No sign that anyone else has ever set foot on this island. And no fresh water, either, unless there's a source somewhere inland."

"Shit!"

"My sentiments exactly. How are the others coping? Did Alita make it back okay?"

"She made it back, mad as a hornet. I don't think she could believe you wouldn't want a piece of what she had to offer."

"Like I had time!" Zach declared, shaking his head in disbelief. "What about the others?"

"I'm about to explode over here, is all," Roberts called out, alerting them to his need.

"Cross your legs and hold your breath. We'll get to you," Gavin advised curtly. To Zach, he added, "The woman died."

"Which woman?" Zach's head came up, and he quickly took account.

"The one we carried down. Jane."

Zach's gaze swiveled to meet Kelly's. She stared at him from her makeshift pallet. "Jane?"

"Jane Doe, if you will," she replied softly, a hint of tears in her green eyes. "We have to call her something. We can't just bury her with no name at all."

"Another nasty little chore ahead of us," Gavin put in. "I have no idea what we're supposed to use to dig a grave."

"Well, you'd better find something," Wynne suggested, levering herself to a sitting position. "In this climate, you can't let a body lie around in the open for long, you know."

"Wonderful thought." This derisive comment came from Frazer, who was now awake as well.

"*Dios mío!* Can't a person get any sleep at all?" Alita grumbled, and peered out through one mascara-smeared eye. "Ach! It isn't even morning yet!"

"Oh, but it is, Alita. The very crack of dawn. We didn't want you to miss the sunrise," Frazer taunted. "We wanted to see if you'd melt, like the witch in *The Wizard of Oz.*"

"Very funny. Go stick your head in the sand and suffocate."

"You've got your stories mixed, Frazer," Kelly informed him dryly. "The witch melted when she got water tossed on her. It's vampires that go up in a poof of smoke on contact with sunlight."

"Good grief, Zach!" Gavin exclaimed in mock horror. "She didn't bite you on the neck out there in the dark, did she?"

"Ha!" Alita pinned Zach with a malevolent look. "He was dashing down the beach much too fast for that. I'm beginning to think there isn't a real man among you." Her head swept to include the steward in her statement. "That should make you a very happy camper, Frazer. It will be like a buffet for you, where you can pick and choose what you like best."

"Hey! I resent that remark!" Gavin told her. "I have a fiancée at home, and a couple of other good-looking women in the wings, hoping I'll change my mind."

Alita raised an eyebrow at him. "So? What does that prove?"

"You are a real bitch, aren't you?"

"Hey! Hey! Not in front of the baby!" Blair cut in.

"Me not baby! Me a big girl!" the toddler refuted on a sleepy whine.

Blair struggled to her feet and held her hand out to the child. "Well, big girl, it's time for us to go potty."

"No." The girl's chin jutted out willfully. "Mommy take me."

"Uh . . . Mommy's not here right now, pumpkin," Blair said. "I'll take you this time, okay?"

"Take me, too, and we'll all be happy!" Roberts declared loudly. "I'm gettin' desperate here, folks."

Everyone ignored him, including the child. "Want Mommy!" she insisted. Her face screwed up as she began to cry. "Want Mommy! Mommy!"

Blair knelt and tugged the girl into her arms, hugging her. "I'm a Mommy," she choked out past her own tears. "I have a little boy named Bobby. He's in third grade. I have a daughter, too. Nancy is just a couple of years older than you. And I have another baby on the way, but I don't know what its name will be yet. We have to wait to see if it's a boy or girl. What's your name, sweetie?"

The child blurted something that sounded like "Cindy."

"Cindy? That's a very pretty name."

The toddler shook her head, making her blond curls bob. "No. Sirdley," she sniffled.

"Shadley?" Kelly echoed with a frown.

"No." The little girl stamped her foot and repeated the strange sounding name again.

"Maybe it's Shirley," Wynne suggested.

The toddler pouted.

"Guess not. What about Susie?" Zach guessed.

Her tiny face puckered.

The others joined in, taking turns.

"Shelby?"

"Sally?"

"Shelly?"

The girl screeched, garbling her name yet again.

"Damn! I can't understand what she's saying. It doesn't even sound like English to me," Gavin admitted in frustration.

"That's because you Yanks have distorted the language so badly," Frazer told him. "She's a little Aussie. Came across on the flight from Sydney yesterday with her folks."

"So, can you understand her?" Alita asked.

"No," he admitted ruefully. "Guess we'll just have to dub her Sheila, which Down Under means a good-looking female, and have done with it."

Everyone grimaced, including the baby.

"That would be like naming her Girl, or Lassie," Zach objected. "Might just as well say, 'Hey, Kid!' Let's call her Sydney."

The child seemed to brighten at that.

"Is that your name, honey?" Kelly inquired gently. "Is it Sydney?"

"No," the child replied blandly.

"But it's a nice name, don't you think?" Blair put in quickly. "Can we call you Sydney?"

The girl smiled, showing off a row of gleaming new teeth. "Uh-huh," she nodded.

"Okay. Sydney it is." Blair took the toddler's hand in hers. "C'mon, Syd. Nature calls, and I can't wait much longer to answer."

"Me, either!" Roberts bellowed. "Hey! Y'all deaf, or what?"

Zach pinched the bridge of his nose with forefinger and thumb, trying in vain to ease the throbbing in his head. "That's one minor problem solved. Only about six hundred and ninety major ones to go—including what to do with our big-mouthed, small-bladdered felon."

Chapter 6

The question of what to do about Jane was turning into a mini-debate.

"If we'd known she wasn't going to make it, we could have left her on the plane. It would have facilitated identification later," Frazer said. "They'd have matched her seat position with the name on the roster."

"They'll just have to figure it out from who is missing from their assigned seats," Zach replied. "I'm sure not going to carry her all the way back up that mountain, just to make it easy for some airline official."

"Don't look at me, either," Gavin protested. "I wouldn't go back up there for all the rice in China."

"Wait a minute," Kelly put in. "Weren't you the guy who wanted to stay up there and man a signal fire?"

"I've changed my mind. A fire on the beach will do just as well."

Kelly grinned. "You know you're only perpetuating the myth that black people are afraid of ghosts, don't you?

What was it your ancestors supposedly called them? Haints, or haunts, or something?''

"Spooks?'' Roberts suggested with a gruff laugh, deliberately rattling the links of his handcuffs, which bound him once more to the palm tree.

"I don't give a rat's ass what they're called, or what I'm perpetuating,'' Gavin insisted adamantly. "I'm not into hanging around a bunch of dead bodies. If I wanted to do that, I'd be an undertaker, like my Uncle Calvin.''

"I vote for a burial at sea,'' Zach said. "Neat, easy, no worry that an animal might come along and dig up the body. We could float her out far enough for the current to carry the body out to sea.''

"No need to dig a grave, either,'' Alita pointed out.

"No.'' Kelly expressed her disapproval. "If we do that, the rescue team won't have a body to match to dental records or whatever. That could be important as a means of identification. Besides, think of her family. Surely, they'll want the body exhumed and transferred for a proper burial in her hometown.''

"Besides,'' Blair added, "there shouldn't be any animals on the island to disturb the grave. At least nothing larger than a lizard or a bird.''

Zach graced her with a dark look. "You and that textbook brain of yours could really become annoying after a while. I'll bet you drive your poor husband nuts.''

Blair returned his gaze with one of superiority. "Actually, Anton is smarter than I am. He's a professor at Laval University in Quebec.''

In the end, they buried Jane a short distance away, a few feet inside the treeline, near a huge palm that jutted out at an acute angle. This landmark, they figured, would make relocating the spot fairly easy. The location was also beyond the tidemark, and sheltered enough that the wind and rain would not uncover the remains. The men dug the hole, using broken coconut shells as tools. The women gathered tropical flowers to throw atop the grave. Wynne led a short, touching ceremony, including in her prayers those who had perished in the initial crash. It was a subdued group that returned to the campsite to contemplate their own fates, and their guilty feelings of relief and wonder at having so narrowly escaped Death's jaws themselves.

Breakfast consisted of coconuts and bananas, a fare that was fast becoming monotonous. Gavin kept gazing skyward, his expression anxious. "Shouldn't we be seeing or hearing some signs of a search?" he worried. "Surely they know something is wrong. They've got to be looking for us by now."

"I'm sure they are," Frazer said. "But this is a big ocean, with thousands of islands. And who's to say we weren't blown off course in the storm? It might take a while for them to find us."

"In the meantime, we're just going to have to fend for ourselves," Zach stated flatly. "And the first order of business should be another attempt to locate fresh water. It rained yesterday. You'd think we could discover at least a puddle or two."

"The sand would have soaked it all up," Kelly bemoaned.

"Here at the beach, yes," Zach agreed. "But in there," he gestured toward the verdant interior, "the ground is hard. Rocky. Look at all the foliage. The flowers. Even the birds must be getting water from somewhere."

"Maybe you can get one of 'em to tell you where," Roberts commented facetiously. "Parrots are supposed to be able to talk, aren't they?"

"They learn to imitate human speech," Blair told him. "As do parakeets and cockatoos, all of which are abundant here, it seems. However, I doubt they've ever encountered people before, especially those who use the sort of language to which you are prone."

Roberts smirked. "You think you are so damned smart, huh? Let's see how high and mighty you are when you're sippin' water from a friggin' birdbath."

"Beggars can't be choosers. I'd drink from a urinal right now, and consider myself lucky," Gavin avowed.

"Shouldn't we be arranging some sort of signal device?" Kelly inquired, changing the subject. "Like a pile of wood for a bonfire?"

"Or a message in the sand, like they do in the movies?" Alita contributed.

"What would yours say?" Frazer asked on a laugh. "Send caviar and champagne?"

She glared at him. "I was thinking more of the word 'help.'"

"Try SOS. It's universal," Wynne suggested. "And it appears the same if you read it upside down."

Zach was impressed. "Wynne, old girl, you're my kind of woman."

It was decided that they should arrange a signal on the shore. The letters would be formed of coconut shells, this being their most ample source of ready material. Also, a bonfire would be erected, using driftwood, tree bark, dried coconut shells, dead palm leaves, and anything else that looked as if it might burn.

While the others set themselves to these tasks, Zach and Gavin went off to explore the northern end of the island again. They returned hours later, more dirty and sweaty than ever.

"We climbed far enough to be able to ascertain that there is no harbor hidden below the rocks," Zach related dejectedly. "It was the only place left along the shoreline that I hadn't been able to investigate last night."

"If there's no port along the shore, there's probably no settlement of any type inland, either," Gavin reasoned.

"You're right," Blair concurred. "For most island inhabitants, fish is their main source of meat. They'd at least have fishing boats, proas or some such, and nets to seine the shallow waters. They'd no doubt leave these near the shore, where they'd be handy."

"So we're really alone here," Kelly murmured, loathe to face that dread fact. "All on our own, until someone stumbles across us and comes to our rescue."

Zach nodded. "That's about the size of it. No phone, no pool, no pets. Left to our own devices."

Kelly gave a wry laugh. "It's really sort of funny, in an ironic sort of way. How many times, when life got so hectic I wanted to chuck it all, did I fantasize about running away to a deserted island? Somewhere with nothing but sand and surf and sun, where I could laze the days away and not be bothered with the daily hassle. As you said, Zach, no phone, no television, no fax machines or computers."

"No traffic jams." Blair took up the tale. "No clock to watch, no washing machine to break down."

"No frantic schedules," Frazer added. "No running at everyone's beck and call."

Zach nodded. "No deadlines looming. Or building materials not delivered when they should be—or worrying if they're of inferior quality."

"No spit and polish inspections. No drill sergeant bellowing, or snippy lieutenant acting as if he's God's right-hand man. No orders, or standing in line for everything from chow to using the latrine," Gavin listed.

Roberts chimed in. "No Feds, no prisons. If y'all would just let me loose, this could be my idea of paradise!"

"Don't kid yourself," Alita rejoined. "This stinking sandbox is just one big prison without bars. There's no way off of it."

"Suits me fine. I'd gladly trade a few comforts for my freedom. It'd be like a long huntin' or fishin' trip."

"But I want all those conveniences!" Alita wailed, her mouth pursed into a pout. "I've earned them, and I deserve them. Already, I miss my spa and all my beautiful clothes. And the costumes I wear when I perform." She stopped, her mouth forming an O. "I am going to miss my concert!" she shrieked. "This cannot happen! I've never missed a performance before."

"Big whoop!" Gavin retorted sarcastically. "As of six o'clock this morning, I was AWOL from Schofield. I think my superiors are gonna be slightly more pissed than your adoring public."

"Geez, you guys!" Kelly exclaimed. "It's not as if you could help it. Given the circumstances, I'm sure everyone will understand and forgive. They'll probably be tickled pink to have you back, if and when we ever get off this isolated speck of land."

"Who's missing you right now, Kelly Kennedy?" Zach asked. "Do you have a husband out there, worried out of his mind?"

She wrinkled her nose at this. "Just a soon-to-be-ex, who's probably thrilled thinking he'll inherit everything I own. And my parents, and my brother. They'll be worried. Brad won't. Knowing him, he'll probably be relieved, though he'll hide it well, of course. Can't have his public image tarnished, and all that. In fact, I'll bet he's already found a way to cover up the fact that I've filed for divorce and is casting himself in the role of the bereaved widower— to the hilt. The conceited ass!"

She returned the question to him. "What about you, Zach?"

"I'm already a widower, for three years now. And I truly was bereaved."

Kelly could have kicked herself for her rash comments.

"Gosh, I'm sorry, Zach! I didn't know. I certainly didn't mean to dredge up hurtful memories for you."

He shrugged off her apology. "It's not myself I'm concerned about now, so much as my daughter. And my Dad. He's having some health problems. We're afraid it might be his heart. If he thinks I've been killed, it could prove fatal to him. I can only pray he's strong enough to hang in there until we're rescued."

"My God!" Blair blurted, her eyes wide with dismay. "You're right! By now, everyone probably thinks we're dead! Oh, my poor babies! Poor Anton!"

"Hey! Slow down! You're getting way ahead of yourselves," Frazer proclaimed loudly. "Right now, all they know is that the plane didn't make its scheduled landing, that we've disappeared somewhere in the Pacific. They might assume we've crashed, but they won't automatically write us off, you know. First, they'll check to see if we might have been hijacked. And they'll keep an ear open to see if any radical faction claims responsibility for a bombing. They'll send out reconnaissance planes. They'll be searching, and hoping to find survivors. Which they will."

At the peak of the day, when the heat was at its most debilitating, they retired to the shade of the palms to conserve what little energy they still possessed. A couple of hours later, Zach decided they really must renew their efforts to find water in the interior. He rallied his reluctant troops, and between them he and Gavin determined that their best plan would be to form a loose line, much as would be done in searching for a missing person. Even with his bum leg, Frazer insisted on being included. Wynne gladly volunteered to stay behind with Sydney, Roberts, and the still-unconscious teenager. Thus, the small party of explorers, numbering six, set off, armed with sticks for beating back the bushes. Zach set out the guide lines.

"We'll start here, and go straight inland. Everyone try to keep pace with those on either side of you, and stay within shouting distance of each other, if not actually within sight. Don't clump up. Keep several yards between you, but scout the area as carefully as you can. A small pool or creek would be easy to miss amid the brush. Call out if you spot something, but don't chat back and forth. We need to listen carefully for the sound of water. Or even the smell of it. If the ground underfoot gets soggy, alert your neighbor. It could mean there's a spring under-ground, or it could just as well mean that you're heading into quicksand, or the equivalent thereof, if such things exist in this part of the world."

Everyone cast a quick look at Blair, who gave an abashed shrug. "Beats me. I haven't read anything to that effect."

"Be careful, then," Zach instructed. "Watch your step. We'll take roll call every ten minutes, just to make sure no one has gotten lost or into trouble. And be on the lookout for other things that might signify that someone else has been here on the island. Cans, bottles, cold campfires, an old shoe. If we're lucky, maybe someone uses this island for a fishing spot from time to time."

They lined up, the men alternated with the women, and headed into the jungle. In the high humidity, they were drenched with sweat within a few minutes. And without the ocean breeze to hold them at bay, the bugs began to attack in swarms. Despite Zach's directive not to talk, Kelly muttered loudly, "This is not my idea of a fun way to spend the day."

To her right, she heard Gavin grouse, "Do I get combat pay for this, or some sort of extra compensation?"

"You'll get a swift kick in the butt, if you don't shut up," Zach warned.

"The man has the ears of a damned bat!"

In spite of her discomfort, Kelly giggled. "Small and pointy?"

"I heard that. Now hush! Pay attention."

"Aye-aye, sir!"

At the first roll call, everyone was still accounted for, with Alita responding peevishly, "*Si!* I now have more blisters than fingernails, but who is counting, eh? I hate this! If I'd wanted to roam the jungles, I could have stayed in Mexico."

Not long after that, Blair let out a startled yell. Everyone immediately deserted his assigned position to rush to her aid, aborting the effort when she called out with a weak laugh, "Never mind! It was just a lizard! He dashed out from under a rock and scared the willies out of me. I think it was one of those things they call a skink, or maybe a gecko. Sorry."

"Whatever it was, you probably scared it clean out of its hide," Frazer commented. "I know you just took ten years off my life, hollering like that."

"Are they edible?" Zach wanted to know.

His query met with united disgust and a clamorous chorus of "No!"

Onward they trudged. A minute or two following the second head count, Frazer announced, "Hey! I think I found more tucker!"

"Huh?" This from Gavin.

"Food," Frazer clarified. "Something else to eat."

They all converged in his area. He pointed to a tree, from which hung numerous greenish globs up to a foot in length.

"What is it?" Kelly asked, looked up at the strange growths doubtfully.

"Breadfruit. The staple of the tropics," Frazer explained. "I've eaten it before, on a stopover in Fiji, and it's not bad at all. Rather akin to a potato in taste, though it looks like a loaf of bread once it's baked.''

"So that's what it looks like," Blair put in. "I've heard of it, but I've never seen one. You're supposed to be able to fry or boil it, too.''

Employing their sticks, Gavin and Zach knocked a few of them down. "We didn't bring anything to carry them in," Alita pointed out.

"No problem," Zach said. "We can bundle them into Gavin and Frazer's shirts, and Kelly's jacket.''

As he approached her, Kelly warded him off. "No way, José. I'm keeping my blazer on.''

His brow furrowed. "Why? You've got to be sweltering in it. As a matter of fact, you look as if you're about to expire from heatstroke at any moment.''

"Obviously, you're not up on current fashion for women," she told him. "I need the jacket because I'm wearing a camisole under it in place of a blouse.''

"So? What's the difference? What's a camisole?''

"It's like the top half of an underslip," Blair supplied helpfully.

Zach stepped nearer. His gaze traversed Kelly's chest, lingering on the exposed triangle of camisole with acute interest and a definite gleam in his gold eyes. On closer inspection, he saw that the raspberry colored material, though not sheer, was light-weight and shiny, adorned with a wide row of lace across the top. He leaned close, his voice low and a husky as he murmured for her ears only. "I'd like to get a closer look at that camisole of yours. Later. If we could arrange a private viewing.''

Kelly stared at him, struck momentarily speechless by his unexpected advance, though she was normally quite adept at handling this sort of come-on. However, for the past five years she'd been rejecting them. Now, with this good-looking stranger, she was actually considering accepting his suggestion, which was, in itself, sublimely stupid. From all indications he was a typical alpha male, too domineering and sure of himself for her peace of mind. Gorgeous, yes, but she needed another bossy, arrogant man like she needed the measles.

Then again, for the purpose of a brief, extremely temporary island fling, Zach just might fit the bill after all. What better than an attractive man to help rebuild her flagging self esteem?

Finally, she managed to kick her brain into gear and reply saucily, "Sure. You can take my camisole and sponge it out for me as soon as we find water. But I want it right back, and if you're into cross-dressing, you'd better not stretch it or split the seams, or I'm going to be supremely ticked."

Amusement danced in his eyes. "That's not really what I had in mind. For now, though, can you tuck the bottom of your jacket into your slacks?"

"Why?"

"Just do it, okay?"

Turning aside, she unfastened her slacks, tucked the tail of her blazer inside, and quickly re-zipped and buttoned. The result was bulky and unattractive, and sure to wrinkle the linen fabric even more. She was still wondering, as were the others, why Zach would make such an odd request, when he reached forward and plopped two plump gourds down the front of her top. They sank to her waist, and lay there in an elongated lump.

Alita burst out laughing. "Hah! He has turned you into a kangaroo with a pouch!"

"A wee wallaby!" Frazer agreed on a chuckle.

"Don't laugh too hard," Zach advised, advancing on the steward. "You're next." He deposited two breadfruit into the man's shirt, then turned toward the corporal.

Blair chortled. "I've always wondered what a pregnant

man would look like, and it's just as ridiculous as I'd imagined it would be!''

Kelly was now caught up in the humor as well. "I wish I had my camera. When we get back to camp, I want a picture of this before you fellows unload!"

"You should get a picture of Alita, too," Blair said. "I'll bet her adoring public has never seen her so disheveled."

"Speak for yourself, you grimy little elf," Alita snapped back. "You look like one of the seven dwarves after a hard day's work in the mine. And you . . ." She pointed a jagged fingernail toward Kelly. "Your hair resembles a haystack. You look . . ."

"Like an adorable ragamuffin," Zach broke in. He reached out a hand to ruffle Kelly's mussed hair even more.

"Great!" Kelly mumbled, grimacing as her newborn notion of having a wild rebound fling with Zach bit the dust. Studmuffin had just called her a ragamuffin. And she had to admit that she felt like one. She was grungy from head to toe. Her hair was straggling, her clothes were torn, her make-up half melted away. Yep, she was every man's idea of a real love goddess, all right! Which proved he'd probably only been teasing her before, with that remark about a private viewing, flirting casually with no real intent behind his words.

Which was a shame, actually. With her marriage on the rocks, and her feminine ego in tatters, statistically speaking she was ripe for a hot affair. Zach might have been the perfect antidote for what ailed her. Tall, dark, handsome, ruggedly built, with just the right amount of muscle— there was something about him, not machismo really, but a sort of raw male magnetism, that made her sharply aware of him, and of herself as a woman. Sort of weak in the knees, a little bit giddy, and most definitely attracted. Even sweaty and grimy, he was amazingly appealing—while she looked like something the cat would refuse to drag in!

It figured. What else could she expect, the way her life and luck had been running lately? She was on a long bout of shooting nothing but craps!

Chapter 7

They dispersed to continue their search for water. Half an hour later, having had no success, Zach called a halt. "I'd guess we're midway across. We really should take the next sector to the south and head back." He tapped his watch. "It's getting too late to continue on, and we don't want to be stumbling around in this tangle in the dark."

"You can say that, again," Gavin agreed. "Besides, we ought to get back and check on the others. Get another fire going and cook these breadfruit things. I don't know about the rest of you, but my backbone is getting real friendly with my stomach. I'm so hungry, I could eat a horse."

"Hungry and thirsty," Kelly contributed. "A big, juicy coconut sounds wonderful right now."

They were still some distance from the shore when they heard the ruckus. Sydney was shrieking. Roberts was bellowing. It was a horrible sound, rivaling the hounds of hell, and it sent chills of terror through them all. Zach broke into a run, loping over bushes like an olympic hurdler. Gavin sprinted besides him, the others dashing and hopping along as fast as they could.

Zach tore onto the beach, making a beeline for the campsite. The first thing to make an impression was poor Sydney, clutched in a tight grip between Roberts's legs, fighting to get free. Raw fury boiled through Zach's veins as he ran to the child's rescue. He skidded to a halt, ripped the toddler from Roberts's hold, promptly thrusting her into Gavin's arms, and plowed a fist into Roberts jaw hard enough bounce the man's head off the tree trunk behind him.

"You animal!" Zach roared, grabbing a handful of Roberts's shaggy blond hair and yanking his face up for another blow. "What were you doing to that baby?"

By now, Kelly had reached them. In turn, Gavin handed Sydney off to her. Still trying to catch her breath, Kelly gasped, "What's going on? Where's Wynne?"

The rage in Roberts expression matched Zach's. "Gone!" he roared, spitting blood. "If you'd gotten here sooner, you might have saved her. Damn y'all! I been hollerin' forever, and tryin' to keep the kid from runnin' off! Why couldn't ya come sooner? What took ya so damned long?"

They were all there now, all firing questions at him.

"What do you mean, Wynne is gone?"

"Where did she go?"

"Why would she go off and leave Sydney?"

"I don't understand."

"Start from the beginning," Zach told him, giving their prisoner another shake. "I want to know exactly what happened. How, when, and why."

Gavin stepped in, tugging at Zach's arm. "Back off, man. Give him a chance to explain."

Zach released his hold on Roberts's hair. "This had better be good," he warned, his eyes blazing.

"Well, it ain't," Roberts countered angrily. "There ain't a thing good about watching a crazy old woman walk into the ocean and drown herself, and not bein' able to do anything about it cause you're tied fast to a friggin' tree!"

"What?"

"How long ago?"

"Oh, sweet Jesus!"

"No!"

"Yeah!" Roberts hissed past his split and swelling lip. "She checked on the boy a while back. Found he'd died, and somethin' just sort o' snapped, I reckon. Not that the old gal was playin' with a full deck to start with. But she started mumblin' to herself, prayin' and such, staring up at the sky. It was when she took up this conversation with her dead husband that things really got spooky."

"James?" Kelly inserted. "She was talking to James?"

"Not at him, woman! With him! Ain't you payin' heed? She'd say somethin', then she'd listen a minute and nod and say somethin' else, then listen some more. To see it sent the hair straight up on my neck! Then, after goin' on like that for a bit, she stood up, brought Sydney over to me, and set the kid in my lap. Told me to watch over her, and not to let the kid loose, no matter what. Then she just walked away, straight out into the ocean, like she wasn't doin' no more than takin' a nice afternoon stroll!"

"My God!"

"Oh, that poor, dear lady!"

"Didn't you even try to stop her? To reason with her?" If looks could kill, Frazer would have been dead.

"O' course I did, you lame-brained jackass! I hollered at her to come back, to sit and talk a spell. I told her I didn't know if I could keep hold of the kid, tied down like

I was. I did everything but pull this damned tree up by its roots!''

"How long ago?" Zach put in again, his voice rife with urgency. "Where, exactly, did she enter the water?"

Roberts sneered. "Give it up, champ. You took too long. She's been under for at least half an hour already. Way past savin'. And it's your fault."

His glare, directed first at Zach, swung to encompass the entire group. "All of you share the blame for this, you know. Y'all think you're so much better than me, but every one of you is a murderer now, same as me. You got her blood on your hands, 'cause if I'd been free I could have stopped her. Let that be on your conscience, and see how it sets. Think about it good and long. Think about how it was for Sydney and me to sit here and not be able to do a damned thing to save her! And thank your stars it wasn't even worse, 'cause it was all I could do to keep Sydney from runnin' after her, to keep her corralled until y'all could get here!"

Despite Roberts's claim that it was far too late to do anything about Wynne, they dashed down to the shoreline. Blinking away tears, and shading her eyes from the glare of the fast-setting sun, Kelly scanned the rolling waves. "I can't see her. Does anyone see her?"

"I thought I saw something bob up, way out there," Gavin replied excitedly. Then, on a depressed note, "No, I think it was just a swell—the way the light caught the top of a wave."

"Maybe we should try to swim out and look?" Zach suggested.

"Too dangerous," Frazer put in swiftly, before Zach could put words to action. "The undertows around these islands are notoriously treacherous. Moreover, it's going to be dark soon, and you won't be able to see worth beans. Also, chances are if you did bump into something in the dark, it would be a lot more menacing than poor dead Wynne.''

"He's right," Alita agreed with a shiver. "We can't risk more lives, especially if she's already past help."

"At least we can search the shore, can't we?" Blair contributed woefully. "Her body . . . she might have washed ashore."

They traversed the beach for over a mile in each direction, until it was too gloomy to see anything but indistinct shadows.

"We'll try again in the morning," Zach said, once they were assembled back at the campsite.

"It would be nice to give her a decent burial," Kelly said sadly. "She was such a sweet woman, and you could tell she loved her husband to distraction. It's all so tragic."

"Which is why she went loco and killed herself," Alita pointed out dismally. "I hope I never love anyone that much."

"I hope I *do,*" Kelly rebutted. "And I hope I find someone who loves me just as greatly. Not that I'd want him to kill himself over me, mind you. I just want him to care for me with all his heart."

"What bothers me," Blair put in, "is that, for all intents and purposes, Wynne committed suicide. Wouldn't that have been against her religious beliefs, especially if she wanted to join her husband in heaven?"

Roberts spoke up for the first time since they'd all gathered together again. "I reckon she thought she got the okay from God, so I don't guess He'll hold it against her. Wasn't like she was in her right mind. When I called to her to stop, she even turned and waved. Had this funny sort of smile on her face, like she was almost happy. 'I'm going to meet my James now,' she said. Then she toddled off again, 'til this wave came along and . . . and that's the last I saw of her." The big man sighed heavily. "She never came up again. I don't reckon she even tried."

"You liked her, didn't you?" Blair surmised quietly. "Beneath all that gruff talk of yours, and all that cursing, you liked Wynne."

"Yeah," he admitted, sounding abashed. "She reminded me o' my granny. Real religious, always tryin' to make you mind your manners, as true-blue as they come. Not many women like that anymore. Mary Beth sure wasn't."

If Kelly hadn't been watching him closely, she might have missed the way his eyes misted slightly, how he bowed his head to hide it, blinking rapidly. On closer inspection, there were faint tracks in the dirt on his face, and his nose appeared more red. She couldn't help but wonder if the man had been crying, and she was very touched by the thought. Maybe he wasn't as cold, as hard-hearted, as they'd all assumed he was. And she could only imagine how traumatic it must have been for him to sit helplessly by, while Wynne drowned herself right in front of him. Not to mention that he had, despite being bound, kept Sydney safe from harm.

On impulse, Kelly turned to Zach and said, "Let him loose."

Zach looked at her as if she'd just grown a second head, one without a brain. "What? Are you nuts?"

"I'm perfectly sane. I'd also like to think I'm a fairly reasonable, humane person."

"But not too smart, apparently," he told her bluntly. "Turning a self-confessed murderer loose in our midst would not be a particularly wise move. It'd be like buying your canary a cat to play with!"

Kelly just shook her head at him. "Can't you see, though? In trying to protect ourselves, we only made things worse.

Roberts is right. We all share in the responsibility of Wynne's death."

"Look, I know you're feeling a little guilty right now. We all are," he acknowledged. "But that doesn't mean we should let compassion rule and go off the deep end."

"He saved Sydney," Kelly argued stiffly.

"So that suddenly makes him a saint?" Gavin asked incredulously. "Guess it's true what they say about dumb blondes." His dark eyes scanned Kelly's figure in a frankly appraising way.

"I agree with Kelly," Alita chimed in quickly, surprising them all. "Just look at his wrists. They are scraped raw. You can tell he fought to get free."

"Sure, but to save Wynne or his own hide?" Frazer countered.

Alita struck a haughty stance, hands on her hips. "So where would he go if he was loose? Nowhere!" she declared, answering her own question. "We're on an island, *estupido!* There is no place to run to, unless one wishes to go round in circles like a mad dog!"

"Which he well might be," Zach reminded her. "I certainly wouldn't sleep soundly, knowing he could creep up and bash me in the head some night."

"Can't we let him free during the day, and tie him up at night?" Blair proposed. "That way he could move around, get proper exercise, feed himself, and we still wouldn't have to worry about being attacked in our beds."

"We don't have beds, but I get your point," Frazer noted.

"For the sake of argument, what's to keep him from attacking one of us in broad daylight?" This from Zach again. "Or from taking off and hiding in the woods, only to sneak up on us when we least expect it?"

"We could watch him during the day," Kelly submitted. "Keep a constant eye on him. At six against one, the odds are in our favor. He needs some amount of movement, at least, Zach. It's criminal to keep him chained up constantly."

"Besides, we'll probably be rescued within a few days, at most," Frazer added, playing Devil's advocate now.

Zach remained firm. "In that event, it wouldn't hurt to keep him bound. He's the actual criminal, after all, and hugging a tree for a couple of days isn't going to hurt him."

"I say we put it to a vote," Kelly suggested, aware that Frazer was waffling and taking advantage of it.

"Do I get a vote, too?" Roberts inquired wryly.

Gavin sneered. "Get real. I say no, keep him tied up."

Zach nodded. "Ditto."

In quick succession, all three women voted to free him, but only during the day.

Frazer hesitated.

"Well, Fraz? What's it going to be?" Kelly prompted. For good measure, she added, "What do you think Wynne would want us to do?"

"Dirty pool!" Zach complained.

"Free," Frazer announced finally. "But not until morning. I want at least one night's decent shut-eye."

"You gonna be able to sleep, with that boy's body lying there, and Wynne likely to wash ashore with the tide?" Gavin asked, his tone intimating that he wouldn't be resting too well under those circumstances.

His comment reminded them that Wynne wasn't the day's only victim. Zach heaved a weary sigh, eyes closed as if in prayer. "Lord, when is this going to end?"

"Soon, Zach," Kelly murmured, reaching out to touch his hand in commiseration. "Help will come."

Blindly, he took her fingers in his and held tightly. "But will it be soon enough?"

* * *

They buried the boy by torchlight, none of them wanting to leave the chore until morning. Their impromptu graveside service included a prayer for Wynne. Afterward, they sat around the campfire, morose and silent for the most part, waiting for their breadfruit to bake in the coals. One by one, they gradually drifted off to sleep, each hoping that tomorrow would bring deliverance—or, failing that, less death and disaster.

There was no sign of Wynne's body the next morning, for which they were all privately thankful—which was about the only thing for which they were grateful at the moment. Again, it was bananas and coconut for breakfast, along with chunks of cold breadfruit. Even little Sydney wrinkled up her nose at the limited fare, as if to say, "Same old, same old."

"Water, water everywhere," Blair quoted drearily, staring out at the ocean, "nor any drop to drink."

"Or to wash with," Kelly grumped. "I hate to think of having to clean up in salt water. In fact, I doubt it's really possible. I know swimming in it leaves your hair sticky."

"You might get the dirt off, but the salt would dry on your skin and most likely itch," Blair agreed. "And I don't think I'd care to try it except as a last resort. I break out in a rash just from lake water. I think it has something to do with the algae, or maybe the fish."

"Well, I'd give my right arm for a bath right now. Or a shower. Even a quick slap with a washcloth."

"And a change of clothes," Alita added wistfully. "Even a hairbrush would help."

"That I've got," Kelly said, brightening. "There's one in my purse, and if you two don't mind sharing, neither do I."

"Oooh! Get it!" Blair cooed in delighted anticipation.

"And a nail file, if you have one," Alita all but begged.

Kelly reached eagerly for her purse. Just then, Zach called out, "C'mon, ladies. Shake a leg! We agreed to get an early start today."

Kelly and Blair groaned.

Alita cursed in Spanish.

"Can't you guys go, and let us girls tend the home fires?" Kelly suggested hopefully.

"No, we really need you. The more people we have looking, the more territory we'll be able to cover at a time."

"What did I tell you?" Alita hissed, shoving to her feet. "He's the Energizer Bunny in disguise."

"Now he wants to explore that blasted jungle again, like Indiana Jones. I'm telling you, if we don't find water soon, he's going to drive us all wacky," Kelly muttered. She tossed her knapsack and purse into a nearby clump of bushes, where they would be concealed until she got back.

"Why'd you do that?" Blair asked, half curious and half amused. "It's not as if someone is going to come along and steal your wallet while we're gone. Really, Kelly, we should be so lucky!"

Kelly paused, then gave a wry laugh. "You're right. I guess it's just a habit with me, to stuff my purse out of sight somewhere. Comes from living too long in crime-ridden cities, I suppose. First Houston, and now Phoenix."

Today, there was no need to leave anyone behind to watch over an injured member of their party. The most badly wounded had already succumbed, everyone else was mobile—and Roberts, no longer tethered to his tree, was going with them. They would all take turns carrying Sydney.

Off they trudged, again spread out in their search pattern as per the day before. Ten minutes later Zach called out the roll, and everyone grudgingly responded.

"Egad!" Kelly groused loudly. "I feel like one of those kids who followed the Pied Piper."

Frazer, next in line, heard her and laughed. "Maybe we can carve Zach a didgerido so he better fits the role."

"I am going to hate myself for asking," Alita called out, "but what is a didgerido?"

Blair, on her other side, instantly supplied the answer. "It's a long trumpetlike instrument that the Australian aborigines make out of bamboo."

"Yeah, just what Zach needs," Gavin contributed sarcastically. "He already bellows like a bull elephant."

On cue, Zach shouted, "Pipe down and pay attention to your areas!"

"I know precisely where I'd like to shove his 'pipe down'!" Blair avowed.

"*Up* with that pipe would be even better," Alita proposed.

A quarter hour later, they stumbled across their first significant find of the day. The lime tree was in Roberts's sector, upon which they immediately converged.

"At least we won't have to worry about getting scurvy," Blair said. "Not that we'll be here that long . . . I hope."

"Hey! This is great! A little rum, and we'd have the makings for banana daiquiris," Frazer noted. "I wouldn't mind getting a little sloshed right now. My leg is killing me."

Roberts considered this a moment. "You know, there just might be a way to make us some home brew out of something on the island. That breadfruit maybe, or fermented coconuts. You can do it with everything from grain to potatoes, so one of these foods ought to do the trick."

"I'd settle for tea or coffee, myself," Blair put in.

"I'd be tickled with lime-flavored water, if only we had the water," Kelly added.

They loaded up on limes, stuffing their pockets full.

"Okay," Zach commanded, hoisting Sydney up on his shoulders. "Back to the search, troops."

Slowly, they began to disburse, dragging their feet like students reluctantly returning to class after recess. They'd taken but a few steps when Zach let out a yell loud enough to send the birds fleeing the treetops. Kelly whirled around, only to stare stupidly at the empty spot beside her—where Zach had been just a second ago.

Chapter 8

Before Kelly could comprehend what had happened, Gavin came dashing across the small clearing, his hands held straight out in front of him, palms up. He dived into Kelly, bowling her aside, and in the next instant Sydney fell into Gavin's open arms.

"What the devil?" Kelly muttered in confusion.

At the same time, Sydney was shrieking and Gavin yelled breathlessly, "Got her! I got her! The kid's okay!"

"Thank God!" Zach's voice floated down from above.

As did the others, Kelly looked up, and gaped in horrified astonishment. Perhaps thirty feet overhead, Zach dangled upside down in mid-air, twirling slowly at the end of a vine which was wrapped around his ankle. The other end of the vine disappeared somewhere in the foliage at the top of a tree, no doubt attached to an unseen limb. Their immediate, amazed exclamations melded together.

"Oh, my lands!"

"How did he . . . ?"

"What in the. . . .?"

"Good grief!"

"Get him down!" Kelly screeched. "We've got to get him down!"

Again . . . "How?"

And from Roberts, "Why? He didn't want to let me loose. Besides, I think he looks real cute swinging around up there like a red-faced monkey."

"Toss me a knife, so I can cut this vine," Zach hollered over the confusion below.

"Dang, mate!" Frazer called back. "You're hangin' higher than most rooftops. Cut that vine, and the fall will surely break your neck."

"Climb it," Gavin offered as a safer solution. "Haul yourself upright, and pull yourself up the vine, the way they do in rope climbing exercises in basic training. Once you reach a sturdy limb, you can work your foot loose."

By folding himself double, Zach managed to grab hold of the vine just above his ankle. The effort made him swing like a human pendulum, but at least his head was even with his foot now, the blood no longer pounding to his brain.

"Be careful!"

"Don't untie the noose! Try to work your foot into it if you can, like a stirrup."

"Oh, God! I can't watch!"

Zach didn't want to watch either, but necessity demanded that he keep his eyes open, no matter how dizzy it made him. Finally, his stomach lurching all the while, he maneuvered the loop over his heel and pulled himself into a standing position, losing his shoe in the process. Again the vine spun wildly, twirling him around like a top. He did close his eyes then, and fought to keep his breakfast down. The thick, twisted vine to which he clung with such desperation was old, dried out to the point of flaking, and creaked ominously beneath his weight—an audible warning of its brittle state.

Praying as fervently as he'd ever prayed, Zach coiled his foot in the loop and his hands around the upper length, and slowly began to hoist himself upward, inch by perilous inch. Several times, his sweaty hands slipped, nearly sending him plunging to the ground. His sore shoulder ached, crying out for relief from the strain.

At last his head cleared the lower cluster of leaves. Daring to look upward, Zach was dismayed to find that the vine was attached to a limb still well overhead. Not that he intended to climb that high. Nor would that particular bough, slim and limber as it was, provide the support he required. Upon viewing it, he was vastly surprised, and grateful, that it had sustained his weight thus far. Surely, it wouldn't do so much longer.

Still spinning, Zach spotted a larger branch some distance out of his lateral reach. It was the only one near that appeared sturdy enough to bear him. There was one major problem, however. In order to reach it, he was going to have to swing himself over to it.

"Okay, I can do this," he told himself, screwing up his waning courage. "If Tarzan could do it, so can I." He deliberately blocked out the fact that Tarzan had purportedly been raised by apes and trained to such daring exploits from childhood—whereas he, Zach, was in his thirties and, though fairly fit, not at all used to acrobatic endeavors of this level. Desperately wishing he could let loose long enough to dry his perspiring palms, Zach sucked in a quick breath and began to rock back and forth. Above him, the vine and its thin support groaned in protest. From below, he heard multiple gasps, echoing those in his own fear-frozen mind.

To and fro he swayed, arcing farther each time, in imitation of a clumsy trapeze artist, one arm and hand extended as far as he could reach toward his intended goal. "One more swing," he thought apprehensively, scared spitless and trying not to imagine his broken body if he failed in his attempt. He'd probably shatter into more pieces than Humpty Dumpty! "One foot closer, and I'll go for it."

He was on the advance swing, headed back toward his chosen target, when the vine suddenly snapped, breaking his forward momentum. Arms flailing, Zach lunged for the branch, praying he'd reach it. Praying it would hold him. His nails scraped at rough bark, his fingers clawing frenziedly. His second shoe flew off, sailing through green-leafed space. Frantic, he twisted, shifted, and somehow gained enough of a hold with his bare toes and fingers to haul himself up and wrap his quivering body around the branch. There he clung, arms and legs firmly grasping the rapidly vibrating bough, his teeth clenched yet still chattering.

Far below, anxious screams died away, replaced by pregnant silence. "Zach?" Gavin called tentatively. "You okay?"

"Y—" Zach had to swallow twice, past petrified vocal chords, to reply shakily, "Yeah. I think so. Just have to get my wind back."

"Can you climb down from where you're at now?" Frazer asked worriedly.

At this point, Zach wasn't sure he could move at all, let alone climb down. His treetop perch was precarious at best. He risked a look around, and promptly wished he hadn't. So far up was he, that between wavering fronds he could see all the way past the eastern shoreline, and when he turned his head to the right, he had a dizzying view of the waves rolling onto the southern coast. And between them, acres of tangled jungle growth, interspersed with massive clumps of rock and tiny clearings.

"I'm facing away from the tree. I think," Zach told them.

"I can't see what's behind me, and that's the only direction I can go."

"You'll just have to crawl backward, then," Roberts instructed, speaking up at last. "Feel your way along."

"Like an inchworm, Zach," Kelly contributed in a bid to help. "A bit at a time, and very carefully."

"Think like a *gatito,* a kitten," Alita added nervously.

"Make that a panther," Blair revised in a strained voice. "I've never heard of one of them getting stuck up a tree."

The branch supporting him groaned, and Zach knew his short reprieve wouldn't last. He had to move. Now. Whether he wanted to or not. Cautiously, he edged backward. Fortunately, the farther he scooted, the thicker and sturdier the branch became, until he eventually butted up to what he presumed was the main trunk. Only then did he allow himself a gusty sigh of relief.

From there he picked his way slowly downward, until his bare, scraped feet finally touched solid, never-more-welcome earth. Weak-kneed Zach slumped to the ground, his back braced against the base of the tree, sucking in deep grateful breaths while the others rallied around him, exclaiming excitedly.

"Thank God, you made it down from there in one piece!"

"I thought you were a goner for sure!"

"You are one lucky son-of-a-gun!"

"What the blazes happened anyway? How did your foot get tangled up so tightly in that vine?"

"It was a snare," Zach explained, shaking his head in amazement. "I stepped into it, and wham! Next thing I know I'm swinging from the treetops, and Sydney is falling like a stone. I'm just grateful to God that Gavin managed to catch her before she hit the ground." He looked wonderingly at the girl, who had long since recovered from her fright and was grinning at him from Kelly's arms.

Satisfied that the toddler was perfectly fine, Zach's gaze swung toward Gavin. "That must have taken some fancy footwork on your part."

Gavin nodded. "For a minute there, I thought I was back on the gridiron, stretching out for a pass. Luckily, that old sliding football dive I perfected in high school panned out. But Syd's by far the prettiest little pigskin I ever caught."

Roberts was frowning, deep in thought. "A snare?" he repeated. "One deliberately set?"

"From what I could see, yes," Zach answered, his frown now matching Roberts's. "The noose appeared to be skillfully fashioned, and the other end was tied in several knots to the upper branch, though how the hell anyone ever got that limb bent to the ground in the first place is beyond me. And I'd be willing to bet my last dollar if we look around, we'll find the stake it was anchored to. Which reminds me, we're all going to have to be more careful in the future. God only knows what other sorts of traps we might inadvertently stumble across."

"I don't understand," Alita said. "Why would there be such things about, when no one lives here and according to Blair there are no animals to catch?"

"They're probably remnants from World War II," Blair guessed. "This entire area of the Pacific was a real hot spot back then, and the Japanese had soldiers stationed on many of these islands."

"She's right. That vine was brittle with age, definitely not a freshly set snare," Zach agreed.

Roberts grunted. "In that case, we need to be on the lookout for other booby traps, like camouflaged pits with bamboo stakes, maybe. We seen plenty of that kind of dirty trick in Nam."

"Whoa! Does that mean there could be things like live

hand grenades lying around somewhere?'' Kelly exclaimed, her eyes wide with renewed alarm and dread.

Zach's response was somber. "It's possible. We'll simply have to be extremely cautious from here on out, especially on any treks into the interior of the island."

Then, on a face still pale from his recent fright, he offered an unexpected grin. "Fortunately, there is a brighter side to all this. You'll all be glad to know that we can stop beating the bushes for a while. As I was clinging to that limb like a limpet, I spotted a small pool. It's about two hundreds yards due south of us."

He paused for effect, and to savor their surprised and elated expressions. "People, we now have water."

The group followed Zach's lead, treading very carefully as they headed toward a big shelf of lava rock. Zach directed them around it, to the eastern side.

"There." He pointed proudly to a small pool, almost hidden by the growth of weeds surrounding it.

"That's it?" Alita declared with obvious disappointment. I've seen wash basins larger than that. And a lot cleaner, too."

She wasn't exaggerating by much. The pool was about the size of a large jacuzzi, and the liquid contained in it more resembled ink than water.

Kelly groaned. "How are we supposed to drink that? It's as black as tar!"

"No, it's not," Zach refuted. "It just looks black. Actually, it's as clear as crystal." He bent down and put his hand beneath the surface. "Look. It's the lava rock on the bottom and sides that's dark, making the water seem black, the way a swimming pool liner might make it appear blue."

"It's also reflecting the dark green of the weeds and trees," Gavin said.

"Look, the pool is being fed from a crack near the top of the ledge," Frazer pointed out.

"That accounts for the trickling sound," Blair concluded.

"It also accounts for the purity of the water," Zach added, and went on to explain. "It's being filtered through the lava rock, probably better than any purification system in any city back home. And see there?" He gestured toward the opposite edge of the pool. "The water is seeping out on the other side, which serves to keep it moving so it doesn't become stagnant."

"Then it's safe to drink?" Kelly asked.

"Probably more so than the water you get from your tap," Zach assured her.

That's all Kelly and the others needed to hear. Like a herd of deer, they converged on the pool, kneeling and cupping the water to their mouths.

"I've never tasted water so good!"

"It's wonderful!"

"Delicious!"

"A fair dinkum little billabong!"

They were laughing and splashing like carefree youngsters.

"It feels so good, I could jump right in, clothes and all!"

"If we took turns, men and women separately, we could undress and really get clean." Kelly suggested further.

"Or we could all get naked and go in together," Roberts proposed slyly, wagging his thick blond eyebrows. "Really get to know each other." His gaze swept over the three women, his expression that of a fox eyeing a hen house.

"Hah!" Alita spat. "Fat chance. Look where it got your wife."

"Get real, Roberts," Kelly added. "Don't make me regret talking Zach into letting you loose."

"The same goes for me," Blair said, making it unanimous on the female count. "If you want to get better acquainted, start with something a lot less significant. Like telling us your full name."

"It's Earl Roberts," he tendered. "And in case you're wonderin', I'm fifty-two years old and I've never had any sexually-transmitted diseases. No thanks to my darlin' wife."

"Oral Roberts?" Gavin echoed on a hoot of laughter. "You've got to be kidding!"

"*Earl,* not Oral, you spear-chuckin' idiot!" Roberts snarled. "And you can quit laughin' fit to give yourself a hernia. It ain't that funny."

"It will be if you tell us you're a preacher, previously from Tulsa," Zach informed him with a chuckle.

Kelly giggled. Blair was almost choking trying to hold back her laughter.

"Aw, shit!" Roberts cursed, his expression one of acute embarrassment. "I knew I shouldn't have told y'all."

"Hush!" Kelly hissed suddenly. She stood, tilting her head, waving for the rest of them to be quiet. "Listen! Do you hear that?"

Silence fell, as they all strained their ears.

"It's a plane!" Frazer cried out. "It's a plane! What did I tell you? They're searching for us!"

Bedlam ensued, as they stumbled over one another trying to thrash through the jungle and still watch their every step, at first heading several directions at once.

"This way!" Zach yelled. "It's to the east side of the island!"

The others rallied behind him, following his lead, shouting and waving, though still in the cover of the trees where it was doubtful they could be seen as yet.

By the time they'd plowed their way nearly two miles through thick undergrowth to the eastern beach, the plane was already gone. Out of sight and hearing.

Scratched, scraped, and out of breath, the disheartened band collapsed on the sand. Blair started to sob. So did Alita. Kelly laid her head on her upraised knees and joined them.

"Damn! I knew I should have stayed near the signal fire!" Gavin swore, berating himself.

"It's not your fault," Zach said wearily. "We were all so intent on finding that water. It was our main priority, and none of us were giving much thought to anything else."

"Maybe they spotted the wreckage," Frazer submitted in an effort toward optimism. "Could be they're on the radio right now, contacting a rescue cruiser."

"We should be so lucky," Blair sniffed.

"Whether they saw anything or not, we should relocate our camp closer to the water hole," Zach interjected thoughtfully. "Perhaps on the eastern or southern side of the island, where the ocean breeze will help keep the mosquitos at bay."

Kelly gazed up at him, her dark, damp lashes framing liquid green eyes. "You don't think they're coming back, do you?"

Zach shrugged. "They'll be back. Trouble is, we don't know how soon. Meanwhile, we need to be nearer the pool."

After another quick stop at the water hole, they returned to their camp to collect their meager belongings.

"Oh, no!" Blair wailed, upon nearing the spot. She gestured toward the message they'd laid out in the sand. "I was holding out hope that they might have seen our SOS from the plane, but look!"

Her companions shared her dismay. In their absence, the tide had washed half the coconuts away, strewing them along the shore. The remainder spelled nothing at all, resembling just scattered dark blobs in the sand.

"Well, at least we have water," Kelly pointed out in a subdued voice. "And as long as the fruit holds out, we won't starve."

"So who are you? Little Miss Sunnyanna?" Alita griped.

"That's Pollyanna, and I'm just trying to look at the good side," Kelly rebutted. "Which is more than I can say for you."

Within a few minutes they'd gathered their small store of gear and were trudging en masse toward the southern end of the island. Kelly, sensitive now to Blair's pregnant condition, offered to carry Sydney. When she tired, Zach perched the little girl atop his shoulders once more. Apparently none the worse for her previous experience there, Sydney squealed with delight.

As the toddler clutched Zach's dark hair and pounded his head with her tiny fists, urging on her makeshift pony, Kelly had to chuckle. "You're taking that beating very well," she commented.

He grinned back at her, and replied simply. "I like kids."

"How old is your daughter?"

"Becky's twelve." His face sobered, as he added, "Going on thirty, most of the time. It was hard on her when her mother died. She seemed to grow up faster after that, quicker than I wanted her to."

"How did your wife die?"

"Rachel was killed in a car accident. The only good thing was, she died instantly. Or so the doctors told me. I hope they're right. I hate to think that she might have suffered."

"Was . . . was Becky with her?"

"No. She was in school. Rachel was out alone, shopping for a birthday present for Becky."

"You loved your wife very much, didn't you?"

"Yes." He didn't elaborate. He didn't have to. The lost look on his face said it all.

"How I envy you," she murmured.

He frowned at her in mute disbelief.

"Not that you lost her," Kelly hastened to say. "But that you loved her that deeply. That you had a child together. That you shared something so precious between you."

"You and your husband didn't have any children?" he asked.

"No. I miscarried a couple of years ago. Brad was relieved, I think. I was devastated."

Zach's brows drew together. "Your ex sounds like a real bastard."

Kelly smirked. "He's a hot-shot lawyer with political aspirations. Does that tell you anything?"

"How long were you married to him?"

"Five years too long. I married him the week after I graduated college."

"Which makes you what, around twenty-seven or so?"

"Twenty-eight next September. A dried-up old prune," she tacked on with a wry grin, only half joking.

"Yeah," he said in a teasing tone, his topaz eyes twinkling. "A real hag. Which explains why Alita acts so jealous of you. Now, if you think you're past your prime, I've got eight years on you, green eyes. What does that make me?"

Kelly pretended to eye him critically. "Oh, I think you've still got a couple of good years left in you. I don't see any gray hair yet."

He slanted her a grin and winked. "Only my hairdresser knows for sure. And maybe Sydney."

Chapter 9

After choosing their new campsite and resting a bit, Zach started organizing a work schedule. "It will be dark in another couple of hours, so we'd better make hay while the sun shines. All right, who gets latrine details?"

"As in digging, or using?" Frazer asked archly.

"Very funny, Fraze," Kelly told him.

As one, the others turned toward Gavin.

"What?" he complained. "You think just because I'm in the army I should get the shit job?"

"I thought that was part of your basic training," Blair said. "You know, digging fox holes and latrines. At least you know how to go about it."

"So the rest of you just automatically volunteer me, huh?"

Earl smirked. "That's about the size of it, soldier boy."

Gavin scowled. "What about you?"

"He's going to set up another signal fire, and lay out another SOS signal, this time beyond the tide line," Zach specified. "Staying within sight at all times."

"The fire, okay. But it probably won't do a diddly damn bit o' good to make another sign," Earl groused. "In order to keep it far enough up from the water, it'll be too close to the trees and too small for anyone to read from a plane."

Zach nodded. "You're probably right, but it's still worth a shot." He turned to the women. "You ladies are in charge of collecting food and water. Coconuts, bananas, and anything else you can find that you know for sure is safe to eat. Stay together, so there's no chance of your getting lost, and keep a sharp eye peeled for any more traps. Frazer, since you're the most incapacitated, you can help set up camp and watch over Sydney."

"What does that leave for you to do, *Señor General?*" Alita inquired testily.

Zach offered a saccharine smile and swept a hand toward the ocean. "Why, I get to go snorkeling, of course. Actually, I thought I'd try to catch a fish or two if I can, and add to our limited menu."

"Good," Blair approved. "We need protein. Meat, to keep up our strength."

"How do you propose to catch a fish without a rod or reel and no bait?" Kelly wanted to know.

Zach snatched up a blanket, and promptly began to tie the opposite ends together. "Using this as a net, I hope. I figure it's better than trying to spear one with a stick, at least until I've had some time to practice. But don't get your hopes up. This is still going to be iffy."

"Don't go out too far," Frazer cautioned. "The currents can be tricky. And don't cut yourself on any coral."

"What about sharks?" Kelly asked worriedly. "Or barracuda?"

Zach grinned at her and jested, "I was thinking more along the lines of something smaller, like a perch or mackerel, that would fit in the blanket and wouldn't put up as much of a fight. Probably better eating, too."

"Go ahead and joke. Just make sure you aren't the main entree for the fish, instead of the other way around," she stressed.

The gleam in his eyes changed to something less humorous, more predatory. "Don't fret, Kelly. I'll do my utmost not to let anything happen to ruin my plans for making love to you."

Kelly's jaw dropped, and she stared at him, wide-eyed and dumbfounded. Stunned that he would announce such a thing so abruptly, and right in front of the others. "Now wait just a blamed minute," she sputtered. "I think I have something to say about that."

He shrugged. "Don't get your Irish up, sweetheart. I'm just stating my intentions." His tigerlike gaze now swept the others, leveling warningly on Earl and Gavin. "Simply staking my claim, so there won't be any misunderstandings later. I trust I've made myself clear, fellas."

"Yeah," Earl grumbled. "Clear as glass."

Gavin held his hands up, as if surrendering. "Aye-aye, Captain. I got no problem with that, as long as she doesn't."

Kelly glared at them all. "*She* will make up her own mind, in her own good time, thank you all very much. Good Lord! It sure didn't take you Neanderthals long to revert back to the law of the jungle, did it?"

Again, Zach lifted his shoulders in a nonchalant motion. "When in Rome, green eyes. When in Rome."

"It's your big innocent eyes," Alita sniped. "And that fake blond hair. Just wait until all those dark roots start to show. "I'll bet Zach won't find you so appealing then. He'll be sorry. . . ."

"Sorry for what?" Kelly interjected nastily. "That he didn't choose you? The Crowned Princess of Pop Rock?

The Mistress of the Macarena? Hasn't it occurred to you that the man might like your music, but he has a little more class than to want to hook up with a woman who wears clothes so skimpy and tight that there can't be a square yard of material covering her boobs and her butt?"

Kelly surveyed Alita's bright red skin-tight mini-dress with disgust. "What did you do? Spray paint that thing on?"

"Reeoow!" Blair rendered a fair imitation of an angry cat. "You two sound like you ought to be on a back fence somewhere, sharpening your claws and fighting over a horny tomcat. Furthermore, I was under the impression that you didn't appreciate Zach's comment back there, Kelly. If that's the case, I fail to see why you're so upset that Alita might want the man."

Kelly's facial expression echoed her confusion. "It's not that I don't want him, Blair. In fact, I find him extremely attractive. It's just his high-handed manner that made me so mad. He as much as issued a proclamation, not an invitation, and he's taking an awfully lot for granted, especially on such short acquaintance."

"In other words, if he wasn't so bossy, you'd be happy to jump his bones," Blair deduced with a knowing grin.

Kelly laughed. "Yep, that just about sizes it up."

"Hey, girl. Go for it," the librarian advised. "Don't let a little thing like too much pride keep you from a good thing."

"Aren't we supposed to be looking for food?" Alita reminded them irritably. She pointed toward a nearby tree, from which hung numerous greenish globes. "Isn't that more of those bland breadfruit things?"

They collected a few that had already ripened and fallen to the ground, and continued their search. A few minutes later, Kelly discovered a papaya tree. Soon after that, Blair tripped over a trailing vine and unearthed, of all things, a large sweet potato! A bit of digging unearthed several others.

"Oh, this is a marvelous cache!" she declared delightedly. "And look there! Unless I miss my guess, that's another lime tree! Now we have vegetables, fruits, and if Zach is successful we'll have meat, too."

"Good. Something from nearly every food group," Kelly assessed with satisfaction. "A nutritious balance for our mother-to-be and her baby. And for Sydney."

"For all of us," Alita said. "You don't suppose we could find some coffee and chocolate on this sandy rock, do you?"

"Hang a left at the ice-cream stand," Kelly snickered.

Blair laughed, too. Then, ever handy with the trivia, she added thoughtfully, "It isn't totally beyond the realm of possibility, you know. There just may be coffee growing somewhere on the mountain."

"Hopefully, we won't be here long enough to find out." Kelly shrugged out of her stained linen blazer and bundled a portion of their foodstuff into it. "I'm going to start back to camp with this load, and see if I can find something better to use to carry some more."

"Going to weave a quick basket or two?" Alita taunted.

"I'd consider it, if I could make one big enough to stick you and your big mouth into and set you adrift," Kelly snapped back. "And I can promise you, I wouldn't bother trying to make it water-tight."

Kelly was almost back to camp when she heard excited shouts coming from the shore. Immediately, she dropped her bundle and sprinted toward the beach, sure that her brash would-be lover must be in terrible trouble to be yelling so loudly. Half expecting to see him being eaten by a shark, Kelly skidded to a halt midway across the sand, and stood gawking.

Still knee deep in the surf, Zach was clutching the blanket to his chest, wrestling with the fish caught within its folds. "Get hold of an end!" he bellowed at Gavin, who was wading out to him. "Quick! Before he wiggles loose!"

"What am I supposed to grab? The fish or the blanket?" Gavin hollered back.

"I don't care. As long as it's not my balls! This sucker is slippery, and all muscle!"

Gavin gripped the edge of the blanket just as the finned tail poked through the gap. Between them, the two men hauled their writhing burden to within a few yards of Kelly before the fish squirmed loose and plopped out onto the sand. Zach quickly tossed the blanket overtop the fish, and straddled it.

"Get a knife, or something to use as a club," he told Gavin breathlessly. "We don't want this beauty flopping back to freedom."

Kelly was feeling a bit breathless herself at the moment. When Zach had tossed down the blanket, she'd caught her first full look at him. Her initial thought was to wonder where he'd gotten a pair of swim trunks. In the next instant, she'd realized he wasn't wearing bathing trunks at all. He'd stripped to a pair of form-fitting navy blue briefs—and brief they were! Cut high along his hips, amounting to little more than a swath of clinging polished cotton and a few bands of elastic, they left very little to the imagination—especially the way he filled them out!

"Oh, my!" she murmured.

Zach looked up to find her staring at his crotch. A broad grin creased his face. "See something you like?" he asked.

Her head jerked up, her cheeks flaming as she met his teasing gold gaze. "Uh . . . what?"

"You're drooling, babe. Do I pass inspection?"

She faced him squarely, denying her urge to run, primarily because she couldn't decide which way to go—toward him or away from him. "I can safely assume there's no conceit in the rest of your family. You obviously inherited it all."

He laughed. "Along with other attributes." His pause was significant, allowing her time to ponder which traits he might be referring to. Then he elaborated, his eyes dancing with mirth. "My nose, for instance. The cleft in my chin. The color of my eyes. And the slight wave in my hair, complete with a very stubborn cowlick. I've often wondered if that kid who played Alfalfa was Jewish."

Gavin chose that moment to come running up with his pen knife in one hand and a big stick in the other. "Got them both, Zach."

Kelly retreated a couple of steps, quickly mustering her lost composure and sense of humor. "I've got to get back to the others. I'll leave you and Buckwheat to your chores, Alfalfa. I'm sure Spanky, aka Earl, will be along soon to lend a hand."

Gavin, totally baffled by her comment, threw her a dark look. "Hey! Watch the name calling, Blondie! What do you mean by that crack, anyway?"

Kelly gave a little wave of her hand. "Ask the guy with the cute cowlick." She walked away, chuckling.

Kelly was almost content as she sat by the campfire later that evening. For the first time in two long, horrendous days, she was finally clean and relatively free of sand. That was to say her body was, and at least part of her clothes. She had sponged out her panties, which had dried in no time, and her camisole top. But her linen slacks were still soiled and looking more than a little ragged at the hems. And she'd been forced to don her dirty blazer again, since her camisole was still damp enough to be fairly translucent. She'd also washed her hair, replaiting it in a neat French braid while it was still wet.

The others had also availed themselves of the pool, their overall appearance vastly improved, discounting miscellaneous bandages and multicolored bruises. The primary advantage for the men was that they were able to discard their shirts, and now lounged around the fire wearing only their trousers. Even Sydney was dressed only in her panties. Of course, being all of two years old, the toddler could get away with such things, whereas the women could not. Everyone, however, was barefoot, having gratefully shucked their socks, hose, and shoes. A little sand between one's toes was immeasurably preferable to having one's skin abraded by thousands of individual granules grating between flesh and leather.

After two days of nothing but coconuts and bananas and breadfruit, supper had seemed like a feast. The fish and sweet potatoes had been wrapped in wet palm leaves and roasted in the coals of the fire. Though lacking seasoning, they'd still been tender and tasty. The papaya was delicious. Kelly had even concocted a new drink for the group, consisting of combinations of papaya and lime juice and water. Sipping it from coconut shells still rendered a tinge of coconut flavor to it, but even Alita had liked the new beverage.

Even with their disappointment over missing the plane, and their assorted aches and pains, their situation was vastly improved. Zach's shoulder and ribs still ached, but Kelly had checked him over and he hadn't yanked anything else out of place. Gavin had found that he could still use his left hand, despite the discomfort of a broken bone or two and a jammed finger. Kelly's fuzzy vision had improved with her headache, which was now merely a dull throb. Blair was hobbling along fairly well on her ankle, and the swelling was beginning to subside. Frazer was worst off, with his mangled leg, yet he still refused to let Kelly tend it for him. And Alita, with only the scabbed-over laceration on her calf, complained more about her puny injuries than any of the rest of them.

Now, however—clean, tired, and replete—they were all feeling quite mellow. "A little Hawaiian music, a few leis, and a couple of hula dancers, and I'd think I was back on Oahu at a luau," Gavin remarked lazily. "There are a few perks to being stationed in Hawaii, even if the cost of everything is totally outrageous."

"It's because of the tourist trade," Frazer said. "They hike the prices, knowing visitors will pay it. They do the same thing in all the popular vacation spots."

"Trouble is, unless you know where to shop, a resident ends up paying the same amount," Gavin groused. "Not that I'm actually a resident. My time's up in four months. Then I'm back to Chicago. I only joined up to get the VA benefits for college, since I missed out on a football scholarship due to a torn ligament that put me on the sidelines most of my senior year."

"Chi-town, huh?" Zach responded. "I've done some work there. I heard the whole town celebrated when the Bulls won the basketball championship last year."

Gavin grinned. "Yeah. It's sure good to have Michael Jordan back. Where you from, Zach?"

"Seattle. At least that's my home base between jobs."

"With all the rain I hear you get up there, I guess it's the extreme opposite from Phoenix," Kelly mused.

Zach arched a dark eyebrow in her direction. "That where you live?"

"Now, I do. I used to live in Houston."

"With the ex."

Kelly nodded. "He still lives there, but even as large as Texas is, it wasn't big enough for the two of us. Not to suit me, anyway. I hired a competent manager for my health club there, and relocated to Phoenix, where I'd just opened a new club six months before."

"How many do you own?" he asked.

"Me and the bank?" Kelly joked. "The new one in Sydney is the third, and that only because one of my most affluent clients moved there and swore she couldn't live in such a foreign locale without one of my specialty salons. She put up half the financing herself, and helped arrange the other half. I just hope the salon goes over as well as the first two, for both our sakes."

"I'm confused," Blair said. "I thought you ran a beauty shop."

"I'm trying a new concept," Kelly explained. "I've combined several operations into one. There's a health club, complete with exercise machines, aerobics classes, a small pool, a whirlpool and sauna, and a massage room and showers. Connected to that is the beauty salon, where ladies can get the full treatment: nails and hair done, facials, hair removal, classes on applying make-up, the whole ball of wax. Then, the piece de resistance—a very exclusive boutique—with the most luscious lingerie you could ever want, a line of fabulous perfumes, and a section devoted to scented candles, wine, caviar, fresh flowers, bath oils, nearly anything you need to create a romantic atmosphere. The idea being that you can walk in one door looking and feeling like a real frump, and exit the other as an entirely new woman, ready for a night on the town or a private evening for two. We've even incorporated classes on how to flirt, since it seems to be becoming a lost art these days, believe it or not."

"Wow! I love it!" Blair exclaimed softly. "If you ever decide to open another one, please consider doing so in Quebec. I know at least a dozen women who would sign up immediately."

"Not I," Alita declared adamantly. "Her salon in Sydney did not impress me."

Kelly smirked. "Oh, can it, Alita. You're just miffed because we don't carry aerosol fashions by Sherwin Williams!" Kelly reached for her oversized canvas carry-on bag. "I've got a brochure in here someplace," she told Blair as she started rifling through the bulging bag.

After a few frustrated seconds of trying to wade through too much in too little space, Kelly began unloading it, item by item. First came her purse, chock full to bursting with all her normal day-to-day paraphernalia. Then a small tote, the kind designed to hold toiletries. A travel steamer for clothes. A mini hair blower, and a fold-up curling iron. A small plastic spray bottle. Several intriguing bits of satin and lace and a pair of panty hose, which she hastily wadded into a ball and stuffed out of sight again. A four-cup coffee pot.

"Oh! I completely forgot this was in here!" she exclaimed excitedly. "Hey, guys! We now have a container for water or whatever, and two plastic cups and a plastic spoon! I think there's even a packet or two of sugar left in here, but I used the last of the coffee. Sorry."

The others sat gaping in amazement. "Good grief, woman!" Zach declared. "I can't believe this! What all did you manage to cram in there? It's like the bottomless pit!"

Kelly ignored him and continued to unpack. Out came a small ring-binder notebook, a paperback novel, an instamatic camera and six rolls of film, a bottle of suntan lotion, two scarves, a battered box of tampons, which she hastily hid. A beach towel, a small stack of postcards, and a travel alarm clock.

"If you've got a carton of cigarettes stuffed away in there, I'll buy them off of you," Earl proposed hopefully.

"Sorry, I don't smoke. But I do have a couple of these." Kelly pulled forth three tiny airline-courtesy liquor bottles.

Gavin let loose a whoop. "Boy, when this lady packs, she does it right!"

Blair leaned in closer, peering in awe-filled expectation at the bag. "I'm waiting for the genie in the magic bottle to appear."

"I'd settle for some soap," Frazer admitted.

"Done." Kelly tossed him a minuscule bar with the name of a hotel on the wrapper. "You should have said something sooner. I've already shared some of my stuff with Blair and Alita, but there's plenty to go around."

Zach reached over and snatched up her toiletries bag. "I'll bet you've got a toothbrush and some toothpaste in here," he surmised. "And some deodorant."

Kelly tried to grab it back from him, but he held it out of reach. "Hey, you big galoot! Where are your manners? It is my property, after all."

"No, as of right now, it's community property," he corrected.

"Fine, but there are some things that I consider personally mine and mine alone. Like my one and only toothbrush," Kelly stressed, shooting Zach a warning look.

Zach had already unzipped the bag and was searching through the contents. He replied without bothering to look up. "Don't quibble over the small stuff. What's a toothbrush shared between lovers?"

"We're not lovers," she reminded him tartly.

"Soon. Don't be so impatient, sweetheart," he ribbed. Then, "Jackpot!" He held up a packet of disposable pink razors and a small can of scented shaving gel. "We're in luck, fellas."

"You can't use those!" Kelly objected. "They're for shaving my legs."

He grinned back at her. "You've got that backwards, honey. You women can't use them, because we men will be using them on our beards. Can't have you dulling the blades, can we?"

"So what are we supposed to do?" Alita complained loudly.

"Go hairy and pretend you're wearin' a pair o' tights," Earl suggested wittily. "We won't care."

"We won't care if you idiots have to grow beards to your knees, either," Kelly countered.

"Okay, we'll draw straws for them or something," Frazer submitted.

"We have no straws," Alita reminded him.

"Maybe we can find a way to sharpen the blades on a rock or something," Gavin proposed. "What else do we have in there?"

Zach sorted through the cache. "A couple of those hotel-size shampoos and conditioners, toothpaste, a mini-mouthwash." He held a plastic container aloft to read the label. "Dental floss? Who packs dental floss to go on a trip?"

"I do," Kelly stated defiantly.

He sent her an amused look. "I guess this means you have your original teeth? You won't be pulling your dentures out each night at bedtime?"

"Cute, Goldstein."

Next he produced a round metal aerosol canister. "What's this? Feminine hygie—"

Kelly lunged forward and yanked the spray can from his hand, retrieving her travel kit at the same time. "Doggone you! This is not Show and Tell!"

He laughed at her embarrassment. "Okay, keep your secrets, as long as you don't hold out on us with the major goodies."

"Like toilet tissue," Blair said longingly. "You didn't pack a roll of that, by any chance, did you?"

"Unfortunately, no," Kelly replied dispiritedly. "I only

wish I had. I don't even have a lousy pack of Kleenex, unless there's some in one of the other purses I collected."

"If not, it's back to grass and leaves and moss, like our great granddaddies used, I reckon," Earl supposed. "And green asses, sure as shit."

"That is disgusting!" Alita wrinkled her nose.

"It's not the color that would bother me so much as the possibility of getting poison ivy," Kelly conjectured.

"I'm not one hundred percent sure, but I don't believe poison ivy is indigenous to this region," Blair announced.

Her fellow castaways glared at her.

"Let us know when you're sure, Mrs. Britannica," Gavin advised smartly, speaking for them all. "Until then, keep a lid on the trivia, will you? I'm starting to feel like I'm trapped on 'Jeopardy.'"

Chapter 10

Kelly was half asleep, snuggled on her side with her head pillowed on her lumpy duffle, when Zach crept up to lie at her back. He edged close, snaked one arm around her waist and pulled her next to him. "Don't scream," he whispered. "It's me."

Kelly's eyes popped open. "Look, Goldstein, when I need a bed-warmer, I'll let you know. Meanwhile, find your own plot of sand." She tried in vain to uncurl his arm from around her.

"Shhh!" he warned. "Lie still. I'm not going to do anything but snuggle a little. It's essential to make a firm impression, so the other fellows don't doubt my word."

"Aren't you carrying this macho Tarzan and Jane routine to extremes?" she hissed. "Dangling by your heels must have rattled a few marbles loose."

"Come on, Kelly. I can't believe you haven't noticed the suggestive looks and comments Gavin and Earl have been giving you. If you don't team up with me, one of them is going to make a move on you. Is that what you want?"

"You're crazy!"

"And you're either incredibly naive, or as dumb as dirt," he informed her bluntly. "Call it male intuition, but those two are sending out signals like radar. Gavin's already said he thinks you're a fox. As for Roberts, two days ago he was on his way to a prison cell, where he wasn't going to get any loving for a long time. At least not from a woman. If I were in his shoes, I'd be gearing up for a last fling, just in case."

Kelly wriggled around to face him and give him a sour look. "Gee, thanks, Zach. You're doing wonders for my feminine ego, not to mention my moral image. According to your assessment, I'm either an over-sexed tart, or the last port in the storm. Whichever, I'm not flattered, buster."

He kissed the tip of her nose. "You're beautiful, and you know it. So do I. So do they. If you don't want my protection, I'll back off, but I won't like it, and I don't think you will either."

She ignored his compliment to point out the obvious to him. "I'm not the only woman here, Zach, and if we're talking sexy, Alita has me beat hands down in that department."

"You think so? I don't, but it'll suit me just fine if the other guys do."

"You're not concerned about her safety?" Kelly questioned.

"Let's just say I think Alita can hold her own against whatever crops up."

Kelly considered this. "Well, they do say a cat always lands on its feet. But what about Blair? She's married, Zach, and pregnant. You don't think she's in danger, do you? I mean, surely neither Gavin nor Earl would go so far as to rape a pregnant woman, God forbid!"

"I hope not. I'd do my damndest to prevent it, but you're my main concern right now, taking you out of the running."

"Sort of like a stallion cutting a mare from the herd? Earmarking her for his own so the other stallions don't claim her?" Kelly equated. "Do you realize how utterly primitive that notion is? How . . ."

"Primeval?" he supplied. "Actually, I do. Under normal circumstances, I wouldn't be reacting this way, or resorting to such measures, but these aren't ordinary circumstances, Kelly. Here, now, for as long as we're all stranded on this island, we're back to survival of the fittest. And I'm damn well going to survive, babe. And I'm going to see that you do, too. If you'll let me."

"Well, I guess you are the pick of the litter," she conceded with a wry smile. "You're fairly easy on the eye, and not totally without charm. I suppose I could handle a short-term liaison with you, but it would help if you could stifle the Lord-of-the-Jungle routine. I've had my fill of supercilious asses."

His mouth twisted in a grin, and his brow rose. "Ah, a master . . . mistress, rather, of back-handed compliments, but I'll take what I can get and count myself fortunate."

"We'll see. I still think your logic is full of holes. Be honest. You just want into my britches."

He nodded. "True, but I also want to protect you, Kelly."

"Said the spider to the fly. Why me?"

He chuckled softly. "I don't know. I was attracted to you when I first saw you. There's just something about you . . . something vulnerable. Infinitely feminine. Soft, warm, sexy. And those green eyes combined with that tail of copper-gold hair—you remind me of a long, lean marmalade cat. I want to stroke you and hear you purr."

Kelly swallowed. Hard. Her tongue crept out to wet lips

gone dry. "I guess if anyone could do it, you could," she allowed.

His sharp golden eyes noted the provocative gesture with avid interest, zeroing in on her moist mouth. "Not just anyone, Kelly. I want it to be me. Only me."

She met his mouth halfway, her hands delving into his dark hair to hold his head to hers. It was not a tentative first kiss. No awkward fumbling to keep noses from bumping. From the initial touch of his lips on hers, it was as if they'd been born to kiss one another, her lips fashioned specifically to fit his. Fire leapt between them. Passion flared, bright and hot. His tongue speared into her mouth to dance with hers, sending shock waves reverberating through them both. She moaned, drawing him closer, deeper.

Forced at last to come up for air, both were reluctant to end it there, but short of creeping off into the bushes there was little else they could do at the moment. "If that wasn't a purr, I've never heard one. We'll finish this," Zach promised, gazing deeply into her passion-glazed eyes. "Tomorrow."

They awoke the next morning to overcast skies. The hovering gray clouds held the threat of more rain.

"Great! Just what we need!" Alita griped. "This weather is ruining my hair."

Indeed, her naturally wavy black hair did seem to be in a perpetual frizz.

"That's the least of our problems," Zach informed her and the rest of them. "I doubt we'll be spotted today through the thick cloud-cover. Any planes flying over will probably be routed above the clouds. Also, once the wood gets wet, our signal fire will be worthless."

"If we don't want to get completely soaked, I suppose

we'll have to huddle together under the trees," Blair said. "Kelly, it might be a good idea to pass that toothpaste and deodorant around beforehand. And if you have any perfume, don't let Alita anywhere near it, please. Coming off that mountain the other day, she had so much on that I had to stay upwind of her or gag."

"Why, you homely little dwarf!" Alita spat out. "How dare you! I should rip your stringy, mousy hair from your head!"

Blair drew herself up to her full five feet. "Try it, and I'll flatten you like a tortilla!"

"Now, girls, try to behave like ladies," Kelly broke in, attempting to head off an all-out scuffle, one she was sure Alita would win.

"Oh, so the pot is calling for the black kettle," Alita retorted. "Those planning to sin have no room to criticize others."

Kelly could not prevent the blush that tinted her cheeks. She'd awakened that morning with Zach still holding her, the two of them curled together like a pair of spoons in a drawer. Naturally, everyone had noticed, though no one had said anything until now.

"I'm out of here, before this turns into a cat fight," Frazer declared as he hobbled past on his crutch. "If anyone needs me, I'll be over there, soaking my leg in saltwater." He pointed toward the shoreline.

"Good idea, Frazer," Blair agreed. "Saltwater's supposed to be very curative for wounds, though it does sting quite a bit. And I wonder if the ocean water is as clean as it should be for your purpose, what with algae and pollution and such."

"I'm sure I've got a small tube of antibacterial cream in my bag somewhere, Fraze," Kelly offered. "Come get it before you rewrap that leg. And we ought to see if we can scare up a new bandage for you. That way, you can wash the other one out, and alternate.''

Frazer nodded. ''Thanks, Kell. I appreciate it.''

''I'd still be willing to help you dress that leg,'' she said.

''No.'' Frazer and Zach spoke at the same time, and everyone seemed to freeze in place.

Kelly broke the ensuing silence first. ''Zach Goldstein, I'll warn you now that I'm just getting rid of one man who tried to rule my life. I will not put up with another.''

''That's tough,'' he countered callously, his eyes like hard gold nuggets. ''You're not going to nurse Frazer. I can't let you chance it.''

''He's right, Kelly. It's too much of a risk,'' Frazer agreed.

''Okay, if *Frazer* doesn't want my help, I'll abide by his wishes. End of discussion.'' Kelly quickly changed the subject. ''I'm going to go through those other two purses, and see what else I can find that might be of use to us.''

''Wait just a minute! The little fag's got AIDS, doesn't he?'' Gavin exclaimed, his eyes narrowing in suspicion.

''No, he does not!'' Kelly rebutted hastily, before Frazer could admit to something better left alone, especially amidst this bunch of bigots.

''Then why doesn't Zach want you touching him?'' Blair asked doubtfully, her hands cupped over her stomach in an unconsciously protective gesture.

''Because he's gay, and I'd rather play it safe than be sorry,'' Zach replied, still frowning at Kelly as if he wasn't altogether sure she was telling the whole truth.

''Hey!'' Earl's face was a putrid shade of gray. ''What about me? I touched the squirrelly bastard! I pulled that rubble off him and got him out from under that cart!''

''You're safe, Roberts,'' Frazer informed him dryly. ''You didn't get any of my blood on you.''

The big man towered over him, fists knotted, the image

of a raging bear. "How do you know? Maybe I did. From off the metal or something. Or your pant's leg!"

Frazer shook his head. "I watched. And I pulled my own leg out when you lifted the cart."

"You sure?" Earl demanded irately. " 'Cause if you ain't . . ."

"Positive."

Earl nearly wilted with relief. "Okay," he grumbled. "But you keep your queer ass as far away from me as you can get, you hear?"

"And from me," Alita echoed in disdain.

"Like you have anything to worry about," Gavin jeered.

The singer's nose went up. "I don't want him touching me, or anything I touch. Not my food, or a cup, or the same blanket. No saliva, no sweat, *nada.*"

Kelly sighed in acute exasperation. "Oh, for God's sake! I can't believe you're all carrying on this way. Even if Frazer was infected, it's not that easy to contract AIDS or to pass it on. Moreover, they're finding out now that some people, about one in a hundred, have some sort of mutated gene that makes them immune to AIDS altogether."

"Yeah, I heard that, too," Gavin admitted. "But I thought they said that was for whites. So, where does that leave me and Alita? Right at the top of the high risk section, I'll bet!"

Alita took exception. "I am Latina. Mexicana. There's a difference."

He smirked. "Maybe so, but you don't qualify as white, either. Put that in your sombrero and dance on it, *Señorita* Snob."

"The rest of you can do as you please," Kelly announced firmly, daring a defiant look at Zach. "But I will not lower myself to treating Frazer as if he were a leper. He's the same person he was yesterday, and if he was good enough to associate with then, he's good enough now. At least in my book.''

With Zach's hand clamped securely around her arm, Kelly trotted to keep pace with him as he led her into the trees. With nary a word from either of them, they walked briskly for several minutes, until they were well out of hearing of the others. There, Zach swung her around to face him. ''Okay, let's have it, sweetheart. The whole truth, and nothing but the truth—and no stretching or waltzing around the truth. What's the skinny on our gay steward?''

''He hasn't got AIDS,'' she stated adamantly. Kelly held up one hand, as if taking an oath. ''Swear to God, Zach.''

''But he is gay, or I'll eat my sandy socks.''

''Yes, he's homosexual. Big deal. A lot of people are.''

''Gay and what?'' Zach pressed. ''I know there's more to it than you're telling me. He's been tested and is waiting for the results, maybe?''

She shook her head, offering nothing further.

''He's had . . . he's HIV-positive?'' Zach guessed. The look on her face told him he'd struck the truth. ''Damn!''

''That's not the same as AIDS, though, Zach,'' she pointed out hurriedly.

''Don't split hairs, Kelly. It's still serious. Deadly serious, if you ask me.''

''I know, and I didn't,'' she replied succinctly. ''Look, Zach, I don't want to argue with you about this,'' she relented. ''But Frazer is a very nice man, and I happen to be of the belief that homosexual tendencies are an inherited factor. I'm not going to get into a deep discussion about whether it's right or wrong, sinful or not. It's just the way some people are. My motto on the subject is, 'live and let live.' ''

''Ordinarily, so is mine,'' Zach told her. ''But in this

instance, with the two of us about to become so intimately acquainted, I sure as hell don't want either of us exposed to something that could prove fatal. Now, tell me I'm wrong to be so cautious," he dared her.

"No, you're being very wise, which is the only way to treat sex in this day and age," she allowed. "Which leads us right into another phase of the same topic. How do I know that sleeping with you, a total stranger, would be safe?"

"I suppose you'll simply have to take my word for that, the same as I'll have to with you. I will tell you this, however. I've been very particular about the few women I've slept with since Rachel died."

Kelly eyed him curiously. "What do you consider a few?"

"Let's just say I can count them on the fingers of one hand, and let it go at that, shall we? What about you, Kelly?"

"I just filed for divorce three weeks ago. The only man I've been to bed with in the last five years has been Brad."

"That leaves your husband and any extramarital activities he might have enjoyed," Zach said pointedly. "Was that what led to your divorce?"

Kelly shook her head. "No, contrary to all that is popular these days, that was not our problem. We have . . . correction . . . we had differences of another sort altogether."

"Mind revealing a few, just to ease my curiosity?" he urged.

"Yes, I do mind, as a matter or fact, but I'll tell you anyway. In a nutshell, Brad wanted the perfect wife, the perfect hostess, a stand-in-his-shadow-and-mirror-only-his-image spouse. He's on the fast track, and doesn't want anyone to slow him down. I tried. I agreed to put off having children, while he got himself established in a prestigious law firm. I gave dinner parties and invited all the right people, until I could recite their boring bureaucratic bull in my sleep. I joined a garden club, a country club, and learned to play bridge. And I hated every minute of it.

"Through it all, I got to listen to Brad harp and deride the way I walked and talked and dressed. Nothing I said or did was good enough. To top it all, I'd started my first salon in our second year of marriage, with money my grandparents left to me. Brad was miffed that I didn't put the money into our savings account, earmarked for his future political career, naturally. Still, he didn't whine too much, since he figured it was just something to keep me busy, something to play with for awhile, like with a hobby. He certainly never expected that I'd stick with it and make a profit.

"Then I started planning the second one, and he flipped out. After all, how could he aspire to a government position, when his wife sold sexy undies? It just wasn't done in the better circles, you know. To hear him rant and rave, you'd have thought I was peddling pornography. To quote an old adage, it was the straw that broke the camel's back. I quit trying to be the model wife and went back to being myself. When that didn't meet with his approval, I filed for divorce, much to dear Brad's surprise and dismay. If he'd listened to me just once, instead of always turning a deaf ear and hearing only his own exalted voice, he'd have seen it coming."

"I suppose a divorce will be a black blot on his otherwise spotless resumé?" Zach presumed. "And Brad is against it?"

Kelly's grin was decidedly wicked. "Tough noogies! We've had presidents who've been divorced. Let him deal with it the best way he knows how."

"Then you feel no remorse over your break-up?" Zach inquired.

Kelly frowned at him. "Of course, I do. Who wouldn't after living with someone for five years and trying to make a go of it? When I first met Brad, I thought he was the best thing since peanut butter! I was crazy in love with him. It's very sad to see all that die. And for what? Lofty dreams of grandeur and glory? A seat on some dreary committee? Status? Not in my book, Zach. If that's all Brad wants out of life, more power to him, but I need more."

"Such as?" he prompted.

"Lasting love. True devotion. Equal respect. Children." Her smile was poignant and shaded with whimsy. "I want that vine-covered cottage, or a fair facsimile thereof—pets, station wagon, toys clogging the driveway, and a couple of rocking chairs on the porch. Someone to grow old with, like Wynne did with James." Kelly slanted him a self-conscious look, and shrugged. "Now, aren't you sorry you asked? I really gave you an ear-full, didn't I?"

He smiled back. "No, I'm not sorry, and I'll bet it did you good to unload. Do you feel better now, with all of that off your chest?"

"Immensely," she admitted sheepishly. "Thank you for letting me snivel."

"Hey, I've got broad shoulders," he told her.

His off-hand comment turned her attention to his broad, bare torso. "I'll say you do," she murmured appreciatively. Her hands came up, splayed, to measure the width of his chest. Her fingers sifted through the dark mat of hair furring it. "God! Just looking at you makes my mouth water," she confessed softly. "And touching you is making my insides melt."

Zach gave a husky chuckle. "Horny little cat, aren't you? How long has it been, Kelly?"

"It's not just that. It's a number of things. For one, I've got this inane urge to celebrate being alive. An aftereffect of such a close brush with death and too much adrenaline, I suppose. And what better way to vent those emotions than by making love, affirming life? Added to that, I guess you'd say I'm on the rebound, looking to assure myself that I haven't lost my feminine appeal. So, be forewarned, Zach. You might only be using me, but I'm doing likewise. Hopefully, we'll both benefit, and can part friends once we're rescued."

"You think our relationship is destined to be that short-lived?" he queried.

She nodded. "I don't see how it can be otherwise. You like being in control of things, and I abhor being manipulated. We're both leaders, and that can only spell trouble in the long run, all this physical chemistry, or whatever, aside."

"I'm glad you're not going to try to deny that, at least," he told her. "We've definitely got sexual attraction on our side. If we were magnets, we'd be stuck fast to each other."

"A case of opposites attracting? Hardly." She shook her head. "It's just raging hormones. Enhanced by the fact that you're so magnificent to behold . . . so absolutely, beautifully male!" She licked her lips, as if hungry for the taste of him.

Zach groaned. "Now you've done it. I've got all sorts of fantasies about what you could do with that moist pink tongue."

"Tell me," she urged.

"I'd rather show you," he countered, his head lowering toward hers. "And vice-versa."

"Show and Tell after all?" she joked.

"Yeah." He nibbled on her earlobe, sending shivers through her. "Speaking of fantasies, I've always wondered what it would be like to 'make it' with a redhead."

"My hair isn't red. My hair is blonde. Straw—"

"I know, strawberry blonde. Close enough." He switched sides, and nipped at the other lobe.

Kelly's knees wobbled. "I should warn you. I'm not on the pill, and I will hold you responsible for any repercussions. Not marriage, mind you, but I don't believe a man should shirk his parental duties.''

"Your warning is duly noted." His tongue traced a wet path across her jawline, and continued down her throat. "Do you have any other remarks or objections, before I make mad, passionate love to you?" He suckled the pulse point at the base of her throat. Warm, calloused hands slid inside her blazer to cup her breasts through the thin, slick fabric of her camisole.

"Yes. Hurry," she commanded on a hiss of delight. As she spoke, she was shrugging awkwardly out of her jacket. It scarcely hit the ground before she was tugging at the button and zipper of Zach's trousers. His hands were just as busy unfastening her slacks. And all the while, his lips were devouring hers. Her mouth frantically mating with his.

He tore his mouth away long enough to mutter, "God! You're not wearing a bra or anything under this flimsy top."

"Camisole," she supplied breathlessly.

"And your panties are nothing but a scandalous scrap of lace. Woman, if I'd known this was all you were wearing under that demure pant suit, I'd have had you on your back much earlier."

"So what's holding you back now?" she goaded, tugging her top over her head and throwing it aside. "Need some help?"

She caught his ankle with hers, sending them both tumbling to the ground. She landed on top of him, their legs tangled, her breasts crushed into the dark pelt on his chest, pelvis to pelvis.

"Shy thing, aren't you?" he commented on a wry chuckle. He shifted, parting his legs and trapping hers wide apart. His hand cupped her crotch, stroking her through the satin panties. "Lord, but you're hot! And already wet for me. I can't wait to taste you there."

She whimpered. "Next time. I . . . oh, please! I want you now!"

Near to bursting himself, Zach didn't waste any more time on preliminaries. He simply freed himself from his briefs, tugged the elastic leg of her panties aside, and plunged into her. It was akin to being imbedded in liquid fire, forcing an immediate groan from deep in his throat. Atop him, Kelly moaned and wriggled, burying him to the hilt in her moist heat, and Zach thought he would die from the waves of bliss pulsing through him. He knew it wouldn't take much to push him over the edge, but he wanted to hold on long enough to take Kelly with him.

He needn't have been concerned. On the third thrust, Kelly stiffened, her head thrown back and her throat stretched taut as she exploded around him. Her muscles contracted in a tight velvet grip that wrenched him into his own violent climax.

Chapter 11

The resultant aftershocks of their lovemaking sent them into a prolonged series of shudders, until at length they lay limp and trembling, still twined together.

Zach stroked Kelly's damp back, savoring the soft texture of her skin. "Was that you shrieking to high heaven, or was it me?"

"Both, I think," she replied on a shaky sigh. "I hope the others didn't hear us."

She felt him shrug. "I don't care if they did, as long as they don't feel inclined to investigate."

She gave a languid laugh. "I'm too weak to move if they did," she confessed. "You melted all my bones."

His chuckle reverberated from his chest to hers. "That good, huh? And we didn't even get around to any of the really innovative stuff."

Kelly poked at his ribs with her finger. "Don't brag. It's not polite."

"I'm not bragging, sweetheart," he informed her bluntly. "I'm promising better things to come."

They lay quietly for a few moments, recouping their strength. Then Zach said, "Hear that? It's raining."

"Can't be," Kelly murmured drowsily. "If it was, we'd be drenched."

Zach twisted beneath her, craning his head. "Kelly, it is raining. Cats and dogs, as a matter of fact. I can see it. And you're right. We're dry. The trees are forming a canopy over us."

She rolled to gaze around. "This is weird. I've never seen trees like these. Look at the trunks. They're as straight and smooth as posts."

"Geez!" Zach slapped at his forehead. "What a dunce I am! Those aren't trunks, Kelly. They're supporting stems. Aerial roots. And not from several trees, but from one. We're lying under a giant banyan tree."

She shot him a look of disbelief. "Honestly," he avowed. "There's one on Maui that covers nearly an acre. It's a regular tourist attraction." He paused, then tacked on excitedly, "Do you realize what this means?"

"No, but I'm sure you're about to enlighten me. And let me add that you're beginning to sound a lot like Blair."

He ignored that last comment. "We now have a shelter. We won't have to erect thatch huts."

Kelly cocked an eyebrow at him. "Planning to settle in for awhile? This does not sound encouraging. Personally, I'm hoping to be rescued in the next day or two."

"So am I, but in the event we're here for longer, it's best to be prepared. Or, in this case, to take advantage of nature's bounty."

"Does this mean we're going to move camp again?" she inquired dryly. "I thought we needed to stay near the beach, close to the bonfire."

"Look." He turned her around and pointed through

the trees. "We're sitting on a knoll, which gives us a good overview of the southeastern shoreline. I could run the distance in a minute or so. It's also closer to the pool. Here, we have shelter, plus the sea breeze to help ward off the bugs. The best of both worlds, so to speak."

"No," Kelly countered. "The best of both worlds would be to have this island in the middle of my backyard. Call me spoiled, but I'm accustomed to my indoor plumbing and to having a shopping mall conveniently located." She rose, adjusted her panties, and assessed their surroundings with a slight frown. "Lacking that, this will have to suffice, however. I just wish it offered more in the way of privacy."

Zach let his eyes skim the length of her incredibly long legs, across the curve of her hips, the indentation of her waist, to the pert jut of her breasts. "I'll second that," he agreed readily. "Let me work on the idea."

She caught his avid perusal and grinned. "Wow! If I'd known having a fling with an architect brought these kinds of perks, I'd have considered it sooner. My kitchen could stand some major remodeling. And I've always wanted a hot tub."

Zach reached up and tugged her down to kneel at his side. His hand guided hers to his revived erection. "Would you settle for a hot rod, instead?" he quipped.

She laughed at his bad pun. "Only if you promise to give me the ride of my life." She flexed her fingers, felt him lurch in her grasp, and winked saucily. "I don't come cheap, Zach, but I am willing to negotiate."

If Kelly thought she'd almost lost her mind the first time, their second round of lovemaking was the clincher. Zach was in the mood to take his good sweet time, intent on exploring her body until he knew it more intimately than she did. And just as eager to have her explore his with equal devotion. There wasn't a spot of female flesh he didn't kiss, lick, lave, or suckle—until Kelly was a quivering mass of desire. Nor did he stint on his praise of her, though some of his comments struck her funny bone.

"You have the sexiest earlobes I've ever come across."

"Sexy earlobes?" she echoed, shivering as he nipped at one with his teeth. "I always thought one set was just like any other, excepting size, of course."

"Uh-uh. Yours are just the right shape. Dainty, delectable, with just a hint of fuzz."

Kelly laughed aloud. "Yeah, I appreciate the fact that you don't have big tufts of hair sticking out of your ears, either, Zach. Chest hair turns me on, but ear hair? No way!"

He practically glowed. "My chest hair turns you on? With your health club, I figured you'd be more into the smooth, oiled, muscle-flexing type."

"Shows how much you know," she countered, feathering her fingers over his chest, relishing the way the hair tickled her palms. "Besides, there's not a thing wrong with your pecs, big boy. Watching you flex these babies could make a dedicated virgin cream her jeans."

He actually blushed, though he was quick to return the compliment. "Yours are something else, too, lady. Satin to the touch, nipples like ripe strawberries set on mounds of whipped cream. Absolutely luscious."

He cupped one in each palm, weighing them in his hands before pressing them together to form lofty peaks on either side of a deep valley. "Perfection!," he declared softly. "And I adore this little mole on your left breast. Sort of X marks the spot, pointing to the sweetest confection a man could want."

"Knock yourself out," she offered generously, tingling in anticipation as his mouth lowered over her breast. "The candy store is open, and all yours."

That mole was the first thing to receive his attention. Kelly had never before realized how sensitive it was. Perhaps it was the rasp of his three-day beard over it, and across the delicate skin of her breasts that excited her so rapidly. And the way he lapped at her nipple, wetting it, then blowing on it to make it crest even more. She was literally panting by the time his mouth finally closed over one turgid peak. He suckled, and nipped, and wrapped his tongue around it, leisurely toying with her, displaying a finesse she'd previously only dreamed of encountering. He treated the other breast to the same slow, sweet torment, making Kelly ache as she'd never ached before.

Her fingers tangled in his dark hair, holding him close, wanting more. Then, suddenly, he drew the nipple further into his mouth, suckling so strongly that she lurched upward with a desperate cry, feeling the tug deep within her. Again, and her insides coiled more tautly, collecting and preparing for the impending upheaval which, to her immense shock, followed immediately thereafter.

She shuddered. She shivered. She clung tightly to Zach and cried out, again and again. When at length she began to descend from dizzying heights, she murmured in amazement, "Good grief! I can't believe it! I've never come that way before, without . . . without . . ."

"Being touched here?" he supplied, cupping her sex with his palm. His smile was smug, but after what she'd just experienced Kelly decided he'd earned the right. The edge of his hand massaged the sensual nub nested there and, on a gasp, she quivered anew.

"Kelly, sweetheart, you're so incredibly responsive." As his fingers continued their foray, his mouth mapped a trail of kisses across her chest, down her stomach, on a direct path to the golden delta at the juncture of her thighs.

She knew where he was headed, what he intended. "No, it's too much!" she gasped, tugging at his hair in an attempt to deflect him from his chosen target. It was wasted effort on her part. He would not be deterred.

"I've got to taste you, or die thinking about it."

"Not yet. God, Zach! Show some pity! I haven't even come down from the last time."

"I don't intend for you to. I want you to go higher, further, time and time again. I love watching you come undone."

His tongue found that tiny button at the same time his fingers delved inside her. For Kelly it was blissful torture.

"Purr for me, Kelly," he urged. "Talk to me. Tell me what you're feeling, what you want."

She writhed beneath him. "Stop!" she whimpered. Then, "Oh, more! More! Harder!"

His fingers, slick with her dew, pushed into her, twisting. His tongue flicked deftly back and forth, his lips tugging at her with wickedly exquisite skill—and she could only hiss, "Yesss! Zach, yesss!"

Within seconds, she was soaring again, feeling as if she'd split apart at the seams. She couldn't tell up from down, and no longer cared. She was on a runaway carousel ride, spinning round and round . . . on and on it went. And just when she thought she'd reached the pinnacle, Zach and his magic mouth sent her flying higher. Vaguely, through the whirling mists, she heard him urging her onward—and herself screaming his name.

Barely missing a stroke, Zach straddled her and plunged into her torrid, quivering depths. He could not recall ever being this aroused . . . this hard . . . this engorged. With a sigh bordering on a sob, he immersed himself fully in a single, swift stroke. It was heavenly—and hot as hell. He could feel her silken muscles pulsating around him, and his own frantic pulse echoing hers.

She bucked beneath him. He answered her need with his. Retreating, advancing. Forcing himself to start out slowly, gradually increasing the tempo, making both of them wait for the grand finale. Anticipating it. Savoring it. Until at last Zach got caught up in his own design—out of control, subject only to nature's urgent demand. On a final, desperate thrust, he let himself go, spewing into her like an endless fount. Spasm after wondrous spasm shook him, and through clenched teeth his cry of triumph emerged as a muted howl.

It was several minutes before either of them could resume breathing normally. "You've wrung me out, woman. All that's left is to hang me up to dry."

"You'll have to manage on your own," she informed him wearily. "I'm about as limp as a rag doll with half its stuffing missing."

He patted her bottom. "Nope. You're stuffing's still there. In all the right places."

"Ssh. I'm trying to nap. And when you talk, the sound vibrates from your chest to my ear. Pillows are supposed to be seen, and not heard."

"I thought that was children, not pillows."

"So pretend you're a big kid and pipe down."

"Got news for you, babe. You haven't got time for a siesta now. Not unless you want one of the others to wander by and catch you as naked as Eve without her fig leaves."

"Crap!" With a great show of reluctance, Kelly pushed herself into a sitting position. "For a deserted island, this place certainly lacks privacy." She reached out and rumpled his hair. "Then again, you're going to do something about that, aren't you? That was part of the deal, wasn't it, Tarzan?"

He arched a dark eyebrow at her. "Tarzan?"

Kelly grinned. "Yeah, aside from your incredible acrobatics, both off the ground and on it, that was some jungle yell you let loose a couple of minutes ago. Sent visions of loincloths dancing in my head."

* * *

As they wobbled into camp a short while later, Kelly had to wonder if she wore the same goofy grin on her face that Zach was displaying on his. Anyone with eyeballs and brains could tell what they'd been up to for the past hour and a half.

Alita was the first to comment, lashing them with a spiteful glare. "Well, I hope you had fun, while the rest of us were sitting here growing mold in the rain."

"Actually, we did," Kelly retorted smugly.

"And while we were at it," Zach added for good measure, "we found the perfect place to set up a permanent camp."

"Not again!" Blair wailed loudly. "Tell me we're not moving to yet another spot."

"Holy Moses, woman!" Earl complained, holding his hands to his ears. "To hear you bellyachin', you'd think we had to move six rooms full of furniture. Lord, if there's anything I can't stand, it's a whinin' female!"

"It's really not that far, and it's more conveniently located between the southern and east shores and the pool," Zach went on to say.

"Best of all, it's dry," Kelly tacked on temptingly, in the manner of a real estate agent. "And the ground is covered with this mossy kind of grass instead of rocks or sand. Nice breeze, lovely view, lots of shade."

"Sold!" Frazer proclaimed decisively. "When can we move in?"

"It's available immediately."

"And we sure won't have to worry about the neighbors cranking their stereo up too high," Gavin quipped.

"So, what are we waiting for?" Alita inquired impatiently. "The sooner I'm dry, the happier I'm going to be."

"R-i-i-ight." Kelly drew the word out mockingly. "The

day you turn genuinely pleasant is the day I'll start believing in Santa Claus again."

"So, who are you? Mother Teresa?"

Kelly gazed in dismay at the pile of items Zach had dumped out of her bag onto the ground. "Look at the mess you've made! If I ever want to find anything, I'll have to repack it all. What in the devil are you looking for, anyway?"

"Safety pins," Zach replied distractedly, proceeding with his search. "I've got the dental floss. Now I need the pins and a couple of rubber bands. Oh, and I'm taking the pocket clip off of your ball point pen."

"What for?"

"Fishing equipment."

"Fishing equipment?" she echoed stupidly.

"Yeah. I'm hoping the floss will suffice in lieu of regular fishing line, and I'm going to file the pen clip on a rock and use it as the hook. Do you have a bright length of ribbon, or something I could fashion into a decent lure? Since we don't have anything to use for bait that I think would attract the fish, I'm going to try a little fly fishing instead." He snapped his fingers as a thought came to him. "I know! That neon pink lace on your panties would be perfect!"

She stared at him in disbelief, then laughed. "Planning to catch a horny fish? One with his *fly* down? Is that why they call it fly fishing?" she mused teasingly. "I've always wondered about that."

"You're a regular riot," he retorted dryly.

"And you're thoroughly demented. Round the bend. A one-man cracker factory. This Robinson Crusoe fixation of yours is short-circuiting your brain cells."

The look in his eyes was roguishly determined. "Are you

going to hand over that lace voluntarily, or make me take it off of you?"

With a grin, she waved her hand at her face, as if warding off a hot flash, and cooed flirtatiously, "Oooh, baby! Talk some more dirt to me! It gets me all hot and bothered!"

From out of nowhere, a raucous voice repeated, "Oooh, baby! Oh, baby! Oh! Oooh!"

Kelly's head jerked in surprise, as did Zach's. She eyed him with a frown. "How did you do that? I didn't even see your lips move."

"That's because they didn't." Zach peered at the bushes at the edge of the clearing. "Okay, you've had your little joke. You can come out now."

No one emerged. Not a leaf stirred.

"Who are you talking to?" Kelly inquired curiously.

"Whichever of our motley companions is pulling a fast one," Zach replied.

"Uh-huh." Kelly nodded. "That would make a lot more sense if they weren't all in plain sight." She gestured toward the center of their "Tree House," where the others were busy forming a new firepit.

Zach counted heads, his brow furrowing in bewilderment. All were present and accounted for, and too far away to have been the voice both he and Kelly had heard. "What the . . . ?"

"Oh, baby! Oh, baby! Oooh!"

Zach gave an involuntary jolt. Kelly emitted a startled squeal. The unseen speaker cackled—a wicked, eerie sound that seemed to waft overhead.

Zach looked up, squinting through the abundant foliage. It took a moment, but then he laughed. "There!" He pointed. "There's our culprit!"

Kelly followed his lead, her heart still pounding overtime. Half-hidden among the leaves, she caught a glimpse of crimson. She couldn't quite make out the form of it. "What is it? Who's up there?"

"A bird. A blasted mouthy parrot!"

"A parrot?" She took a closer look, and sure enough, camouflaged in the branches was a big green and red parrot. "But . . . Blair said these birds wouldn't know how to speak."

Zach's eyes gleamed with unholy glee. "This one does, and it's my guess he's an incredibly fast learner. After all, he's imitating you, Kelly."

"Oh, he can't be! I only just uttered those words a second before he said them! And just that once."

Zach shook his head, chuckling. "Oh, he's quick, but he's not that quick. Unless memory fails me, you repeated that same phrase, several times over, earlier this morning— beneath this very tree, when we were going at it hot and heavy. It wouldn't surprise me if he learned more than 'oh, baby' from you."

On cue, the parrot squawked. "More! Oh, baby! More!"

Kelly's jaw dropped, her face turning as red as the bird's feathers. Zach doubled over, laughing uproariously.

"Oh, shut up!" Kelly screeched. "It's not that funny!"

"Wanna bet?" he choked out.

"I mean it, Zach! Shut up! Now!"

"Now!" the parrot shrilled. "Now, baby! Oooh!"

Zach went into renewed fits.

Kelly scanned the ground. "If I find a rock," she warned on a feminine growl, "I'm going to bash you and that dratted bird brainless!"

All the commotion had drawn the others to investigate.

"What's going on?"

"What's so funny?"

"Hey! Let us in on the joke!"

Zach could only point helplessly overhead, holding his aching ribs as tears of mirth rolling down his cheeks.

Kelly, having failed to find a worthy missile, stood flapping her arms and shouting, "Shoo! Go away, you blabber-mouthed pest!"

If birds could grin, she swore this one did—at her. It remained firmly atop its perch and called back, "Ooh, baby! Oooh!" Then, adding to his repertoire, he made loud, unmistakable kissing noises.

The others gaped, then burst into hoots and giggles. Kelly, sank to the ground with a mortified groan, and promptly hid her blazing face against her knees.

Zach's laughter was cut short as the bird managed a fair imitation of his "jungle yell." Momentarily stunned, it took him a second or two to recover. "You," he yelled tree-ward with a humor-skewed scowl, "are parrot stew!"

Chapter 12

"Do you have a pair of scissors in that magic bag of yours?" Blair inquired. "I'm about to melt in these hot jeans, and even though I hate to cut up a new pair, I'm thinking of making them into shorts."

"Sure," Kelly said. "I always carry scissors with me. Hazard of the trade, I suppose. And I was considering doing the same thing to my slacks." It took her but a moment to produce them, but prior to handing them over, she eyed them and Blair speculatively. "Before we ruin a good pair of scissors, would you like to play beauty shop? After cutting cloth, they'll probably be too dull to use on hair again."

Alita's ears perked up. "Did someone say *beauty shop?*"

"Yes, I'm itching to get my hands on Blair's hair, if she'll agree to a new cut."

"What did you have in mind?" Blair hedged. "Nothing too drastic, I hope. I like to keep it simple, easy. With the kids and all, I don't have time to mess with a complicated hairstyle."

Kelly nodded and assured her, "What I have in mind would be perfect for you. A few shorter wisps to properly frame your face and accentuate your eyes, a little more lift at the front and crown. I'll shape it to fall into place, and all you'll have to do is tease it a bit here and there. You can fluff it with your fingers, or a hair dryer if you prefer. You won't even have to use a curling iron, unless you want a more elegant look for special occasions."

"That's good," Alita put in drolly. "Because for now we don't have anyplace to plug in a curling iron, and there is no social life. I'll be so glad to get off this stinking island!"

"As will we all," Blair said, at the same time gesturing for Kelly to begin cutting her hair. "I miss my children dreadfully, and I can't fathom the misery Anton is experiencing. Moreover, he doesn't know the first thing about dealing with kids or running a house. He's used to associating with adults—fellow professors, college students, and the like. I suppose he'll have his mother or mine in to cook and clean and watch Bobby and Nancy. I can't imagine him trying to operate the washing machine or the sweeper. If he can't do it on his computer, or read it in a book, he's practically helpless."

"Maybe it will do him good to learn," Kelly suggested, turning Blair's head to a more convenient angle. "If worse comes to worst, he can always resort to instruction manuals."

"*Si,* and perhaps he will learn to appreciate you all the more," Alita added. Then, to Kelly, "While you are doing that, do you have some make-up in your purse that I could borrow?"

"In the plastic case in the zippered side," Kelly told her. "None of it is probably your preferred shade, but you're welcome to use it. There's a mirror in there, too, and a nail-care kit."

Blair chuckled. "Anton is always making fun of my big purse. I've told him I could live for a month on what I carry in there. You are proving my theory, Kelly."

"I hope not. A week here will be too long."

"Even with Zach to make it more pleasant?" she teased.

"Well," Kelly drawled. "Now that you mention it, if I have to be marooned, he's the perfect man to do it with."

"I rather guessed that," Blair said. Then, unable to resist, she cooed impishly, "Oooh, baby!"

Kelly whacked her lightly on the head with the comb. "Don't you dare get that blasted bird started again!"

Half an hour later, Kelly fluffed Blair's new "do," and sat back to admire her work. "I like it," she pronounced.

"So do I," Alita admitted, albeit a mite grudgingly. "She looks like a . . . what is the word . . . an elf?"

"A pixie," Kelly corrected. "An adorable pixie."

"Let me see." Blair reached for the mirror Alita was already extending toward her. She stared into it for a minute, then grinned. "I love it. Thank you, Kelly. Anton is going to have fits, but I think it's cute."

"Piss on Anton," Alita declared, wrinkling her nose. "The man sounds like a real nerd."

Blair shrugged. "He is a nerd, but a nice one. I didn't mean to give you the impression that he's not. It's just that he gets so wrapped up in his academic endeavors that they just naturally take precedence over everything else. I suppose you could say he's the proverbial absent-minded professor."

"Ignoring you and the kids and the outside world in general?" Kelly conjectured.

"And puffing himself up, while he makes you feel inferior?" Alita blew on her newly polished fingernail to aid the drying. At Blair's acknowledging look, she added ada-

mantly, "Then it is high time you did something to make
him stand up and take notice. You are his wife, not his
servant. I am sure you are superior to him in many ways,
Blair. You must make him see this and give you credit for
it."

"Alita is right, Blair. Unless you're truly comfortable in
his shadow, don't resign yourself to staying there. That's
what I did with Brad, and I was miserable."

"But I love him. And while I wouldn't mind having him
pay more attention to me and the kids, I certainly don't
want a divorce."

"I'm not suggesting you do. I'm just saying that you
deserve some praise and acclaim in your own right. Every
woman does."

Blair looked uncertain. "Well, I can't blame it all on
Anton. I have let myself go more than I should have. But
with the house and the children, and my job, and another
baby on the way, there just don't seem to be enough hours
in the day anymore. By the time I get off work, rush home
and put supper on the table, help Bobby with his homework and get him and Nancy off to bed, pick up the house
and do a couple of loads of laundry, I'm so tired I can
scarcely see straight. And before you say anything, we can't
afford household help or for me to quit my job at the
library."

"What about your lazy husband?" Alita suggested with
a sneer. "Is he so completely helpless that he can't pick
up toys, or help his son with his school work? It seems to
me you should teach that old dog a few new tricks."

"He's usually busy grading papers, or preparing for his
classes."

"While you take up the slack and let him get by with
shoving most of the work onto you," Kelly told her. "Hey,
girl, you've let him slide for too long. The modern husband
does his fair share around the house, especially if his wife

is also holding down a job. And he should also be contributing in the fatherhood category, helping to raise your children. After all, it's not as if you carted those kids home with the groceries. Unless I miss my guess, he had plenty of fun making them. The least he can do is help rear them. Changing a few diapers wouldn't kill him, but it might wake him up to all the dirty little chores you've been doing for years."

"I suppose he could pick Nancy up from his mother's on his way home from work," Blair allowed. "And learn to use the laundry hamper instead of letting his clothes litter the bedroom floor. And hang his wet towel on the bathroom rack, where it belongs, and shut his dresser drawers and closet properly. It's those little things that really irritate me." She was starting to get into this now, her gray eyes shining with fervor.

"And the kids could help out, too, with smaller chores like taking out the trash and making their beds and keeping their rooms neat. My mom was a stickler for all that," Kelly recalled. "She had us doing dishes when we had to stand on a chair to reach the sink."

"At least you had a sink," Alita muttered.

That remark gained their full attention, as Kelly and Blair turned questioning looks her way.

"What?" she snapped. "You think I was born with a silver spoon in my mouth? Hah! Both of you were probably raised like little princesses compared to me. Even this place," Alita waved a hand to encompass their surroundings, "little as it offers, is better than the place where I grew up. At least the water does not come from the gutter or a polluted well. The food does not come from garbage cans, alive with worms and bugs. The very spot where we sit is more comfortable and offers more shelter than the hovel I called home." She gave a gruff laugh. "Even the company is better, and that is not saying much."

"You grew up in the slums?" Kelly inquired incredulously. "That's not the story your public has been told, not by a long shot. I've read in interviews that you are the product of a nice, average family from Mexico City. Your father was a factory worker—"

"My father was a good-for-nothing drunk!" Alita interrupted bitterly. "He worked at odd jobs just enough to get money to buy more beer or liquor and go on another bender. We, my sisters and brothers and I, lived in a tiny, ramshackle town near the west coast, about halfway between Manzanillo and Acapulco. I never saw Mexico City until a couple of years ago."

"What about your mother?" Blair asked hesitantly.

"She ran off with another man when I was seven years old. Left five kids behind to fend for themselves or starve. Not that I blame her entirely. She saw a way out, and she took it, just as I did."

"What about your brothers and sisters?"

Alita gave a careless shrug. "Geraldo turned out like our father, but not so lucky. He was killed in a knife fight over a lousy bottle of tequila. Juanita married, and already has a passel of kids tugging at her skirts. Pedro has a good job at a hotel in Ixtapa. Maria works there, too, at the hotel, as a maid. So did I, until the night the female singer of the band playing in the lounge got sick. A friend told them I could sing even better. They gave me a try and, as they say, the rest is history." Her dark eyes shimmered with acrid memories. "No more making beds and cleaning rooms for a dollar a day, no more begging for kitchen scraps, and no more kissing up to rich tourists."

Her smile was more of a snarl as she faced the other women defiantly. "Now, do you see why it is so important to me to have nice things? To have more money than I can count? To never go hungry or dirty again?"

Kelly let out a low whistle. "Yeah, Scarlett, I sure as hell do!'' she said. "I can also understand how you got the reputation for being such a hard-assed bitch. If I came up the way you did, I'd be one too.''

"Amen!" Blair intoned in sympathetic agreement.

"I am not always so disagreeable," Alita told them. "But just now, I must stay ahead of the game, and getting stuck on this island is not helping. I have a chance to audition for a lead in a movie, an opportunity I would kill for, and I have been very nervous about it. Now, if they think I am dead, they will give the part to someone else. I may never get such a chance again. Not to mention that the recording business itself is a dog-eat-dog world. To stay on top, you must work harder, sing better, and make hotter videos than anyone else. If you sit back, for even a day, someone else will come along and take your place. I cannot let that happen. I will not be a flash in the pot.''

"Pan. A flash in the pan," Kelly amended. "And I doubt you have to worry much about that happening. You've already made your mark in the recording industry, and once we're rescued the publicity alone will send your sales soaring. You'll be a very hot commodity. In fact, I wouldn't wonder that someone will want to make a movie about all this.''

"About your whole life, maybe . . . with you as the star," Blair added excitedly. "Oh, gosh! Just imagine it!''

Alita's black eyes flashed, first with enthusiasm and then with dread. "No! I would agree to a movie about the plane crash and our time here, but I would never want the whole world to know how I grew up. I should not even have told you. If I was not so worried and depressed, I would never have done so. If this gets out to the tabloids, I will be ruined!" She grabbed Kelly's arm so tightly her nails dug into flesh. Her face was twisted with apprehension, her voice tight with alarm. "You must not tell anyone the things I have revealed to you. If you do, I will . . . I will . . .''

Kelly peeled Alita's stiff fingers off her arm. "You can stop with the mad threats of death and disfigurement, Alita. I promise you, your secret is safe with me."

Blair held up her hands to ward off similar treatment. "That goes for me, too. Just don't ask me to sign it in blood."

Alita remained unconvinced. "Why would you do this for me? The papers would pay you money for the real story. A lot of money. You, Blair, could quit your job or hire a maid. Kelly, you could pay off your loan on your business. Why, when I have been so . . . so . . ."

"Hateful? Snotty? Bitchy?" Kelly submitted with a sardonic grin.

"*Sí.* Why would you do this kindness for me?"

"Because we're in this together, sink or swim," Kelly told her. "Besides, I'm used to keeping confidences. Didn't you know that all hairdressers are substitute shrinks? We just don't get paid as well as psychiatrists for listening to women spill their deepest darkest secrets. I swear, once you get your fingers into their hair, these gals let it all hang out. It's got to be some sort of medical phenomenon."

"And friends don't rat on friends," Blair put in solemnly. "I wouldn't want you telling Anton how we've talked about him."

Alita's mouth worked, until finally the words emerged in a disbelieving whisper. "You would be my friends? My *amigas?* Truly? You would not just be sucking in to me?"

"Sucking up," Kelly corrected again.

"And real friends don't do that," Blair assured her.

"They don't betray each other or deliberately hurt each other, either by word or deed," Kelly counseled, by way of warning. "They offer advice, they listen, they're there when you need them. They joke around and tease each other, but all in good fun. If, and I stress the word *if,* we were to become friends, could you hold up your end of that bargain?"

Tears swam in Alita's eyes as she held up her hand, palm out, as if taking an oath. "I swear it. But I am sure to make a mistake now and then, to be not so nice sometimes."

Blair nodded. "As long as you're not intentionally vicious, we'll forgive you. That's part of being friends, too."

Kelly's grin was decidedly mocking. "Besides, if you suddenly turned sweet as syrup, we wouldn't know you. But I would suggest you learn to keep your claws to yourself. I've been known to scratch back, kiddo. Also, if you're serious about wanting to be friends, pals don't poach, so you can ditch any designs you might still have on Zach. He's mine, and while I don't mind sharing my make-up and hairbrush with you, I'll be damned if I'll share my lover."

Revising their wardrobes took a bit more effort and ingenuity. Fortunately, Kelly had her travel-sized sewing kit, and they supplemented its meager supply of thread by carefully salvaging strands from the clothes they had on hand.

For Kelly, aside from turning her slacks into a pair of shorts, she also added a loose inner panel on the inside of her camisole—the material appropriated from the lining of her blazer, which she could now forego and still be decently clothed. Once Blair's jeans had been converted to cut-offs, Kelly showed her how to inset wedges of the extra denim at the front pleats, to enlarge the waist and tummy.

"Egad! I can actually breathe again!" Blair declared delightedly. "What a relief! It was pure vanity, and not wanting to resort to maternity clothes yet, that made me keep wearing these tight jeans, even when I had to undo the top button most of the time.''

Alita had no problem with vanity. She was all for it. She did have one dilemma, however. How to revamp her mini-dress into more serviceable and comfortable attire.

Kelly shook her head. ''There is no way that scant amount of fabric is going to stretch into a top and a pair of shorts. You've already got it straining at the seams.''

Alita's lip poked out in her trademark pout. ''There has to be something we can do, perhaps with another piece of cloth. Something lighter. I tell you, I am sweating like a pig in this dress.'' She eyed Kelly's discarded linen blazer with longing. ''Can we make a pair of shorts out of that?''

''Sheesh! Talk about taking the shirt right off of a person's back!'' Kelly grumped. ''Still, if it will keep your abundant buns covered, I guess we can try it.''

It took some doing, and added material from the cut-off pant legs which they utilized in extra-paneled sides and a waistband, but they finally fashioned Alita a pair of button-up, boxer-style shorts.

''Not bad, if I do say so myself,'' Kelly approved. ''Maybe you'll start a new trend, Alita. Madonna's got nothin' on you!''

Alita surveyed the garment critically. ''It needs more pizzazz, don't you think? And I still need a blouse. I can't just wear my dress over these.''

Kelly tossed her the scissors. ''Stop whining and make yourself a crop top or something. Be inventive.''

Alita's idea was more than creative. It was downright exotic. By cutting her dress from neck to hem, she came away with a long strip of material about ten inches wide. This she wound around her chest like a scarf, tying it into a knot between her breasts, leaving her shoulders and entire midriff bare.

"It's like the bandeau top of a bikini swimsuit," Blair marveled.

"Shades of Dorothy Lamour!" Kelly exclaimed, more than a little jealous of Alita's generous endowments. "I just hope the darned thing stays put when you take a deep breath."

Alita experimented with a series of exaggerated jiggles. "It is fine. See?"

"I still think you should sew some straps on it, just in case. And for heaven's sake, don't bend over! And don't stand close to anyone if you do, because when you pop of out of that, you're sure to jab someone in the eyeball! And it had better not be Zach!"

Chapter 13

"I'll give it two more days, and if they haven't found us by then, I'm gonna build a raft," Gavin said.

"Oh yeah? Outta what?" Earl asked.

"Out of logs and vines, Goober."

"So, what ya gonna use for a saw, or an axe, smartass?"

Gavin was temporarily stymied. "I guess I'll have to look for fallen limbs and deadwood, and strap it together."

"You get hollow wood, or some that's all punky, and that raft o' yours will take on water like the Titanic," Earl warned.

"Well, we can't just sit here forever, twiddling our thumbs and growing beards," Gavin argued.

"Ya can't go off half-cocked, neither, unless ya want to be blowing salty bubbles."

"Have you got a better idea?"

"No," Earl admitted smugly. "Then ag'in, I'm not wantin' off this island, like the rest o' y'all are."

"A raft really might not be such a good idea, Gav," Zach

put in. "God only knows how far we are from another island. And you'd be just a speck in the ocean. You could die of thirst before anyone spotted you. Or run into a storm and have the thing break apart. At least here, we can survive until they find us."

"They're right, mate," Frazer agreed. "I wouldn't chance it out there on a raft. An ark, maybe, but nothin' smaller. I've seen some of those Great Whites they've pulled out of the waters around Australia, big as boats and teeth like giant razors. I sure wouldn't want to meet up with one—me on a dinky raft and him 'bout four times longer and hungry."

Gavin frowned. "I'm still going to try building one," he insisted stubbornly. "If nothing else, it will give me something constructive to do."

"Suit yerself," Earl drawled. "Me, I'm gonna try making some home brew."

Zach lifted a skeptical brow. "Try not to poison yourself while you're at it."

Earl grinned. "Gee, Zach. I didn't know ya cared."

"I don't actually. I just have better things to do with my time than to dig another grave."

"Like what? More fishing?" Gavin inquired.

"That, and I thought I'd try to devise a way to divert some of the water at the pool, to make a spout of sorts, for drinking water and maybe a shower. Ingesting the same water we're bathing in is only asking for trouble."

"I'm already working on a project of my own," Frazer informed them. He held up a piece of wood, on which he'd spent most of the day whittling.

"I give up," Gavin said. "What's it supposed to be?"

"When it's finished, it'll be a boomerang, mate."

"A damned toy?" Earl exclaimed with disgust. "You've spent all day making what amounts to a fool Frisbee?"

"You're the fool, Roberts," Frazer rebutted smoothly.

"It shows every time you open your mouth and say something so completely stupid. For your information, a boomerang is anything but a toy. It's a weapon. With one of these, an aborigine can lop a man's head clean off his shoulders."

Gavin whistled. "No shit? I hope you're not planning on throwing it my way."

Frazer's smile aped one Boris Karloff might have dredged up. Then he laughed. "No, but I do hope to knock me a pigeon or two in the noggin. They make good tucker, and fish can get real tiresome after a while."

Despite himself, Earl was impressed, as were the other men. "Well, I'll be hornswoggled. I just might try making a slingshot, and give you a tad o' competition, you little runt."

Frazer gave an amiable shrug. "Whatever floats your boat, mate. It'll just put more meat in the pot."

Three days went by—three days of constantly being on the lookout, ready to light the signal fire, to wave blankets, to flash Kelly's small hand mirror into the sun—anything to attract attention toward them. The first day, they thought they heard the distant drone of an airplane, but it was too far off to see. The next day was bright and clear, perfect weather to conduct a rescue mission, yet no planes came. The third day was also clear, but the sole plane flew over just before dawn, rousing them from their sleep and sending them dashing to the beach. However, when Zach and Gavin attempted to light the signal fire, the wood was too damp to catch. Even the small amount of smoke generated was quickly whisked away on the wind, not nearly enough to notice.

"Damn! I don't understand this!" Zach ranted, spearing his fingers through his hair in exasperation. "This wood should have dried out by now. Not a drop of rain for the past two days, and it's been hot enough to fry beef on the hoof!''

It had been terribly hot. If not for the ocean breeze, they would have sweltered even more than they did. As it was, the humidity was stifling, combining with the intense heat to make them all highly irritable, which they were anyway, for assorted reasons.

Earl had run out of cigarettes and the lack of nicotine was having its predictable effect, while Kelly swore she was having caffeine withdrawal. Poor Blair had morning sickness that often lasted all day. Hourly, Zach was more worried about his father. And Sydney . . . Sydney was cranky, feverish, and had a runny nose. Blair suspected the toddler was cutting teeth, at least they all hoped it was nothing more serious. With no children's aspirin on hand, they resorted to sprinkling a small amount of powder from adult Tylenol capsules into Sydney's food.

''I wish we had something to rub on her gums, or something cold for her to chew on,'' Blair bemoaned. The best they could come up with in lieu of a teething ring were lime rinds, which made it difficult to tell if Sydney's continual pucker was a result of the sour fruit or a cantankerous sulk.

As for Alita, she developed a monstrous case of PMS. Jittery didn't begin to describe her, and her moods swung wildly from nearly exhilarated to thoroughly depressed.

''If I didn't know better, I'd swear she was on drugs,'' Kelly confided to Blair.

''How do we know she's not? Or wasn't, prior to the crash?'' Blair said in return. ''Lots of people in the entertainment field are, or are reported to be.''

''Well, nuts! That would be all we'd need. A junkie trying to go cold turkey!''

"Should we ask her?" Blair inquired dubiously.

Kelly's brows shot up. "Beard the lioness in her den? That might not be too wise."

Their question was answered when they found Alita rifling through pockets and purses.

"What are you looking for?" Blair queried mildly.

Her hands shaking, Alita replied on a frantic sob, *"Caramba!* You would think there would be something stronger than Midol in one of these bags! I would sell my soul for a single Valium! Or even a marijuana joint!"

"What have you been on, Alita? Crack? Cocaine? Heroin?"

"Mostly cocaine, though I only snort a little now and then, and a few pills. I'm . . . I'm not hooked, really."

"If you're not, you're the next thing to it," Kelly told her. "Look at you. You're about to jump out of your skin. You're shivering and clammy in one hundred degree temperatures. Your pupils are jerky little pinpoints. Honey, you're a wreck if ever I've seen one."

For a moment, Alita looked as if she might physically attack Kelly for daring to say such a thing. Then, she collapsed into a sobbing, quivering heap. *"Dios mío!* I am coming apart! I am either on fire or freezing, and sometimes my heart starts pounding so hard it is all I can do to catch my breath!" She scratched her nails across her arms, where a patchwork of welts already decorated her flesh. "My skin itches so awfully! What am I going to do?"

Blair and Kelly shared a desolate look.

"I doubt there's anything you can do, but try to weather it through," Blair said.

"And trim your fingernails back so you don't inflict anymore damage to yourself," Kelly suggested. "Maybe we can make you a balm, from coconut oil or something. There's got to be something that will ease the itching, at least." She shook her head. "How did you get sucked into such stupidity, anyway? Did you do it simply because everyone else was? Did your show-business friends push you into it?''

Alita grimaced. "I have no friends. Only acquaintances who are either jealous of me or wanting something from me. At first, I just wanted to fit in, to not feel so awkward at their fancy parties. Then it seemed like the drugs made things easier . . . the hectic schedules, the constant traveling. If I was dragging, they picked me up. If I couldn't sleep, I could take a pill. And Eduardo could find it all, whatever I needed. But he cannot help me now, can he?'' Her laugh was bitter. "Poor Eduardo, reduced to a pile of ashes, cannot help himself, let alone help me.''

"I realize this can't be easy for you, but if you can get clean now, you ought to stay clean. Imagine how much harder it will be later, if you go back to the drugs once we're rescued and then try to quit,'' Blair advised.

"If I survive quitting this time, it will be a miracle!'' Alita claimed, swiping at her tears.

"Maybe this is your miracle,'' Kelly offered quietly. "Your wonder cure. The one sure way to beat your addiction—by finding yourself in a place where nothing stronger than aspirin is available to you.''

Blair squatted down beside Alita and put her arm around the singer's shoulders. "You can do it, Alita. You can kick the habit. You just have to hang in there and believe that you are stronger than it is. And be smarter next time. Say no.''

Kelly joined them, kneeling in front of Alita where she could look the girl straight in the eye. "Never, ever, let yourself in for this brand of misery again. It's not worth it, Alita. It will sap your bank account, your career, and your health. Don't risk your fantastic looks and talent for a sham sense of security. And if you're truly tempted, give Blair or me a call. We'll remind you just how lousy you felt today and all you have to lose if you don't stay straight."

If anyone actually and desperately needed drugs at this point, as opposed to craving them as Alita did, it was Frazer. His mangled leg was not responding to anti-bacterial ointment, a few aspirin, and daily saltwater baths. Kelly was sickened by the sight of it, her first since their second day on the island. It appeared worse, much worse than it had at the start.

Frazer's calf was now swollen more than twice its normal size. The gashes were deep, and seeping a putrid mixture of blood and pus. One look, and even an untrained amateur could tell from the acute inflammation that infection had set in. But it was the red line tracing its way up Frazer's leg that alarmed Kelly most.

"Good heavens, Fraz! I had no idea it was this bad! You could have blood poisoning or . . ."

"Or gangrene," Zach inserted somberly, studying Frazer's injury from over Kelly's shoulder. "Damn man! If we don't get you to a hospital soon, you're liable to lose that leg." Unvoiced was the threat that it might well be his life Frazer would lose as well.

"I know." Frazer's tone was dismal. Still, he managed a rough, humorless laugh. "I never thought I'd go this way. Pneumonia maybe, I figured, and pumped full of painkillers to make it easier. Guess my immune system is pretty well shot."

"I wish there was something more we could do," Blair said. "If only I knew which plants might be safe to use for medicinal purposes, but I'm afraid my limited knowledge doesn't extend that far, and trial and error could prove fatal."

"Like it's gonna make much difference, at this point?" Gavin mocked. "Jesus! If you think something might help, try it. What's the poor devil got to lose?"

"I reckon a few swigs o' my coconut beer will take the edge off some, when it's ready," Earl contributed with awkward sympathy. "Should be fermentin' real well in another week or so, in this heat."

Frazer mustered a half smile. "Thanks, Roberts. I'll look forward to it."

Again, unspoken, was the worry that Frazer might not last that long—and to add to their distress, they could do nothing to relieve Frazer's pain, an agony which could only build as the infection raged on, unarrested.

Gavin was out exploring, trying to find the best material for his raft. Earl had gone with him. Zach and Frazer were busy rigging up that water spout/shower at the pool. Blair was searching for roots and herbs that might draw the poison from Frazer's leg. Kelly was in camp, attempting to weave reeds and leaves into a sun-hat for Sydney; while Alita kept herself and Sydney entertained by rehearsing her latest songs.

"Teach her the macarena," Kelly suggested, laughing as the toddler tried to sway in time with the singing. "I think the kid's got rhythm."

Alita chuckled. "You should make her a drum, and give up on that stupid hat. You've really made a mess of it."

Kelly grimaced. "I know. This is a lot tougher than trying to macrame a plant holder out of yarn."

"I hope our overgrown Boy Scouts are doing better than you," Alita said.

"They do resemble a misfit troop, don't they?" Kelly

agreed with a grin. "Especially Gavin and Frazer, with their uniform pants cut short."

"They have only themselves to blame for envying our new shorts and wanting some of their own. Even Zach looks like . . ."

Alita's comment was cut short as a shrill scream coming from the interior overrode it. Alita and Kelly stared at each other, eyes wide. "Was that a bird, maybe?" Alita ventured.

"It sounded more like Gavin."

"As a boy, perhaps, before his voice deepened," Alita allowed.

"Or in a terrible panic," Kelly added. As another wavering screech reached them, followed closely by a third, Kelly dropped the hat, scooped Sydney into her arms, and started to run toward the sound. "C'mon, Alita! Hurry! Maybe he stepped into another one of those snares."

"Then watch where you are going!" Alita called from right behind her. "This is *muy estúpido*, you know, the two of us dashing to his rescue when we have no idea what kind of trouble he has encountered. Surely the men are better equipped to help him."

"But Earl was with him," Kelly reminded her, huffing now with the effort of running with Sydney clasped to her hip. "Maybe something happened to Earl, too. Gavin may need all the help he can get."

"Something might happen to us, too," Alita panted. "I've got a bad feeling about this."

Since there was no actual path, Kelly was simply taking the course of least resistance, dodging through and around the tangled underbrush. Several minutes later, she spied Zach ahead of her, running on a tack diagonal to hers. Just as she neared the juncture of their two routes, through a veil of trees she spotted Frazer hobbling along in Zach's wake, and Blair coming from yet another direction—all of them about to converge within yards of each other.

Suddenly, for no apparent reason, Frazer let out a yell and dived headlong at Blair, shoving her hard enough to send her flying backward. Then Frazer just seemed to disappear before Kelly's eyes. It was only when she got nearer that she saw the huge, gaping hole in the earth, precisely where Blair had trod mere moments before.

Zach, hearing Frazer's yell, quickly backtracked, reaching the scene while Blair was yet on the ground, trying to get her legs back under her. Kelly and company were still several feet away, closing fast. Zach took one look into the hole, motioned to Blair to scoot farther from it, and spun around in time to catch Kelly before she could get close enough to see.

"No," he rasped in a strangled-sounding voice. "Don't look. Any of you. You don't want to see this, believe me."

"What?" Kelly demanded. "What is it? Is Frazer hurt? Is the hole deep?"

"It's a bunji pit. Frazer's dead, Kelly."

As she gazed up at him, not yet fully comprehending, Kelly noted that Zach's face was literally gray, as somber as his words. He looked deathly ill.

"A bunji pit?" Alita echoed. "Earl warned of those earlier, did he not? But I still don't understand how . . ."

"I want to see," Kelly demanded. "Frazer might still be alive, and if there's any way to get him out of there and treat—"

"Damn it, woman!" Zach exploded. "Do you have to argue about everything? Can't you take my word for it? He's dead, Kelly. D-E-A-D. He's impaled on what amounts to dozens of long, sharp spikes. There's one straight through his heart. Now, do you get the picture? Have I been graphic enough, or do you need to hear specifics?"

"Oh, my God!" Kelly stared at Zach in horror, her own color fading. "No! No!"

Alita sank to her knees and crossed herself. "Santa Maria! This is too awful! Too ghastly!"

"He . . . he shoved me out of the way," Blair whispered from across the pit, her eyes huge and glazed with shock. "He pushed me to safety, risking his life for mine."

Gavin burst through the bushes, skidding to a halt a scant yard from the pit. Apparently, he didn't even notice. His dark, panic-filled eyes sought Zach's as he immediately began to babble between breathless gasps. "Back there!" He pointed toward the north. "Cave. Man. Dead!"

"Earl?" They all asked the same question simultaneously.

Gavin shook his head.

"Then he can wait," Zach tersely informed the young soldier. "If he's dead, he's not going anywhere, and we have a more immediate problem. Where's Earl? You were supposed to be keeping an eye on him."

"Right here, boss." Earl crowded into the small clearing. "What's goin' on?"

Alita waved a trembling hand toward the pit. "Frazer. Pitiful, *galante* Frazer."

Earl walked up to the pit, gazed down for a moment, and swiftly stepped back. "Aw, shit!" He hunkered down, his head on a level with his knees, and Zach wondered if Earl was fighting not to pass out. It would have been perfectly understandable.

Either not fully comprehending the situation, or curious beyond his own reasoning, Gavin peered into the hole. He gagged, his hand coming up to cover his mouth. For a moment he swayed dangerously before stumbling hastily backward into the bushes, where he promptly lost his lunch.

"Do you know anything about this dead man Gavin claims to have seen?" Zach directed his query at Earl. "And a cave?"

Earl nodded. "It's little more than a hollow space in a rock, compared to most caves, but evidently it was home to this Jap soldier. There he sits, an honest-to-God skeleton, all decked out in his uniform, like some freakin' Halloween decoration." He pulled in a deep breath and let it out. "Scared poor Daniels shitless, but I have to admit it spooked me some, too." He glanced toward the pit, and shook his head. "Then, this. Jesus! After findin' that snare, I warned y'all not to run around with your heads up your asses! Even a friggin' fairy like Frazer don't deserve . . ."

"That 'fairy' saved Blair's life!" Kelly declared, rounding on Earl in righteous fury. "He may have been gay, but he was brave and gracious, which is more than a lot of 'he-men' can claim."

"Well, one thing's certain," Zach said grimly. "He won't have to worry about dying of gangrene or AIDS, slowly and miserably. At least this way was quick. Maybe even more merciful. And he went out as a hero."

"He . . ." Kelly gulped back tears and stammered, "He couldn't understand why he was spared in the crash. Perhaps this was the reason, so he could save Blair and her baby."

"May God bless him for that," Blair murmured, hugging her stomach.

Earl grunted what amounted to an assent. Then, "At the risk of soundin' even more crude, I suggest we bury Frazer right where he is. That way, none of us have to mess with the body, and you gals can mark the grave any way you see fit." He rose to his feet. "I'll go see if I can find us some more coconut shells or somethin' to use as shovels."

It was when he turned to leave that Zach saw the pistol stuck into the back of Earl's waistband. It looked old and rusty, but menacing nonetheless. A shiver ran through him. "Earl!" he barked. "Hand over the gun."

Earl whirled around, his hand hovering over the butt

of the weapon. "Not a chance, chief. Finder's keepers, as the sayin' goes. That old Jap won't be needin' it no more, but I just might." His smirk was tinged with malice. "And you can forget tyin' me to any more trees at night."

Chapter 14

"I can't take much more of this! It's like waiting for the other shoe to drop! Just wondering who is going to be next to die, and in what horrible, macabre manner! And now, to make things even more frightening, Earl has that gun!"

Zach rubbed his hand along Kelly's spine, trying to impart some comfort and calm through his touch. They were lying in the semi-dark, in a spot apart from the others and away from the fire, yet still beneath the shelter of the banyan tree. "I suppose you expect me to do something about that," he replied quietly. "I would, if I was certain I wouldn't get myself killed in the process, because if that happened, you ladies would really be at Earl's mercy. I doubt Gavin, by himself, would be much help."

Kelly sighed. "I don't want you to risk your life, Zach. It's just that . . . I don't know. I just wish Earl had never found that gun. I suppose I'm just used to the idea of big strong men protecting smaller, weaker women." She made a disgusted noise. "Ugh! I can't believe I just said that!"

"White knights and damsels in distress?"

"I guess. Stupid, fairy-tale notion, isn't it?"

"Not really. Archaic, maybe, but still very romantic. I wish I could meet those expectations, Kelly, to be your shining knight. But I seem to have misplaced my armor and my trusty steed. I do however, have the Japanese sword that Earl conveniently overlooked, so we're not totally defenseless."

She turned toward him, stroking his cheek with her palm, her eyes seeking his. "You are the best knight I've encountered in a long, long time. It's not your fault Earl found that gun . . . or that the plane crashed . . . or that no one has found us yet . . . or that Wynne drowned herself, and Frazer fell into that pit. I'm just feeling overwhelmed right now, and trying to make some sense of it all, and frustrated that I'm having so little success! The best I can figure is that God has decided to play with our lives, and there's nothing we can do to prevent it. And that makes me angry, damn it! And scared."

Zach cuddled her close. "I know. On one hand, you want to reach out to God for help, and with the other you'd like to punch Him in his omnipotent nose. Everybody's felt like that at some time or other. And we've all felt guilty just thinking such sacrilege, too."

Kelly gave a weak laugh. "Golly, maybe it's not the other shoe I'm waiting for, after all. Could be it's a bolt of lightning striking my nasty little self."

"Got news for you, babe. The lightning has already struck, but it missed us and hit the plane instead. If we're fortunate, God has used up his quota for awhile."

"I hope so, but I'm beginning to wonder if this blasted island isn't possessed—by demons, or the spirit of that dead Japanese guy, or something totally evil." Kelly shivered and snuggled nearer still to Zach's comforting bulk. "Twelve of us escaped the crash, and now, within days, our number has been reduced to a mere seven, counting Sydney."

"Maybe that's our lucky number," Zach proposed. "It beats calling ourselves the Devil's Dozen, which was one of my first impressions of our ragtag group."

"Which would make this what? Devil's Isle?" Kelly submitted recklessly. "How uncannily appropriate."

Out of nowhere, something dark and furry suddenly buzzed by her head—so close that Kelly could hear its wings flapping—and flew into the tree above them. Kelly let out a startled shriek and burrowed into Zach's chest. "Oh, my Lord! What was *that*?"

"A bat, I'd imagine," Zach answered, apparently not nearly as disturbed by the creature as she was.

"A bat?" she screeched, totally terrorized. "A bat! Oh, crap and corruption! This is all I need!"

Zach patted her quivering back. "Hey, settle down. The poor thing's probably a lot more scared of you than you are of it. I wouldn't be surprised if you just frightened the heck out of it."

"How can you be so . . . so calm!" Kelly smacked him in the shoulder with her fist, then quickly replaced her arms over her head as a shield. "Those things bite, you know! And they carry rabies! And lice! Oh, holy Moses! He's up there squeaking!"

Zach chuckled, which only made her more peeved at him. "If you'd hush up, he most likely would do the same," he told her. "He and his buddies are not going to hurt you, Kelly. They're after bugs, and those figs growing up there."

"They?" she echoed frantically. "There's not just one? How many are there?"

"Off hand, I'd guess about fifty. But that's just a rough

estimate. It's hard to do an accurate head count in the dark, you know." Humor resounded in his voice, though he did his best to curb his laughter.

"Darn you, Zach Goldstein!" Kelly pummeled him again. "This is not funny!"

"Honey, they've been up there every night since we set up camp here. Probably before that," he corrected. "I can't believe you haven't noticed them before."

"Well, I didn't! And I want them to go away!"

"I wouldn't doubt they wish the same of you."

"Hey! What's the problem over there?" Gavin called out.

"Nothing," Zach called back. "Kelly's just having a hissy fit over the bats in the tree."

"Bats?" Another pair of female voices rose in dual alarm.

"Oh, criminy!" Earl griped loudly. "Now look what you've started. I ain't seen a female yet who didn't go into the screamin' meemies over snakes, rats, or bats—or an itsy-bitsy spider."

"Look, ladies, they're just like tiny winged mice," Zach assured them, or tried. "Only better, because they keep the insect population down."

"Yeah. Some folks even build bat houses, to attract 'em," Earl added.

"Then they are loco!" Alita avowed in a shaky tone.

"You trying to say they have bats in their belfries?" Gavin joked.

"One of you big brave men could get off your duff and throw some more wood on the fire," Blair suggested, her voice muffled by the blanket she'd thrown over her head and Sydney's. "Bats don't like light, do they?"

"Better yet," Kelly whined, "why don't you put that dratted cannon you're toting to some good use, Earl? Pop off a round or two, and scare them away."

"I ain't wastin' ammo on a bunch o' measly bats, missy,"

he retorted with a snort of disgust. "But if you don't think ol' Zach can keep you safe, you can crawl over here with me."

Kelly nearly choked on that. "Never mind. I'd bed down with the bats first, thank you very much."

To everyone's surprise, including Earl's, Alita scurried over to his spot, dragging her blanket with her. "Scoot over, big boy," she ordered testily. "I'm taking you up on that offer. But I warn you, unless you are swatting at a bat, you had better keep your hands to yourself. My teeth can do as much damage to you as theirs."

Thus prompted, Gavin moved closer to the fire, and to Blair. After adding a chunk of wood to the dying flames, he positioned himself an arm's length from her back, with Blair and the baby between him and the fire. "It's okay, Blair. I'll keep watch. You go to sleep."

Kelly had wriggled beneath Zach, so that he was lying over her. "Getting mighty friendly, aren't you?" he teased.

"Not tonight, dear. I have a headache," she countered tritely, smothering a yawn. "Actually, I just want to make sure that if anybody gets bat-bit on the butt tonight, it's not me."

Zach chuckled. "Gee, and they said chivalry was dead!"

Kelly waited until the men had left the campsite before confronting Alita. "Okay, what gives?"

"Yes," Blair added suspiciously. "All of a sudden you're cozying up to Earl as if he owned the crown jewels."

Alita's smile was canny. "Not quite, but he is hung pretty well for an old guy."

Kelly shook her head. "I'm not buying it. You're up to something."

Alita gave a careless shrug. "Can you think of a better way to know what the man is doing all night, other than sleeping with one eye open? I tell you, every time he twitched in his sleep, I knew it. I did not have to wonder where he was or what he was doing, and if he was to try to sneak away or creep up on anyone, I would have been aware of it.''

"Alita!" Blair gave an astounded gasp. "Don't you realize how dangerous that could be for you? The man could slit your throat, and none of us would be the wiser until it was too late!"

"If he were to try, I could just as easily cut his," Alita returned, her dark eyes gleaming brazenly. She lifted the hem of her floppy shorts, exposing the knife she had tucked into her panties. "You forget, I am not some silly, frail female. I learned very early how to protect myself, and I am quite skilled with a knife. Believe me, I know where to stick it, whether merely to wound or to kill."

"So, you've set yourself up as our guard dog," Kelly said.

"Sí. You can all rest easy, except for Earl." She gave a wicked laugh. "Even in his sleep, the man is as stiff and hard as a tire iron from wanting me."

"He's also as strong as an ox," Kelly reminded her. "He could overpower you. Rape you. Good God, the man killed his own wife! Alita, this is an awful chance you are taking. None of us would want you to get hurt, just trying to keep watch on Earl at night. We could all take turns standing watch, if it came down to it."

"There is no need," Alita insisted. "I can handle him. And if the opportunity arises, I will steal his *pistola* from him, even if I have to trade my body to get it."

"Good grief, Alita! We'd never expect you to prostitute yourself on our behalf!" Blair exclaimed.

"Never!" Kelly agreed. "I can't tell you how guilty I would feel if you felt you had to resort to that."

Again that nonchalant shrug, though Kelly thought she glimpsed pain in Alita's eyes. "Do not concern yourselves about such a small matter. After all, it would not be the first time I've had to do so—for food, for favors, for drugs. Eduardo wasn't working only for money, *comprende?*"

Their dismay showed clearly on both Kelly and Blair's faces. "Now I suppose I have given you yet another reason to despise me," Alita concluded with a sigh. "You consider me no better than a *puta*. A whore."

"No! I'm sure your life was not an easy one. Who is to say, that under similar circumstances, we wouldn't have done the same?" Blair told her.

Kelly nodded. "I, of all people, have no room to condemn you. Technically, I'm still married, though the divorce papers have been duly filed. Which, in the eyes of the law and the church, makes me an adulteress. But frankly, I don't give a rat's whiskers. I'd rather have Zach, for as long as I can, than have Brad served up to me bareassed naked on a silver platter."

"Not even with a nice shiny red apple in his mouth?" Alita quipped, the corners of her mouth twitching.

"Or with a diamond-studded collar and leash around his neck?" Blair added, surprising them with her risqué contribution.

Kelly pretended to consider this. "Maybe . . . if it was a choker collar. Around his balls."

Alita laughed with genuine appreciation.

Blair's eyes widened. "Whew! You really loathe the man, don't you?"

"I don't actually hate him, I don't think, but I certainly don't have any love for him anymore. He destroyed that when he wouldn't accept me for the woman I was. Instead, he tried to make me over into the wife he wanted—someone I simply couldn't be. And in doing so, he nearly destroyed me as well. His constant harping, his unmitigated conceit, became more than I could stand and still retain an ounce of self-respect. Believe it or not, I may have bailed out just in the nick of time, though Brad will never see it that way. All that matters to him is that, by divorcing him, I may be ruining his chances at a political career.''

"He sounds very egotistical," Blair said. "Much more so than Anton."

"Even if he did not concede much to you, Kelly, he must at least have to suck up to his superiors. Or to those people who might influence his career." Alita deduced thoughtfully. "Let that be your consolation."

Kelly's laugh was understandably bitter. "You've got that right, Alita. I'm willing to bet Brad has kissed more rear ends than a public toilet. He just would never bend far enough to kiss mine. Not once."

Blair could not hold back her smile. "Considering where his lips have been, you should consider yourself fortunate, indeed!"

"Hear! Hear!" Kelly raised her coconut shell in a toast. Her friends did likewise. "To womanhood, and being true to oneself!"

"To womanly wiles. Long may they prevail!" Alita chanted.

"To everlasting friendship," Blair added sincerely.

"Amen!"

"Amen!" Sydney chimed in innocently, struggling on tiptoe to raise her cup to theirs.

The three women chuckled at the baby's antics. Kelly lifted Sydney onto her lap, making the toddler's reach easier. "To Sydney, with love."

Gavin wanted to use the sword to cut down small trees to use as the base for his raft. Zach refused to relinquish the weapon until they had cleared safe paths from the camp to the beach and the pool. "Your raft can wait, Gav. This won't. We can't afford to have anybody else stepping into some sort of trap. We need to establish at least a few trails we know we can travel safely."

Even Earl agreed with that, and made it his mission to scout out other areas in search of any additional snares or pits the Japanese fellow might have set.

"What's the story on this Japanese soldier, anyway?" Kelly asked curiously. "Did he die of a wound, or what?"

Zach had gone back with Earl and Gavin to investigate further. Now, he said, "We couldn't find any evidence that he was shot. At least there were no bullets lodged in his skeletal frame, as far as we could tell without disturbing the scene too much, or any tell-tale holes in his clothing, which was fairly worn and tattered."

"So your guess is?" Blair pressed.

"That he's been dead for years. It wasn't as gruesome as it could have been, as I'd first feared from Gavin's reaction. The body was totally decomposed, nothing left but dry bones and what remained of his uniform."

"How do you suppose he got here?" Alita inquired.

"During the War," Earl said. "World War II. Leastwise, that's when his uniform and weapons date from. Could be he was sent here as a scout or signal operator."

"Then where's his radio?" Gavin queried. "And why would they just leave him here?"

"Maybe he missed the boat, so to speak, when everyone else left," Blair proposed.

"Or maybe his boat or plane sank, and he swam to the island," Kelly put in.

"Well, however he made it here, he obviously didn't make it off again," Zach noted.

"Do you think he's not the only one? That there are more skeletons lying around?"

Zach shrugged. "Who knows?"

Kelly shivered. "There . . . couldn't be anymore Japanese soldiers still alive on the island after all this time, could there?"

"I honestly doubt that," Zach answered. "The war ended in 1945, and if the average soldier was around twenty or twenty-five years of age then, he'd be in his seventies now. That's a hell of a long time to survive being marooned on an island."

"How do you think this guy died?" Gavin asked.

Zach shook his head. "Hard telling, Gav. Could be he caught some sort of disease, or maybe he *was* wounded and died of infection. Or thirst, perhaps, if all the fresh water was still hidden underground back then. It might have taken an earthquake or some sort of tremor or violent storm to crack the lava and let the water through to the surface."

"More recently than his lifetime," Earl concluded.

"Possibly."

"Could he have been here for so long that he died of old age?" Blair inquired with a quiver in her voice. "I mean, as far as we know, we're the first to discover his body."

"Which would lead to the conclusion that no one ever comes to this island," Kelly deduced bleakly.

"And we could be stuck here until we die, too," Alita added anxiously, her panic rising with every syllable. "We could all grow old and die right here on this stinking pile of weeds and rock!"

Blair caught the hysteria. "With no medicine, or doctors! I don't want to have my baby here! I want a nice, sterile hospital, with anesthetic available if I need it, and help for the baby, and Anton holding my hand and coaching me!"

"Cripes! Some pioneer woman you'd have made!" Earl

scoffed. "My granny had eight young'uns right there in her cabin, and lived to the ripe old age of ninety."

His mockery did nothing to calm Blair, who was sobbing inconsolably now.

"Oh, shut up, you insensitive bozo!" Kelly railed. "You may not mind the idea of spending the rest of your natural days here, but the rest of us have lives we'd like to resume."

"As soon as possible," Alita appended angrily. She stalked past Earl, pausing only to punch him hard on the arm as she passed. "You really piss me off, you know that?"

Contrarily, Earl took her swat with good grace. In fact, he stood gazing after her with a smitten grin on his face. "By gum, I think that hot little tamale likes me," he commented to no one in particular. Then he trotted after Alita, like a hound on a scent.

Gavin let loose a hoot of disbelief. "Ha! That dumb ridgerunner's been playin' with himself too much if he thinks a famous star like Alita will give him a spin. Besides, if she really wants a tumble, I'm younger and better lookin'. What's Earl got over me?"

"A big gun, Gavin," Kelly told him, deadpan. As he and Zach stared at her, mouths agape, she said, "I mean that literally, not sexually. She intends to sweet-talk him out of that gun somehow, by hook or by crook. Blair and I both tried to drill some sense into her, to tell her it was too risky, but she's determined that she can do it."

"Then, by God, we'll help her," Zach decided. "If she can distract him and get him to let down his guard, Gavin and I might have a chance to grab the pistol. It's worth a try, but we'll have to coordinate our actions with hers. Maybe set up some type of signal between us ahead of time. In the interim, if she can just string him along. . . ."

Kelly's lips wrapped around a sly, purely feminine smile. "Oh, she has every intention of doing just that, Zach. She's not about to give up the goodies until he's paid the dues, and something tells me that before Alita is through with him, old Earl is going to be tied up in more knots than a Chinese puzzle.''

Chapter 15

The ship was too far out for anyone on board to spot the half-dozen people shouting and waving from the island.

"They don't see us! Use the mirror, Zach!" Kelly yelled.

"The ship is to the east of us, and the sun is too low in the west for that to work. They wouldn't catch the gleam."

Gavin called from the signal fire. "Zach! The fire won't light! The damned wood is soaking wet! It won't even catch enough to smoke!"

Zach swung around, his eyes blazing as he searched for Earl. The man was leaning nonchalantly against the trunk of a tree some distance away, his expression smug as he watched the others exhaust themselves in their useless attempts.

"You lousy son-of-a-bitch!" Zach snarled, advancing on Roberts with ground eating strides. "You doused the wood with water, didn't you? You've been doing it all along!"

Earl grinned. "Yup. And I'll keep right on doin' it, too." He straightened slightly, his hand hovering over the butt of the pistol stuck into the waistband of his pants, the gesture reminding Kelly of a gunslinger's move in a grade B movie. "So, Goldstein. Whatcha aim to do about it?"

When Zach's steps didn't slow, Kelly began to panic. "Zach! Stop! For heaven's sake! Think what you're doing!" Even as she shouted the warning, she was running across the beach toward him.

"Zach!" Kelly launched herself into Zach's back, knocking him to the ground in a flurry of sand.

Reflexively, he tried to buck her off, but she clung to him, pleading all the while. "Please, Zach. Don't. Please! I don't want you to get shot. Don't make me watch him kill you! Please!"

For a few, desperate seconds Kelly's words fell on deaf ears. Then she felt Zach's muscles relax as his initial blind fury began to fade and common sense took root. On hands and knees, Zach's head sagged in defeat. "Damn it!" he grated through clenched teeth. "Damn that man to everlasting hell!"

"I'm sure God's already got that on the agenda," Kelly assured him, sliding off of him to the sand at his side.

From his place by the tree, Earl jeered. "You gonna let the little woman fight yer battles, Goldstein? Ya gonna let her interfere in yer business?"

"I'd wipe that smirk off my face, if I were you," Gavin told him.

"Yeah, you dumb clod jumper!" Alita spat out. Her own eyes were practically spewing flames as she marched toward him.

"Clodhopper," Blair corrected automatically.

"Whatever," Alita hissed. Upon reaching Earl, she grabbed a fistful of exposed chest hair and yanked. Hard enough to rip half of what she held from his flesh.

Earl yelped in pain, too surprised to react immediately. "And to think I was considering giving myself to one

such as you! Someone who would betray me so readily!"
Cursing him in rapid-fire Spanish, Alita strutted past him,
the enticing sway of her hips exaggerated all the more by
her ire, a motion Earl could scarcely miss.

"Hey now! Come back here!" Ignoring the others, Earl
bolted after her, his gaze all but riveted to Alita's backside.

"Geezow!" Gavin exclaimed softly. "If anybody's in danger of being pussy-whipped, it's old Earl! And if Alita's
strategy wasn't working so well, I'd be the first to tell him
so."

"Not until we get that gun away from him," Zach advised
on a frustrated breath. "He's got the upper hand right
now, and reveling in it, which makes him doubly dangerous."

"We can't let him provoke us like that again," Kelly
added miserably. "We've got to play it cool, no matter
what the provocation, until we can disarm him."

Zach and Kelly were walking along the beach, just the
two of them.

"You saved my bacon back there, Kelly."

"Maybe."

"There's no *maybe* about it. A couple of more steps, and
Earl would have drawn on me." Zach still couldn't believe
he'd come unglued to the extent that he'd rushed an
armed man the way he had. He hadn't even had the sword
for defense. "If Earl would have shot, at that range . . ."

"But he didn't, and the more I consider it, even if he
had, I'm not sure that rusty old antique would have fired.
For that matter, how do we know it's even loaded? Or that
the bullets are any good after all this time? So, you see, I
may not have saved you at all."

"On the other hand, that old pistol may be in perfect
working order. In which case you did come to my rescue,

very valiantly I might add. That was your intention, wasn't it—behind that flying tackle and all that screeching?"

"Well, I couldn't just stand there like a stump and watch you tempt fate. That was a pretty dumb thing for you to do, Zach."

"I agree. But when Earl admitted to dousing the firewood, and dared to act so damned smug about it, something snapped. There was that ship, with no way to signal it. And my ailing dad waiting in Seattle. And Mom and Becky. And me figuratively knocking my head against a stone wall all this time, trying to convince myself that we can stay alive 'til we're found, that it won't be too late, that sooner or later a plane will fly by and we'll signal it and all be rescued. And all the while, Earl was sneaking around behind our backs, sabotaging our chances."

"I know," she put in glumly. "I've had to re-align the coconuts in our SOS sign for three days running, and I'll bet it's not birds or lizards or the wind messing it up, either."

By now, they'd traversed several miles of shoreline on their solitary trek. Kelly hadn't come this far along the eastern coast before. "Shouldn't we be heading back now?" she asked.

"Not yet. Since we've already come this distance, there's something I want you to see."

"Your etchings?" she teased.

He laughed. "Not precisely what I had in mind, but if that's what turns you on, I'll gladly grab a stick and draw a few in the sand for you. Would you prefer an architectural rendering or a still life?"

"A self-portrait of you would do nicely, thank you."

"That might take some time."

"From all indications, that's what we have most of around here."

"Then let's put it to good use," he suggested. He took

her hand in his, leading her on for another half mile or so. "There." He pointed ahead of them. "What do you think?"

At first Kelly didn't see anything unusual, just more beach, shaded by palm trees. Or so she thought. Upon closer scrutiny, she discovered that the sand was not dark because it was shadowed, but because the granules under-foot were actually black! In the few places where the sun-light struck directly, they shone like tiny pieces of polished onyx.

"How fantastic! Black sand! I've never seen such a thing! How did it form? Why here, of all places?"

Zach grinned. "Neat, isn't it? There are only a few places like this in the world. The conditions have to be right for it. Basically, you need hot lava flowing into the cooler ocean, and a rough enough surf to pulverize the cooled lava into minuscule fragments."

Kelly scooped some into her hand. "It looks like millions of black diamonds, all heaped together!"

"Don't I wish!" Zach exclaimed, laughing. "I'd never have to worry about funding for a project again. I could build the Taj Mahal, or its equivalent, if I wanted, and never borrow a dime from anyone else."

"I could quit buying lottery tickets and build my own house, with everything exactly the way I want it." She grinned up at him. "Of course, I'd hire the very best architect. Would you help me design and build my dream house, Zach?"

"Would you let me live in it with you?" he countered with a look more serious than she'd expected.

"Wow!" Kelly's eyes widened. "That sort of came from left field, didn't it?"

"It happens that way sometimes, so I'm told. How about it, Kelly? Did your first experience with marriage make you totally gun-shy, or would you be willing to give it another try? With me?''

Now he was talking marriage, not just living together, which was even more scary. "Don't dig yourself in any deeper than you want to be, Zach,'' she advised him quietly, biding for time to adjust her thoughts. "After all, you don't know me very well yet, and certainly not under normal conditions.''

Zach shrugged. "They say extraordinary circumstances reveal a person's true nature. If that's so, I already know the best and worst about you, and I like what I've found, Kelly.''

"I do, too," she admitted, "but that still doesn't assure that you'd like me in the real world, or vice-versa. Aside from any major differences, there could be a thousand small things I might do that would drive you thoroughly nuts.''

"Such as?'' He sprawled comfortably on the sand beside her, prepared to hear her out.

With a frown, she did likewise. "Okay, sometimes I forget my manners, even at important functions—like propping my elbows on the table, and whenever possible, I kick off my shoes.''

He tugged playfully on a strand of her hair. "Yeah, I can see where that would really send me over the edge. Go on.''

"I sometimes grind my teeth at night. I wear a special guard my dentist made for me.''

"News flash, babe. I already know that. I've heard you. I can live with it, if you can stand to hear me crack the occasional knuckle.''

Kelly grimaced. "Not too often, I hope.''

"What else?'' he prompted.

"I like being in charge, and I hate being ordered around.''

"So, we'll take turns being the boss, on alternate days."

"I like running my stores, and being independent, and I sell sexy undies."

"Lucky me. Is there more?"

"Whenever I chew a piece of gum, I can't help cracking it. It's an unconscious habit."

"I tend to blow bubbles and pop them. So does Becky."

Kelly jumped on that possible stumbling block. "Speaking of Becky, she might not like the idea of having me for a stepmother."

"We'll deal with it. What's not to like?"

"Just because you like me, doesn't mean she will, Zach. Lots of girls resent another woman marrying their fathers, especially teenage daughters."

"Then we'd better not waste any time about this. Beck turns thirteen in another ten months."

"Good grief, Zach! My divorce won't be final for several months, especially if Brad decides to fight it, which I suspect he might."

"Too bad bigamy's a crime, isn't it?" he mused. "Oh, well, we'll do the best we can. Are you deadset on staying in Arizona, or would you be willing to live in Seattle? Or, I suppose we could commute, but that's a hell of a way to conduct a marriage."

Kelly got to her feet and glared down at him. "You are not taking this seriously, Zach."

His expression turned solemn, his smile and good humor evaporating. He, too, rose, to stand facing her, his stance one of challenge. "Yes, I am. You're just looking for trouble, and maybe a way out. If you don't want to marry me, just say so," he told her stiffly.

"Don't I even get any time to think about it? To get to know you better?"

She was hedging, skirting around binding herself to him in any serious way, and Zach was getting angry now.

"Hell, woman! We've been living out of each other's pockets for weeks here. If you don't know me by now, you never will."

"Don't yell at me, Zach. I'm simply suggesting that maybe we should just live together for awhile, when we get back to civilization. Try it out and see how it feels there, before committing ourselves to something more permanent."

"Get real!" he sneered. "I've got a daughter to consider. What kind of moral example would I be setting for her if we're shacking up?"

"I just don't want to make another mistake, not with something this important. Surely you can understand that."

"Actually, I'm having trouble with it," he snapped back. "From my side of the fence, it seems you're determined to paint me with the same brush as your dip-shit husband, and I don't mind telling you I resent it mightily. Open your eyes, Kelly. Take off the blinders. I am not Brad. If you're going to judge me, judge me on my own merits and faults, not his."

"I'm trying, but you're not making it easy. Especially when you get all belligerent and bossy. I hate that, Zach. I put up with it for five long years, and I won't tie myself up in that particular ball of wax again, or one even remotely similar."

"So what are you saying? You need someone perfect or not at all? Well, good luck finding him. And you'd better brush up your own character while you're searching, because you're not all that ideal yourself."

"That's what I've been trying to tell you, you mule-headed ape! Marriage is supposed to be forever, and until I'm sure we can make it work, I don't want to take that big a step."

He scoffed at that. "Life doesn't come with a guarantee,

like a toaster, Kelly. Neither does love. There are some
things you have to take on faith.''

"There you go, getting all snotty with me! God, I could
just bash you when you do that!''

He thrust his chin out at her, gesturing toward his jaw.
"Go ahead. Give it your best shot, if it will make you feel
any better.''

To his surprise, her small fist landed solidly—in his gut.
The air whooshed out of him in a gush. "Hey!'' he
wheezed. "If you're going to fight, fight fair. No hitting
below the belt, you under-handed little witch!''

"You're not wearing a belt,'' she pointed out in a superior tone, though inside she was appalled that she'd actually hit him, even if he had goaded her into it, and half
afraid of how he might choose to retaliate.

"I can play dirty, too,'' he informed her, even as his
foot snaked behind hers, landing her in a heap at his feet.

He didn't have time to enjoy his sneaky maneuver before
her hand caught his ankle, jerking him down beside her.

"Take that, Goldstein!'' she boasted.

He grabbed her arms, hauling her atop him. They glared
at one another, eye to eye.

"Let go of me, you muscle-bound worm!''

"Make me,'' he taunted. "You're so all-fired independent and intent on demonstrating that you're so superior
to the male species in every way. So prove it. You want
loose, get loose.''

"I'm warning you, Zach,'' she hissed.

"Words,'' he jeered. "All blow and no show.''

She attempted to knee him, but he anticipated her move
this time, and trapped her leg between his. Then he had
the gall to laugh, which made Kelly all the more furious.

She stretched far enough to tangle her fingers into a
hank of his hair and yanked. Hard. In turn, he wound her

braid around his wrist, anchoring her face mere inches above his.

"Check and checkmate," he mocked. "So, now what are you going to do?"

He'd released her arm to bind her braid, and she used her free hand to latch onto his earlobe, pulling and pinching it between her fingernails.

"Ouch!"

"I'll let go, if you do," she offered.

"Hah! Like I'm supposed to believe that, you blood-thirsty viper?"

He tugged her face closer to his, until his features blurred before her. "You want to play rough, sweetheart? How rough?"

His teeth clamped over her lower lip, trapping it between them just securely enough to sting. Without letting loose, he asked, "You ready to cry 'uncle?' Or are you going to go all weak and weepy, and cry big alligator tears so the big bad bully will take pity on you?"

"I'll cry 'uncle' when they're serving frozen daiquiris in hell!" she muttered.

"In that case, I guess we'll be here awhile, won't we?" He chuckled then. "I know it sounds trite, but you're beautiful when you're angry. Your eyes are shimmering, your face is all aglow, and you're literally trembling with fury." One hand crept up her thigh as he pressed his arousal against her. "Are you getting as turned on by this as I am?"

She hadn't been, at least she hadn't been aware of it, until he'd introduced the notion. Then, suddenly, all the fire in her veins seemed to pool in her loins. Her tongue crept out, to lick at her upper lip—and tasted his. Her fingers stopped pinching, only to skim the shell of his ear in a tingling caress. "Kiss, me, Zach," she said huskily.

His teeth released her lip, his own tongue taking a

moment to soothe the ache before delving deeply into her mouth. To his surprise, instead of biting him as he so justly deserved, she met his fervor with equal intensity.

He pulled back to suck in a shaky breath. "God, I want you!"

"So, shut up and take me," she murmured. Her breasts brushed tauntingly over his bare chest as she ground her pelvis against his thigh.

His hand, still twined in her hair, held her head still as his mouth again sought hers. His tongue traced her lips, teasing them for long moments before his lips settled fully onto hers. Passion, hot and sweet, arced between them.

Kelly was melting faster than a chocolate bar in the hot sun. "It isn't fair!" she protested softly. "What you do to me."

His chuckle was slightly wicked, and oh, so seductive. "All's fair in love and war, my pet."

Kelly couldn't hold him close enough, hard enough, to satisfy the longing that erupted in her with volcanic force. Her tongue duelled with his, her fingers clutched at his hair, her nails dug into his shoulders—urging him nearer, though her breasts were practically crushed against his broad, muscled chest. She didn't know he'd loosened the band at the end of her braid until he spread her unbound hair over her shoulders, wavy strands of it sifting slowly through his fingers.

"Burnished gold," he murmured. "So soft and silky and shining. I want to wrap myself in it—in you. I want to feel you in every cell and pore of my body."

Her hair tumbling down to enclose them in a sheer amber veil. Amid urgent, heated kisses, he slid the straps of her camisole off her shoulders. Kelly slipped her arms free, and the garment slithered to her waist. His hands cupped her breasts, molding them, kneading them, his

work-coarsened fingertips rasping across the rosy crests.
She moaned and wriggled in response.

Zach broke off their kiss. "Too rough?"

She shook her head, setting her tresses shimmering.
"No. I love it." She pressed forward, wordlessly inviting
more of the same. "Oh, yes! You have such . . . marvelous
hands!"

Her own were flexing against the muscles of his bare
chest—rubbing, stroking, inciting him. He pulled her up,
her breasts now within reach of his greedy mouth. As he
suckled avidly, his hands grasped her bottom, rocking her
pelvis against his iron-hard arousal. Her breathing became
more erratic, reduced to sexy little pants and gasps.

"I can't take much more of this," he growled, his hands
fumbling at the clasp of her shorts. "I want you. Now."

Of the same mind, Kelly tugged his snap loose and
yanked his zipper down. Kicking and thrashing, they
fought free of their clothes. Gloriously naked at last, they
came together like a pair of lusty animals, heedless of all
else but satisfying their most urgent, basic needs.

Only afterward, when they were thoroughly sated, did a
myriad of nagging discomforts come to their attention.
"Move, love," Zach said, shoving gently at her. "There's
a rock poking me between the shoulder blades."

Kelly groaned as she crawled off of him. "Darn! These
tiny black crystals have permanently dimpled my knee-
caps!" She brushed the offending granules from her legs
and feet, frowning at the remaining red marks. "That was
like kneeling on kernels of uncooked rice!"

"You think that hurts? You should feel my rear end!"
he informed her. "I swear I'm lying on a bed of sharp
cinders and they've scraped half the skin off my backside!
You're lucky you were on top."

Kelly grimaced as she shook out her panties prior to pulling them back on. "Making love on a beach certainly isn't as romantic as it sounds, is it? At least, not in retrospect. For one thing, I've never heard anyone in a book or movie complain about having sand in their pants or in other assorted and intimate crevices, which could soon become extremely irritating. I wish the pool were closer. I can't wait to wash off."

"I'll second that." He presented his back to her. "Brush me off, will you please?"

"Shake your head, first. You've got sand in your hair."

When he complied, she swatted him. "Not right here! Geez! You just sprayed sand all over me again!"

"Sorry."

"What did you do with the rubber band for my braid?"

He peeled it from his wrist and handed it to her. Their eyes met. Their dual frowns melted into rueful grins.

"I've never been this grumpy after such great sex!"

"Me, either!"

Zach held his arms wide, and Kelly walked into his embrace. "Marry me, you harridan," he entreated. "I love you to the point of total distraction and desperation. I never thought it was possible to fall for someone this fast, or this hard. I need you, Kelly Kennedy, for better or worse. I don't care if you turn out to be Lizzie Borden reincarnate. I just want to spend the rest of my life with you."

She laughed. "Such a brave man! However, you'll be glad to know there's no history of major mental deficiency in my family. Aunt Harriet's a bit eccentric, but nowhere near dangerous."

"No split personality?"

"Nope."

"Nuts! I was hoping to get a little variety without having to stray from home," he joked.

She jabbed a finger into his ribs. "No straying, Zach. Ever," she instructed firmly. "That is rule number one."

"Yes, ma'am. Is there a rule number two I should know about?"

"More than that, but none you need to worry over until after the wedding."

He jerked back, putting enough space between them to study her face. "Is that a 'yes?' You're accepting my proposal?"

She returned his earnest perusal. "I guess it's time to swallow my fears and trust that our love is strong enough to carry us through all the problems ahead. And I do love you, Zach. When I thought Earl might shoot you, I nearly died of heart failure! It might not be smart, and we might both live to regret it, but I've definitely fallen heart over head in love with you. If you still want me when my divorce from Brad is final, we can get married then."

His head lowered, his mouth seeking hers. "Sweetheart, I'll still be wanting you, and loving you, when we're old and gray and hobbling around on canes and walkers. That's not to say we won't quarrel. Every married couple has their spats. But you've got to admit that making up the way we just did has its merits."

"So let's practice making up again," she suggested in a sultry murmur.

Within seconds, they were lying in the sand once more.

"You do know what this means, don't you?" he murmured, nipping at her thigh.

"What?" she gasped.

His tawny eyes held a devilish gleam as he met her gaze from between her legs. "You're about to get sand in your pants again—and a few more interesting places."

Chapter 16

The incoming tide was lapping at their feet by the time they roused themselves to dress again. As Kelly sloshed through the foamy surf to retrieve her shorts before they washed out to sea, a wad of seaweed twined about her leg. "Oh, yuck! I hate this slimy stuff."

Tugging on his own pants, Zach laughed at her. "Just another delight of life on the beach. Why don't you save it? Maybe once its cooked, it'll taste like spinach."

"So, who likes spinach?" she retorted smartly. She was standing on one foot, shaking the other and trying to dislodge the clinging mess when a knife-sharp pain shot through her calf. With a loud scream, Kelly fell to the sand.

In three running strides, Zach was at her side. He didn't even have to ask what was wrong. Kelly was clutching her left leg, just below her knee, shouting, "Oh, God! It hurts! It hurts! What is it? Get it off me!"

Zach's confusion turned to horror when he reached for Kelly's leg. The greenish glob attached to her calf wasn't seaweed at all. Zach's best guess was that it was some sort of jellyfish, though it more resembled that revolting snot-like goo appropriately called "slime" that his nephews used to play with. The thing's tentacles were hooked to Kelly's flesh, and from her continued screams, it was evidently biting or stinging her.

Zach's first instinct was to rip the creature off of her. His fingers were a scant inch from it when common sense asserted itself. He jerked back, seized Kelly's foot instead, and turned her leg into the sand and began dragging it back and forth. Within seconds, the friction convinced the animal to release its hold. Before it could resume its attack, Zach quickly grabbed Kelly and hauled her farther up the beach, out of harm's way.

"Don't touch the wound, Kelly!" he ordered sharply, seeing she was trying to clutch at her injured calf. "You've been stung by a jellyfish, but it's off now. Lie still. Let me look."

"Oh, God, Zach!" she wailed. "Do something! It hurts so badly!"

"I know, love. I know. There are still some tentacles attached. Just keep your hands away, or you'll likely get them stung, too."

As would he, if he touched the tentacles which had come loose from the jellyfish and were still clinging to Kelly's flesh. For a moment, he was stymied as to how to loosen them without causing her additional injury. Finally, for lack of anything more inventive, he daubed her entire calf with a thick paste of wet sand. Then, employing his pocket knife, he carefully scraped it away again, tentacles and all.

By now, Kelly was sobbing and trying to brush his hands back to make way for her own. He seized her wrists tightly, aborting the move. "Stop it, Kelly! I got it off. It's going to be all right now. Just don't rub or scratch at it, love.

You'll only irritate it all the more. And don't thrash. You'll grind sand in the wound.''

Her calf was dotted with nasty red puncture marks that were seeping blood and whatever poison the creature had injected. The wounds were red, and already swelling. Zach knew they should be washed, disinfected, and probably bound, but at present his resources were severely limited. For lack of anything else, he used his own cotton briefs as a bandage, wetting them first with saltwater. The emergency measure granted Kelly a modicum of relief, though Zach speculated it would be temporary at best.

After quickly dressing her, he scooped Kelly into his arms and started jogging down the beach. "Just hang on, darling. We'll get you back to camp, and maybe Blair will have a better idea how to treat this. Lord knows that woman is knowledgeable about nearly everything else.''

By the time Zach staggered into camp with Kelly in his arms, she was whimpering pathetically. Tears tracked endlessly down her cheeks. "Lay out a blanket for her. Somebody fetch some water,'' he called out.

"Good heavens! What has happened?'' Blair hastened to spread a blanket on the ground.

Gently, Zach deposited Kelly onto it, careful not to bump her leg. "Something bit her, or stung her. I think it was some variety of jellyfish, though I can't be entirely sure.''

"Oh, dear!''

Alita paused in passing, the coffeepot in hand. "Ay! That looks awful! And painful!''

"It is!'' Kelly whined. "It stings something fierce! As if someone is holding a hot poker against my leg!''

"I will hurry with the water, *amiga.*''

"Wait!'' Gavin told her. "One of the guys in my unit in Hawaii got stung by a jellyfish a few months back, and they told us it's best to rinse the wound with salt water instead. It has something to do with the sacs or cells the tentacles shoot into the victim's skin. They react to fresh water, releasing even more venom into the system. And you've got to wipe all the tentacles off, too.''

"I've done that," Zach said. "But I'm glad you told us about the water. I don't want to cause her any more pain. What else did they do for the soldier? Do you remember?''

Gavin nodded. "They made sure his tetanus was up to date, gave him some type of shot to stop the itching and swelling, and kept applying alcohol to the wound.''

"To sterilize it, I suppose," Zach reasoned.

"I guess it helped hold the pain down by neutralizing the stinging cells, somehow. At least, that's what the lieutenant told us when he was instructing us what to do if it ever happened to another one of us." Gavin snapped his fingers. "Hey! He said if you didn't have regular rubbing alcohol, you could use the kind you drink. Kelly's still got those little freebie liquor bottles in her bag, doesn't she?''

"Get them," Zach instructed. "And that bottle of aspirin.''

Kelly groaned. "Oh, Lord, Zach! My leg is cramping up just like when you get a really bad charlie horse! Can't you rub it out for me? Please?''

Gavin heard, and yelled back, "No! That'll break more of those sacs open, and make it hurt worse.''

"Maybe a couple of Midol would work better than plain aspirin," Alita suggested. "If it works for menstrual cramps, it might help her leg.''

"It certainly couldn't do her any more harm," Blair agreed. "And a dab of that antibacterial ointment wouldn't be amiss, either.''

Zach dragged a hand through his hair in agitation. "Is there anything on this entire, blasted island that isn't a peril to mankind?'' he fumed. ''Can anything else possibly go wrong?''

''Don't, Zach.'' Kelly reached out a trembling hand to pat his arm. ''It will be okay.'' Tears still welled from her eyes, even as she tried to console him. ''After all, it can't hurt like this forever. And it's not as if I got attacked by a shark. It was just a creepy little jellyfish.''

Her breath was emerging in short, pained pants. ''My head is starting to ache more than my leg,'' she added weakly. She tried to roll to her side, moaning with the movement.

''Lie still, sweetheart.''

''Can't,'' she wheezed, her eyes and teeth tightly clenched now. ''Gonna throw up.''

That set the pattern for the following, seemingly endless hours. What little fluid and medication they managed to get into her usually came back up. Her muscles cramped abominably, knotting and twisting until she writhed in agony. She had a headache that made a migraine seem tame. But those times when she couldn't seem to catch her breath were what scared Zach the worst. That, and being virtually unable to do anything to ease her suffering. Moreover, he and the others knew, even if Kelly apparently didn't, that stings from some jellyfish could be fatal.

He kept a vigil at her side, hardly daring to leave for a quick trip to the latrine, watching as she managed to snatch a few minutes of pain-racked sleep at a stretch. For the most part, she was lucid, but in this instance, being fully aware was scarcely a blessing. The others offered to spell him, to give him time to stretch and eat, but basically it was Zach who sat with her. She was most calm when he was beside her, as if he and he alone could lend her strength enough to carry on. His name was the one she called; his hand was the one she clutched so tightly that the bones soon felt bruised.

He talked to her, encouraging her until his voice was hoarse. Sometimes he just rambled from one topic to the next, telling her about his childhood, his college years, his family, the different places he'd worked. During the worst spells, he reminded her, "You can't leave me now, love. You and I have a date to be married, and it wouldn't be kosher to stand me up at the alter."

"I know. I won't," she rasped, forcing her words through gritted teeth, attempting in turn to keep his spirits up. "I'll beat this. No spineless little blob of jelly is going to get the better of me. That would be the height of humiliation, wouldn't it?"

Around noon the next day, after being up with Kelly throughout the night, Zach had drifted into a light sleep. If it hadn't been for Gavin's excited yell, he might have missed hearing the aircraft that buzzed directly over the island, so low it sounded as if he could reach right up and shake hands with the pilot.

Zach leapt to his feet, instantly alert. "Stay with her!" He was halfway across the campsite, headed toward the path to the beach as he shouted the order to Blair.

"Go! Go!" Blair waved him on, pausing only to scoop Sydney out of the way. "Hurry!"

Zach knew he'd never run faster in his life—that he was probably breaking all kinds of track records—yet the beach had never seemed further away. It was like one of those weird dreams in which you run in slow motion and everything stays the same distance from you, frustratingly unattainable, no matter how hard you try to reach it. Though logic told him it had taken mere seconds to cover the short span, it seemed an eternity.

He was two strides from the end of the trees and the open beach when something cracked him on the head with the force of a hammer. The earth spun crazily as his feet went out from under him. Just before he hit the ground, before everything went black, he caught a quick glimpse of Earl on the path behind him, hand raised and holding the pistol aloft.

Zach awoke feeling as if his head had been split open with an ax. It was when he tried to raise his hand to his head that he discovered he was in an even worse predicament. Through slitted eyelids, he peered dazedly at the metal cuff encircling his wrist. Comprehension dawned.

"Damn!" he groaned.

"You can say that again," Gavin intoned miserably from his place next to Zach.

Zach lifted his lids a fraction more, and saw that Gavin's hand was attached to the other cuff. They were linked together, with the short connecting chain looped beneath a slight arc of exposed tree root. The ends of the root were still underground, with only a foot-long curve visible above the surface.

Zach gave an experimental tug at the cuff, a move that elicited an immediate grumble from Gavin. "Hey! That hurt!"

"Sorry. I was just testing to see how sturdy this root is, if there was any chance of pulling it loose or breaking it."

Gavin eyed the four-inch thick root skeptically. "I doubt it. That thing looks like it's there to stay for another hundred years."

"Shit!" Zach eased back against the tree, careful not to slam his head against it. "I take it Earl clobbered you, too?"

"Yeah. Makes me wonder why we didn't try the same trick with him days ago."

"Mainly because he's carrying a gun, and we aren't,"

Zach replied sardonically. "So, did anyone make it to the beach to signal the plane?"

"No. Blair and the kid were here with Kelly, and Blair didn't have any idea we were out of commission. Alita tried, I guess, but Earl threatened to shoot her, so there wasn't much she could do except back off. She's mad as hell, by the way."

"That makes two of us." Zach gazed around, taking stock of the situation. The root to which he and Gavin were secured was part of one of the aerial supports beneath the canopy of the banyan tree, just a few yards from the central firepit. Kelly lay on her blanket nearby, with Blair in attendance. Sydney was cuddled in Alita's lap, on the other side of the campfire. Earl was nowhere in sight.

"Where is the bastard?" Zach growled.

"I don't know," Gavin said. "Guess he got tired of Alita cussing at him."

Zach's gaze rebounded to Kelly. "How is she?" he called out to Blair.

Blair shook her head. "About the same."

Zach cursed. "Damn that son-of-a bitch! She needs help! This might have been our best chance at being rescued, and he had to screw it up! All because he doesn't want to get arrested again! It really doesn't matter to him if the rest of us rot here with him, or that Kelly might die without medical attention, as long as he doesn't wind up behind bars."

"It was bad enough before," Gavin agreed with a dismal sigh, "but now we're the ones shackled to a tree and he's runnin' around with that pistol, making like he's king of the mountain or something. Lord only knows what that crazy ass will do next."

"We've got to get loose," Zach said, "before he takes it into his head to rape the women or kill us all."

"Yeah, but how? Earl has the key, and I don't think

Alita, as sexy as she is, is gonna be able to sweet-talk him out of it."

"He'll have to let us loose sooner or later, if only to go relieve ourselves. Maybe, between us, we can overpower him."

"While he's holdin' a gun on us?" Gavin inquired doubtfully. "Get real, man. I don't plan to get myself shot any sooner than necessary."

"We'll think of something. We have to. And speaking of weapons, whatever happened to that sword? Last I recall, you were hacking trees with it. Maybe we could use it to sever this root. At least then we'd only be tied to each other."

"I dropped it when I heard the plane. It's still layin' back where I was working . . . unless Earl has found it already."

"I wonder if one of the girls could get to it before he does," Zach speculated. He called Blair over, not wanting to chance that Earl would suddenly appear and overhear their conversation, and briefly discussed the possibility with her.

"I'll send Alita right away," Blair declared. "One of us has to stay and look after Kelly and Syd."

"Is her breathing any better?" Zach asked worriedly.

Blair's expression was bleak. "It's hard to tell, Zach. At this point, with all that poison in her system, all we can do is hope she's strong enough to fight it off."

Zach's eyes misted. "I can't lose her now, Blair. I couldn't bear it. I've already lost one woman I love. I can't lose Kelly, too."

Blair patted his shoulder. "She's young, Zach, and healthy—or was until this happened. She could pull through just fine. We just have to wait . . . and pray. Pray for all you're worth."

* * *

Alita, following the vague directions Gavin gave her, located the sword. She smuggled it into camp right under Earl's nose, hidden in an armload of firewood.

"You are one worthless *hombre,*" she railed at Earl. With her back to him, she dumped the pile of limbs near the fire, close to where Kelly lay. Kneeling, she tossed a branch on the fire, at the same time covertly sliding the sword under the edge of Kelly's blanket. She resumed her tirade. "The least you could do is bring water from the pool, or collect wood for the fire, or do something other than mess with that damned pulque you are concocting."

"Pulque?" Earl repeated grumpily. "Is that another one o' them Mex words you're so fond o' tossin' around, like it was supposed to impress me?"

"For your information, you big jackass—or should I say *burro?*—pulque is a liquor made from the agave plant."

"You know, I'm gettin' right tired o' you actin' so high and mighty, and spoutin' off at the mouth all the time. 'Specially when you do it in Spanish. If ya got somethin' to say to me, say it plain out in English."

"Hah! Like you speak that language, either!" she taunted. She rounded on him, her fists braced on her hips in a provocative stance. "Okay, you want it in words you can understand? Get off your dead ass and do something useful, you lazy bum! And you talk about me? Instead of shooting off your own mouth, why don't you shoot off that lousy gun of yours? Go hunting and bring back a nice plump pigeon or two. I'm tired of fish, fish, fish!"

"I ain't wastin' ammo on a blasted bird, woman," he rebutted.

"Then strangle one with your bare hands, for all I care. Just bring me meat!" She threw her hands up in an exasperated gesture. "Isn't that what a man is supposed to do, after all? Supply meat for the table? You are a man, aren't you?"

She'd thrown down the gauntlet, in front of everyone, and quite deliberately. It was one he couldn't ignore, any more than a bull could ignore a matador's cape.

"I'll show you who's a man," he snarled, tossing down the piece of wood he'd been whittling and starting to rise. "You probably ain't never been with a real man before."

Alita faced him with a haughty sneer. "That is so typical! A man trying to prove himself by what he has in his pants! Which makes him no better than any other animal roaming the earth! But even the male beast knows when to rut and when to provide for his mate. He brings her meat to please her. Can you really call yourself a man and do less?"

Earl paused, dumbfounded. "You want me to court you with a pigeon?" he asked with an incredulous half-laugh.

She smirked. "Again, I will say it clearly. I am totally pissed at you, that you have again prevented us from getting off this island. You have a lot to make up for—a lot of kissing up to do, as they say. At this point, the only cock I will gladly accept from you comes with a beak and feathers attached to it. You bring me that kind, first. Present it to me plucked and cooked to perfection. Then, and only then, will I consider the one you so braggingly think I should admire."

To everyone's amazement, Earl bought into her spiel. He puffed up like a strutting rooster. "You got a deal! I'm gonna bring you the fattest, juiciest damn bird you ever did see. Maybe a whole slew of 'em. But don't you try to wiggle out o' your part afterward."

Alita couldn't help getting in one last jab. "We will see. From where I'm standing, a bird on the plate is worth two in the bush."

Nobody bothered to correct her misinterpretation of the old adage.

Chapter 17

"Dang, woman! Watch it with that thing! You trying to lop off a hand, or what?"

Kelly nudged Blair's leg to get her attention. "What are they doing now?"

Blair had already explained that Earl had knocked both Zach and Gavin out and handcuffed them to the tree root. "Alita is trying to hack through the root with the sword, but there's not much space in which to work. In order to give it a good whack, she has to swing it hard, and the guys are nervous. Not that I blame them. I sure wouldn't want someone chopping at a slippery root mere inches from my hand."

"Maybe if she used her knife, she could chip away at it," Kelly offered weakly.

"Hear that?" Blair called out. "Kelly says to try your knife instead, Alita."

For several minutes, Alita alternately poked and sawed at the root with her knife, with little appreciable results.

"At this rate, we'll be here 'til doomsday!" Zach grumbled.

"And Earl sure isn't going to be off hunting that long," Gavin added. "Does anyone know how to pick a lock?"

"Don't you?" Alita asked archly.

Gavin took exception. "Hey! Just because I'm black doesn't automatically make me a criminal, you know."

Alita shrugged. "Just asking. I simply thought you might be better at it than I am."

"Say what?"

Zach, too, couldn't believe he'd heard her correctly. "You're into jimmying locks?"

"Used to be," she admitted readily. "But I was never really good at it."

"Good, bad, or otherwise, give it a try," Zach told her.

Alita studied the hasp on the cuffs. "I don't know. It has one of those funny little holes that takes a special key. I will need something narrow to stick in there, but it must also be strong enough not to bend or break. I don't think a hairpin will work, and this knife blade is much too wide."

"Let me see that knife," Zach told her. She handed it over, and after inspecting it for a moment, he pulled a long, thin piece of metal out of the end of it."

"What is that?"

"It's a toothpick, and fortunately it's metal instead of wood," Zach explained. "Most Swiss pocket knives have them. They also have these." Again, he retrieved a metal object from its compartment in the knife, holding it up.

"My goodness!" Alita exclaimed. "It's a tiny pair of tweezers!" She grabbed both items and set to work.

Half an hour later, she sat back, thoroughly discouraged. "I'm sorry. It's no use."

"Then we're stuck," Zach conceded. "The only thing left to try is to cut the links apart, and we don't have anything that will do the job. We'd need a hacksaw, at the least.''

"Could we melt the metal?'' Gavin proposed. "Or weaken it with heat, so Alita could pry the links apart?''

Zach shook his head. "You'd need a blow torch to get it hot enough, and I wouldn't recommend that even if we had one handy. With our luck, all we'd achieve would be to set ourselves on fire.''

"I suppose it wouldn't work to try to grease your hands with coconut oil and pull them free,'' Blair submitted doubtfully.

Kelly tugged at her arm. "That gives me an idea. Help me over there.''

"Good grief, girl! Just lie still and tell us what to do,'' Alita said.

"No. Not unless you know how to pop a bone out of joint and put it back in again,'' Kelly argued with more force than she'd exhibited in two days. "Now get over here and help me. I don't care if you have to drag me, blanket and all.''

"Just whose bones are you talking about?'' Gavin inquired worriedly.

"And which ones?'' Zach wanted to know. "And why?''

Kelly didn't bother explaining just yet. She was too busy trying to contain the moans rising to her throat as her two friends towed her toward the men. As of waking that morning, after a terrible night during which she'd almost wished she would die, she was feeling remarkably better. However, though the nausea and the muscle spasms had subsided to a tolerable level, her head still ached horribly and the most agonizing pangs would shoot up her leg unless she kept it absolutely immobile. Just now, she was in god-awful pain.

Even after they stopped moving, Kelly needed several minutes to recuperate. Finally the misery abated, allowing her to speak. "Houdini used to deliberately dislocate his own shoulder in order to maneuver out of a straight jacket. Therefore, it stands to reason that if we were to do the same with your thumb, it is quite possible that you could slip your hand out of the handcuff. As soon as it's free, I'd pop the bone back."

"Oh, Jesus! It makes me sick just thinking of it!" Gavin groaned. "Isn't it bad enough I've got one hand broken up, without you wanting to ruin the only good one I've got left?"

"That's why I think it's best that Zach volunteer," Kelly informed them both. "Besides, he's right-handed, and his left one is cuffed."

Zach frowned down at her. "Honey, I know you're trying to help, but this sounds painful as all hell."

"So is getting shot," she pointed out succinctly.

"Right. Okay." Zach nodded. "So, are you sure you can do this?"

"Yes. I can even manipulate a couple of pressure points first, to numb the joint. That way, you'll hardly feel a thing, and it should only ache a bit for a short while afterward."

"Should, could, would," he intoned dubiously. "Famous last words."

"The only thing I'm concerned about is the size of your hands, and whether this will allow you enough leeway to pull your hand loose," Kelly went on to say. "The thumb I can work with. The rest is up to you."

"I say we go for it," Gavin said.

"Sure, now that your hand isn't the one in question," Zach noted wryly.

"Look. Guys." Alita called for their attention. "We either do this or we don't. We haven't a lot of time to decide."

"And fewer options," Blair stressed.

Zach held his hand out as far as he could reach toward Kelly. "All right. Do it."

Blair plopped Sydney into Gavin's lap, so she wouldn't get into mischief while the adults were busy. Then she aided in steadying Zach's hand, while Alita helped prop Kelly into a better position.

As she had told him, Kelly first kneaded the applicable pressure points. When the lower half of Zach's hand had gone numb, she swiftly twisted the ball of his thumb out of its joint. She and Alita, working together, compressed his remaining fingers as tightly as possible and pulled in one direction—while Zach and Gavin tugged the metal cuff in the other. It was a tight squeeze, and for a minute it looked as if their efforts were in vain. Then, though the skin was scraped from his knuckles in the process, his hand broke free. Quickly, before the feeling could come back, Kelly popped his thumb back into place.

Exhausted, but triumphant, Kelly fell back on her blanket. Zach, after planting a fleeting kiss on her brow, scrambled to his feet. Gavin dumped Sydney off of his lap, pulled the handcuffs from under the root, and did likewise. "Maybe I should let Kelly get my hand out, too," he debated, eyeing the cuffs dangling from his right wrist. "These things could be a problem, just hanging like this."

The numbness wore off suddenly, and feeling rushed back into Zach's hand with a vengeance. "Oh, crap! Oh, nuts!" Zach grabbed his wrist, oubling over. "Kelly! I thought you said this was only going to ache a little!"

"That's just the blood coming back. It's only temporary. Flex your fingers," she ordered. "Like you would for a cramp. Work it out. Shake it. Get the blood flowing properly again."

Gavin backed off. "I've changed my mind. I'll keep the cuffs until we can get the key away from Earl."

"Chicken!" Alita taunted. She rolled her eyes. "Why are men such big babies?"

"If they had to have babies, the way we do, they'd know what pain really was," Blair agreed. "And there would be only one child per family, no matter what the Pope decreed."

The pain had subsided by now, and Zach was looking somewhat abashed.

"Think you'll live after all?" Kelly teased.

"I might."

"Me, too," she told him, mustering a smile.

"And if we all want to stay that way," Gavin announced, grimly bringing their primary problem to the fore, "we'd better come up with a foolproof plan to deal with Earl. Real fast."

Earl couldn't have announced his imminent arrival more clearly if he'd been wearing a cow bell. The man was whistling, apparently feeling quite pleased with himself. The minute the others heard him, they went into action. Gavin and Zach resumed their positions, as if still chained to the root. Kelly, with the sword again concealed beneath her blanket, was lying in the same spot she'd been before, a few yards from the fire. Alita and Blair stood on either side of her, facing one another across Kelly's prone body.

Earl had yet to enter the camp when Blair and Alita began screaming at each other.

"You might be a famous singer, but you're no better than a slut! A rich bitch!" Blair shouted.

"You are just jealous that I have a big strong man wanting me, and you have no one!" Alita countered loudly.

"I could have him if I wanted him!"

"Ha! I've seen pigs less homely than you! And in a few months, you will be as fat as one!"

"And what would you be without your big boobs and your big hair?" Blair retorted angrily. "I've a good notion to snatch you bald! Let's see how sexy you look then!"

Earl had just stepped into the clearing when Blair launched herself at Alita, grabbing a huge handful of the singer's hair. On an enraged screech, Alita countered by clutching the front of Blair's T-shirt, holding onto her as she slapped Blair's cheek. The brawl, with both women yelling and kicking and scratching and pulling hair, was taking place directly above Kelly—who was helpless to move out of the way. The best she could do was to shield her face, hope neither of them happened to kick her by mistake, and plead with them to stop. Poor Sydney ran to hide behind Zach and Gavin.

Earl stood stock-still for a moment, staring in dumbfounded awe at the female cat fight erupting before his eyes. Then, as if suddenly recalling that he was the only male free to physically intervene, he dropped the brace of pigeons he was carrying, and stomped into the fray. "Hey, you dizzy broads! Knock it off! You're scarin' the kid!"

He had one paw wrapped around Blair's forearm, and the other gripped around the back of Alita's neck, trying to pry the battling women apart, when Kelly made her move. Drawing the sword, she slid it alongside Earl's leg, until the point rested at his groin.

Watchful and waiting, though they certainly hadn't appeared to be, Alita and Blair abruptly ceased their scuffling. In the sudden hush, Kelly's warning rang clear. "I wouldn't make any hasty moves, if I were you, Earl. Unless you want to sing soprano from here on out."

Before he could even think to react, or try to disarm her, Zach and Gavin were there. Zach yanked the pistol from Earl's waistband. Gavin relieved Kelly of the sword.

"Let loose of the ladies," Zach commanded.

Blair immediately went to reassure Sydney that all was well. While Zach held Earl's arms wedged behind his back, rendering him defenseless, Alita quickly and efficiently frisked him. She came away with the two knives he'd taken from the other men the previous day, the handcuff key, Earl's handmade slingshot, a wallet, a butane lighter, and a handful of extra bullets. When his pockets hung empty, and she was sure he had no other weapons hidden on his person, she used the key to free Gavin of the cuffs, and handed them out to Zach.

"Do you want the honors, or should I do it?"

"I'd better," Zach said. "Keep him covered, Gav."

Between them, they hauled the big man to the sturdiest support post and anchored him to it, with his hands bound behind him.

"This time, you can stay tied to the damned tree until you grow moss," Zach informed him tightly. "And I don't think you'll be getting much sympathy from the women, either. You conned us once, thanks to Kelly's soft heart. It won't happen again."

"You'll have to let me loose to go to the bathroom, and to eat," Earl snarled defiantly, his face twisted into a scowl.

"I don't have to do anything but die and pay taxes," Zach stated flatly. "I just might figure it's safer to let you starve and wallow in your own filth. You see, Earl, you made a tremendous blunder when you sabotaged our rescue efforts, especially when it endangered Kelly's life. And threatening us with this gun wasn't a really wise move on your part, either."

"Hell's bells, man! The damned gun don't even work!" Earl shouted. "And Kelly sure wasn't going to croak off from no bite from a danged jellyfish! Not that it wouldn't have served her right, cheatin' on her hubby the way she is with you. I kind of liked her 'til then. 'Til she proved she weren't no better than Mary Beth.''

Gavin couldn't grab Zach's arm in time to prevent him from plowing his fist into Earl's jaw. Earl's head hit the tree trunk with a force that sent figs falling from the branches like rain. He slumped, unconscious, blood seeping from the corner of his mouth.

"I hope he bit his foul tongue in half!" Zach declared, shaking off Gavin's restraining hand and backing away from the temptation to hit Earl again.

"Is he right?" Kelly called from her blanket. "About the gun, I mean? Has he been holding us at bay with a weapon that won't even shoot?"

"We'll find out right now," Zach decided. "Blair, you hold onto Sydney in case this thing does go off with a bang. I don't want her to be frightened." With that, Zach marched out of the clearing and headed for the beach, with Gavin and Alita close behind.

Kelly strained her ears, as did Blair, but try as they might they heard nothing that sounded like a gunshot. Silence reigned, stretching into long minutes. Finally, when they thought they couldn't bear the suspense much longer, the others trooped back into view.

"The lousy bastard was right," Zach grumbled. "The years and the high humidity have rusted the barrel, bound up the firing mechanism, and basically turned the ammunition into hunks of worthless powder and metal. In its present condition, the pistol probably doesn't even have any antique value, except maybe as a war memento."

"Well, that's a relief!" Blair sighed. "What with bats and bunji pits and snares, at least we won't have to worry about Sydney getting hold of a loaded gun. It's hard enough to keep her out of mischief as it is."

"We might have used it to signal help, though," Gavin said. "A gunshot can be heard for miles."

"No use crying over spilled beer," Alita misquoted. "The good thing is, none of us are going to get shot and Earl is now the one in handcuffs again."

"And you don't have to make the ultimate sacrifice to save us," Kelly reminded her. "None of us would have wanted you to resort to that."

"Gracias a Dios!" Alita cast a glare in Earl's direction. "If that miserable excuse for a man wants to get laid, he can crawl up a bird's butt and make like an egg!"

"Speaking of birds," Blair put in. "I believe there are a couple of pigeons awaiting their turn on a spit."

"Well then, what are we all standing around for?" Zach clapped his hands, as if calling them to order. "I, for one, can't wait to sink my teeth into a plump, succulent breast."

In chorus with Gavin's choked guffaw, and despite Kelly's bright blush, Alita rolled her eyes dramatically. "Aye, chihuahua! Watch out for this guy, Kelly. He is one rowdy puppy!"

Chapter 18

Murphy's Law was in full play. With Earl unable to sabotage their efforts, the planes now ceased to fly over the island. A week went by without sighting or hearing any sign of a rescue attempt.

"This is asinine," Kelly said. "Why would they stop looking for us?"

"And why, even if they didn't see any evidence of us, didn't they at least spot the wreckage?" Blair queried despondently.

"I've been wondering the same thing," Zach admitted. "I think I'll take a hike up the mountain tomorrow and have another look around."

Unencumbered, and fully recovered from his initial injuries, Zach made it up and down again in good time. He arrived in camp a full hour before dark. "Bad news, folks. I climbed as far as that knoll where we stopped the first day, and from what I could see, it's doubtful that anyone flying over would recognize the charred remains as that of a 747. The blackened debris blends in too well with the lava rock.''

''What about the part that didn't burn?'' Gavin asked. ''The tail section was fairly intact.''

Zach shook his head. ''Some of the trees supporting it have since given way. The tail section has slipped further into the foliage, and my guess is that some fronds and branches which were previously bent have sprung back up around it. You can barely see a trace of it through the brush. In fact, it's so well camouflaged that if I hadn't known exactly where to look I might not have found it.''

''And the cockpit?'' Kelly inquired.

''Too mangled to distinguish it from much else. Even if a piece of metal would reflect sunlight, a pilot might assume it was simply glare off a pond or a patch of snow.''

''Snow?'' Alita echoed. ''Here?''

Blair nodded. ''It sounds ridiculous, doesn't it? But I've read that there are many places in the tropics that have snow-capped peaks even in the summer. It has to do with the elevation. It can be hot on the coast, and freezing on the mountain tops.''

''So, what you are saying, Zach, is that unless they see us or our signal fire, we're fairly well S.O.L.,'' Gavin concluded.

Zach sighed. ''That's about the size of it.''

''And since they've stopped coming around, we can assume they've already searched this area and decided to look elsewhere?'' Kelly proposed.

''For the time being, perhaps,'' Zach agreed.

''Then it's a darn good thing I've got that raft nearly finished,'' Gavin declared with resolve. ''Another week or so, and I should be able to set sail.''

Zach frowned. ''I still think it's an immense risk to take. That's an awfully tiny raft, and a tremendously big ocean.''

Gavin shrugged. ''So, what other choice do we have,

other than sitting here watching our toenails grow? If they can't find us, we'll just have to find them."

"Or die trying?" Kelly voiced the awful thought for all of them.

Life went on, with the castaways trying to make the best of it. They also sought to keep busy, in an attempt to keep themselves from dwelling on the passing of each successive day without rescue. Zach helped Gavin with the raft. Blair set herself to the task of learning to leaf-weave hats and baskets. Alita practiced her singing, strung leis, and helped watch over Sydney. Kelly created several hanging lamps by making macrame hangers in which were suspended coconut shells filled with coconut oil. The oil, pressed from the nutmeat, burned very well as a substitute for candles or lamp oil. The makeshift pots, hung at intervals beneath the banyan tree, served to ward off the pesky bats at night—which made them all sleep a little easier, whether the men admitted it or not.

On subsequent forays of the island, they uncovered two more bunji pits, which the fellows filled in, and half a dozen snares, which they dismantled without mishap. Some new discoveries were infinitely more appreciated, among them a mango tree, a guava shrub, and a small papaya tree. Sydney was the one to find the first gull nest, and the trio of edible eggs it held. From then on, they scoured the beach for more. They also experimented with various ways of preparing their food, as another means of providing themselves more variety.

Sydney soon found herself with a few primitive toys. A doll, made of macrame pandanus leaves. A crude ball, similarly fashioned. A miniature raft for floating in the pond at bathtime. Kelly even devised a ball-in-the-cup game for her, by employing a mango stone, half of an undersized coconut shell, and her ever-handy dental floss. Even the adults, in need of some form of recreation of their own, enjoyed an occasional game of papaya football. The trick was to use an unripe papaya, or risk getting spattered with the juicy fruit.

As beautiful as the island was, with its dazzling display of exotic birds and blossoms, its flower-fragrant breezes and pristine beaches, the lack of modern amenities made it difficult to truly appreciate it as a tropical paradise. It became routine for them to list those things in the real world which they missed the most.

"I would kill for a butterscotch milkshake," Blair said. "With Bobby I craved sauerkraut, of all things. When I was expecting Nancy, I wanted green peppers, despite the indigestion they caused me. This time, milkshakes. Go figure."

"It must be something your body needs," Kelly surmised. "I guess coconut milk just isn't cutting the mustard. As for me, the first thing I want to eat when we get back is a BLT with mounds of mayonnaise."

Zach shook his head. "Give me a nice, juicy sirloin steak, and my morning coffee, and I'd be in heaven."

"Lasagna," Gavin put in. "With garlic bread."

"Chocolate," Alita contributed wistfully. "A whole meal of nothing but brownies, chocolate mousse, mocha mint cake, and fudge—with about a gallon of hot cocoa and marshmallows."

Earl had his own choice. "Venison roast with carrots, taters, and gravy. And buttermilk biscuits."

Other than daydreaming about foods they yearned for, there were the conveniences they missed. At the top of Blair's list was her microwave.

"Air conditioning," Kelly countered. "Just a decent electric fan would be bliss."

"A chain saw," Gavin proposed. "The better to cut the

poles for the raft. Or, if I'm really gonna fantasize here, a
yacht would be nice, complete with crew and a couple of
well-built babes."

"Any kind of car or truck, even an old beater," Earl
said.

Zach agreed, with provisions. "My BMW. That, and a
kingsize bed with big fluffy pillows, soft cotton sheets, and
a comfortable mattress."

"Clean, decent clothes," Alita added, eyeing her soiled,
mis-matched ensemble with disgust. "And somewhere to
actually wear them would be great! A restaurant, a show,
a party, even a tacky amusement park. I'm too desperate
to be picky. I just want to be able to go anywhere other
than here. Someplace without sand."

Laundering their clothing, sans soap, was a feat in
itself—primarily because they either had to put it back on
wet and let it dry on their bodies, or find among their
limited attire something else to wear in the interim. Sydney
had no difficulty. She could dash around in her panties
while her abbreviated playsuit was drying, or vice-versa. As
for the adults, being far less modest than the women, the
men did likewise. It didn't seem to bother them one whit
to prance around in their skivvies. In truth, they tended
to preen, somewhat akin to male models.

"Born exhibitionists!" Kelly declared. "Not a bashful
bone in their bodies."

"Well, I wish they would cover up more," Blair complained. "I'm pregnant, not dead, and my hormones are
standing on end here! No matter how big I am by the time
I get home, Anton is going to be in for the surprise of his
married life."

The women elected to be more discreet, and inventive.
Blanket togas came into vogue. As did donning a man's
jacket, or Gavin's uniform shirt or T-shirt, which he gallantly lent them. Kelly's decorative silk scarf often served

as a skirt, or sometimes as a bandeau top, whichever was most needed at the time.

"You know, you could save yourselves a lot of trouble if you'd just whip up a couple of grass skirts," Zach told them with a naughty grin. "Go native."

"In a brisk breeze," Gavin added enthusiastically.

"Go away."

"Dream on."

"Amuse yourselves elsewhere," Blair suggested.

"I think that's their problem," Kelly commented with wry wit. "They've been playing with themselves too much. I've heard that causes a number of medical and physical repercussions."

"Hey, girl! That's hitting below the belt!" This from a disgruntled red-faced Gavin, his exclamation eliciting chuckles all around.

"Strictly rumor," Zach rebutted smoothly. "And not applicable in my case, thanks in large part to Kelly."

Now it was Kelly's turn to blush. "Between you, Sydney, and that blabber-mouthed parrot, I have no secrets anymore!"

Sydney was, indeed, a gabberbox. Whatever entered her ears, exited her mouth. Daily, her vocabulary and pronunciation were improving. Unfortunately, she was also picking up a number of nasty words in the process. As was her feathered friend, Fricassee, so named because that's how Kelly envisioned the pesky bird on his worst days—in a stewpot!

"For two cents, I'd wring his scrawny neck," she claimed.

"First you have to catch him," Blair reminded her.

"I think he's cute," Alita said.

Kelly shot her an annoyed look. "If it were you he was repeating all the time, you wouldn't."

Alita laughed. "Ooh, Baby! Oh, Zach! Go, baby, go!" she mimicked tauntingly.

From above, Fricassee sprang into action. "Ooh, baby! Move that thing! Yeah!"

"Now, that was Zach, not me," Kelly refuted peevishly.

"Likely story."

"No, I believe her," Blair stated. "I've heard that bird repeat other words I know didn't come from Kelly's lips. B-O-O-B-S for instance." She spelled the word, aware that Sydney was seated nearby, her little ears perked.

"Gee, thanks," Kelly grumbled. "Now, if you really want to help, give me a good recipe for white sauce, one that will enhance Fricassee's flavor."

Gavin considered his life one long series of missed opportunities. He'd missed entering kindergarten with his best friends and had spent his school years a grade behind them, simply because his birthday was six measly days beyond the deadline. In high school, his girlfriend had gone to the junior prom with another guy, because Gavin came down with, of all things, the chicken pox two days before the big event. Once, he'd even lost a mega-buck betting pool on a super bowl game by a single point. His father's life insurance policy, which would have gone a long way toward easing the family's financial distress, expired for lack of payment a month before he had died. Gavin had even been passed up for a football scholarship, only to have the college change its mind three weeks after he'd already enlisted in the army.

It was the story of his life. He always seemed to be a day late or a dollar short in the good-luck department. Like his R&R to Australia, for instance, which had ended with the plane crash and almost killed him. Now he was AWOL, or maybe just missing-out-of-action, if there was such a thing. Whichever, knowing the army and the screwed-up way they handled matters, they would probably make him serve extra time, to make up for what he'd lost, before giving him his discharge.

To beat all, he was stranded here in the prime of his sexual life, with three attractive women, and was living the life of a monk—except he doubted a monk would be half as frustrated. Once again, life had dealt him a lousy hand, when it could have been a winner. Blair was pregnant, and married, not that that would have deterred Gavin if she'd indicated an interest in him. But she hadn't given any sign of wanting him as anything but a friend, and Gavin wasn't the type to use force. He hadn't survived growing up in Chicago—avoiding gangs, drugs, and a rap sheet—just to screw up now. As for Kelly, Zach had made it clear that she was exclusively his, and Gavin couldn't blame him. With those emerald eyes and long braid, she was a walking, talking Barbie doll!

Which left Alita, Super-Star and Queen Bitch. Yet, even knowing he didn't stand a snowball's chance with her— or maybe because she was so unattainable—Gavin had developed a kingsize crush on her. God, that woman was beautiful! And built—with a set of maracas sure to set any guy between the ages of six and ninety-six to drooling. When she'd come on to Earl the way she had, though it had all been an act, Gavin had been so jealous he could scarcely see straight.

Now, for some reason, probably just to drive Earl nuts, Alita had suddenly started flirting with Gavin. She had him hornier than a three-peckered billy goat. Worse, she knew it. He could see the amusement lurking in her big, dark eyes every time she batted those long lashes at him. Laughing eyes. Teasing eyes. As that old song had phrased it, Spanish eyes, that had him thoroughly entranced. Moreover, Gavin was sure she was just playing with him, luring him on with no intention of putting out, the way she'd done with Earl, which truly ticked him off. This game of hers, whatever it was, was fast driving him up the proverbial wall.

That wall came tumbling down on him much sooner than Gavin would ever have suspected. He and Zach had finished their day's work on the raft and had stopped by the pond to clean up prior to going back to camp. Gavin had put in a grueling day, and his muscles were aching worse than they had that first week of basic training.

"I'm going to soak a while," he told Zach. "Maybe that will work out a few of the kinks."

Zach, ready to head back, sluiced the excess water off his chest with his hands. "In that case, I'll leave the string stretched across the path."

They'd rigged a signal of sorts, to warn each other when the pool was in use—just a vine with a bright piece of cloth tied to it, strung between two trees along the path to the water hole. Crude as it was, it served the purpose and kept the men from intruding on the women when they were bathing, and vice-versa.

Zach left, and Gavin was soon blissfully relaxed, his eyes closed as he lounged, naked and half-afloat, with his neck propped on the narrow ledge encircling the pool. He was contemplating how remarkable and fortunate it was that the lava forming the mini-lagoon had cooled to form such a smooth surface here. It was almost like lying in one of those pre-poured hot tubs, one built to accommodate several people comfortably, with plenty of room to stretch out. Which led him to fantasizing about what fun it would be to frolic in the pool with Alita. He could picture her naked, her creamy toffee-tan skin glistening, her hair streaming across her shoulders in wet waves. Just imagining her that way gave him an erection that made him grit his teeth.

"My, my! Something has you immensely aroused. I hope it's me."

Alita's lilting voice cut unexpectedly into Gavin's musings of her. With a startled jerk, he lost his grip on the ledge, and slid beneath the surface. He came up choking, to find her at the edge of the pool, laughing at him.

"Dammit, Alita!"

Whatever else he might have added was swept from his brain as she calmly and deliberately proceeded to undress. While he sat there, tongue-tied and bug-eyed, she stripped for him—slowly, tauntingly, with a smile to rival Mona Lisa's. Then, with the grace of a doe, she stepped into the pool and sank onto her haunches beside him. Her hand dipped into the clear water to stroke his thigh.

"You know, I always envied the other kids, the ones with more money and nice families," she told him, her ebony eyes sparkling above that tantalizing smile. "They got to do all the fun things, especially on the holidays. Do you know that I have never once bobbed for apples?"

"That . . . that's a darn shame!" he croaked out.

"I agree," she said with a nod. "Perhaps you can show me how it is done."

Gavin nearly swallowed his tongue. "Uh . . . what do you plan to use for apples?"

She cupped his genitals, sending goosebumps chasing across his flesh. "These would do nicely, don't you think?"

Gavin could feel beads of sweat popping out on his forehead. "I suppose, as long as you don't intend to take a bite out of them."

She gave him a wounded look. "You don't trust me?"

"About as much as I'd trust a strange rottweiler," he muttered.

"Oh, but they can be very friendly animals, once they get to know you," she assured him. Her fingers curled more firmly around him. "Think of me as one of the nice ones, the kind that love to lick you all over." She gave a little shimmy that set her breasts quivering and the water rippling around them. "Pet me. Stroke me. Teach me some new tricks, Gavin."

"Like how to retrieve apples and big sticks?"

"*Sí.*" She gave her head a playful toss. "And perhaps, if you are a very good teacher, I will even sit up and beg for you."

"Dear Lord!" he murmured, reaching for her with eager hands. "If I'm dreaming, please don't wake me until after the good stuff."

For once, Gavin lucked out—big time.

Chapter 19

Despite his new and exciting liaison with Alita, Gavin was determined to finish the raft and still insisted that he would leave on it when it was done. His work was going more slowly, though, his mind and body often being otherwise engaged.

Thus, the small group of survivors had been marooned on the island for three weeks by the time Gavin finally announced that his tiny craft was ready and he would be sailing soon. As luck would have it, however, now that the raft was complete, the weather was taking a turn for the worse. His long-planned launch would have to wait until conditions improved.

If Gavin was disgruntled, Zach was worried. The usually gentle ocean breeze was stiffening daily, almost hourly, strengthening into a gale. The tides were running higher than normal, the waves pounding ashore with growing force. Dark clouds built on the eastern horizon and scuttled across the sky in ever-building masses—sometimes dropping significant rain, but often traveling too fast for the precipitation to amount to much. Each day, the weather deteriorated more.

"I don't like the feel of this," Zach admitted to the others. "Even the birds are acting weird, as if they know something is going to happen. I've heard that animals are sensitive to changes in the atmosphere, the barometric pressure, and such."

"Fish, too," Earl put in from his post. "A storm can really mess up a fella's fishing. 'Course, sometimes they bite real good just beforehand, like they know they ain't gonna feed for a while with the water all stirred up."

"I've read that cattle and sheep have behaved oddly just prior to an earthquake. Supposedly, they can feel those slight initial tremors much sooner than humans can," Blair related.

Gavin huffed an exasperated breath. "Darn! If I'd just finished the raft a couple of days ago!"

"Right!" Alita scoffed. "And then where would you be?" She pointed toward the churning sea. "Out there bouncing around like live shark bait, that's where."

Kelly agreed. "She's right. You wouldn't want to be out there on that raft now. I'll bet even seasoned sailors, on those huge transport ships, will be seasick before this is done."

"I just wish we knew how bad it's going to get," Zach said. "It would be nice to know what to expect, what to prepare for."

"Yeah, where's a reliable meteorologist when you really need him?" Kelly mocked.

"Back on cable TV, with the Weather Channel and CNN," Alita informed her wryly. "Probably bringing us an update as we speak."

Zach had to laugh. "No doubt, and that's another thing I've always thought so ludicrous. Have you ever noticed how they'll announce on television that a certain area is without power, then tell those affected not to phone in because the electric company is aware of the problem and attempting to fix it as soon as possible. Pray tell me how those people are supposed to be watching that broadcast if their power is out?"

"Well, we don't have any electricity to start with, so I guess we're just going to have to prepare for the worst and hope for the best," Kelly suggested. "But, like you, I wish we had some way to determine how strong this storm may be."

Zach nodded. "Are we talking mediocre, a series of relatively harmless rainstorms, or a major typhoon? Are we directly in its path, or are we just going to catch the edge? Will there be a resultant storm surge, possibly even a tsunami? As it is, we don't know whether to dig a hole, or climb to higher ground—or both. And to procrastinate too long could prove disastrous."

They spent a miserable night huddled beneath the banyan tree, which was now offering very little shelter. At dawn, which amounted to no more than a slight lightening of the darkness, Zach decided they must act immediately. Once again, they packed up their meager belongings, but this time they bundled up a couple of baskets full of fruit as well.

"We'll stop by the water hole and fill up the coffee pot," Zach told them. "What I wouldn't give for a thermos bottle about now!"

"Where to after the pool?" Kelly asked, ducking her head as several figs blew loose from the branches overhead and pelted her.

"The cave."

Kelly stared at him, aghast. "The cave? As in, the same

cave with the decayed soldier? We're going to share quarters with a corpse?"

"A skeleton," Zach corrected succinctly.

"Semantics. It's still gruesome, any way you cut it. I vote we find someplace else."

"There is no place else. If this turns into a full-blown typhoon, it's the only site likely to withstand the storm."

"Then, historic relic or not, old 'Harry-Kari' has to go," Kelly insisted with a shiver that had nothing to do with the wind-driven rain dripping down her back. "Out on his bony butt."

In good conscience, there was nothing they could do but unchain Earl and take him along with them. Zach even relented enough to couple Earl's hands in front of him for the short jaunt to the cave, making it easier for Earl to negotiate the rough spots along the way.

"Just don't try anything, Roberts," he warned, pushing him ahead of him on the trail. "I'll have my eye on you all the while."

"You're worse than a damned cop," the big man retorted sullenly. "Shit! I ain't no better off now than if I'd gone to prison. Probably worse. At least there I wouldn't be tied up to a danged tree day and night."

"It's your own fault."

"Yeah, yeah, yeah."

They'd hoped that once they were farther from the shore, the trees would act as a buffer from the wind and rain, but the storm was gaining momentum faster than they were. The wind swirled and gusted around them, forcing them to turn their backs to it in order to breathe, and to crab-walk sideways—while the earth beneath their feet was quickly turning into a slippery river. The rain didn't fall, it slashed in blinding, horizontal sheets, carrying with it sand and debris. Each step was a strain, like wading through the surf, against a surging tide.

Once, Kelly lost her footing and tumbled down a slight incline, garnering several bumps and bruises. Alita, too, slipped and gashed her knee on a piece of lava rock. A particularly strong gust sent Zach stumbling into a tree trunk. Fortunately, his back and shoulders took the brunt of the blow, and Sydney, cradled against his chest, wasn't hurt. Blair, nearly blinded by the grit aggravating her contact lenses, was reduced to hanging onto Gavin's waistband and hoping the two of them could remain upright.

Communication between them was soon impossible— words too feeble to be heard above the roar of the wind and vision reduced to a few hazy feet. Such were their circumstances when a palm tree came crashing directly in front of them, the serrated trunk missing Zach and Sydney by scant inches. The mighty thump as it landed vibrated the ground, sending them all tumbling and skidding. One by one, gasping and trembling, they crawled into a hasty huddle.

"Anybody hurt?" Zach yelled.

Each, in turn, shook his or her head.

"Okay, let's go on. I estimate we're about three-quarters of the way there."

Kelly tugged at his arm. "Wait!" she hollered. "Where's Earl?"

Zach's frown deepened. "He's either under the tree or on the other side of it, I guess. Here, you take Syd." He handed the frightened child over to her. "I'll go have a look."

Gavin went with him, and was back in a few minutes. "Come on. Zach's clearing a path on the other side."

"Earl?" Kelly inquired on a shout.

"We couldn't find him. He's probably somewhere ahead of us."

It took another forty-five minutes of muscle-straining labor before they finally, gratefully, stumbled into the cave.

On leaden legs, unable to see where she was going in the murky interior, Kelly tripped over something and landed on her knees. Her hand connected with several small, cylindrical objects. Only as her vision adjusted to the dim lighting did she recognize them as the finger bones of the Japanese soldier's skeletal remains. Her frantic scream echoed off the rock walls as she jerked away, scrambling on all fours to the opposite side of the cave, as far from the dead man as she could go. There she drew herself into a quivering, teeth-clattering ball. Blair and Alita, joined her, staring in abject horror at the macabre object still dressed in tattered uniform.

Zach approached them to hand over Sydney. "I know you women get the willies over this sort of thing, but face it. The guy can't hurt you."

"Get . . . rid . . . of . . . him." Kelly forced the words out.

"Just toss the old boy out in the storm, huh?" Zach said. The wide-eyed feminine trio nodded in tandem.

"We need the cave worse than he does," Gavin contributed. "And it's not as if he's in danger of catching pneumonia or anything."

Between them, though neither was happy about performing the chore, Zach and Gavin disposed of the remains, hauling the body, clothes and all, outside. The one thing in their favor was that enough time had elapsed since the man had died that all organic matter had long since decomposed, leaving behind nothing but dry bones, dust, and moth-eaten cloth.

With a grimace, Gavin wiped his hands on his pants. "I guess it could have been a lot messier."

Zach dredged up a chuckle. "Yeah. Give me 'dem bones, dem bones, dem dry bones' anytime."

All in all, once the skeleton had been removed, the cave wasn't that dreadful. The opening faced away from the wind, which helped keep the rain from entering. And once they'd lit the coconut oil lamps, it wasn't nearly as gloomy. The light revealed a small stack of age-dried wood just inside the entrance, and after claiming a few logs from a nest of disgusting insects, they soon had a cheery little fire going as well. They clustered around it, drenched to the skin and all but numb with fatigue.

"How long do you suppose the storm will last?" Kelly inquired.

"Your guess is as good as any," Gavin replied wearily. "I just hope my raft is still intact afterward."

"You lashed it down, didn't you?" Zach asked.

"As best I could, yes. I wedged it partway under a dead-fall, where the wind wouldn't catch it so easily."

"Speaking of wind," Blair said, "it nearly blew my contacts right out of my eyes. I really need to get these things out and clean them before they do permanent damage."

"Did you pack up your eye-cups?" Alita asked. In the first week, Blair had devised a unique system for cleaning her contact lenses. She did so by employing two well-scrubbed lime halves partially filled with salt water, which substituted fairly well in place of her usual saline solution.

"Yes, would you mind fetching them for me?" Blair replied. "They're in that red purse. But I don't have any salt water handy."

"You'll just have to use fresh water this time," Kelly told her. "I hope we have enough to last for a while. It doesn't look as if the storm is letting up at all."

"As long as it keeps raining like this, we don't have to worry about getting our water from the pool," Zach inserted. "Just set the coffeepot outside, and it will fill up in no time."

"Or be blown to China," Gavin claimed.

They sat quietly for a time, shifting once in a while to aim another portion of their clammy bodies and clothes toward the fire. Gavin was first to break the silence once more.

"Where do you think Earl made off to?"

"Who gives a flying fig?" Blair muttered.

For a moment no one answered, that in itself a condemnation of Roberts. Then Kelly spoke.

"You're sure he wasn't caught beneath that tree?"

"Fairly certain," Zach averred. "He wasn't under the trunk, at any rate, which is where he should be if the palm had fallen on him."

Kelly nodded. "As much as I resent the man, I would still hate to think of him lying out there, trapped and bleeding to death, with the rainwater slowly rising to drown him."

"I doubt he'd return the sentiment," Alita declared. "That is one bad *hombre*. Rotten through and through."

With none of their usual projects to occupy them, nothing to do but watch the storm rage on outside the cave, the hours passed slowly. Alternately, they napped, nibbled on the food, played with Sydney, and carried on desultory conversation.

"If I'd known we were bound to be so bored, I'd have carved a deck of playing cards," Zach grumbled. "Or a set of dice."

"We could play Twenty Questions," Kelly offered.

"Or Charades," Blair added without much enthusiasm.

"How about trivia?" Gavin suggested. Immediately he thought better of it. "Forget that. Blair would know all the answers before we got the questions out of our mouths."

Alita brightened. "I know what will entertain you. I could read your palms. You know, foretell the future for all of you."

Zach snorted. "So where were you with this offer when I was standing in the airport ticket line? You sure could have saved us all a lot of trouble if you'd proposed this about three weeks ago."

"And why, if you can predict what is going to happen, were you on that disastrous flight?" Gavin insisted.

"Oh, lay off, guys," Kelly told them. "This could be interesting. Lord knows it's got to be better than counting flies on the wall." She scooted closer to Alita and held out her hand. "Do mine first."

Alita studied Kelly's palm very seriously for several sec-'onds. "This," she intoned, tracing a line on Kelly's hand, "is your life line. Very long. Your love line is broken only once, which probably indicates your divorce from Brad. These two marks below your little finger are marriage lines, the lower one being your marriage to Brad, which would lead me to believe you will marry once more." She curved Kelly's thumb into her palm and counted the creases formed by the lower knuckle. "Four, one faint and three strong, which could mean one miscarriage and three full-term babies."

"I've already had the miscarriage," Kelly said.

"Then you will have three more natural children, not counting any you may adopt or otherwise inherit."

"What about me?" Blair asked curiously. "What does my future hold?"

Again, Alita took a moment to study Blair's palm. "Your life line has a narrow arc to it, which says you are a private or shy person, as a rule. You need time to yourself to revive your energies. Your head line is deep, with a long curve, to indicate that you are an intellectual who is very creative and good at communication, possibly in the field of writing."

"Oh, my gosh!" Blair gushed. "I've always dreamed of someday writing a book. While I was in Australia, I did a lot of research on a possible idea I have for one."

"If we ever get rescued, you'll have one heck of a story

line," Gavin pointed out. "All about our island adventure."

Alita went on with the reading. "Your love line is very strong. You love deeply. I hope you love Anton very much, for I see only one marriage line." She curled Blair's thumb over and added, "I also see five children for you."

Blair grimaced. "Five? Are you sure? Anton is not going to be thrilled to hear that. Three is pushing it, for him and our budget."

Alita gave a definite nod. "Five. But perhaps your money problems will ease once your first book is published, no?"

"This is a bunch of bunk!" Zach declared.

"But entertaining," Kelly countered. "I want to hear what she has to say about you, Zach."

He frowned, and she wheedled, "Oh, come on. If it's all in fun, where's the harm? Let her see your palm."

Reluctantly, he held it forth for Alita's perusal.

"Your life line is strong, long, and widely arced. You like being around people and are very creative. Your love line is also long and deep, and when you give your heart to someone it is for always. I see two marriage lines. Your head line indicates that you are very good with facts, numbers, and logical thinking. Ah, see here? There is a three point fork in it, which means that you are exceptionally intelligent." She folded his thumb over. "You will father four children in your lifetime."

"This life or the next?" he jeered.

Alita smiled. "This one, and may they all be smartasses, like you."

Next, she reached for Gavin's hand. "Your life line is strong, but it has a few problem areas which signify illnesses or injuries. Your heart line is shallow. That usually means you hold back your affections, or do not love as deeply as most people. You are going to have to work hard to achieve the success you want. You will marry or be involved in serious relationships three times, and have two children along the way."

"What hocus-pocus bull!" he grumbled. "And what about you? What does your own palm say about your life? Or is that a big dark secret?"

"I, of course, am very talented and creative. My life line is strong and wide. But like you, my love line is lightly grooved. I do not trust enough to give my heart fully to anyone, yet I will probably marry four times and have one child."

"Too bad Earl isn't here. It would be interesting to hear how his palm reads, wouldn't it?" Blair commented.

"Probably like a murder novel," Kelly said with a shiver. "Or a nightmare."

"He can't be sane, to prefer being out in this storm," Zach stated flatly. "Look at it. The wind is blowing so hard that some of the trees are bent nearly in half and are being stripped of their leaves."

Kelly peered out. The rain was coming down sideways in thick sheets. The wind was howling, in a loud mournful bellow. Loose debris, mostly foliage and branches, were whipping around as if caught in a giant blender. The storm seemed to be getting progressively worse with each passing hour, with no let-up in sight.

Much later, in the middle of the night, they were awakened by a huge thud, which literally shook the earth beneath them.

"What was that?" Kelly wondered aloud. In the wavering light of their little fire, she scanned the rock ceiling overhead, relieved not to find any menacing cracks or signs that it might be ready to cave in on them.

"My guess would be that a tree just blew down," Zach answered. "Somewhere close."

"It must have been a big one, to make the ground shake like that," Alita surmised warily.

Now, along with the moan of the wind and the steady pounding of the rain, they could hear a variety of mysterious creaks and groans from outside the cave, though they couldn't see a thing in the black-as-pitch night.

"This is terrible, hearing all these ominous sounds and not being able to tell what is making them," Kelly said. "It reminds me of those slumber parties we used to have as teens, where we'd sit up all night and scare the peanut butter out of each other by telling ghost stories."

"We did the same thing around the campfire at scout camp," Zach admitted. "Eerie tales of ghouls and goblins and escaped convicts on the loose. We'd frighten each other simple and think it was great fun."

"I should have figured you for a boy scout," Gavin commented. "And to make it even more realistic, we've got our very own real-life murderer wandering around out there somewhere, probably trying to concoct ways to bash in our heads."

"More likely trying to find a way to breathe water," Blair argued. "It's still raining cats and dogs. You should have built an ark instead of a raft, Gavin."

"I'm wide awake now," Alita complained.

Kelly nodded. "Me, too, but I'd rather not exchange ghost stories tonight, if you don't mind. This weather has me jittery enough as it is. Let's talk about something more cheerful."

"Like what?" Blair yawned. "The bedtime fairy tales I read to my children?"

Kelly shrugged. "I don't know. Old movies? Good books we've read. Whatever. Anything to take our minds off the storm."

"Okay, I'm game," Zach surprised her by saying. "Name the seven dwarves."

"You've got to be kidding!" Gavin scoffed.

"I'm as serious as a grave," Zach assured him. "My daughter and I used to do this sort of thing all the time."

For five fairly intelligent adults, it took them considerable time and mental effort to finally name all seven. They kept forgetting about Happy. Even when Zach finally recalled him, the others were skeptical. "Are you sure his name was Happy? I don't remember him."

Next, they recalled all of Santa's reindeer. That accomplished, they went on to list the items for the Twelve Days of Christmas, and nearly wound up in an argument over whether the maids were milking or dancing, and whether the geese or the swans were a'laying.

Then Kelly suggested something more challenging. "Name all the Waltons."

"From the T.V. show?" Alita asked. "How many kids did they have, anyway?"

"A whole slew of them," Gavin replied. "Plus the old couple and the Mom and Dad."

"Seven or eight, I think," Blair said. "I remember three girls and at least four boys."

At length they remembered all of them, though no one could recall the grandparents being called anything but Grandma and Grandpa. They even recalled Ike, who ran the general store. But the stumper was remembering the two old-maid sisters who still brewed the family "recipe" in their kitchen. Nobody had a clue, and they finally gave up, though Blair swore not knowing would drive her nuts until she finally thought of their names.

In retaliation, she said, "List the seven seas."

"Which seven?" Alita wanted to know. "There must be hundreds."

"The seven referred to in books and in songs," Blair clarified. "As in, 'he sailed the seven seas.' "

"Of course, Miss Trivial Pursuit already knows the answers to this one," Gavin presumed correctly.

They tried, but eventually had to worm the answer out of Blair before going on to the seven wonders of the world. After a series of movie titles, song lyrics, and famous actors, they tired of the game and settled down to try and sleep again.

Kelly, punch drunk from lack of sleep and trivial overload, yawned and called out, "Goodnight, John Boy."

Alita giggled. "Sleep tight, Mary Ellen."

Zach got into the act. " 'Night, Ben."

"Back at you, Jim-Bob," Gavin grumbled.

"Darn it, you guys!" Blair groused. "Now you'll have me trying to remember those two old ladies again!"

As one, the others chorused, "Goodnight, Elizabeth!"

Chapter 20

A couple of hours past dawn, the storm stopped as suddenly as if someone had flipped an electric switch. The rain quit, the sun shone brightly, the wind ceased so completely that not a leaf stirred. The small tribe of temporary cave dwellers ventured out into the open for the first time in twenty-four hours.

"Thank God that's over and done!" Kelly exclaimed, turning her face to the clear blue sky. "I was starting to develop claustrophobia."

"But it might not be," Zach said. "This may be just a short respite, the eye of the storm, with more to come."

Alita gazed about, at the cerulean sky stretching as far as the eye could see, at their rain-washed sun-dappled surroundings. "Couldn't be. There's not a cloud in sight. No storm brewing on the horizon. No haze. Just hot, glorious sunshine."

"And no breeze whatever," Zach pointed out. "Which is odd in itself, as if we've been locked inside a vacuum."

"Or the center of a typhoon," Blair agreed. "If it's large enough, we could have hours of calm weather before getting hit by the backside of the hurricane."

Zach nodded. "In which event, we'd better stick close to the cave today. Just for safety's sake."

In scouting their immediate area, they discovered the storm had done more damage than they'd suspected. Numerous limbs, branches, and whole trees had been felled. Most of the flowers that had been in bloom were now denuded, as were some trees, many of which now sported windblown seaweed in place of leaves. Several dead birds were strewn about amid the debris. But the strangest sight were the fish—swept ashore by the gale and deposited willy-nilly three-quarters of a mile inland, some landing on rocks, others high in treetops, like some type of bizarre ceremonial decoration.

"This is downright weird!" Gavin declared.

"Weird or not, it's food. Manna from heaven," Zach insisted. He turned to Blair. "Have you ever studied how to dry meat in strips?"

"Like jerky?" she asked. At his nod, she said, "I've read about it, but I've never tried it. I think it needs to be smoked over a fire, and salted."

Alita wrinkled her nose. "Sounds like a lot of work to me, especially when we already have fresh food to eat."

"I suppose so, but I hate to think of all this food going to waste, particularly the pigeons. They're hard enough to kill with that slingshot, and these have all but landed in our laps."

"Then let's preserve the pigeon meat, and bake a couple of fish for dinner," Kelly suggested. "I can't say fish jerky sounds very appealing to me, except as a last resort."

"To me either," Gavin granted, "but it might be a good thing to take with me on the raft."

"Okay, I'll try it," Blair agreed. "But the rest of you have to help."

Other than what had been stored inside the cave, there was no dry firewood to be had. There was, however, plenty of available seaweed, without having to trudge down to the shore to get it. Kelly also discovered that, as the sun dried small pools of saltwater atop the lava rock, it left behind a deposit of salt, ready and waiting to be harvested.

Their project was soon underway. Together they toted a dozen big flat rocks inside the cave, on which to lay the meat to dry. They cleaned fish, plucked birds, sliced the meat into thin strips. All that remained was the actual smoking and drying by the time the weather began to reverse once more. They moved their venture indoors, lest their providential harvest be waterlogged or blown away, and were soon inundated with the fishy odor.

"Sheesh! This must smell worse than a dockside tuna cannery!" Kelly declared.

"It's making my eyes water," Alita complained.

"If there are any cats hiding away on the island, they'll show up at any moment," Zach said in a nasal voice, the result of trying to breathe solely through his mouth and not his nose.

Gavin echoed that. "Yeah, the nine-lives dinner bell has definitely been rung!"

Blair, declining comment, bolted for the cave entrance, one hand clamped to her mouth. Much to her surprise, Kelly followed suit within seconds. Zach found them hunched against the outer wall, pale and shaky. He urged them inside again before they got completely drenched. "Sit by the entrance, where you can get some fresh air and still stay dry. Now that we've got the gist of how to do this, Gavin, Alita, and I can handle it from here."

Alita cocked a sassy brow at him. "Thank you so much for volunteering me, Zach. It's so gallant of you."

Zach returned the arch look. "You're so very welcome, my dear Alita. Now kindly can the lip and flip. The bird," he added, when she just stood there. "It's burning. Turn it over. Flip it."

Alita ignored the charring pigeon long enough to flip Zach the bird, in fluent sign language.

The backside of the storm hit with a vengeance, dumping torrents of rain while the wind wailed like a demented banshee. It was as if all the furies of heaven and hell had been unleashed en masse. Trees crashed earthward, sand-littered debris hurled past the cave entrance in a endless, deadly whirl. Even large rocks were tossed about, as if they were weightless bits of dandelion fluff. The earth trembled in awe of this mighty assault. The very walls and floor of the cave seemed to echo this quaking, as did the people huddled within.

"Dear Lord! I've never seen anything like this!" Kelly exclaimed in fearful wonder. "And look at the fire, and the lanterns." She and the others watched in anxious amazement as the madly flickering flames inclined in a severe angle toward the entrance, akin to a plant being drawn toward sunlight.

"It's as if all the air is being sucked out of the cave," Blair noted.

"There is definitely an outward draw," Zach concurred, "but I don't think there's any danger that we'll suffocate, if that's what is worrying you. Nor, regardless of the unstable sensations, do I think the cave will collapse. To be out in the storm, with no protection whatever, would be a far greater peril."

"Makes me wonder how Earl is faring," Kelly said.

"If he's lucky, he's not airborne or clinging to a treetop right now," Gavin stated with a smirk.

"Like the Flying Nun?" Blair suggested.

"More like the Flying Felon," Zach quipped.

"For all we know, he could be a phantom by now," Alita contributed on a more serious note. "A real one—as in dead, deceased, departed."

"I wouldn't wish that on anyone, not even him," Kelly said. "Especially not him, at this point in his life. Maybe, given enough time, he'll see the error of his ways and repent."

Blair nodded in accord. "And escape having to spend eternity in hell."

Gavin groaned. "Oh, stop with the evangelistic moralizing. It's starting to feel like a tent revival in here!"

"Not such a bad idea, under the circumstances," Zach commented, staring out at the fierce storm. "I think all of us would like to feel a little closer to God at this moment. Not necessarily face-to-face close, mind you, but assured that He's watching over us."

The storm finally wore itself out several hours later, and everyone heaved a grateful breath of relief. They also abandoned the cramped, smelly cave as quickly as possible, eager to be back on what they now considered home turf, beneath the old banyan tree. The return trek was almost as long and hazardous as their trip to the cave had been. This time, they had to skirt fallen trees, heaps of branches and rubble, and sodden quagmires.

Again, they stopped at the pool to fill their coffee-pot/ canteen, only to find that the water was strewn with leaves and murky with sand and lava grit. It would take a day or two to settle properly. The water pouring from the spout Zach had rigged was much clearer, however, saving them the necessity of filtering it through a cloth sieve.

Upon arriving at their previous haven, they discovered,

to their united dismay, that it was in similarly sad shape. Limbs littered the small clearing, as did a variety of dead and injured birds and bats. The rocks surrounding the fire pit had been scattered. The wind had ripped away a good portion of the leafy overhead bower, leaving half of the original area now uncovered and the ground underfoot soggy. Fortunately, the section still protected was spacious enough to accommodate them in comfort, once they cleared away the clutter.

There was no sign of Earl, or that he had been back here. Nor had they seen him along the way. A quick survey of the beach gave no evidence of him, either. It did reveal that the storm had completely dismantled their SOS and signal fire, which was disheartening, though not entirely unexpected.

When Gavin went to check on his raft, they got their first clue as to what might have become of their missing castaway. Gavin came running, his face flushed with anger. "It's gone! The raft is gone!"

Zach's primary response was, "Are you sure you looked in the right place? The storm destroyed a lot of trees and landmarks we've become accustomed to."

"I'm sure."

"Could it have blown away?" Kelly asked.

"Or floated off?" Blair added. "The tide must have risen far beyond its normal mark."

"No," Gavin fumed. "I checked the tide mark, and it isn't anywhere near the spot. And I doubt the wind carried it off, or there would be pieces of it scattered everywhere. As it is, I can't find so much as a splinter of the raft or the oar I made, but the rocks I used to anchor it are still there, all pushed to one side in a nice tidy pile—almost as if someone stacked them there on purpose. Someone by the name of . . ."

"Earl!" came the united cry.

Immediately, Kelly thought better of their conclusion. "Surely not! Surely he wouldn't be dumb enough to attempt setting off on the raft in the middle of such a terrible storm. That . . . that would be suicidal!"

"Besides," Alita cut in, "he was the only one of us who wanted to stay on the island. Why would he decide to leave now?"

"Because, to use his own words, he was as much a prisoner here as he would have been if the plane hadn't crashed," Zach explained, his expression grim. "As for leaving in the middle of the storm, I presume that's precisely what he did. It's entirely possible that when the eye hit and the weather cleared, Earl thought the storm was over and it was safe to light out on the raft. He'd have been in a hurry. He wouldn't have wanted us to catch him in the act."

"Which would have made him all the more desperate and impetuous," Kelly deduced.

"Damn!" Gavin cursed, pounding one doubled fist into the other. "Damn that man to hell and back!"

"Which is where he's at now, no doubt," Blair said solemnly. "I truly doubt anyone could have survived a tempest of that magnitude on a rickety little craft such as that. Why, the waves must have been several times as high as the raft was long!"

"We may be wrong," Zach told them, offering another scenario. "Earl might still be holed up somewhere on the island, with or without the raft. If he did take it, he might be hiding it to keep Gavin from setting sail and bringing back help. Or he could be biding his time, waiting for the sea to calm before leaving on it himself."

Gavin considered this. "Maybe, but other than searching the entire island inch by inch, how would we find him, preferably before he decides to launch the thing or destroy it? The rain and wind have washed away any tracks he would have made.''

"There is no easy way," Zach stated. "We can search, we can keep our eyes and ears open for any sign of him, but there's little else we can do.''

"I hope he did set off on the raft," Alita declared adamantly. "I'd rather he be drowned and out of our hair once and for all, than skulking about on the island with us.''

Kelly nodded. "You do have a point there, Alita. But, either way, we are still without a raft.''

They started all over again, practically from scratch. In fact, for two days, until the wood dried out, they couldn't even light a campfire, though they still had the coconut oil lamps for light at night. Until then, they were back to eating fruit, a lot of which was now lying about on the ground—squashed, bruised, but within easier reach. While the women set the camp to rights, Zach and Gavin began work on a new raft. They even found something constructive for Sydney to do. Unlike the adults, the tot thought it was great fun to scoop the sand and dead bugs from the pool and toss the muck aside.

On the third day, Zach decided to make a return trip to the cave, on the off-chance that Earl had taken up residence there after they'd abandoned the site. "I also want to take another look around that entire area," he told them. "It's struck me odd, ever since we first discovered it, that we never found a rifle. You'd think that Japanese soldier would have had one, wouldn't you? He was wearing his uniform, complete with sword, pistol, and helmet. So where is the rifle he should have been carrying?''

From the start, Earl had not only claimed the pistol, but the helmet as well. He'd been wearing it the day of the storm, on the way to the cave. It was gone now, too, along with Earl. Presuming Earl has set off on the raft, the others figured he must have taken the helmet with him, possibly employing it as a container for fresh water. Likewise, they assumed he'd used his shirt or trousers or something that would serve as a makeshift pouch in which to carry a store of food—for surely even Earl, hunter that he'd professed to be, would not have sailed without those simple but essential provisions.

Zach returned with no news of Earl, but he was carrying an old, half-rotted canvas knapsack. Contained within its worn interior was a standard-issue metal mess kit and canteen, both a bit dented but otherwise functional. These discoveries were most welcome, providing them with additional utensils, a divided plate, a shallow cooking tray, a cup/soup container, and—saints be praised—an honest-to-goodness water flask with a screw-on cap! In addition to a few faded letters, photos, and coded operations maps, all printed in Japanese, there was another useful item, one they wished they'd had sooner. A field shovel.

In Gavin's estimation the most valuable item, aside from the canteen, was the old compass, for with it he would be able to navigate on the open sea and know which direction he was headed. "We'll have to test it out, but it looks as if it still works," he declared excitedly.

"With the canteen, you'll have a means of carrying water and not spilling it," Alita pointed out. "Every drop will be precious, I imagine."

"Now all we have to do is get that raft built again," Zach said. "I just wish there'd been a hatchet hidden away in that field pack, but the storm did aid us in that aspect, by putting more broken limbs and branches at our disposal."

"I take it you didn't find the rifle, but where in heaven's name did you find this stuff?" Blair inquired.

"In the cave, stuffed back in a crack in the far corner.

It was there all the while. Amazingly, none of us spotted it in all those hours we spent waiting out the storm.''

"Imagine that!" Kelly exclaimed. Her sharp green eyes studied Zach's face, noting the pleased, almost exultant expression he wore. She could swear he wasn't revealing all to them. "What else did you find up there?"

He replied evasively, not quite meeting her gaze. "Nothing worth mentioning at the moment. You'll be glad to know I took the time to bury Harry-Kari's bones. After all these years of peace with his country, I thought even a former enemy deserved a proper interment—particularly since he's donated, albeit posthumously, all this worthwhile equipment."

"Decent of you," Kelly murmured, still not satisfied, but willing to let it pass for now.

It wasn't until later, lying next to Zach in the dark, that she hissed, "Okay, buster. Fess up. You've been as twitchy as a bug on a hot rock ever since you got back from that cave. What gives?"

"Was it that evident?" he queried, "I was hoping no one would notice.''

"The others might not have, but I did. Now, are you going to tell me, or do I have to wring a confession out of you?"

"Kelly, you wouldn't have believed it!" he whispered excitedly. "I almost didn't, and I saw it with my own eyes."

He hesitated, and she jabbed a finger between his ribs to prod him. "What? What did you see?"

"Gold. The old guy discovered gold, right there in the cave. He'd been digging at it, using his rifle as a pry bar. I suppose his shovel wasn't strong enough to hack away at the rock, so he used the rifle barrel, instead. It was still there, stuck in a deep crevice—the same one where I found the field pack.''

Kelly eyed him skeptically. "Oh, give me a break, Zach! Do you really expect me to believe this outrageous fairy tale? That 'there's gold in them thar hills'?'' she drawled in imitation of an old western line. "More likely, you found a stash of Saki and got yourself looped. Let me smell your breath.''

"I'm not drunk, sweetheart, and I'm telling you the God's honest truth. It's not all that inconceivable, you know. There are precious metals to be found in this part of the world. In fact, we're not that far removed from Fiji, and I know for a fact that gold is one of their leading mineral products.''

"I still say you're getting all enthused over nothing. It's probably just fool's gold, or some other shiny substance you've mistaken for gold.''

"Maybe," he allowed, "but I'm planning to stake a claim when we get back to the States. Better than that, I'm going to see if I can buy this whole blasted island, if I have to hock my underwear to do it.''

"Gold fever," she muttered in disgust. "Just listen to yourself, Zach. One whiff of what you only *suspect* might *possibly* be gold, and you're ready to bankrupt yourself. That's an awful lot to risk on a chancy proposition, don't you think? Are you going to throw poor Becky's college tuition into the pot, too? Her entire inheritance?

"Furthermore," she went on, before he could reply, "I'm willing to bet that soldier had the same idiot notions you're having now, and that's probably what got him stuck alone on this island for all these years. I can just see him, hiding his discovery from his fellow soldiers, then deliberately missing the boat or plane or whatever transportation the others used to get off of this place. He probably hid out in the jungle until they all left, hording his find. And where did it get him, Zach? Nowhere. He died a lonely man, all for greed and dreams of riches, because no one ever came along and he had no way to get himself away from here to spend his wealth—if that's what it really is."

Zach frowned at her. "Are you through preaching at me? Can I get a word or two in edgewise here?"

"Fine. Go ahead. Convince me otherwise, if you can," she murmured.

"You might give me a little more credit for intelligence, babe. I'm not going to go off half-cocked." He reached into his pants' pocket and drew out several small objects. Even in the dark, with only the moon and stars for light, they glittered enticingly. "I've taken a few samples, which I intend to have analyzed before I do anything rash. In the meantime, I'd like to keep my potential strike under wraps, at least until I can file a legitimate stake."

"Don't want to chance any claim jumpers getting in ahead of you?" she mocked. "Is that why you didn't tell the others about it?"

"I'm not being stingy, if that's what you're thinking," he alleged. "I just don't want anyone shooting off his or her mouth and blowing a fantastic opportunity to smithereens. Once I've gotten the assayer's report, and have negotiated a claim on the property, I fully intend to cut Gavin, Alita, and Blair in on the deal."

"What about me?" Kelly inquired. "Don't I get a piece of the pie, too?"

Zach's smile would have rivaled that of a pirate. "You, my fair-haired beauty, will be amply rewarded. Between your share and mine, if all pans out, we'll be able to honeymoon anywhere our hearts desire, for as long as we wish. We'll make oil barons looks like paupers by comparison."

Kelly sighed. "I don't know, Zach. It sounds like prosperity could make you extremely pompous, and I'm not altogether sure I like that idea. I'm kind of fond of you just the way you are."

"Fond?" he questioned haltingly. "Fond? That's a rather lukewarm sentiment from someone who, just a few short hours ago, professed undying love."

"I do love you," she assured him. "I just don't want to see you turn into a money-grubbing rat."

"That will never happen, darling." He held up his hand, as if taking an oath. "You have my word of honor. And if I get at all pompous, you have my permission to give me a swift kick in the rear to set me straight again. Does that meet with your approval? Do you have any other objections or suggestions to add?"

"Just one that I can think of off-hand. If you even consider buying me one of those humongous, gaudy, overly ostentatious rings, our engagement is off."

"Fair enough. With that in mind, I promise to find you the smallest, cheapest engagement ring I can locate," he teased. "Would one from a bubble gum machine suffice?"

She grinned at him. "Actually, it would," she surprised him by saying. "As long as your heart is presented with it."

"My heart is already yours, green eyes," he whispered, his lips hovering over hers. "You're holding it in the palm of your hand."

Chapter 21

Pieces of the first raft, or what looked like it, began washing on to shore toward the end of the week. The mini-logs were all the same length, a couple of them still lashed together with vines, and Gavin was sure he recognized the way he'd tied the knots and notched some of the limbs. Then, as if to seal their suspicions once and for all, one of the branches arrived with a boot tied to it by means of the laces. Though battered and waterlogged, the boot was the same type Earl had worn.

"I think we can stop looking over our shoulders and waiting for Earl to pop out at us from behind the bushes," Zach stated solemnly. "I'd bet my last dollar this boot is his." His voice held a note of self-condemnation as he added, "I wonder if he'd have made it if he hadn't been hindered by those handcuffs?"

"Don't blame yourself for what was his fault, Zach," Kelly advised gently. "After all, his hands were tied in front of him, and he managed to maneuver well enough to steal the raft and float off on it—so he must have had some measure of mobility, much more than he had before, when his hands were behind him.''

"If he wasn't such a dumb shit-heel, I could almost feel sorry for him,'' Gavin declared. "He screwed up all the way along, and was too stupid to see it. In fact, he was such a witless wonder that a good lawyer could probably have gotten him off on an insanity plea with no problem.''

"What a shame,'' Blair said. "Some people just never think before they leap.''

"Too late for him now,'' Alita added.

Kelly nodded. "She's right, but there is still hope for us. We still have a fighting chance, and I'm not about to give up yet. There are too many people out there who need us as badly as we need them, and even though we haven't seen any search planes lately, I can only pray they haven't given up, either.''

"I think it's going to be up to us to plot our own rescue,'' Zach said. "Especially now. The navy and coast guard are going to be busy with new emergencies, compliments of the storm. Too busy to bother searching for a plane that went down over a month ago, presumably killing all aboard.''

With that sober thought, they redoubled their efforts toward constructing the new raft as quickly as possible, while trying to make this one stronger, more sea-worthy. They even rigged a mast for this second, more improved model, employing one of the blankets as a sail. All this took two and a half weeks of steady work, but finally the raft was deemed ready. For safety's sake, and bearing in mind what had happened to Earl, the men decided that a test run in the bay was in order, before an actual ocean voyage was attempted.

The women watched from shore as Zach and Gavin launched the raft on its maiden trial. Even on the bay, the small craft looked pathetically tiny, and it was a very good thing that they'd decided to test it first. It listed to one side, terribly, and the men had to bring it in and add another log to the width to correct the problem. Then the mast wouldn't stay upright, tending to lean to one side, and they had to make several adjustments before it would remain in position.

Finally, when they'd done everything they could, there remained one major obstacle. Even with a large pack of coconuts and foodstuff lashed aboard, it was not enough to compensate for Gavin's weight on the opposite end of the raft. Unless he sat in the center continually, which made it impossible to row with the oar, and difficult to maneuver about at all without threat of tipping over, the raft tilted up on the lighter end. They debated tying rocks to the underside to even it out, but didn't really consider that a wise alternative. Moreover, they doubted the rocks would stay lashed in place for long.

"There's no help for it," Zach said. "We'll have to double up on the logs on the weak end, and hope they stay put. Which means you'll have to keep to the other end most of the time. It's that, or move the mast over. We should have mounted the mast more to one end in the first place, instead of the middle. I should have known to take your weight into consideration. My only excuse is that I've never before tried to build anything that's supposed to float."

"Hey! With you helping, this one turned out a lot sturdier than the first one," Gavin claimed. "I just hate having to take the extra time to revamp the thing. I was all geared up and ready to go, and the sooner I leave, the sooner help will be on the way." He thought a minute, then added, "When we were both aboard, we didn't have any problem. Another solution would be for you to go with me."

Zach considered this, but only briefly, before shaking

his head. "No. One of us has to stay with the women. But, if you prefer, I can go and you can stay."

Now Gavin shook his head. "No way, man. I'm so sick of this island I could spit. Besides, if anything bad happens, I'd rather it be to me. You have a kid at home, waiting for her daddy. I don't."

"I'll go."

All heads turned toward Alita, their expressions as surprised as hers appeared to be.

Gavin was the first to reply. "Woman, are you crazy? I wouldn't want anything to happen to you, either. Jesus! Your fans would scalp me! Besides, how do we know you're not pregnant or something?"

Alita tapped her left arm, near her shoulder. "I don't take those kind of risks, Gav. I got the implants—you know, the birth control they put under your skin. They last for years."

"Yet you're willing to take a more dangerous risk on that raft?" Kelly asked incredulously. "I don't believe this!"

Alita tried out a nonchalant shrug that didn't quite fly. "Life's just one big crap shoot anyway, isn't it?"

"But we're talking life and death here, girl. That's a mighty high ante," Gavin maintained. He tried a rougher tactic, to discourage her. "Besides, just because we had some fun in the bushes doesn't mean I want you around for the long haul."

Alita simply wrinkled her nose at him before thrusting it higher into the air. "Tough toenails, *amigo*. I'm going. You need someone for balance, bal—what is the word I want?"

"Ballast," Blair supplied automatically.

"*Sí*, ballast. You need another person for ballast, and it might as well be me. Also, I can help you with the sail, and take turns watching for ships. You have to sleep sometime."

"We should have made the blasted raft bigger, then we

could all go," Gavin grumbled. "We could take our chances together."

"Bad idea," Blair said, patting her tummy. "On top of this, I can't swim, and neither can Sydney."

"I could go," Kelly proposed hesitantly. "I don't have any kids, or an adoring public."

"Think again," Zach put in gruffly. "You're not going anywhere without me, sweetheart."

Kelly scowled. "I didn't say I wanted to go, but . . ."

"No but about it," he stated flatly. "As for that little comment about kids, once more I say, think again. According to my calculations, we've been here for more than six weeks now, and unless you're normally irregular, you should have had a period by now, shouldn't you?"

Kelly stared at him, stunned speechless. The others waited, and could almost see her counting out the days on her mental calendar. "Uh, maybe it's the stress . . . of the crash . . . and all," she stammered.

"Get real," Blair told her with a smirk. "You turned as green as grass cooped up in that cave with those smelly fish. And I know you've tossed your cookies a couple of times since then. What's more, you can't seem to make it through the day anymore without taking a nap or two. Face it, honey. You've got a bun in the oven."

Gavin nodded. "Knocked up higher than a kite."

"Muy preñada," Alita agreed with a grin. "Or, to put it another way, more 'Prego' than spaghetti sauce."

Kelly's hands flew to her flushed cheeks. "Oh, my gosh! I'm going to have a baby!"

"We're going to have a baby," Zach corrected gently. "So, what do you think? Are you mad, glad, or indifferent?"

He didn't have to wait long for her reaction. She literally threw herself into his embrace, her arms wrapped so tightly around his neck that she was practically choking him. "Oh, Zach! I'm thrilled! Elated! Delirious with joy!"

With a laugh, he lifted her off her feet and spun her in circles. "Me, too. I just wish we could be married right now. don't want our little papoose to be born on the wrong side of the blanket."

"All the more reason why Gavin and I had better shove off tomorrow morning," Alita announced decisively. When Gavin would have argued further, she faced him defiantly. "Just shut up! I'm going, if I have to swim alongside the whole way! Hollywood has waited long enough, and I'll be damned if I let someone else have my turn at fame and fortune in the movies! I've earned it, I deserve it, and by heaven I'm going to demand it."

Amid hugs and kisses, tearful goodbyes and last minute admonitions, Gavin and Alita set sail with the outgoing tide early the following morning. The others stood on the shore and waved until the tiny craft was no longer in sight. Finally, with mixed feelings, worry warring with excitement, they returned to their camp. Already, the site seemed too quite, almost forlorn.

"So this is what empty-nest syndrome feels like," Blair commented sadly. "Can't say I'd recommend it."

"Me, either," Kelly agreed with a sorrowful face.

Zach tried to reassure them, and himself. "They'll be alright. We'll see them again. It's only a matter of time. The weather is fine, the seas are calm. They couldn't have picked a better day to set off."

A day went by. Then two. Blair occupied herself by weaving more baskets. Kelly helped her watch over Sydney, and began plaiting a wide panel out of pandanus leaves.

"What's that going to be?" Blair asked curiously.

Kelly shrugged. "I don't know. I don't particularly care. It's just something to do."

Zach began carving wooden blocks for Sydney. He

fished, and somehow managed to beach a big sea turtle. The meat was tough, but tasty—a welcome change from fish and pigeon.

On the third day after Gavin and Alita's departure, Kelly finally found a use for her woven mat. She anchored it between two of the support posts beneath the banyan tree. Along a second abutting side, facing the fire, she hung a blanket. Combined, the two items formed crude walls, separating and shielding her and Zach's sleeping area from the rest of the campsite.

Zach was impressed. "I wish you'd come up with this weeks ago, when privacy was really at a premium."

"Hey, hotshot architect! You were supposed to be in charge of this project, if I recall correctly," Kelly reminded him. "I hope you're not going to prove as lax about your promises in the future. And if you value your hide, you won't make any comments on how I could or should have done it differently or better."

Zach held his hands up in a plea for clemency. "I wouldn't think of it." He surveyed her work with a swift glance, and said, "Actually, you didn't do half bad, but I've got to say that this is going to give the term *shacking up* a whole new meaning for me."

From the shelter of the leaves, a raucous voice squawked, "Shacking up! Shacking up! Awk!"

Kelly glared upward. "Of all the birds that croaked off during the storm, Frick had to survive! I'm telling you, Zach, if I ever get my hands on him, he's a goner!"

The days became a week, and still no sign of rescue or their friends returning on the raft. Either would have been preferable to the eternal waiting and worrying.

"They've got to be out of drinking water by now, or close to it," Kelly fretted.

"Unless they found some on another island or managed to collect some rainwater," Zach said.

"A few clouds wouldn't be bad, to shield them from the worst of the sun. Maybe a light shower or two. But I hope they didn't encounter any storms," Blair brooded.

Kelly sighed. "I hope we discover something soon. This is so nerve-wracking! I keep imagining them out there, dying of thirst. Or worse yet, being attacked by sharks."

"I suppose you saw *Jaws* and both sequels," Zach presumed.

Kelly gave a morose nod. "Several times over. If I'd known then what I know now, I would have avoided those films like the plague."

Fortunately, with their preoccupation over Gavin and Alita's plight, the next couple of days were fairly calm. The most traumatic event was when Sydney got her fingers caught in the claw of a large coconut crab. Zach pried her loose. Kelly bandaged her fingers and dried her tears. Blair cooked the offending creature, and it turned out to be the most delicious meal they'd had in all the time they'd been on the island. They all went out the next morning in search of more of the appetizing rascals.

Which was precisely what they were doing when they first heard the distinctive whop-whop-whop of helicopter blades. Zach, who had located a crab hole at the base of a coconut tree, tossed aside his shovel and raced out onto the beach. Within seconds, he was joined by Kelly, Blair, and Sydney. Clustered together, they all frantically searched the sky.

"Where is it?" Kelly wailed, upon failing to sight it.

Blair shaded her watering eyes against the glare of the sun and railed, "Curse these contact lenses anyway! Whenever I need to see something, they blur or make me tear up. I can't see a bloody thing!"

"There!" Zach pointed at a tiny silver speck nearly out of range. "There!"

Kelly thumped him on the back. "Quick! Light the signal fire, Zach!"

Contrarily, now that the wood was dry, the lighter wanted to malfunction, much in the way a car tends to flood when the driver is in a rush. After several false starts, during which Zach wondered if they'd depleted the butane at precisely the wrong moment, the flame flared. The dry coconut husks that formed the base of the stack caught like tinder, and within mere seconds, the entire underside of the large pile was ablaze, licking hungrily at the larger pieces of driftwood atop it. Even as a fledgling fire, long before the flame would be visible from afar, smoke bellowed upward, beckoning in the breeze like a flowing gray banner.

"Oh, please let them see it!" Kelly prayed aloud. "Please let them find us!"

Blair was hopping up and down excitedly, resembling a rotund rabbit. "They're coming closer!" she shrieked. "It looks like they're heading straight for us!"

Indeed, the minuscule speck in the distance had become noticeably larger, the noise of the rotor louder. Kelly and Blair began waving their arms at it. Sydney, thinking it a game of some sort, did likewise.

"Save your energy," Zach advised. "They're too far away yet to see or hear us, though they can probably see the smoke."

Kelly dashed toward the path to camp, calling as she went, "They'd see a blanket, wouldn't they?"

It only took a few minutes to collect the blankets and scoop their most important possessions, including her tote bag, into them. She arrived back on the beach, dragging it all behind her, as Santa might have hauled an overstuffed toy sack. Zach spotted her and ran to help.

"Good grief, woman! What all have you got there?"

"Everything we might want to take back with us," she huffed. "including your precious turtle shell."

Zach laughed. "Afraid you might miss your ride out of here?"

Kelly gave a vigorous nod. "I'm not leaving anything to chance."

Zach grabbed one of the blankets, and began waving it over his head like a flag. The helicopter had advanced toward them considerably in the short time Kelly had been gone. She estimated it was halfway to them now, from where it had been when they'd first seen it. With Sydney tugging at a flapping corner and trying to help, Blair and Kelly hoisted a second blanket and began awkwardly flinging it up and down.

The chopper kept coming, getting larger with each anxious minute. Then, much like a plane might tip its wings in acknowledgment, it sort of wagged its tail section from side to side in a single, deliberate motion.

"They've spotted us!" Zach yelled exuberantly. "This is it! This is really it! We're being rescued!"

While Zach continued to wave and shout, Blair and Kelly dropped their blanket, joined hands with Sydney and each other, and launched into a joyous impromptu jig. "We're saved! We're saved!" they chanted giddily, while Sydney piped repeatedly, "Ring-a rosie, ring-a-rosie."

Then, emotionally overwhelmed, they collapsed onto the sand and sat there, tears of gladness and relief streaking their faces. "Oh, God!" Blair sobbed happily. "We're going home! I'll see my babies again!"

Kelly hugged her, rocking with her. "I know. I know. Isn't it wonderful?"

Their celebration was interrupted as Zach bellowed, loudly and angrily, "What the hell?"

They glanced first at him. He was shaking his fist and cursing now. Their gazes followed his, and to their vast bewilderment and disappointment, saw that the chopper was now retreating just as speedily as it had advanced.

Kelly leapt to her feet, jumping and waving at it in wild, jerky actions. "Wait! Come back! Don't leave us! You can't!"

Chapter 22

Blair was inconsolable. Kelly was in a near-numb state of disbelief. Zach was beside himself with fury. Poor Sydney was simply confused and upset, unable to understand what had put the adults into such a dither.

"I don't understand it!" Zach ranted, thrusting his fingers through his thick hair in frustration. "They saw us! I could swear they saw us and signaled to us!"

"Then why would they just fly off like that?" Kelly muttered, emotionally drained.

"I don't know, damn it!" he snarled. "I just don't know! Maybe they're waiting for an engraved invitation to tea!"

Kelly glared at him. "You don't have to be so sarcastic! And don't yell at me. It's not my fault!"

"I'm sorry, okay?" he barked. "It's just so blasted maddening!"

"So close," Blair sobbed. "So close! It's not fair!"

"Maybe they'll be back," Kelly said. "Maybe they were running low on fuel or something."

Zach rolled his eyes. "How much more fuel would it have taken to set down here and load us up before heading back to wherever they came from?"

Kelly shot him another irritated look. "How should I know? Do I look like a pilot?" She suggested another reason. "Maybe they didn't have enough space to land. The beach isn't very wide."

"Maybe," Zach grumbled. "They certainly wouldn't want to hit the trees with the blades and crash the thing."

"Yeah, then we'd have been stranded with a new set of greenhorn castaways," she retorted with a snort. "I don't think I'm up to training a whole new batch."

"If you're right," Blair sniffled, "perhaps they went for other help. Like a ship, or something."

Zach considered this. "That would take awhile, I suppose."

"How long awhile?"

He shrugged. "Depends on how far from us the nearest one is. Maybe a day or more, I'd guess."

"I don't care how long it takes, I'm going to sit right here until someone shows up," Kelly stated stubbornly. "I'm not moving from this beach."

"Me, either," Blair concurred. "This is where they'll look for us, and if we go back to our regular camp, they won't see us."

"All right, we can spend the day, and the night, here. We won't even have to build a new fire," Zach reasoned. "We'll just keep feeding the signal fire."

As the day progressed, they did move into the shade to escape the hot sun, and when necessity demanded they go for water or visit the latrine or gather food, at least one of them always stayed behind, to keep watch. Hours passed. Hope waned, despondency taking root.

It was about an hour from sunset. Blair was napping. Zach was trying to spear a fish for supper. Kelly was sitting on the damp sand, desultorily helping Sydney build a sand fort, when she heard an odd tooting sound, just loud enough to be heard over the pounding of the surf. Shielding her eyes from the glare of the slanting sun, she peered out to sea. A dark shape bobbed on the waves. She blinked, and when she focused on it again, she could just make out the silhouette of a ship.

It was too soon to tell if it was just passing by, farther out, or if it was actually coming in their direction. Kelly didn't know if she should alert the others or keep silent until she was more certain. She didn't want to get their hopes up, only to have them dashed again. She waited anxiously—wishing it nearer, praying, hardly daring to hope. Slowly, at what seemed a snail's pace compared to her thudding pulse, the ship crawled closer, the bow now pointed toward the island. Again, louder this time, the horn sounded.

Kelly couldn't stand it a moment longer. She jumped up and dashed into the surf, calling Zach's name. She halted only long enough to turn and tell Sydney, "Go wake Auntie Blair, Syd. Now!"

Zach was just making his move with the sword-spear, when Kelly yelled at him. Involuntarily, he jerked, missing a good-sized grouper. "Damn!" he cursed, watching the fish swim away. Then Kelly came thrashing through the water, creating waves and stirring up sand like a human Mixmaster. "Crap! With all that racket and fuss, you've probably scared away every fish within ten miles!" he snapped.

"I don't care!" she trilled. "Look, Zach! Look! A ship!"

He whirled around so fast, he nearly lost his footing. She caught hold of his arm, and they both teetered for a moment before catching their balance.

"Oh, Lord!" Zach breathed, scarcely believing his eyes.

"I don't know whether to laugh or cry. If this one goes by, I'm going to sit down and bawl like a baby."

Behind them, on shore, Blair was dashing around like a headless chicken, screeching, "The fire! Help me build up the fire!"

They scrambled for shore, and hastily tossed the last of their collection of wood onto the fire. In no time, it was roaring like a blast furnace. Zach's only worry was that the wind might kick up and set the whole island ablaze, but if that's what it took to get the ship to stop, he was willing to do it.

As it turned out, measures that extreme weren't necessary. A quarter hour after she'd sighted it, the ship dropped anchor some distance out, but close enough now that they could see the sailors milling about on deck. It followed that the crew could also see them waving and dancing around on shore. As they watched in wired anticipation, a rubber dinghy was lowered over the side. Three men climbed aboard, revved a small outboard motor, and began bouncing their way over the waves, toward the island.

Kelly thought surely her heart was going to explode in her chest from sheer excitement. "Where do you suppose they're from?" she asked. "I hope they speak English."

"I don't care if they speak Swahili," Zach claimed. "In fact, as long as they get us off this island, I don't care if they're Mongolian headhunters or a traveling ballet troupe decked out in pink tights and tutus."

Blair giggled. "They're Americans, I think. That's your flag flying off the mast, isn't it?"

Zach caught a glimpse of the pattern as it fluttered in the breeze, but enough to identify the red-and-white stripes and the blue corner of stars. His eyes misted and his throat closed up. Never had he been so glad to see that flag, and never would he take it quite so much for granted again.

The rubber craft, after first heading directly for them,

veered to the right. After the morning's experience, Kelly began to panic. "Where are they going?"

Zach drew her close, holding her to his side. "Calm down, love. I imagine they're just trying to find a better place to negotiate past the reef. They don't want the coral ripping the raft to shreds. C'mon. Let's go meet them."

Kelly needed no more urging. Grabbing Sydney into her arms, she loped down the beach, Blair and Zach right beside her. They arrived just as the craft drew onto the beach.

Blair let loose a delighted shriek, and ran toward the black man alighting with two men in sailor's suits. "Gavin!"

Kelly had to chuckle. The way Blair launched herself at Gavin, anyone would have thought the two were long-lost lovers. He endured the embrace for a moment, then set her on her feet in front of him, complaining in pure-Gavin style, "Whoa there, little mama! Watch the lips! They're blistered to beat hell, along with the rest of my body. This sunburn business is the pits!"

At this, everyone else burst out laughing. Gavin blessed them all with a frown. "What? Did you think only white folks suffered from this sort of thing?"

Kelly hugged him lightly, pecking at his cheek with her lips. "I love your tan," she teased. "Sure hope you don't peel." Before he could comment, she asked, "Did Alita come along? Is she okay?"

"She went on to Honolulu, but she's fine. As beautiful and bitchy as always, even if she does look a little like Rudolf."

Zach stepped up, and enveloped Gavin in a loose bear hug. "Man, it's good to see you! We were worried out of our minds."

"So were we," Gavin admitted. "Especially after our water ran out. Then, just when Alita started eyeing my jugular with this really weird look on her face, this cruise ship appeared. Next thing I know, we're guzzling champagne and lolling around in a bubble bath as big as a swimming pool, and getting the royal treatment—after we informed the captain about you and the location of the island, of course. He passed the word on to the navy, and they picked me up on the way.''

Kelly gave an ironic shake of her head. ''Leave it to Alita to get rescued by a cruise ship instead of an oil tanker!''

''I'd settle for a garbage scow, and not mind a bit,'' Zach declared.

''Will a U.S. navy vessel do, sir?'' one of the sailors inquired politely.

''Yes, indeed.''

''Are you ready to board, then?'' He waved toward the dinghy. ''Ladies, first. Here, let me help you with the little girl.''

Kelly had one foot over the rim when she remembered her traveling bag and bundle, still several yards down the beach. She backtracked hastily. ''Wait! I'll be right back! I've got to get something!''

''Her bottomless bag,'' Gavin surmised.

Zach nodded and laughed. ''I guess, like American Express, she never leaves home without it.''

''And aren't we all lucky she doesn't?'' Blair put in with a feminine smirk.

''Cozy, wouldn't you say?'' Zach ushered Kelly into the tiny cubicle which would serve as their sleeping quarters for the next several hours.

She looked around at the postage-stamp size room. ''You, Zach, are a master at understatement. I've seen broom closets larger than this. Superman's telephone booth had more space.''

He chuckled and drew her close, not merely because

he wanted to have her crushed to his chest, but to enable him to shut the door behind them. "I know it's a bit cramped, but it's all ours, darling. Privacy, at long last, and perhaps the last we'll get for a while. Once we get to Hawaii, I imagine things will be rather hectic."

She had to agree. The captain had already told them that their families had been notified, and were being flown, courtesy of the airlines, to Honolulu to meet the ship when it arrived. Moreover, they were now the top news story of the week, which meant they stood a fair chance of being swamped by the media.

"I thought I was supposed to share a room with Blair and those two women sailors, or sea-women, or whatever they're called," Kelly said. "And you were supposed to bunk with Gavin and a couple of male crew members, weren't you? How did you finagle this?"

"By talking myself blue in the face and throwing myself on the mercy of two lonely sailors with sweethearts waiting for them at home."

"I see." She eyed the double bunk skeptically. "So, which teensy-weensy bed do you get? I'd prefer the lower one, if you don't mind."

He grinned at her. "If you think I'm taking that top bunk, you can just think again. We'll be sharing the lower one. It'll be a tight squeeze, but we'll make it work, with a few innovative contortions, I suppose."

"They'd better be awfully inventive, lover boy," she informed him drolly, "because this is going to be like trying to make love in the backseat of a Volkswagen bug."

He drew her over to the bunk, a mere two steps backward, and began undressing her. "Do you want to ride top, or shall I?"

She ducked her head to peer at the metal underside of the upper bunk. "I'll take the mattress, thin as it is. This being your bright idea, you can bump your backside on the overhead frame, thank you. I just hope it doesn't sound like someone beating on a bass drum."

He gave her a lopsided, rascally grin. "I'm sure your cries of ecstasy will drown out any noise I make banging it—and you."

She tugged playfully at the dark lock of hair drooping across his forehead. "So gallantly put, you silver-tongued devil. But might I remind you, I'm not the one who lets loose with that warbling yell, like Tarzan sliding down a greased tree vine."

After one extremely awkward session in the bunk, they piled pillows and blankets onto the floor in the narrow walkway beside the bed, and proceeded from there. Much, much later, Kelly collapsed atop Zach with a sated sigh. "One of these days, we're actually going to get to do this in a real bed, and we probably won't know how to act."

"We need a soundproof bedroom to go with it," Zach told her. "You nearly smothered me, pushing my face into your chest that way."

She giggled. "I was only trying to muffle your shouts. And we can't have a soundproof room. How would we hear the baby when it cries?"

"That's why they make monitors, darling. So Mommy and Daddy can have their private moments and still hear the little rug rat."

"Speaking of dads, it was nice of the captain to patch your call through so you could check on your father's condition."

Zach sobered. "Yes, I just wish the news was better. I'm thankful that Dad's alive, and that he went ahead with the tests, but I wish they could have found a blood donor and done the heart bypass. Mom says they've been trying medication in the interim, but he's got to have surgery soon."

Kelly stroked his chest soothingly. "Now that you're back, they'll probably schedule it as quickly as possible."

"Will you be there with me, when they do? I'd really like to have you there."

"Of course. I just hope your family won't see it as an intrusion."

Zach knew Kelly intended to go to Phoenix to check on the status of her shops and her divorce. On the flip side of that same coin, he had to attend to his own family and business matters in Seattle. For a time, they would be communicating via phone and fax, and commuting back and forth whenever possible.

"Once they meet you, they'll love you as much as I do."

Kelly wasn't as optimistic on that score, but loving him as she did, she kept her concerns to herself for the moment. Zach had enough on his plate to worry about right now, and she was a big girl. She could fend for herself, and their baby, until they could work things out. In the meanwhile, they still had several hours to themselves, and she intended to make the most of them. Her hand wandered southward, to that lumpy nest between his legs.

Zach gave a chagrined groan. "Sweetheart, you're beating a dead horse. The spirit's willing, but the flesh is comatose."

"Poor pony," she crooned, shooting him an impish wink. "Maybe a little resuscitation will get him pumped up."

"Mouth to mouth?"

"So to speak." She wriggled around, sprinkling kisses along his abdomen as her lips trailed downward, toward their ultimate goal.

"It's worth a try," he volunteered, gasping as her tongue painted a warm, wet design on his already reviving member. "Just promise me you won't resort to anything as drastic as the Heimlich maneuver. That could put me out of commission for good."

Kelly laughed. "Gosh, Zach. Where's your sense of adventure? Sometimes you're just no fun at all!"

Chapter 23

When their ship finally docked at nine o'clock the next morning, the pier was jammed with people. From the deck, while waiting for the stair-ramp to be secured, the rescued castaways scanned the crowd. Blair was first to spot her family. "Oh, look!" She waved and pointed excitedly. "There's Anton and the kids! And my mother and father, too!"

It took a minute more, and Zach sighted his family. "Oh, no! They've got Dad in a wheelchair. Does his color look a little gray to you?"

Kelly followed his gaze. "It's hard to tell from this distance, Zach. And don't go borrowing trouble. They wouldn't have let him come all the way from Seattle if his condition was terribly critical. He's probably just using the chair to conserve his energy."

"I hope so, but he doesn't look good."

"Well, he's had a couple of terrific shocks this past couple of months," she reminded him. "First thinking you'd been killed, and now the joy of knowing you've survived. That would take a lot out of anyone, let alone someone with a heart condition.''

"They should have kept him in Seattle, where his doctors could keep a close eye on him.''

"Honolulu is a very large city, Zach. If he needs immediate attention, I'm sure the doctors and medical facilities here are excellent. Besides, he'll have a couple of days to rest up before the flight back to the mainland.''

The naval captain had informed them that they would be met in Honolulu by representatives from the airline and the FAA—officials who would be investigating the crash and wanted a day or two to interview them and gather whatever first-hand information they could concerning the accident. These people would also act as mediators during a scheduled press conference. As a courtesy, the crash survivors and their families were to be installed in a plush hotel, all expenses paid by the airline, for the duration.

"They're hoping if they're nice to us, we won't sue their wings off,'' Zach had said upon first learning this.

"Damn straight,'' Gavin concurred. "Especially if it turns out to be pilot error or a mechanical malfunction.''

"Oh, come on,'' Kelly had said. "I thought we had all agreed it was that direct hit by lightning. We certainly can't hold anyone responsible for an act of God.''

"I'm just glad they'll be able to retrieve all the bodies and give those people decent funerals,'' Blair had added gravely. "And they'll want to hear about Wynne, and Frazer, and Earl, too, and the other three we brought down off the mountain.''

Now, within seconds of disembarking, Kelly finally caught sight of her own relatives. "Wow! They brought the whole clan!'' she exclaimed. "There's Mom and Dad, and Cole and his wife, and their children.'' She pointed them out to Zach. Then, on a choked curse, she gasped,

"Oh, rats! Oh, dang! Of all the times and places, why did he have to turn up here?"

"Who?"

"Brad, damn it all!"

"Where?"

"Right down there. The self-important idiot in the blue three-piece suit and the Gucci loafers. I can see his diamond tie tack winking at me from here. I'm surprised he left his briefcase at home. Correction, he probably brought it, and left it at the hotel."

Zach studied him with a critical eye. "So that's Brad Kennedy. After all you've told me about him, I guess I didn't expect him to be such a handsome cuss."

"Pretty is as pretty does," Kelly muttered. "And his name is not Kennedy. It's Bradley Charles Sanders—Esquire, of course. I reverted to my maiden name even before I filed for divorce."

Blair interrupted by tugging at Kelly's arm. "Do I look all right? Is my make-up okay? I wish I'd thought to ask you to do my hair for me. Oh, nuts! I'm so nervous!"

"You look wonderful," Kelly assured her, patting a stray strand into place. "Tan. Fit—as fit as a woman five months pregnant can be, that is. If I didn't know better, I'd swear you just came back from a trip to some expensive spa."

"You look lovely," Zach confirmed. "That hairstyle suits you, and the sun has added lighter streaks to it. Very becoming."

"Hey, you guys!" Gavin called for their attention. "We can go now."

Kelly took a deep breath, held it, and exhaled heavily. "Okay, I'm as ready as I'll ever be. I just wish I didn't have to meet the press wearing these stained, wrinkled clothes."

"Is it the press or Brad you want to impress?" Zach asked with a frown.

"Don't be an ass. I wouldn't walk across the street to

impress that jerk, and that was before I fell head over heels in love with you."

Zach grabbed both her arms and turned her toward him. "Prove it. Kiss me, Kelly. Right here, right now, in front of God, Brad, and everybody."

"I wouldn't insult God by pronouncing his name and Brad's in the same breath, if I were you," she warned. Then, "What about your family, Zach? Your daughter? They're watching us."

"I don't care. They're going to find out about us sooner or later, anyway. I guess we might just as well give them a preview of what's to come. Besides, it could be a while before I get to kiss you again. I need one to tide me over."

"One for the road?" she teased. She stood on tiptoe, arching her body and lips toward his. "Me, too. Make it good, Zach. Nice and sweet and hot. Make me burn for you."

His mouth slanted over hers, his lips nudging hers open to make way for his invading tongue. His arms closed around her, holding her so close their heartbeats seemed to merge. Her arms locked around his neck, anchoring his mouth to hers. Her fingers speared through the hair at his nape—clutching, caressing. Throughout the prolonged embrace, they were oblivious to all else around them—Gavin and Blair leaving them behind, camera bulbs flashing, cheers and whistles from the sailors, the mixed reactions from those in the crowd below.

When, at last, they drew apart, Zach turned his back and surreptitiously adjusted his pants. "Darn things are going to cut off my circulation. I should have known that, even if public, you'd turn me on with more voltage than a power plant."

She gave a self-conscious laugh, her face flushed. "Come to my room tonight, if you can get away, and I'll take care of that problem for you."

"What am I supposed to do in the meantime? It's a rather obvious condition, you know."

She laughed harder. "Hunch over and limp. Maybe you can make them believe it's an injury from the plane crash." She bent down and retrieved the huge turtle shell and slapped in against his groin, "Better yet, hold this in front of you. If they ask, tell them it's the latest in Polynesian loin cloths!"

They walked down together, but the minute they reached the pier, their individual families claimed their immediate attention. Zach's daughter, Becky, flew into his arms—a sixty-pound human missile with braces on her teeth. Clinging like a barnacle, she sobbed, "Oh, Daddy! Daddy! I thought you'd left me forever, just like Mommy did! Don't ever go away again!"

He held her tightly, reveling in the feel of her, the sound of her voice. Tears stung his own eyes. "Oh, pumpkin! I'm sorry, so very sorry. I thought about you every minute. It broke my heart not to be able to let you know I was okay."

Finally, when she calmed a bit, he set her down gently, though he kept hold of her hand. "Let me say hello to Gramma and Grandpa, sweetie."

He enveloped his mother in a one-armed hug and kissed her tear-stained cheek. "Mom." His voice cracked on the word.

Sarah's palm came up to cradle his jaw. "It's a miracle, our very own miracle. We thought we'd lost you. It nearly killed your Dad."

"Now, Sarah, don't load the poor boy with guilt. I'm here, aren't I?" Ike admonished gruffly. "Dave. Pete." He gestured impatiently to his two sons-in-law. "Help me up out of this contraption. I want up on my own two feet when I greet my son."

They helped him rise, and Zach was there before the older man could take more than a single step away from the wheelchair. "Dad." They embraced, thumping one another on the back.

"It's good to have you back," Ike said, his voice quavering with emotion. "You'll never know how good. It's the answer to our most fervent prayer."

"I know, Dad. Mine, too." Zach urged his father back into the chair. "But now we've got to get you taken care of. I heard about the tests."

Ike waved that comment away. "We'll talk about it later."

Zach's sister, Leah, stepped forward to give him quick squeeze. "I told them you were okay, that they were grieving for no reason. But would they listen to me? No."

Next came Beth, his second sister. "I'll admit it. Leah's right. And I couldn't be happier. Now, tell me, brother dear, who's the chickie who was trying to suck the fillings out of your teeth?"

Zach laughed. "That's Kelly, the woman I intend to marry as soon as her divorce is final."

A stunned silence ensued, broken only when Sarah frowned and murmured, "Kelly? That sounds like an Irish name to me."

"It is, and before you ask, no, she's not Jewish. And it doesn't matter to me. I love her. So will you, when you get to know her."

Kelly was dealing with the same issue, a few feet away. The first person to reach her was Brad, who grabbed her arm in a tight grip and hissed, "You've made a spectacle of yourself, as usual. Who is that guy, and why were you allowing him to kiss you like that?"

Kelly stared pointedly at his hand, but Brad didn't take

the hint and release her. "His name is Zach Goldstein. He's my fiancé."

Brad's plastic smile, the one he presented to the public and the media, slipped briefly. "It's not appropriate to have a husband and a fiancé at the same time, darlin'."

She sent him a saccharine smile of her own. "Maybe not, but since our divorce will be final soon, it hardly matters, does it?"

"That's what you think. Once you were assumed dead, the divorce was dropped, honey," he informed her in that smooth Texas drawl she'd once found so charming. "They don't schedule court time for a corpse."

"Then I'll get it reinstated," she declared, her eyes shooting green flames. "Retroactively. Now, let go of my arm, or I'll knee you in the groin, and you can watch it replayed on the evening news, coast to coast."

He released her, and Kelly swiftly retreated the short distance into her mother's waiting arms. "Mom! Oh, I missed you so much!"

"My sweet Kelly! We were so worried! So stricken! I can't believe I'm holding you again!" Eileen Kennedy's joyous tears dampened both of them.

Ryan Kennedy approached, to envelop them both in a warm, hard embrace. "Kelly, lass, you're a glorious sight for these poor sore eyes! Here we were, grieving ourselves sick, and you were off growing more beautiful than ever!"

"Yeah, Dad, it was a real picnic," Kelly muttered. "But we can discuss all that later. The main thing is, I'm back now, and you can cancel plans for my wake."

"Too late," her brother Collin, more familiarly known as Cole, piped up. He wedged his way to her side for a quick kiss. "It's already been held, and you should have seen the grand turnout. Dad even sang 'Danny Boy,' though he revised it to 'Kelly Girl.' He had us all cryin' in our beer."

"Most likely because he accosted your ears with his off-key singing," Kelly joked. In truth her father had a wonderful tenor, and they all loved to hear him perform. "Still, I'm sorry I missed it. I think."

"It was lovely, and very touching," Cole's wife, Kathy assured her. "Now, we're dying to hear about that handsome devil who was kissing you on deck. From a distance, he resembles Mel Gibson."

"Really? I'll have to tell him that. He'll get a kick out of it."

"So, who is he?" Eileen prompted.

"Zach Goldstein. He's an architectural engineer and your future son-in-law—as soon as I can unload the dud you've got, that is."

Kathy and Cole's eight-year-old twins finally managed to pop through the circle of adults. "Aunt Kelly!" they shouted in tandem, throwing themselves forward and grabbing hold of her from each side. "We missed you! Did you bring us something?"

Kelly laughed, and clutched at her brother's arm for support. "Just look at you two! Shane, you've sprouted up at least two inches since I've been gone. Shannon! You're wearing your hair like mine now. Are we twins now, too?"

"Did you bring us something?" they asked again.

Kelly stooped down to their level. "Well, the present I bought for you in Australia got burned up in the crash, but I brought you something else you might like."

"What? What?" they chorused eagerly.

Kelly patted her still-flat stomach. "I've got a baby in here. In a few months, you're going to have a brand new cousin."

Shane frowned, evidently preferring a toy of some type. Shannon was fascinated. "Really?" she cooed. "Will I get to play with it?"

Kelly nodded. "When it's big enough." She looked up

to see the adults gaping at her in stunned silence. She wondered if Brad, hanging back on the fringes of the family gathering, had heard her news, and what his reaction might be to this revelation.

But before anyone could say anything more, a commotion a few yards away claimed everyone's attention. A child was screaming, as if in dire pain or stark fear. Between shrieks, Gavin was shouting at someone.

Kelly came upright, her head swiveling as she tried to peer over heads in the direction of the disturbance. "Sydney!" she exclaimed, already pushing her way through the milling crowd. "Gavin!"

"Kelly!" he called back. "Over here!"

Kelly jostled the last man out of her way, just as Zach appeared at her elbow. Together, they rushed forward to find a strange woman trying to wrest Sydney from Gavin's arms. The terrified toddler was having none of it.

"What's going on here?" Zach demanded loudly. He rounded on the woman. "Who are you?"

Kelly, less diplomatically inclined, grabbed the woman's wrist and commanded sharply, "Let loose of her! What do you think you're doing?"

The woman backed off a step, no longer tugging at Sydney, but did not retreat. "I'm Olivia Newhart, from Social Services. I'm here to take charge of the child."

Kelly met her, nose to nose, her eyes ablaze. "Over my dead body! Sydney stays with us!"

By now, the throng—relatives, media, and airline representatives alike—was amassing around them, curious to know what was causing such an uproar. Gavin had handed Sydney over to Zach, and the little girl was whimpering, her face hidden in the curve of his neck.

"I'm sorry, but those are my orders," Ms. Newhart insisted. "I must take the child. She'll be placed in a foster home until her relatives can be located."

"You lay one hand on her, and I'll break it, bone by bone," Kelly warned darkly. From the corner of her eye, she caught the flash of the bright light of a nearby video camera and bit back an exasperated groan. Here she was, caught threatening bodily harm to a civil servant! On tape, no less! Then a thought came to her. Why let this opportunity pass, when she could use it to her own advantage, and Syd's? Perhaps a little public sympathy was in order, to help turn the tables.

"This child has been through hell and back again," she claimed loudly. In her peripheral vision, she saw the man with the camera edge forward, and was pleased to note the camera sported the logo of a TV station. "Sydney's parents were killed in the plane crash, and for the past two months she has considered us her family. Hasn't the poor tyke been traumatized enough? Now you want to take her away from the people she trusts most, and place her with strangers? Good Lord, woman! Where is your heart? Doesn't anyone care about what's best for her? Any one of us," Kelly gestured toward Gavin, Zach, and Blair, who now stood close, "are perfectly capable of caring for her."

"But I have papers," the social worker argued adamantly. "There are certain procedures that must be followed."

"Screw your papers and your procedures," Zach growled. "Until Sydney's true family is found, she belongs to us."

Blair stepped forward, despite the fact that her husband tried to hold her back. "That's right. Possession is nine-tenths of the law, so I've heard. We've got her, and we're keeping her."

"And we defy anyone to take her from us," Kelly added belligerently.

"Furthermore," Zach put in, "if none of her relatives

want or can care for her properly, Kelly and I intend to adopt her.''

Kelly scarcely kept her chin from dropping open in surprise. Somehow she managed to rally and snap out, ''That's right. Now, you just march back to your office and tell your superiors to get their priorities in order!''

At this point, an airline representative stepped into the fray, placing himself between Kelly and Ms. Newhart. ''I think that might be best for all concerned,'' he told the social worker. ''The child is obviously in good hands, which is where she should be. We'll be striving diligently to locate her family, and I'm sure all this can be ironed out in an amicable fashion, if we all just stay calm, reasonable, and put the child's welfare above all else.''

The woman gave a haughty sniff. ''You'll be hearing from us, and most likely from a judge.''

''Likewise, I'm sure,'' Zach retorted sharply. ''We'll have our lawyer call yours.''

The woman gave them all a final glare and stomped off in a huff.

Kelly gave a shaky sigh. ''Well, things have really started off with a bang. Not back into society for half an hour, and we're already embroiled in legal tangles.''

''Welcome to the real world, tied up in a snarl of red tape,'' Blair commiserated. Turning to Zach, she inquired quietly, ''Did you mean what you said about adopting Sydney, or were you just spouting off? I'd love to be able to take her, but . . .''

''I meant every word. Unfortunately, I didn't have time to confer with Kelly beforehand.'' He gave Kelly a sheepish look. ''Sorry, sweetheart. Was I out of line?''

Kelly gave a bewildered shake of her head. ''You know I love her. I do have one question, though. Just how large is this family of ours going to be? We haven't even exchanged vows yet, and it's growing by leaps and bounds.''

"That's hard to tell. As they say, love knows no bounds."

"Then I hope we can find a good sale on those baby monitors, buster, because twins run on my side of the line."

"Twins?" he repeated dumbly. "You're kidding."

Kelly shrugged helplessly, and gestured toward the two red-haired imps on the sidelines, flanking their father. "Meet Shannon and Shane, and my twin brother, Collin. We call him Cole."

"Your twin brother?" Zach's tone revealed his confusion. "The osteopath? I thought you said he was older than you."

Kelly offered a lame nod. "He is, by three whole minutes."

Chapter 24

After the most hasty, perfunctory introductions between Blair's family, Gavin's, Kelly's, and Zach's, with promises to get better acquainted later, they were all shepherded onto the bus the airline had provided to take them to their hotel. Kelly wound up in a window seat, holding Sydney on her lap. There was little she could do, aside from creating another scene, to prevent Brad from claiming the seat next to her, though he all but pushed Shannon aside to accomplish it.

"Do you have to be such a bully?" Kelly snapped irritably.

"I want to talk with you."

"Well, I don't want to talk with you," she told him tartly. "Butt out, Brad. You and I are history."

"What's this about you and lover boy wanting to adopt the kid?" he asked, ignoring her rebuttal.

"That's between Zach and me. It has nothing to do with you."

"You think so? I'll remind you again, darlin', you're still my wife, and you will be for as long as I want it that way."

Kelly slid a glance at his hard-set face. "How do you figure that?"

He smirked. "I'm a lawyer, honey. We know how the system works, all the ins and outs, the tricks of the trade. With delays and whatnot, I can drag this divorce out 'til doomsday, or at least until I get elected to the Senate."

"Employing the 'good-ol'-boys' network, I presume. Calling in markers from your attorney friends?"

"Not to mention a few judges," he concurred smugly. "You might as well give up and give in gracefully, Kelly. There's no way you can win in a legal fight against me. The deck is stacked in my favor. Besides, as things stand now, you don't have a plug nickel to your name."

Kelly scowled. "Would you care to expound on that last remark?"

"After the plane disappeared, I used my power of attorney to transfer the money in your separate checking and savings accounts into our joint account. A few days later, when it was assumed you were dead, I paid off your credit cards, and the companies cancelled them. They do that, you know, so no one else can charge things to your account, claiming to be you. You don't have a red cent to call your own, and absolutely no credit. As of this moment, you're broke, totally reliant on my benevolence, so if I were you I'd give some thought to being nicer to your ol' hubby."

"In your dreams, Brad. And I won't be without funds for long," she continued confidently. "Now that everyone knows I survived, they'll re-issue new credit cards to me, and I expect—correct that, I demand—that you repay every last dime you took from my bank accounts, less the outstanding balances on the cards, of course."

Brad crossed his arms over his chest, a self-satisfied expression on his face. "It's gonna take some time, maybe a very long time, to sort out what's rightfully yours and what's mine, sugar. What with the funds combined now, and all. It might even take an accountant, or a court order, to get it done."

"You're a real sleazeball, Brad. I suppose you made an insurance claim, too. How much was I worth to you—dead, that is? A million? Two? Too bad you won't be collecting on my untimely demise. And the picture isn't as bleak as you've painted it, dear heart. I've still got my health clubs, and the income they bring in."

Brad shook his head. "You haven't got jack squat. As your power of attorney, I closed the clubs, and the boutiques. I'm very close to sealing a deal on them with a prospective buyer."

"You what?" she shrieked, her blood pressure shooting through the roof. Sydney, who had been half asleep, gave a jerk and began to wail again. Most of Kelly's fellow passengers had turned in their seats to stare at her.

"Everything okay back there, Kelly?" Zach called from the front of the bus.

"Other than the fact that my dearly bereaved, soon-to-be-ex-husband has been stealing me blind in the past two months?" she yelled back. "Sure. Everything's just dandy!"

She turned back to Brad, fury on her face and venom in her voice. By now, those sitting closest to her, especially her family members, were hanging on every word. "If you think you have me over a barrel, you're sadly mistaken, Brad Sanders. I'm going to beat you at your own game, you sneaky weasel. By the time I'm finished with you, you'll wish you'd never been born, let alone filch from me. I'll ruin you so badly you won't be able to run for dogcatcher, let alone the Senate."

"You don't have the guts or the connections."

"We'll just see about that, and you can kiss that deal with the buyer for the clubs goodbye. I'm back, and in

charge of my own affairs now, and I don't intend to sell.
Any contracts you made on my behalf are null and void."

"It might not be that easy," he informed her arrogantly.
"After all, I did have the right to negotiate in your stead,
which makes it all perfectly legal and binding."

"Surely, when I filed for divorce, that power of attorney
foolishness was revoked. Who, in their right mind, would
believe I'd still want you conducting my business dealings?"

"But there is no divorce pending," he reminded her
again. "And I'm still the beneficiary of your life insurance
policy and your will, as well as executor."

"Something I'll remedy immediately, I assure you," she
replied through clenched teeth. "Thank you for
reminding me of it. Do I still have a car, or did you sell
that, too? What about the things in my apartment in Phoenix, my personal possessions, like my furniture and
clothes?"

"I didn't have time to bother with the small potatoes,
or that clunker you're so fond of driving. I assume your
stuff's still in your apartment above your club, unless someone has broken in and burglarized the place. You'll have
to move out, once the business is sold, unless the new
owners agree to rent it to you. But, you don't have the
money to do that, do you?" he smirked. "Guess that means
you'll be coming back home to Houston. It'll be just like
old times, only better, because you won't be working anymore."

Kelly fumed. She could barely restrain herself from
reaching out and strangling him with his expensive silk
tie. If not for Sydney, and about a dozen avid witnesses,
she might still have tried it. "I wouldn't move back in with
you if you owned the last house in the universe. In fact, I
wouldn't spit on you if your pearly white, perfectly-capped
teeth were on fire! How could you possibly do this, yet still
expect me to come back and be your wife, as if everything

was all sunshine and roses? Do you have any idea how much I detest you?''

"Dad and I will loan you some money, and you can move back home with us, sweetie," her mother offered from the seat behind Brad.

"Or with us," Cole said from the seat ahead.

"Thanks, but only if it's a necessity," Kelly told them. "If Brad wants to play hard ball, and not willingly transfer my money back to me, or give me my divorce without making a fuss, so be it. I'll make a stink so bad they'll smell if from coast to coast. Then we'll see what his political future looks like, won't we?"

Brad jeered, "Do you really think anyone outside your family will care? I can sling mud, too, Kelly. Remember that. You could come away looking like a candidate for the laughing academy."

"Thinking of having me committed, Brad?" she countered snidely. "I hope not, because I have witnesses."

"And I have clout," he claimed pompously. "If you really want that divorce, you're going to have to fight for it every inch of the way, which will be mighty costly. Take me to court, sugar, and by the time all is said and done, you'll come away looking like a slut, and I'll be the poor, wronged husband who is still willing to forgive and forget."

She sneered at him, all bluff and righteous anger. "You've got it all figured out, right down to the last little detail, don't you? You've been a very busy little snake while I was gone. But you never really planned on me coming back from the grave to louse up your best plans, did you? Well, I'm back, Brad, and raring for revenge. I'm going to nail your hide to the barn door and use it for target practice—and that's a promise you can take to the bank!''

* * *

Kelly marched into the hotel lobby, at the tail end of the line, all but speechless with rage. After waiting nearly half an hour for the guests ahead of her to check in, she approached the desk. "I'm Kelly Kennedy. I'd like the key to my room, please. Oh, and what kind of beds are in there? I'm going to need a place for the baby to sleep."

The desk clerk checked his register. "Ma'am, the room is equipped with a king-sized bed. I can have a cot or a crib sent up for the baby, if you wish." The fellow looked past her shoulder, spotted Brad, and gave a congenial nod. "Your husband already has both key cards."

Kelly whirled around. "Okay, hand them over, you rat. Both of them."

Brad shook his head. "Nothing doing. I've already unpacked."

Turning back to the desk, she said, "I want a separate room please, for me and the child."

The clerk was momentarily nonplussed. "I'm sorry, ma'am. We're booked solid. Every room is already taken."

"You don't understand," Kelly told him. "Mr. Sanders and I are separated and getting a divorce. I cannot possibly share a room with him."

"May I find you a room elsewhere, perhaps at a neighboring hotel?" the clerk suggested.

Kelly sighed. "Will the airline pay for it?" she inquired impatiently. "It seems my credit cards have been cancelled, since everyone assumed I was dead."

"Oh! You're that Ms. Kennedy!" the clerk exclaimed. "I should have recognized you from your picture on the news. Welcome back to civilization, ma'am. If there's anything you need, anything at all, just let us know."

"My room?" she reminded him, wearily shifting Sydney to her other arm and hip.

The clerk frowned. "Ma'am, the room Mr. Sanders has taken is the room the airline reserved for you."

"Then toss him out of it," she commanded curtly. "It's my room, and I don't want him in it. And be sure he gives you both key cards. I don't want any nasty surprises in the middle of the night."

"But, Ms. Kennedy . . ."

"Now, Kelly . . ." Brad began.

She rounded on Brad with murderous intent. "Get out, Brad. With or without your clothes. I will not aid and abet your schemes by cohabitating with the enemy, if that's your game plan. You've got to have a screw loose to think I would agree to such an asinine arrangement, especially after all you've done, the misery you're causing me."

The clerk cut short Kelly's tirade. "Sir, please hand over your keys." When Brad hesitated, the fellow added reluctantly, "I'll be forced to call security if you don't comply."

Brad dug into his breast pocket for the key cards, and tossed them onto the desk. "Have my clothes packed and stored until I can find other accommodations," he instructed the clerk. To Kelly, he said with a snarl, "Enjoy your piddling victory, sugar. It'll be your last." With those parting words, and a sullen glare, he stalked out of the hotel.

"Well done, daughter," Ryan commended proudly. "I'd have intervened, had it been necessary, but I know that stubborn, independent streak of yours."

"You're right. I'd probably have bitten the hand that was trying to feed me," she admitted ruefully.

"I knew you could handle him, with one arm tied behind your back," Cole told her. "We're two of a kind, Kelly girl. No snot-nosed puffed-up lawyer's going to get the best of us. But if you get into something deeper than you can tread, give Dad and me a whistle. We'll come running."

"I will," she promised. "But right now, I'm going to give it my best shot on my own. I guess I want to prove to myself that I can, after knuckling under and letting him try to run my life for the past five years.''

Her mother frowned. ''You know, dear, I didn't say much. I figured it was your own business. But I never could quite understand why you let him get away with bossing and belittling you the way he did.''

''Me, either.'' Kelly gave a derisive laugh. ''Chalk it up to having stars in my eyes, or youthful stupidity. But the blinders are off, and so are the gloves. From here on, it's all-out war, one I intend to win.''

Zach was presently dealing with his own problem—namely Becky, who had glued herself to his side and had scarcely let him loose long enough for Zach to shave, shower, and change into some fresh clothes his family had thoughtfully brought along from home. Zach was equally thrilled to have his daughter near again, and he fully understood her need and her fear. She'd been traumatized, thinking she'd lost him a mere three years after her mother had died, and now she was afraid to let him out of her sight. In fact, Zach's mother had confided that Becky had been so desolate that they had started sessions with a child psychologist to help the girl deal with her loss and depression, and the angry tantrums she'd begun throwing as a result.

Zach understood all this, and regretted it deeply, but he also realized that they were going to have to get their lives back on track, the sooner the better, for everyone concerned. He and Becky both had issues that needed to be resolved—she, her lingering fright of being orphaned and thus the tendency to cling so tightly, and he the panic that rose whenever he thought of flying again, plus his fears for his father's health. It seemed they each had to learn how to trust again, and there was no time like the present for taking that first step.

Zach, his parents, and Becky were staying together in the suite Zach had been allotted. Zach's sisters and their families had visited for a while, then went to their own rooms down the hall. His father was resting in one of the two connecting bedrooms included in the suite. Sarah was chatting with her son and granddaughter in the living area. Becky was snuggled next to Zach on a small loveseat, clutching his arm with such force she was cutting off the blood flow to his hand.

Gently, he loosened her grip and flexed his numb fingers. "Hey, princess, take it easy on your old dad," he teased. "If you want to arm wrestle, you've got to give me a fighting chance."

Becky giggled. "Sorry. I'm just so happy you're back."

"I know. Me, too. So, catch me up on everything you've been doing while I was gone."

Becky's smile melted away. "I cried a lot."

"Yeah, I suppose you did. I'm awfully sorry about that, but there wasn't any way of letting you know I was okay." He changed the subject. "Has school started yet?"

"Two weeks ago," she told him, not sounding terribly enthused about it.

"How do you like seventh grade?" he prompted. "Are your teachers nice? Do you like going to the new junior high school?"

Becky shrugged. "I guess so. There are a lot of different kids in my classes, though, from some of the other elementary schools."

"Then you must be making lots of new friends, huh?"

"Not really."

"Why not?"

Just like that, Becky's temper flared, taking Zach by surprise. "I'm just not, okay? I've had a lot on my mind."

Sarah immediately scolded her granddaughter. "Young lady, that is no way to speak to your father! He simply asked you a question, and you might answer in a respectful manner."

The girl leapt from the love seat, her face twisted with anger and her hands bunched into fists. "You're always yelling at me! I'm not perfect! Just leave me alone!"

She started to run to the other bedroom, and Zach momentarily considered letting her go. Then he thought better of it. This was something best nipped in the bud at the outset. In his sternest father-means-business voice, he called her back.

"Rebecca Ann Goldstein! Get your huffy little rear end back here this minute."

She stomped back, to stand in front of him. "What?" she asked belligerently.

"Apologize to your grandmother, please." His tone indicated it was an order, not a request.

"Sorry," Becky muttered.

"Not good enough," Zach told her. "Say it like you mean it."

"I'm sorry for sassing you, Gramma." Becky glowered at Zach. "Can I go now?"

"May I," he corrected.

"May I go now?" Each word emerged with exaggerated precision.

"No, you may not. Sit down and try to behave yourself."

Becky plopped herself onto the floor, her lower lip protruding in a pout.

Zach swallowed a sigh. "I understand you've developed quite a temper lately. That's got to stop, Becky. I suppose you're angry with me, the same way you were with your mom after she died, but you can't go around taking it out on other people. If you've got a bone to pick with me, do it, and let's clear the air right here and now."

Becky glared at him, tears glistening in her eyes. "You left me!" she shouted. "You didn't even let me come visit you in Australia when school let out for the summer!"

"I've explained that I was too busy finishing up last minute details to spend any time with you then. Besides, if you'd been with me on that flight home, you might have been hurt or killed, and I'd never have forgiven myself if that had happened. This way, it turned out all right in the end, didn't it, even if we did all have a tremendous scare?"

"No, it's not all right!" Becky insisted adamantly. "You came back with that . . . that woman! And that kid!"

"Oh, dear!" Sarah murmured. "The plot thickens."

"Ah, so that's it." Zach nodded. "You're jealous."

"I am not! I just don't like them. I don't want them hanging around us . . . me . . . you."

"Me, most of all," Zach deduced. "Becky, honey, you don't have to be jealous of them. Making them part of our family isn't going to mean I'll love you any less than I always have. I've loved you since before you were born, and I'll love you forever. Moreover, I thought you, of all people, would sympathize with Sydney and want to help her. She's just a baby, and both her parents were killed in the crash. Without us, she's all alone in the world, with no one to love her. Besides, weren't you the one who was always whining about wanting a brother or sister?"

Becky wasn't so easily swayed. "That was when Mom was alive. I wanted someone to play with. I'm older now, and have my own friends, and Sydney's too little. She'd just be a pest. And you're wrong about her not having anyone to love her but us. She has those other people, too."

Zach tried to explain it more clearly. "Gavin has to go back to being a soldier, Beck. He can't take Sydney with him to the army. And Blair already has two children and another one on the way. As for Alita, she can't watch a baby very well while she's on a music tour or making a movie. She'd have to hire a babysitter, a stranger, to take care of Sydney.''

''That other woman can take her,'' Becky insisted hatefully. ''The one you were kissing on the boat. The one you said you want to . . . to marry!''

''Her name is Kelly, and you might as well get used to calling her that instead of 'that woman.' I know you're not happy that she and I are going to be married, I know it's an unwelcome surprise, but I think you'll really like her once you meet her. I've told her all about you, and she's looking forward to getting to know you.''

Becky's face clouded even more. ''I've already met her, and I don't want her, or anybody else, for a mother. Gramma and Aunt Leah and Aunt Beth and I are doing just fine, without anyone else butting in.''

''You met Kelly long enough to say hello, and that was it,'' Zach pointed out. ''As for the rest of it, Gramma has been great, but she has Grandpa to take care of now that he's going to need an operation on his heart, and your aunts have their own families keeping them plenty busy.''

He tried another, more persuasive tack. ''Wouldn't you like to live at home all the time, instead of shuffling off to Gramma's every time I have to go out of town to work? Kelly would be there, just like Mom used to be, and she's terrific when it comes to girl things, like buying clothes and doing hair. She runs a health club, and a beauty shop and a boutique, so she knows all about the latest styles and ways to keep fit. It could be a lot of fun for you.''

Becky made a face. ''She'd be my stepmother, just like in *Cinderella*. She'd probably make me scrub floors and wear rags and watch Sydney all the time. And I'll bet she's real bossy, too. I heard her yelling at that guy on the bus, and that lady who wanted to take Sydney away.''

''I was yelling at the lady, too,'' Zach reminded her. ''I'd yell just as loudly at anyone who wanted to take you away from me, too. You're my princess, the best part of your mom and me all rolled into one special package and sprinkled with pure Becky sugar and spice."

"But you don't love Mom anymore," Becky choked out, her tears rising again. "You love that other wo—Kelly, now."

Zach dropped to the floor and tugged Becky into his arms. "Oh, baby! No! I'll always love your mom, just like I'll always love you. Nothing will ever change that. Only now I love Kelly, too, and little Sydney. Just like someday you'll grow up and fall in love with some nice boy and have children of your own. You won't stop loving me, just because you have them to love, will you?"

Becky shook her head, which was still buried against his chest as she hugged him tightly. "No. I guess not."

"That's the way love is, Beck," Zach assured her. "It just grows and grows, enough to spread around to everyone, with plenty to spare." He lifted her chin in his palm, tilting her head so he could look into her face. "Just promise me you'll give Kelly a chance, all right?"

Becky grimaced, relenting with reservations. "Okay, but if I really, really hate her, will you change your mind and not marry her?"

Zach's mother laughed outright.

Zach groaned. "Oh, no, Miss Conniver, that's not the way it works at all. Nice try, sweet pea, but no deal."

Chapter 25

After having become accustomed to the leisurely pace of the island, it was something of a culture shock to be thrust once more into the hectic, high-tech, watch-the-clock pace of the modern world. Even the ringing of the phone nearly sent Kelly jumping out of her skin, and it definitely felt strange to be surrounded by four walls and a ceiling, nearly claustrophobic, in fact. This return to civilization was going to take some major readjustment.

As she sat on the edge of the bed—an actual honest-to-God king-sized bed!—and watched the bellman pack up Brad's clothes, Kelly wanted nothing more than to be able to lie back, wallow in the pillows and covers, and snuggle up for a nice long nap. That would have to wait, however, because she already had a dozen things to do before the press conference, which was scheduled for early afternoon. The first of which was to obtain a decent change of clothes. She certainly didn't intend to appear dressed in the same tattered, soiled outfit she'd been obliged to wear for the past two months!

Brad, the self-centered rat, had packed enough clothes for an army of executives, but had neglected to bring along so much as a pair of socks for her! She suspected he'd done so purposely, to make her all the more dependent on him and his benevolence. At this point, Kelly would have chewed ground glass before giving him that satisfaction.

It was while she was watching the bellman transfer the contents of a dresser drawer into a suitcase that a wondrous thought came to her. Kelly could barely wait for the man to finish his task and depart. The minute the door shut behind him, she dashed to the dresser, yanked open the top drawer and began feeling along the backside of the front facing of the dresser, above the actual drawer opening.

Her eyes widened with delight, and she had to squelch her immediate exclamation of triumph as she drew forth a plastic packet. "Brad, you big stupid idiot!" she declared softly. "If you hadn't been so blasted mad at me, you wouldn't have forgotten your hidden treasure."

Swiftly, she unfolded the packet and pulled out the bundle of traveler's checks inside. Flipping through them, she estimated she held in her hand approximately three thousand dollars, or the equivalent thereof. Another quick glance revealed that Brad still hadn't revised one of his principal bad habits. Each of the checks was already endorsed, with only the payee's name left blank. Kelly couldn't remember the number of times she'd warned him about doing exactly that.

"One of these days, Brad," she'd told him time and again, "you're going to be very sorry. Someone is going to find the entire lot and cash them, and it will all be perfectly legal, simply because you insist on signing these darned things ahead of time. As smart a lawyer as you claim to be, you should know better. In fact, it surprises me, because you're so methodical about everything else."

Brad had always pooh-poohed her admonitions. "It's not as if I carry them all with me in my wallet. That's why I hide most of them away, and only take what I think I'll need for the day, in case some street punk decides to mug me. The rest, I stash away, and pretty well, if I do say so myself. Who would ever think to look for them there, taped inside the dresser frame? Even if someone ransacked the room, and pulled out all the drawers, they'd never find them, and I'd bet my law degree no maid has ever cleaned in that spot, or ever will."

Now, as Kelly thumbed through the folded stack, she grinned widely. "But your wife remembers all your bad habits, Brad old boy, and it's finders keepers. Now, all I have to do is get down to the bank and cash these before you remember and come looking for them. Not that I'd give them back to you. You've stolen far more than this from me, so it's only fair that I should get to keep this pittance for myself—and the great thing is, you can't even prosecute. Since you've signed these, in your own handwriting, it's all strictly within the bounds of the law."

Kelly took her purse from her canvas bag and stuffed the wad of traveler's checks inside a zippered compartment. Though she hated waking Sydney from her nap, there was no help for it. She was ready to leave, her hand on the doorknob and Sydney riding on her hip, when someone rapped from the hall side. "Oh, crap!" she muttered, sure it had to be Brad on the opposite side of the door. "You couldn't have given me five more minutes to make a clean get-away, could you?"

"Kelly?"

Kelly sighed in relief and yanked the door open. "Alita! You're just in time to go shopping with me." She thrust

Sydney into singer's arms and steered them toward the elevator at a trot.

"Hey! Slow down!" Alita complained. "Where's the fire?"

"Under Brad's butt, I hope," Kelly retorted. Fortunately, when the elevator arrived, it was empty. On the way down, Kelly filled Alita in on Brad's nefarious doings, and her recent fortuitous find. "That's why I'm in such a rush. I want to get these cashed before Brad can do anything to prevent it."

"Can't he still claim they were stolen?" Alita asked. "Like in all those commercials where people lose their traveler's checks and get them reissued?"

Kelly grinned. "He could if he had the serial numbers, or the slips listing them, that he's supposed to keep separate from the checks." She patted her purse. "Not only does the dumb jackass endorse the things prematurely, but he always keeps everything in one nice, tidy little place, receipts and all."

Alita laughed. "Boy, I'd like to see his face when he finds out what an imbecile he's been, to leave all that right where you could find it!"

For the convenience of the hotel guests, there was a branch bank attached to it, part of a small but elite shopping complex. Within minutes, Kelly had completed her transactions—cashing Brad's checks, accepting a few hundred dollars in bills, and taking the remainder in traveler's checks issued in her name.

"Where to now?" Alita inquired. "Someplace we can buy a baby stroller, I hope." She shifted Sydney to the other arm and tweaked the toddler's chubby cheek, making her giggle. "This *niña*'s been eating too many bananas."

Instead, Kelly guided her toward a fashionable boutique. "This will do, for starters. I need some clothes, everything from undies on out. I hope they have something smart enough for that press conference, because I don't have long to shop and get ready. And we still need to find someplace that sells toddlers' apparel."

Alita glanced at her watch. "It's scheduled for one o'clock, which only leaves you about an hour and a half."

"I know, and I still have to shower, fix my hair and make-up, and do my nails, and get Sydney cleaned up to boot. I'll have to hustle like crazy."

"You should have made an appointment at the beauty salon," Alita told her. "Not that they could do any better than you, but they could probably do it faster, with one person doing your nails while another works on your hair."

Kelly flashed her an annoyed look. "When did I have time to make an appointment, Alita? I was in my hotel room all of fifteen minutes before you arrived. Sydney barely got started on her nap."

"Oh, yeah. I forgot. Tell you what, you look here for what you need, and I'll take Sydney and scout around for some clothes for her."

"Oh, Alita! You're a life-saver, in more ways than one!" Kelly declared gratefully. "But first, let's ask the saleslady if there's someplace close to shop for Sydney. That way you won't be running in all directions, and I'll know where to meet you."

Kelly went through the boutique like a whirlwind, whipping items off the racks and tossing them into the waiting arms of the attending saleswoman. Fortunately, Kelly knew her sizes, and had an excellent eye for coordinating colors and fabrics. Even in her rush, she chose things she could mix and match, which would give her varied combinations with the fewest pieces. After all, she'd only be needing enough for a couple of days, and she had closet and drawers full of clothing back home.

She found a chic, basic black sheath, perfect for dinner, dancing, or just about any occasion, depending on how it was accessorized. She paired it with a hip-length paisley-print jacket, in vibrant hues of blue, emerald, ivory, and lavender. She chose three solid-colored blouses to match. Then came two pairs of slacks, one gray and one in sapphire blue. On a sale rack, she discovered another dress that was made-to-order for the upcoming press conference. Just a modest teal-green shirtwaist adorned with a wide belt, stand-up collar, and gold buttons, it was nonetheless elegant in its simplicity. If the need arose, it could also be teamed with the paisley jacket.

Heading for the lingerie section, Kelly selected a couple of bras, panties, and a slip. Then, with Zach in mind, she bypassed the pantyhose in lieu of a black lace garter belt and sheer stockings. Disregarding the price, she threw in a slinky full-length burgundy satin nightgown, which she knew she could have gotten through her usual distributor for a fraction of the cost.

In a store just across the mall corridor, she found a black pair of sling-back heels and purse, which completed her list of personal purchases, at least for the moment. Time was running low, but with the complimentary kit in the hotel bathroom, and her remaining cosmetics, she could get by—and Kathy or her mother might have a necklace or a pair of earrings she could borrow.

She met Alita and Sydney as they were departing the children's store. "Grab Syd or a couple of these bags before I drop them," Alita wheezed. "I can't believe these places don't have carts! I feel like a one-armed paper hanger!"

Kelly relieved her of the parcels, juggling them with her own. "Good grief! What all did you buy?"

"Everything, including a couple of toys. Now, follow me. You're five minutes late for your beauty appointment."

"My what? How did you wrangle that?" Kelly exclaimed.

"I browbeat them until they felt like worms!" Alita declared with a laugh. "By the time I was done, they were all but begging to perform their miracles on a celebrity such as you."

"Ha! In other words, you threw your weight and star status around until they gave in just to shut you up."

Alita attempted a shrug, which wasn't easy while carrying Sydney. "Hey, whatever works! Don't complain. Just remember to tip well."

"Which reminds me, how much do I owe you for Syd's stuff?"

"*Nada*. Nothing. It's on the home."

"House. On the house," Kelly corrected, "and you really should let me pay you back."

"Forget it. Save your money for a good lawyer, so you can rub Brad's nose in his own dirt."

Alita must have impressed upon the trio of beauty operators that time was of the essence. They whisked Kelly into a chair almost before she could unload her packages and, working in tandem, proceeded to give her "the works" at record speed—hair, facial, make-up, manicure, pedicure. She emerged forty minutes later feeling like an entirely new and revived woman.

They hurried back to her room, where Alita took charge again. "You take the shower, while I bathe Sydney in the sink."

"Bless you," Kelly intoned reverently. "Take your dress off first, or she'll have you soaked."

"Like it would matter!" Alita groused. "Carting her around already has me wrinkled from head to toe."

Kelly examined the fabric with a critical eye. "Put it on a hanger and hook it on the bathroom door. We'll steam the wrinkles out."

"Don't muss your hair or make-up," Alita adjured. To Sydney, as she peeled the toddler out of her worn playsuit, she added, "And you, you ornery imp, keep your pudgy fingers out of my curls. You've wiped half my make-up off as it is."

They finished with three minutes to spare. Sydney was dressed, fluffed, powdered, and looking absolutely angelic in her "Pebbles Flintstone" hairdo, a frilly pink dress, lacy white tights and patent leather shoes. Alita's dress was now wrinkle-free, her hair and make-up restored to their previous order. Kelly looked smart in her new shirtwaist, though she debated the wisdom of having let the beauticians talk her into leaving her hair flow free, with only a pair of clips holding it back from her face.

"Oh, well, too late now," she decided, transferring the last of her things into her new purse. "Let's get this dog-and-pony show on the road."

"Only if I get to be the pony," Alita quipped. "I'll deck the first person who dares to call me a dog."

They ran for the first elevator, missing it by a hair. The second one looked as if it might take forever to get to them, so they decided to take the stairs down the four flights to the main floor. As the stairwell door was closing behind her, Kelly heard the elevator bell ding. She chanced a look, then did a double take and hurried after Alita, who was half a flight ahead of her by now. "I could swear that was Brad getting off and heading toward my room," she panted. "Probably wanting his traveler's checks."

"Screw him," Alita retorted caustically.

Kelly laughed. "Not on a million dollar bet!"

The press conference kicked off as planned, though it lasted longer than anyone had anticipated. The media had numerous questions about how they had managed to survive for so long on the island, alluding to them as modern-day Robinson Crusoes. They were also impressed that such a diverse group, small as they were, had gotten along so well together.

"We pooled our resources," Zach told them. "Each of us, in his or her own way, had something valuable to contribute. Even Earl Roberts, who came up with the idea of a slingshot for shooting pigeons."

One reporter said, "I suppose it had one of those leather slings, like David had in biblical times."

Zach laughed and shook his head. "No, it had an elastic sling, believe it or not. Much easier to use."

"Where'd you get the elastic?" the man inquired curiously.

Zach nodded toward Kelly, who, with a charming blush, took up the tale from there. "Actually, it came from the waistband of my pantyhose."

Everyone laughed. "Very ingenious," someone called out.

"We thought so," Kelly admitted. "Zach also employed my dental floss in lieu of fishing line. It worked very well. And Blair, with her vast store of knowledge was a godsend. I don't know what we'd have done without her. As Zach said, we all contributed something: Gavin, his army training, Zach's leadership and engineering expertise, Alita her bravery and Latin lore, and Frazer his familiarity with the islands and selfless heroism."

"And Kelly's skill at popping bones back into place, and her sewing talent," Alita put in. "Not to mention her endless optimism. She and Zach became our leaders from the start."

"Didn't you argue, or get on each other's nerves?" another reporter asked.

"Did we ever!" Gavin confessed, as the others nodded in avid agreement. "But we learned to put up with each other, to make allowances for our differences, and to pull together for the good of all. In the end, we've become good friends. I'll always be grateful for having the opportunity to get to know these people. I hope we'll continue to stay in touch with each other.''

"We're like family now, regardless of race, religion, gender, or nationality,'' Blair put in proudly. "I wish the world at large could learn to get along as well. It would certainly solve a host of problems and eliminate a lot of strife.''

The next question was directed toward Alita. "Rumor has it one of the major movie studios wants to make a film about your experiences on the island and would like to have you star in it, Miss Gomez. Is that true?''

Alita flashed her beautiful smile. "They have contacted me about it, but I told them I want Blair to write the script, or the book from which it is adapted. Nothing is settled yet, of course, but we are negotiating.''

"Corporal Daniels, how did your fiancée react upon discovering you'd spent the past couple of months marooned with three lovely ladies, most particularly Miss Gomez?''

Gavin grimaced. "She's not thrilled about that part of it, but she is happy to have me back alive.''

"What about you, Ms. Kennedy?'' another reporter asked. "Or should I say, Mrs. Sanders?'' she added slyly. "Your husband appears to be rather irritated with you, especially after that kiss you and Mr. Goldstein exchanged aboard ship. We've heard he even moved out of your hotel room.''

Kelly's face hardened, her eyes like emerald glaciers. "I would suggest you check your so-called facts more carefully. I filed for divorce from Mr. Sanders three weeks prior to the plane crash, and fully intend to pursue it to its conclusion, which is why Brad and I are not sharing a room. Not that any of this is your business.''

"Were you acquainted with Mr. Goldstein previously? Is that why you want a divorce and went to Australia?" the reporter persisted.

Zach jumped in to reply, "Kelly and I met for the first time aboard the jet, mere hours before it crashed, and, on her behalf, I resent your implications."

Someone else called out, "Be that as it may, there's still that kiss, and the report that you and Ms. Kennedy intend to adopt the Australian child. That would suggest the two of you have formed some sort of close relationship. Would you care to comment, Ms. Kennedy?"

"I consider that a private matter, sir," she answered stiffly. "Since there are other people involved, I will leave it to Zach to respond at the appropriate time." She couldn't help glancing at Zach's family, at Becky in particular, seating in the front row.

Zach caught the gesture, and immediately realized that Kelly was trying to protect his daughter. He also knew that it was no longer necessary, and that the news media would persist relentlessly until they ferreted out the truth, so he might as well give them enough to satisfy their curiosity.

"Kelly and I intend to marry, once her divorce is final," he announced. "Then, if Sydney's family cannot be located, we intend to make her a part of ours. That's it, in a nutshell, plain and simple. No love triangle, no scandalous affair, just two fellow castaways who have fallen in love." He ended with an endearing grin, "Sorry to disappoint you, but that's basically all there is to it, nothing more interesting to add." His smile grew. "Except, perhaps, that Kelly has expressed a strange desire for an engagement ring from a bubble gum machine."

Chapter 26

The press conference concluded on that lighter note. The reporters filed out, leaving the friends and their relatives behind. One look at Becky's petulant face, and Kelly was almost tempted to call the media back, sure she'd rather go another round with them than Zach's daughter. There was no help for it however. Zach wanted her to get to know his family, just as her folks were anxious to meet Zach. Plus, Blair wanted to introduce her husband and children to them, Gavin wanted to introduce his family and fiancée, and everyone was eager to make Alita's acquaintance.

"Just a quick chat," Zach told Kelly. "We'll get together again for dinner later."

At the mention of dinner, Kelly's stomach growled, loudly enough for Zach to hear. He chuckled. "Too busy getting beautiful to take time to eat?"

"Something like that," Kelly acknowledged. "I had to get in some speedy shopping for Syd and me. When I say 'we simply had nothing to wear,' you can take me at my word."

"Oh, babe, I'm sorry. It was thoughtless of me not to realize that and offer to take you and Sydney down to the stores. My folks brought clothes from home, and I just assumed yours did, too. Still, I should have remembered Sydney would need things."

"Mom and Dad presumed Brad would bring some of my things, but he didn't pack so much as a hair bow for me, though he brought three suitcases full of clothes for himself. Alita helped with Sydney, and we managed to time it right to the minute. While I was getting spruced up, she and Syd chowed down on cookies and soft drinks at the beauty shop, but I didn't get a chance to eat and Sydney hasn't had her nap."

"What about money? Did you have enough?"

"I'm okay for now. It's a long story, and I'll fill you in later."

On their way across the room to greet Zach's family, they passed Blair and her small entourage. Anton, in a very superior tone, was saying to Blair, "What makes you think you have the talent to write a book? While I admire you for wanting to try, dear, I wouldn't want to see you humiliate yourself."

Kelly pulled up short, tugging Zach to a halt with her. Determinedly and quite deliberately, she approached Anton, thrusting her hand out in a manner he couldn't ignore. As they shook hands, she said, "You must be terribly proud of Blair, Mr. Chevalier. Her intelligence must be legendary around campus. I'll bet she puts all the professors with their masters and doctorate degrees and diplomas to shame with her quick mind and wit."

Zach took his cue from Kelly. "I have never met anyone with as rounded an education as your wife, Chevalier. She amazed us at every turn. She knew more about the flora and fauna of the islands than all of us combined. She was the one who showed us how to wrap our food in seaweed and palm leaves and bake it in the coals of the fire, among other invaluable information. Gavin swears she's a walking encyclopedia."

"Thank you, but . . ."

"Oh, I simply can't wait to read her book when it comes out!" Kelly interrupted. "I'll bet it's a bestseller, and after all she's been through she certainly deserves the acclaim, not to mention the royalties she'll no doubt earn."

Blair beamed. "Thank you."

Anton frowned. "I can't fathom where she'll find the time to write."

"That's where you come in, old fellow," Zach announced, giving the man a companionable slap on the back. "It's a new age, and with the number of single parents, or both working in order to make finances stretch, we men have to pick up the slack at home. No more excuses for us. We have to pitch in with the cooking, the laundry, and the child care, which is only fair. If wives are supplementing the family income, we men have to help hold up the housekeeping end of things."

"I . . . I wouldn't . . . I've never . . ." Anton sputtered.

"High time you did your part, then, I'd say," Kelly proposed curtly. "After all, slavery was abolished a long time ago. A woman has as much right to follow her dream as a man, and much more opportunity these days. The working market is really beginning to open up to the female population. Moreover, I would hope the average male has the mental capacity to figure out how to operate a microwave or a washing machine. He'd be a sorry specimen if he didn't. And any literate person should be able to follow the instructions in a cookbook or on a package of diapers, or read a grocery list, which should put you ahead of the game from the start."

"Besides, a man should get to know his children, to spend quality time with them while they're young," Zach added helpfully. "They grow so fast, and before you know it they're off and married. What a pity, to be too busy with professional obligations in those precious years, only to retire and find them gone, involved with their own lives, little more than familiar strangers. Believe me, if there is one thing I've learned from being marooned on that island, it's that family is important, life is short, and we need to make the best of our time with them."

"I'm sure you're right," Anton said. "Still . . ."

Sydney chose that moment to start fussing. Kelly jostled her and patted her bottom. Zach reached out and plucked the little girl out of her arms, cuddling the toddler close.

"You just think about it, Anton," Kelly suggested. "Listen, Syd's getting tired. We'll talk again at a better time."

Zach shook Anton's hand and said in parting. "You've got a wonderful woman there. Cherish her." He leaned to give Blair a kiss on her cheek. "We'll see you later, pixie. You look adorable."

"Zach, you were terrific!" Kelly praised.

"You weren't so bad yourself, champ," he returned with a wink. "If nothing else, we certainly gave him food for thought."

Kelly rubbed her tummy. "Don't mention food again, unless you're prepared to feed me."

"First my family, then yours," he cajoled.

Kelly would rather have faced the Inquisition, but she stiffened her spine and forged ahead, pasting a smile on her face. "Did you tell them about our plans earlier, or did they just learn the good news along with the media?"

"I told them all right away, everything except that we're

already expecting a baby. I thought I'd spring that on them later, after they've had time to absorb the first shockwave.''

''And?''

''Everyone seems to be reserving comment until you all get better acquainted—except Becky.''

''I knew it! She resents me already.''

''What about your side?'' he asked.

''Same as yours. But they know about the baby. They're all curious about the handsome man who got me pregnant so quickly.''

''Great!'' he groaned. ''They're probably planning the shotgun wedding as we speak. Does Brad know?''

''Not about the baby, unless he overheard one of us talking. Not that it matters much. Everyone will know in a couple of months.''

Zach chuckled. ''Nah, they'll just think you're getting fat. Letting yourself go to pot, now that you've got me properly hooked.''

Kelly swatted him, careful to maintain her smile as she muttered, ''Conceited ass!''

Ike Goldsten's first queston was, ''Are you related to President Kennedy?''

Kelly shook her head. ''I doubt that, sir, since they're Catholic and my family is Protestant. Unless the clan split allegiance somewhere down the line,'' she qualified.

''That's a shame,'' one of Zach's sisters remarked. ''I was hoping you could introduce me to Arnold and Maria so I could get their autographs.'' She smiled and presented her hand in greeting. ''Hello. I'm Beth Moyer, in case you don't recall. I know how hard it is to remember names and faces when you meet so many people at once.'' She gestured over her shoulder. ''This is my husband, David, our son Gabe, and our daughter Myra, ages twelve and ten respectively."

Kelly shook hands all around. "Pleased to meet you. Again. Sorry about the autographs, but at least you'll have Alita's."

"Zach was telling Becky that you run a health club and beauty boutique of some sort," Zach's mother put in. "Does that mean you intend to keep working once you and Zach are married?"

"I suppose I'll hire a competent manager for the club in Phoenix, just as I have for those in Australia and Houston," Kelly told her.

Sarah's brows rose. "You have three of them?"

"At the moment," Kelly replied evenly. Privately, she wondered if she would still own any by the time she and Brad were finished fighting it out.

Zach's second sister spoke up, rattling off rapid-fire introductions. "Hi. Leah, Pete, and Seth Levy," she listed, pointing to herself, her husband, and infant son. "What kind of clothes do you carry in the boutique?"

"Mostly ladies' intimate apparel and exercise outfits, though we are expanding into other areas."

"Oooh, sexy stuff!" Beth enthused. "Do you carry teddies? I simply love those things—and so does Dave. For me, not himself," she clarified with a blush.

Kelly chuckled. "I rather assumed that."

"And you own beauty shops as well?" This from Leah. "That explains your fabulous hair, I suppose. Doesn't she have lovely hair, Becky?"

Becky shrugged in apparent disinterest. "I guess so. Is it real?"

"Becky Ann, what a question!" Sarah declared.

"Well," the girl pouted, "Dolly Parton wears a wig a lot."

"Kelly's is real," Zach said, hiding a grin. "Color and all."

In an aside to Pete, Dave murmured, "Zach should know, I would imagine."

"Hush!" Leah jabbed her husband in the ribs. "You're embarrassing Kelly. What sort of impression is that to make?"

Kelly fought to ignore the comments, remarking to Becky. "You've got your daddy's thick black hair, and I'll bet you got those big brown eyes from your mother, didn't you? Zach showed me a picture of her, one he carries in his wallet. She was a beautiful lady, just like you're going to be someday."

Becky lifted her chin in a haughty pose. "My mom was the most beautiful woman in the world. Daddy loved her. He still does. He told me so."

Into the strained silence, Kelly said, "Of course he does, Becky. I know that, and it's one of the first things I liked about him."

Becky maintained the attack. "Gramma says you already have a husband, but you're getting a divorce from him, just like you'll probably do with Daddy after you get all his money."

Beth let loose a startled gasp. Sarah's abashed groan was echoed by Ike's. Leah grimaced.

Zach took a step toward his daughter. "Rebecca," he warned, "You're way over the line."

Kelly waved him back. "It's okay, Zach. I understand." To Becky, she added, "How can I explain this to you? I made a mistake when I married Brad. He turned out not to be the nice person I thought he was, and I'm very sorry about that, but it made me fall out of love with him. You see, Becky, among other things, Brad didn't tell me he didn't like children. But I do, and so does your dad. In fact, your father and I have much more in common, which makes me very sure that he and I will love each other for always. At least I hope so, because I love him very much, with all my heart. I've never loved anyone more than I love your daddy. And I'm here to love you, too, anytime you're ready.''

"I'm not ready," Becky insisted stubbornly.

Kelly sighed. "Somehow I figured that. Let's just give it some time, shall we? There's no rush."

Sydney begged to differ, and voiced her complaint loudly. "Pee pee! Gotta pee pee!"

The tension broke as everyone laughed.

"Another country heard from, and this one *is* in a rush!" Zach exclaimed. "Do you want to take her, Kelly, or shall I?"

Kelly reached for the toddler. "I will. She needs her nap, and I need something to eat. I'll put her down in her crib, and order up from room service. I wouldn't mind a short rest myself, before we have our first session with the airline officials."

"I'll carry her, and walk up with you," Zach offered. "Becky, you go with Gramma and Grandpa. I'll be along soon, and you and I are going to have a little talk about your manners, young lady."

"Sorry about that," Zach told her as they entered the elevator. "We didn't even get to spend any time with your family."

"That's all right," Kelly assured him with a grim smile. "I'm sure they'll keep the rack oiled and ready for you. We come from a long line of ancient Irish warriors, and from everything I've heard, they really knew how to turn the screws."

Zach pulled a face. "Ah, something to look forward to

with anxious anticipation. Thank you, sweetheart. You've just made my day.''

Kelly opened the door to her room, and almost backed over Zach when she saw Brad reclined comfortably on her bed. "How did you get in here?" she demanded.

Brad gave her a cat-in-the cream smile. "I had the maid let me in." His mile dissolved, his eyes hardening into ice-blue chips. "I want my money, Kelly. Now. Give it to me, and I'll leave peaceably.''

"You'll leave regardless of your mood, mister," Zach informed him bluntly. He set Sydney on the floor, aiming her in the direction of the bathroom. "Can you go potty by yourself, like a big girl, Syd?''

Sydney nodded and toddled off, already tugging at her panties.

Kelly headed for the phone. "I'm calling the desk and having them send up the security guard," she threatened. "I'd advise you to leave before he gets here, Brad.''

"I want my money. I know you have it. You're the only one who could have found those travelers' checks. Now hand them over, or you'll be the one in hot water, sugar. I'll have you arrested faster than you can spit.''

"What travelers' checks?" Zach asked. "What's he talking about?''

Kelly addressed her remarks to Brad. "I warned you, how many times, about leaving those things in your hotel room? And pre-signing them, to boot? Also, you can forget the intimidation tactics. You know perfectly well that once they've been properly endorsed, it's absolutely legal for anyone to cash them. If they've come up missing, it's no one's fault but your own, hot shot.''

"Are you saying you don't have them?" Brad questioned with narrowed eyes.

"Actually, I don't." Which was the truth, as far as it

went. She now possessed a whole new batch, in her own name.

"I don't believe you." Brad grabbed for her purse, a move she hadn't anticipated.

Zach grabbed for Brad.

Kelly grabbed for the phone and quickly dialed the front desk.

As the two men tussled over Kelly's purse, the thing popped open, spilling the contents across the bed and floor. Brad snatched up her wallet, tearing it open, even as he continued to wrestle with Zach. A stack of bills and a few crumpled receipts fluttered out. Zach quickly swept them off the bed before Brad could claim them. The missing traveler's checks were nowhere in sight.

Concluding her phone conversation, Kelly knelt and began scooping her possessions back into the purse. "Are you satisfied now, you louse?" she inquired archly. She seized her wallet from him, plunking it into her purse as well. "Now get out! And stay out!"

"Where are they, Kelly? Where have you hidden them?" he persisted angrily. "Or have you already cashed them? Is that it? I can check, you know, to see if your signature is on them."

"Go right ahead," she told him, as Zach latched onto Brad's collar and yanked him off the bed and toward the door. "It would serve you right if I have, you rotten, underhanded sneak. After all, you left me with no credit, no checking or savings accounts, and you're trying to sell my clubs out from under me. Now, tell me, who's the bigger thief, Brad? Better yet, we can let the courts decide that issue."

The house detective arrived just in time to catch Brad as Zach shoved him out the door. "Mr. Sanders entered Ms. Kennedy's room illegally," Zach explained. "They're in the process of getting a divorce, and he's harassing her."

The man frowned and grabbed Brad by the arm. "I'll take care of it," he stated. "Is he a guest here?"

"No," Kelly piped up. "And I don't want him coming anywhere near me again. If he does, I'll press charges."

The detective gave Brad a rough tug in the direction of the elevator. "Come along, Sanders. You're trespassing and creating a public nuisance. Consider this your last warning. Step one foot on hotel property again, and we'll have you arrested."

Zach watched until the elevator doors closed behind Brad and the detective. Then he shut and locked the door to Kelly's room and turned to face her. "Is there any truth to Brad's claim?"

She gave him a smug look. "Absolutely. The moron always tapes his travelers' checks inside the frame of the dresser. Has for years. And he always endorses them, too. Don't worry, Zach. As I said, it's perfectly legal for me to have cashed them, and that dirty so-and-so only got a portion of what he deserves. He's left me virtually penniless, aside from those checks I found."

She went on to outline her current dilemma to him. At the end of her diatribe, Zach threaded his fingers through his hair, ruffling its neatly combed state. "I should have beaten the bastard senseless while I had the chance," he growled.

"No." She shook her head. "If either of you lands in jail, I'd rather it be Brad. But I am going to have to get in touch with a good attorney immediately, someone out of Brad's circle, and with a lot of clout. I've got to get the divorce going again, get a new will made out, make sure Brad no longer has power of attorney when it comes to my affairs, and stop the sale of my clubs. Then we'll see about the rest of the mess, like getting my pilfered funds back."

"We'll find you a lawyer who specializes in this field,"

Zach promised. "One who will stake Brad out to dry, preferably over an anthill."

"I wonder if we can get someone who will work on
a contingency basis. This sounds as if it could get very
expensive."

"Don't worry about it, sweetheart. I'll take care of it."

"Zach! Your family already suspects I'm a gold-digger.
Having you foot my legal expenses would only confirm it,
at least from their perspective."

"Then we won't tell them. There's no reason they'll
ever have to know."

Kelly opened her mouth to argue the point, then shut
it again with a frown. "Where's Sydney?"

Zach blinked in surprise and looked around the room.
"She went to the bathroom. Good grief, I hope she didn't
get stuck, or something!"

They both made a beeline for the bathroom—and there
was Sydney, sound asleep on the bath mat, her tights and
panties still around her ankles, her bare behind hunched
into the air.

Kelly chuckled softly. "Poor baby! She's just all tuckered
out."

Zach lifted the child from the floor, and laughed. "She's
as limp as an overcooked noodle. A bomb could go off
right now, and she'd sleep right through it." He deposited
her in her crib, and Kelly removed her shoes and tights
and tugged her panties back into place.

Then, Kelly covered the toddler with a light blanket,
commenting, "I'd forgotten how cold air conditioning
could feel. Not that I'm complaining mind you, but it's
going to take some getting used to again."

"By the way," Zach said, "there were no travelers checks
in your purse that I saw, in your name or otherwise. Where
did you stash them?"

"Not where Brad did his, that's for sure!" Kelly informed

him. "That would have been the first place he looked, which I'm certain he did." She speedily unbuttoned her dress from hem to neckline, spreading the two panels apart to reveal her lacy new undies. "Want to go treasure hunting for traveler's checks, Zach?" she cooed.

His smile spread to his bright gold eyes. "Forget the checks. I'm more interested in booby and bottom booty."

Kelly laughed. "Bet you can't say that three times, real fast."

He reached for her, and they both tumbled onto the big bed. "Bet I can get you to do something else three times real fast," he boasted.

She gazed at him, her green eyes dancing with devilment. "Give it your best shot, Tarzan! I double-dog dare you!"

Chapter 27

Zach swatted Kelly on her bare posterior. "Let that be a lesson to you. I'm not one to allow a dare to go unchallenged."

She giggled. "That's nice to know."

Zach reached for his pants as Kelly reached for the phone.

"I'm going to call room service. Do you want something?"

He leered playfully at her nude form. "Yeah, but it will have to wait. Becky's probably breaking out in hives by now."

Before she'd touched it, the phone rang, startling Kelly. She laughed. "Bet that's someone from your tribe, trying to track down the prodigal son."

Zach shrugged into his shirt as she picked up the receiver. He heard her say, "Pardon me?" Followed almost immediately by, "Is this a joke?"

"What?" Zach mouthed. "Who is it?"

"The President," she whispered, covering the mouthpiece.

"The president of the airlines?"

"No!" she hissed. "The President of the United States!"

"You're kidding."

Evidently she wasn't, for she nearly snapped to attention as she said to the person on the other end of the line, "Yes, Mr. President, I'm here."

Pause.

"Likewise, I'm sure."

Pause.

"Yes, sir. Thank you sir."

Pause.

"It was quite a frightening experience, one I wouldn't care to repeat anytime soon."

Pause. A smile for Zach.

"Yes, it certainly did. I'm very happy. Thank you."

Pause.

"Yes, we do. That would be wonderful."

Another pause. Kelly's face grew thoughtful.

"Actually, sir, now that you've offered, there is something you may be able to do for me."

To Zach's utter amazement, his intended bride launched into an explanation of her problems with Brad, her businesses, the whole enchilada—at the end of which there was another extended lull while the President spoke. Finally, Kelly said, "That would be great, but I have to consider the expense you know." Then, "Really? Are you sure this wouldn't get you or anyone else into trouble?"

Pause.

"Yes, I guess they are public servants."

"Monday would be fine. Phoenix. I'm in the book. Thank you. I can't imagine how I'll ever repay you for this." Kelly laughed. "I certainly will. I hope it works out well, too."

Pause.

"He's right here, or would you prefer to speak to him when he rejoins his family in his own room?"

"Right. In about fifteen minutes, then? I'll tell him. Goodbye, sir."

Kelly hung up and stood there, dazed. "He's going to help, Zach. He's going to contact the Attorney General's office and see if someone there can sort this nonsense out for me immediately. In fact, he said someone would get in touch on Monday, as soon as I get back to Phoenix. He's appalled that Brad would use his auspices in a manner so unbecoming a member of the bar. Oh, he saw the clip of us and Sydney on T.V. earlier, and said not to worry about anyone from Social Services trying to take Sydney from us. He's taking care of that, too." She stopped long enough to draw a deep breath. "Can you believe this? The President of the United States is going to help little old me! Us! Isn't this incredible?"

"What's more amazing," Zach told her, shaking his head in wonder, "is that you had the nerve to ask him to do it. Whatever possessed you?"

Kelly's face clouded. "He offered first. I'm not that brazen, Zach. He asked if there was, and I quote, 'anything, anything at all I can do for you, to make your transition back into civilization smoother.' I swear, it was almost as if the man had read my mind!"

"I wouldn't credit him with that much power, darling. He's the President, not God. Besides, I already told you I'd help you find a lawyer."

"Yes, but you've got to admit, having the Attorney General's office breathing down your neck is a tad more threatening, and it just might break up that close-knit legal network of attorneys and judges that Brad's so proud of throwing in everyone's face. Which would be a benefit to a lot of folks who are beating their heads against a stone wall trying

to get justice from a very select and discriminating system.''
She approached him with an apologetic look. "Not that I
don't appreciate your offer, love. I just think this way will
be faster and a whole lot more effective. Moreover, it will
scare Brad right out of his BVDs.''

"Speaking of which,'' Zach commented, allowing a grin
to creep over his face, "do you realize you just held a very
lengthy conversation with the President, and you don't
have a stitch on? He'd likely have had a coronary if he
knew you were standing there, prancing back and forth
in the nude.''

Kelly mouth gaped. "Oh, my lands!'' Then she giggled.
"It's a good thing we didn't have one of those viewer
phones, isn't it? Or some sort of audio-visual computer
link-up.''

"Was there some other bit of information you were
supposed to relay to me?'' Zach asked. "Just before you
hung up, it sounded as if he wanted to speak to me.''

"Good grief, yes!'' Kelly couldn't believe she'd nearly
forgotten. She pushed him toward the door. "He going
to call you, too, in about fifteen minutes. No, more like
seven minutes now, I suppose. You'd better hurry down
to your room and alert your family. I'm sure they'll all
want to be present when he does. After all, it's not every
day the average citizen gets a personal message from the
President!''

"And not everyday Jane Q. Public has the gall to take
him up on a polite but meaningless gesture,'' Zach
reminded her.

"You're not really mad at me, are you?'' she inquired
uncertainly.

Zach shook his head. "More like awestruck by your daring, especially when you did it stark staring naked!'' Thus
reminded, he urged her to the blind side of the door.

"See you at dinner, if not before." He kissed her soundly, and quickly slipped out.

A mere second later, the door popped open again, just enough for Kelly to wedge her head through the crack. "Zach!" she hissed. When he turned, she whispered. "In honor of such a momentous call, maybe you ought to do better than I did and zip up your pants!"

Kelly had time to wolf down half a sandwich and a dill pickle before her first solo meeting with the airline officials in charge of investigating the crash. Then she hurried back to relieve her parents of babysitting duty.

"Holy Neds! What a day!" she declared, flopping into a chair in their room. "I'm so tired I can hardly hold my head up! I can't remember the last time I was this busy— and that dill pickle isn't setting too well, either."

"You do look a little green around the *dills,*" her father joked.

"Was Sydney good for you?"

"Better behaved than you are today," her mother complained. "I can't believe you didn't bother to notify us when you got that call from the President!"

"Mom! What was I supposed to do, put the President on hold while I dashed down the hall to get you? Besides, I wasn't even dressed."

"I thought you said Zach was there," Eileen said, frowning.

Kelly wriggled in her chair, just the way she always had when she'd gotten caught doing something wrong as a child. "He was," she admitted in a small voice.

"Then you might have sent him to fetch us," Eileen pouted.

"Heavens above, Eileen! Don't be dense!" Ryan exclaimed. "If she was naked, it stands to reason Zach was, too. After all, they are engaged, and she is pregnant, and I'll wager she didn't get into that condition by swallowing watermelon seeds."

It was a toss-up who blushed the reddest, mother or daughter.

"Well, I suppose it doesn't matter how much they carry on now," Eileen allowed. "The damage is done, as you said, and she can't get pregnant twice over." She glowered at her daughter. "I just wish you could have waited, at least until your divorce from Brad was final. This is somewhat embarrassing, you know."

Ryan chuckled. "Probably wasn't much else to do on that island, and nature will take its course, after all. By the way, Eileen, do you remember that old '65 Mustang I used to have when we were dating?" he inquired, with a nostalgic expression. "Of course, it wasn't so old then, and neither were we. As I recall, that car had some pretty good shocks, too. Especially the rear ones."

"You just hush, Ryan Kennedy!" Eileen warned, wagging her finger at him. "You can be the most exasperating man! You and your habit of telling tales out of school!"

"Oh, come on, you two," Kelly said with a laugh. "It's not as if Cole and I didn't figure most of this out on our own, years ago. As for my 'condition,' you're both as thrilled as I am, so why don't you just forego the indignant parent act and admit it?"

Eileen threw her hands up. "You're right. We know how badly you've wanted a child, and how you grieved over the one you lost. We're very happy for you, and we're looking forward to having another grandchild."

"Or two," Ryan put in. "Did you warn Zach that twins run in our family?"

"Only after the fact," Kelly confessed. "It sort of slipped my mind for a while."

"How did he take it?" her dad wanted to know. "With

Sydney, and his daughter, you might end up having quite
a brood.''

"Fortunately, he adores children.''

"So, do we get to meet this paragon sometime before
the wedding?'' Eileen queried. "I thought you were going
to make time for that this afternoon, after the press conference.''

"That didn't pan out the way I'd planned it,'' Kelly explained. "After we rescued Blair from her knows-everything,
does-nothing husband, we spent a few minutes with Zach's
family. Then, Sydney had to go potty and was whining for
her nap, and we ended up having to boot Brad out of my
room. Then the President called, Zach left, and I had this
blasted meeting to attend.'' She stared up at her parents
in weary confusion. "Did they shorten the hours in a day
while I was gone?''

"No dear, you're just not used to such a fast pace, after
lolling around on that island for the past two months,''
her mother said. "I'm sorry I was so short with you. It's
just that I would so have loved hearing your conversation
with the President. Why, I'd have been the hit of my
pinochle group.''

Kelly glanced at her watch. "Nuts! Here we go again!
I'll just have time to get freshened up before dinner and
put a shine to Sydney. I promise you'll get to talk with
Zach this evening. You might even get to make a few points
for me with his daughter, Becky. As things stand now, she
despises me.''

"That won't last,'' Ryan predicted. "No one can resist
Irish charm for long. Just wait until she hears a few of my
stories, sweetie. She'll be all agog wanting to know more
about wee people and magic fairies and leprechauns and
such.''

Kelly laughed as she scooped Sydney off the floor, where
the toddler had been playing with a stack of coasters.

"Come on dumplin'. Let's let Papaw rehearse his tall tales." Over her shoulder, she waved and called back, "Don't forget to tell Becky about the blarney stone, Dad, and how you swallowed it."

The airline had set up a buffet dinner in honor of the survivors and their families. Kelly wore the paisley jacket over her new black dress, hoping that if Sydney took a notion to paint her with food, the splatters would blend in with the pattern. Slowly but surely, she was learning to take this sort of "baby thing" into consideration, and actually revelling in it. She'd certainly waited long enough to be a mommy, and wanted to enjoy every delicious moment—the good, the bad, and the messy.

Evidently, someone had done their homework, or at least taken enough notice to place Zach's family directly across the table from Kelly's. To make it even more convenient, the parents were seated opposite each other, the better to become acquainted, and the children had been grouped together for like reason, to insure that their conversation would not interfere overmuch with that of the adults. To further facilitate matters, high chairs and oversized bibs had been provided for Sydney and Leah's baby. On the adult end, Gavin's family sat opposite Blair's, with Alita rounding out the party.

There was one rather delicate moment at the outset, when an airline delegate invoked the blessing prior to the meal. The prayer, while touching on the lives of those lost in the crash and expressing gratefulness on behalf of these few survivors, was nonetheless decidedly Christian. Kelly, seated across from her future Jewish relatives, could not help but wince. Then she caught Zach's reassuring wink, and relaxed a bit. If it didn't bother him, she wasn't going to worry over it.

Then her own father started the dinner conversation off with a bang, by asking Ike who he'd voted for in the last election. Kelly groaned. Eileen gave Ryan a sharp nudge, and said, "How many times have you heard me tell our children not to discuss politics or religion at a public function? Now that they're grown, I suppose I'm going to have to teach you those same manners."

"You're absolutely right, Mrs. Kennedy," Sarah agreed. "More wars have been fought over those two issues than anything else."

"Oh, call me, Eileen. It's much less formal."

Thus it began, the initial exchange of information between the families, the gradual discovery of subtle differences and similarities among them. Naturally, much of the talk centered around Zach and Kelly.

"Where do you two plan to live?" Ryan inquired.

"We haven't decided that yet, Mr. Kennedy. There are a lot of factors to take into consideration, Becky's school, for one."

"I could always relocate one of the clubs to Seattle," Kelly proposed. "I'm just not sure how I'd like that climate year-round. I'm rather used to more sunshine, but I suppose I'd adjust."

"If you could adjust to that island, you could do it anywhere," Alita put in from across the way. She changed the subject by indicating the buffet table. "Can you believe they put seafood on the menu? *Caramba!* As if we haven't seen enough of it in the past months to last us a lifetime!"

"At least this is shrimp and lobster," Blair pointed out.

Gavin wrinkled his nose. "Still smells fishy to me."

"How did your talk with the President go, Zach?" Kelly inquired. "Did you wind up apologizing for my presumptuous behavior?"

Zach chuckled. "No. In fact, I took your lead and asked him about the island. As it happens, it's U.S. owned, and he's going to have someone get back with me on the possibility of purchasing it.''

This set off a whole new exchange of ideas and comments about possible uses for the land and the improvements which might have to be made—everything from a helipad to a runway, even trenching out a channel deep enough for cruise ships to dock.

By the time the evening ended, everyone had become comfortably acquainted. It all went very well, so well that had Sydney not been nodding off in her high chair and Kelly about to do likewise, Kelly would have enjoyed prolonging it. After hiding several yawns, however, she gave it up.

Again, Zach saw her to her room, checking to make sure she didn't have another unwelcome visitor, namely Brad. Assured the room was empty, he lingered over their parting kiss. "Sleep light," he whispered. "I'll be back later, after Becky's asleep, to tuck you in.''

Kelly gave a drowsy chuckle. "I don't know if it will be worth your effort, unless you have a thing for making love to zombies.''

He grinned. "Didn't I tell you? They're my favorite fiends. Besides, I love more than just your body, sweetheart, and I've become so accustomed to snuggling up with you I'm not sure I can sleep alone anymore. I'd miss having you sprawled all over me, and I probably couldn't breathe properly without a big wad of your hair in my mouth.''

"I'll get it cut first thing in the morning," she pledged, just to see his reaction.

"Oh, no you don't! I like it just the way it is.''

"What about that line you just fed me about not loving me for my body alone?" she taunted.

"True," he vowed, "but I really do adore your hair. In fact, I have this fantasy that if you grow it long enough, we can use it as an escape ladder in case of a fire," he teased. "Sort of like Rapunzel."

She gave him a shove toward the door. "Goodnight, sweet prince."

"Does that mean you don't want me to come back later?"

She reached into her jacket pocket, withdrew her key card, and pressed it into his palm. "Wake me gently, love, or I might mistake you for Brad and bean you with the bed lamp."

Chapter 28

Monday morning, they parted at the airport. Zach, Becky, and family were booked on a direct flight to Seattle, while Kelly was headed for Phoenix with Sydney. Single-handedly coping with the toddler, while attending to the multitude of problems facing her, was going to prove quite a challenge. But Kelly was determined to give it all she had, despite her qualms and Zach's.

"Sweetheart, I can take Syd. Mom and Dad would be tickled to help babysit, and it would give Becky a chance to get used to her. You don't have a crib, or highchair, or any of the million and one things you'll need. Becky's old stuff is packed up in the attic, just collecting dust."

"I've already got a plan for that," Kelly informed him. "Mom and Dad are going to bring me some of the twins' things, and Mom intends to hit the garage sales for anything else we need."

"They're going to haul all that from Texas to Phoenix? What will you do in the meantime?"

"The same thing I've been doing, love. Punting. Playing it by ear. Making do with what I've got and relying on my creative genius. Face it, Zach. Syd's been free-wheeling it for so long that she'd go nuts cooped up in a playpen, and she'll probably be just as thrilled with a set of pots and pans and a pile of Tupperware as she would with a fortune's worth of toys."

"You're right there," he conceded. "But I was thinking about you and all your legal tangles with Brad. You'll be stretching yourself pretty thin, trying to manage everything at once. I don't want you wearing yourself out, darling. You have to take special care right now, for your health and our baby's. I don't want anything happening to any of you."

"I'll be careful, Dr. Goldstein," she pledged teasingly. "I'll drink all my milk, and take my vitamins faithfully, and I'll schedule an appointment with an obstetrician the minute the plane lands. I promise."

"And call me, every day. Reverse the charges."

"I will not. I'll dial direct. It's cheaper."

He laughed. "Mom would be proud of you. We'll alternate, every other day. I'll call you this evening."

They were announcing her flight. Zach pulled her into his arms for a quick, last-minute hug. "I'm going to miss you like the devil."

"Me, too," she vowed, blinking back her tears. "It won't be for long."

Zach kissed her and Sydney, and waved them on their way. Suddenly, Kelly swiveled around and headed back toward him, her face as white as school paste. "I can't do this!" she gasped. "I thought I could, but I can't."

"What? What can't you do?" he asked worriedly. His heart nearly stopped for fear she was about to tell him she couldn't marry him.

"Fly," she squeaked out. "I'm scared out of my mind

to get on that plane. I know the odds of crashing twice running are probably astronomical, but I've turned into a quivering coward."

"That makes two of us," he confessed. "I'm dreading the flight home, and praying I won't make a complete fool of myself in front of my daughter by having an attack of the screaming meemies."

"Maybe we can hop a ship home, instead," she proposed.

"Honey, they book those things months in advance, and it would take you days to get home, rather than a few hours. And isn't that liaison from the Attorney General's office going to contact you this afternoon?"

"I know! I know!" she wailed.

They announced her flight number again, the final boarding call. Gently, he turned her around and urged toward the gate. "You've got to go, sweetheart. You can do it. I know you can. Would it help if I walk you to your seat?"

"Not really. The only thing that might help would be to have you beside me, holding my hand the whole way."

"Syd will hold your hand, and I'll be there in spirit," he told her. "Be brave. You don't want to scare Sydney or the other passengers, do you?"

They'd made it to the gate, where the attendant quickly checked her ticket. "You're the last to board, Ms. Kennedy. You'll be in seat 22B. Have a nice flight."

Kelly paled, and Zach feared she might faint on the spot. "Oh, God!" she exclaimed. "That's the same seat I was in before, when the plane crashed!"

"Your lucky number," Zach comforted, with an over-bright smile. "You survived then, and you'll do even better this time."

The attendant's eyebrows rose, and it was clear she sensed Kelly was very close to full-fledged panic. "Maybe you could see her onto the plane, sir, and alert the stewardess to her . . . uh . . . extreme anxiety.''

Kelly was a trembling mass of jelly by the time Zach helped buckle her and Sydney into their seats. "You'll be fine. I know it. I'll call you tonight.'' He kissed her forehead and left her with a final word of advice. "Think of this as the alternative to root canal, only quicker.''

Kelly didn't open her eyes or release her death-grip on the armrest until well after take-off. Fortunately, Sydney didn't appear to be experiencing the same residual fears, and didn't seem affected by Kelly's. She was jabbering a mile a minute, to Kelly and the new dolly Alita had bought her, as content as a well-fed kitten. Gradually, Kelly's nerves calmed to the point where she didn't think she'd have to resort to the airbag. But she remained tense for the remainder of the trip, grateful only that this was a direct flight, and she wouldn't have to transfer to another plane and go through all this again just to get home.

When they finally touched down in Phoenix, Kelly could have kissed the tarmac. With undue haste, she and Sydney exited the craft, wound their way through the airport, and flagged down a taxi. Halfway home, she burst into laughter, which immediately turned to tears. She'd forgotten about her car, which was still parked at a valet parking site adjacent to the airport, unless they'd had it towed away by now. Either way, she was going to owe one whopper of a bill!

Zach was handling his own trauma only slightly better than Kelly. Despite his own advice, his jaw was clenched so tightly it was a wonder his teeth didn't crumble under the pressure. The thought crossed his mind that if he didn't ease up a bit, in addition to having to suffer this torment, he might just have to endure a root canal as well.

In a situation where he, as the adult, should have been reassuring his daughter, she had assumed that role and was now comforting him. "It's okay, Daddy," she said, patting his clenched fist. "Try to remember how much fun flying is." Then, on a streak of generosity, she offered, "Would you like to trade seats with me, so you can look out the window?"

Zach swallowed hard, and gave her hand a quick squeeze. "No, thanks, sweetie. You enjoy the view. Daddy's seen it before." Silently, he added, *Up close and all too personal!*

Thankfully, the flight ended before he could start to hyperventilate or otherwise humiliate himself. Still, he was glad to leave the driving to his brother-in-law. He was much too shaky to trust himself behind the wheel of a car.

After being closed up for so long, Kelly's apartment over the boutique was musty, and hot as an blast furnace. Her first move was to flip on the air conditioner, only to find that the electricity had been shut off. So had the water, and the phone.

"Crap and corruption!" she cursed. "This returning from the dead certainly has its drawbacks!"

Leaving her bags there, she collected Sydney and they both trotted downstairs to the closed health club, only to find the same there. Which meant she had to go next door, to the drug store to use the phone.

Upon seeing her, the elderly proprietor nearly dropped his dentures. "My God! It's you! We thought you were dead!"

"Join the club, Mr. Handel. I suspect you haven't watched the news in the past couple of days. We were finally rescued from the island where the plane went down."

"I hope you're going to sue that airline to its last rivet," he declared.

"No, but I'm going to sue my husband for ripping me off while I was gone," she informed him. "First, however, I've got to see about getting my utilities restored. I guess they figured I wouldn't need a phone where I was going."

Mr. Handel reached under the counter and produced the store phone and the directory. "Here, use this instead of the pay phone."

Kelly sat Sydney on the counter, while she looked up the numbers.

"Who's this little one?" Mr. Handel inquired, clucking Sydney under the chin.

"We call her Sydney. She's from Australia. Her parents died in the crash, and we've sort of adopted her. If her family can't be found or don't want her, I intend to adopt her for real."

Mr. Handel scooped Syd off the counter. "I'll watch her while you make your calls," he volunteered. "Bet she'd like a lollypop, wouldn't you, Sydney?"

Getting her utilities reinstated was a bit tricky. The fellow at the phone company had seen the news on TV, which was the only reason he promised to send someone out within the hour to restore service. After a few minutes of impatient debate, the lady at the water department decided to give Kelly the benefit of the doubt. But the woman who answered at the electric company was a different kettle of fish altogether. She adamantly insisted, despite Kelly's arguments to the contrary, that Ms. Kennedy was dead.

"I am not dead," Kelly contended. "I wouldn't be speaking to you if I were, at least not over the phone."

"I'm sorry, but our records show . . ."

"Listen up, dearie. I am not dead, deceased, or decaying, and I want my electricity turned back on!"

"That's quite impossible, Miss . . ."

"Kennedy!" Kelly supplied in a shout. "Kelly Maura Kennedy!"

"As I was saying," the woman went on in her irritatingly polite way, "it's quite impossible to reinstate that service and that particular account. Now, if you'd care to come up to the office, pay the connection fee, and initiate a new account, we'd be happy to assist you."

"I don't have the time, or the patience for this tripe!" Kelly growled. "I'm telling you, I had an account with you, I always paid my bill on time, and I want my power back. Now!"

"Well, if you really are Miss Kennedy, and you could provide some form of proof, I suppose we might be able to arrange something," the woman submitted doubtfully. "But I really doubt we could do anything about your situation until tomorrow or the next day."

"And what am I supposed to do in the meantime? Baste myself in butter and broil in a sweltering apartment? Moreover, I have a two-year-old living with me, and if she succumbs to heatstroke you'll truly think I'm the devil's dearest daughter. I'll come after you with a pitchfork!"

"Now, there's no reason to be nasty. Obviously, you are overwrought."

"Lady, you don't know the half of it. I'm tired of this hassle. Put your supervisor on the line."

Kelly was on hold for so long, she could have walked to the office and gotten faster results. Finally, just when she was about to give up, the supervisor answered and Kelly went through the whole spiel again.

"All right," the lady relented. "We'll send a man out, but this had better not be some hoax. There are laws against that, you know. And you'd better have proper identification, as well as someone to vouch for you."

Kelly was tempted to ask if the President of the United

States would suffice, but she thought better of it. Instead, she asked Mr. Handel to be her witness, and he readily agreed.

"My goodness!" he exclaimed. "This is a pretty pickle, isn't it?"

Kelly sighed. "This is just the tip of the iceberg, Mr. Handel. I have yet to haggle with the bank, my future ex-husband, the insurance companies, the realty company that's listing my salons, and only God knows who else. It's going to be a long, long week or more."

"I've got water, electricity, and phone service back, at least," Kelly related to Zach that night. "My car is another story. Agent Anderson—that's what the guy from the Attorney General's office is called—located it for me in an impound lot, stripped to the frame. Legally, they were supposed to wait three months before ransacking it for parts, so now they have to either pay me the money or replace my car with one of equal value. They're providing me with a free loaner in the meantime. They dropped it off earlier this evening. Boy, Zach, it sure makes a difference when you've got someone as powerful as the President and his cohorts behind you. They can really grease those skids!"

Zach laughed appreciatively. "I suppose you didn't have time to get anything started, like the divorce."

"Hey! We don't mess around! Anderson and I walked into the courthouse half an hour before closing time, and once they found out who he was, those people bent over backwards to appease us. My original divorce petition has now been reinstated, and scheduled on the court docket for a mere three weeks from today," she informed him in a pleased-as-punch tone. "Not only that, Anderson got an injunction to stop the sale of the salons, pending further investigation."

"Wow! I'm impressed! Did you manage to make an appointment with an obstetrician, by any chance?"

"No, but I'll do that first thing tomorrow."

"Don't forget," he told her. "Do you want me to call you in the morning to remind you?"

"No, I've written myself a note. But you can call me anyway, if you want. I already miss you like crazy."

"I miss you more," he contended. "I miss the sight and feel of you, the sound of your voice whispering in my ear. Hell, I even miss the smell of you, all warm and fuzzy and uniquely you."

"Would it help if I sent you a bottle of my favorite perfume?"

"It wouldn't be the same, love. Now, if you sent me a pair of your panties, that might do the trick."

"Lord, Zach! I hope my phone line isn't tapped. They'll think you're a pervert."

"A horny one," he supplied. "What are you wearing? That sexy nightie you bought in Hawaii?"

Kelly laughed and groaned at the same time. "Actually, I'm in my rattiest terry bathrobe. I'd just stepped out of the shower when you called."

"Oh, God! It's worse than I thought," he rasped. "You're all soft and clean, and scented like soap and shampoo. And totally naked under that raggy robe, aren't you?"

"As the day I was born," she confessed softly. "And aching, Zach. Aching for you."

"We've got to stop this," he declared. "I'm as hard as a brick. I'll never get to sleep tonight, or if I do manage it, I'll probably have the first wet dream I've had since puberty."

"See you in the funny papers, darling," she crooned.

"I'll be the one dressed as Daisy Mae. Talk to you tomorrow. Meanwhile, don't do anything I wouldn't do."

"What's that supposed to mean?"

"Do the expressions 'Get a grip' or 'take yourself in hand' give you a clue? Good night, love."

"The obstetrician's office had a cancellation, and they got me in right away. He says everything is fine, and he gave me some pre-natal vitamins. The baby is due sometime in April."

"Did he do one of those ultra-sound things?"

"It's too soon yet. Why? You hoping this one will have a little something extra, like three legs, maybe?"

Zach laughed. "Yeah, but as long as it and you are both healthy, that's all that matters."

"Well, just for the record, I'm hoping it's a boy, too. We've already got Syd and Becky. You need another male around, so you won't feel so outnumbered."

"How's Syd doing?"

"Fine, but I think she misses you as much as I do. On the contrary, I imagine Becky's delighted not to have to share you with us."

"She'll come around. Your dad really got her going with those Irish tales of his."

"Oh, hang on a minute, Zach. There's another call coming in. It might be Anderson with an update."

A few seconds later, Kelly returned to say, "Can I call you back, darling? Brad's on the other line, sounding frantic as all heck. Evidently Agent Anderson has him in a tizzy, and I'm dying to hear all the grizzly details."

"Can't you just find out from Anderson?" Zach suggested irritably. "I don't like you having any more contact with Brad than necessary. The guy's too damned good-looking to suit me, and I suppose when he wants to exhibit it, he must have a smarmy kind of charm, or you'd never have married him.''

"Don't worry. That Texas honey-and-sugar routine wore thin a long time ago. Listen, I'll call you as soon as Brad and I hang up. Trust me. I love you.''

Chapter 29

"Call off your dogs, Kelly," Brad demanded.

"Whatever are you talking about?" she asked with feigned innocence.

"You know damned good and well! That Anderson guy from the Attorney General's office is making a lot of waves, and some of my friends don't appreciate the way the boat's rocking. In fact, we're all practically up in arms."

"As in toting guns, or up to your armpits in your own stink?" she inquired with a chuckle.

"Damn it, Kelly. It's not funny. He's talking about calling in the IRS for an extensive audit, and investigating court cases dating back five years or more. He's also implied that I could even be disbarred!"

"My! Sounds as if he's really got you sweating. Not that you don't deserve it, you and your little clique of bloodsucking leeches."

"Call him off, Kelly. I mean it. Before this goes too far."

"Gee, Brad, I don't know if that's in my power, even if

I were so generously inclined. Seems Anderson knows a rat when he smells one, good government terrier that he is. He might not want to abandon the scent now, just when he's got you by the shorts."

"Look, I'll make a deal with you. I'll give you back all the money from your bank accounts, if you tell Anderson to back off."

"Oh, you'll have to do better than that, Brad. Much better. Like nixing that power of attorney thing, which probably isn't worth the paper it's printed on to begin with, since I can only recall signing something like that once, when I was going out of town, and it was only supposed to be a temporary proviso. I'll bet Anderson can easily prove that you have taken advantage of an expired document that no longer has any legal basis. Which also means your realty deal is as fraudulent as you are. For that alone, you could be sitting right alongside some of your clients, maybe even in the same cell."

"Okay, I'll relinquish power of attorney," he agreed testily. "Will that satisfy you?"

"Not by a long shot," she replied nastily. "I want it in writing, along with the original paperwork and any and all duplicates thereof. The same goes for the copies of my will, those naming you as benefactor and executor. Which reminds me, my new lawyer is drawing up my revised will as we speak. He already has all the particulars, and Anderson as my witness—just in case you're entertaining any stray and stupid thoughts of bumping me off for my assets."

"For God's sake, Kell. I know you're not thrilled with me right now, but I'm not a murderer."

"Just a thief and a first-class cad?" she rebutted cattily. "Well, I just thought I'd warn you, on the off chance you'd decided to branch out into more dastardly territory."

"Anything else you'd like, sugar?" he snarled. "Like my balls for Christmas ornaments, maybe?"

"Now, there's a cheery notion, but they're really sort of small," she taunted. "There is one more thing that comes to mind immediately. If you haven't received notification yet, our divorce hearing is scheduled for three weeks from today. I expect it to go through uncontested. No muss, no fuss, no last minute snarls or snafus."

"Giving you what?" he demanded to know. "Everything but my underwear?"

"Unfortunately, I've never been as greedy as you. I'm only asking for my fair share. I think you'll find the split quite equitable, all things considered. Moreover, agreeing without a fight will leave you more time and money to spend on other matters, like defending yourself against any charges Anderson might still want to press."

"All right, you've got your blasted divorce!" he snapped back. "But you will speak to Anderson on my behalf, won't you? Get him to pull his teeth out of my backside?"

"Oh, what I'd give for a picture of that!" she chortled. "It's got to be a Kodak moment!" Then she relented. "I'll talk to him, but I can't promise how much good it will do. Oh, by the way, Brad. This entire conversation has been recorded," she fibbed. "I have all concessions on tape, in your own words and very distinctive voice, so don't try to renege on anything you've agreed to tonight. If you do, I'll sic Anderson on you like a fox on a field mouse."

"Hell, Kelly, he's already sniffin' everything but my crotch!" Brad claimed disgustedly.

"When I have all the documentation in my hot little hands—signed, sealed, and delivered, not to mention inspected with due care by my attorney—I'll see about getting Anderson to ease up some. But not a moment sooner, mind you. I trust you about as much as I would a riled rattlesnake. And don't call me again, or I'll have you charged with harassment."

* * *

At eleven o'clock the next morning, all the documents she'd requested arrived at Kelly's apartment by overnight delivery. She could only assume Brad had rushed down to his office the minute they'd hung up and hurriedly assembled the pertinent paperwork. There was even a signed declaration of his intent not to contest the divorce, and a certified check for the exact amount he'd taken from her bank accounts, correct to the penny.

When Agent Anderson learned this, he grinned like a kid with a new bike. "Man, I'm better than I thought! I must have really put the fear of God into him!"

"Or the fear of Uncle Sam. Actually, I think Brad would be less intimidated by God," Kelly said. "Does this mean we can void the real estate contract? I'm anxious to get my salons up and running again."

Anderson perused the text of the paper she'd signed two years prior, giving Brad power of attorney. "This wouldn't hold water, let alone stand up in court," he concluded. "I'm going to fax a sternly worded message to that effect to that fool realtor, and unless I miss my guess, both parties will shy away from a law suit. Most likely, your imminent buyer will have a sudden decline of interest in the property. Just give me a few more days to stir the cauldron, and you should be back in business."

"What about Brad, now that he's given me most of what I want?" Kelly inquired.

"From the look of things, I've only scratched the surface on his corrupt conduct, but as a favor to you on behalf of myself and the President, I'll cool my heels until after your divorce is final. Then I'm going after that devious son-of-a-gun and his crooked cronies with all the fervor of a missionary in pursuit of a potential convert. They're the type that give decent lawyers a bad rap, and there's nothing that makes me madder.''

Four days later, Kelly was in possession of a new set of credit cards, new bank accounts, a new will, and a van-load of used baby paraphernalia. She and her father were unloading the last of the boxes, when the phone rang. From the upstairs window, Eileen called down, "Kelly, Zach's on the phone.''

"In the middle of the day? Gosh, I hope nothing's wrong," Kelly told her father.

She ran up the steps, taking two at a time, and barely had breath left to wheeze, "Zach? Is everything okay?''

"Kelly? You don't sound like yourself.''

"I was downstairs, helping to unload all the baby equipment Mom and Dad brought. I'm just a little winded at the moment. So, what's going on?''

"I called to tell you that all the tests are back and the doctors want to do Dad's heart bypass right away. They've scheduled the surgery for eight o'clock tomorrow morning.''

"So soon? My goodness, Zach! I'll bet you're all just about frantic. How does your father feel about this mad rush?''

"He's as nervous as a long-tailed cat in a room full of rocking chairs. Still, it's best this way, since it doesn't give him any time to change his mind.''

"And your mother? How is she doing?''

"About the same, but she's glad it's all going to be over soon. She's just worried that something might go wrong in the operating room.''

"What about you? How are you holding up, darling?''

"Other than feeling like I've been the main course for a fleet of vampires, I'm doing fairly well. With all the pinpricks in my arm, I look like a junkie. How soon can you get here?''

Kelly could tell from the sound of his voice and the way he was running his sentences together that Zach was a bundle of raw nerves. He really needed her support now, in the worst way.

"Oh, Zach! I wish you could have given me a little more forewarning. It's got to be over fifteen hundred miles. Even if I can average sixty or sixty-five miles per hour, it's going to take me a whole day to get there, and that's driving straight through. What's more, I'm still using the loaner car, and I'm not sure it would hold up under a trip of that length.''

"Fly," he directed succinctly. "I never expected you to drive the distance."

Kelly groaned. "Zach, I was nearly catatonic just getting from Hawaii to Phoenix. I don't want to fly now any more than I did then. Maybe I can take the train. Is Amtrak still running in your neck of the woods?''

"It would still take too long," Zach pointed out. "And you'd be beat by the time you arrived. I'm telling you, Kelly, flying is your best option. And don't think I don't sympathize with you, sweetheart. I'm not comfortable on a plane, either. I suppose I won't be for some time to come, but you know the old adage about getting back on the horse after it's thrown you. There's got to be some truth to it.''

"I suppose there is, but it's a lot shorter distance to the ground from the back of a horse." Kelly sighed. She'd promised Zach she would be there for him during the operation, and she couldn't go back on that pledge now. "Okay. Maybe if I take a handful of Valium, I won't even know I'm on the damned plane!''

Zach came undone. "Don't you dare do anything of the sort! My God, Kelly! You're pregnant! You're not even supposed to take a cold capsule without consulting your doctor first, let alone a potent drug like that!''

"Whoa, Nellie!'' she exclaimed. "Calm down! I'm aware of all the do's and don't's. I've never taken Valium in my life, and I don't intend to start now, so get off your high horse, cowboy. I was just spouting off, trying to convince myself that I can get through another flight.''

"Sheesh! Don't scare me like that, woman!'' he declared. "They'll have me on the operating table next to Dad.''

"You do have a talent for the dramatic, Zach,'' she wise-cracked. "Maybe you should consider a career in the theater. I'm sure Alita could give you a few good contacts.''

He ignored that and asked tersely, "Are you coming or not?''

"I'll be there. I'll call the airline right away and book the first possible flight, though they might have to put me in a straight jacket to get me aboard.''

"I've already done that, and reserved your seat. Your plane leaves at eight o'clock this evening, with an estimated time of arrival in Seattle at ten-fifteen.'' He gave her the name of the airline and the flight number. "You can pick your ticket up at the counter when you check in your luggage.''

"What about Sydney?'' she inquired.

"Nuts! I forgot to reserve a separate seat for her, but since she's only two she should be able to fly for free and sit on your lap if necessary.''

"I have a better idea. I'll see if Mom and Dad can stay for a couple of days, or just Mom, perhaps. We'd have to hire a babysitter in Seattle anyway, if we're going to be spending so much time at the hospital.''

Zach was disappointed. "I was looking forward to seeing the little munchkin, but I suppose you're right. Listen, I've got to go now, but I'll meet you at the airport tonight.''

"Did you make a reservation for me at a convenient hotel?"

"Hell, no! You're staying with me, at my house. With me and Becky."

Kelly's eyebrows rose. "I bet Becky's going to be ecstatic to hear this! Did you at least make up the guest room? I'm sure she's not going to want me sharing a bed with you, especially in her mother's house."

"This isn't the same house I owned when Rachel was alive. The memories were just too much for Becky and me to take, so I sold it and bought another one. Also, in case you're wondering, I even bought a new bedroom suite, too. You don't have to worry about treading on hallowed ground, Kelly."

Her grateful smile carried over to her voice. "Thanks, Zach," she murmured. "I didn't want to come right out and ask, but I was wondering. Becky's still going to have a fit, though."

"She'll get over it, and you're not staying in the guest room, either. You're going to be snuggled next to me, right where you belong. Now, have I allayed all of your major concerns?"

"Yes, but I have a minor one left. Do you have any dental floss in your bathroom cabinet, or should I pack my own?"

Zach was waiting just inside the gate, as impatient as a child waiting for recess. She walked straight into his open arms, immediately overwhelmed by the familiar feel of him.

"It seems like a year since I last held you," he breathed. "This has been the longest week of my life, but I could swear you've grown even more beautiful."

"You're as full of malarkey as my Dad," she teased. "If I look as haggard as I feel, I must resemble someone who's been pulled backward through a knothole, one leg at a time.''

"Was the flight that bad?" he inquired sympathetically.

"The flight itself was very smooth," she allowed. "All the turbulence was in my stomach and the spot where my heart is supposed to be when it's not lodged in my throat."

He curled his arm around her shoulders, offering a comforting hug. "Come on, let's get you home."

"Where's Becky?" Kelly asked.

"I dropped her off at Beth's. She's going to spend the night with them."

"Becky's idea, or yours?"

"Becky's, and Beth's, but when I thought about having you all to myself, I was all for it."

Once they'd collected his car and headed away from the airport, Zach said, "By the way, I got that assayer's report on those pieces of gold. I sent David in with them, rather than going myself, since my ugly mug has been in the news so much recently."

"And?"

He chanced a glance at her, his teeth flashing in a wide grin. "The samples show a very high, very pure gold content. Now, if we can just negotiate a price for the island, within the realm of reason, and get full mineral rights, we'll be set."

"Have you spoken to anyone, other than the President, about purchasing the island?" she asked.

"Yes, but we've barely scratched the surface. Other matters have taken precedence, like Dad's operation and my engineering business. Pete has tried to keep things running, and has done a pretty good job of it, but we did lose that Las Vegas hotel project, which hurts our overall annual income."

"Leah's husband works for you?"

"Yes. That's how Pete and Leah first became acquainted."

"What does David do?"

"He and Beth are both CPAs, like Dad. They all work together in Dad's office, which is attached to the house. It's all very convenient for everyone, particularly since Mom acts as their receptionist/secretary. When Gabe and Myra were little, Beth and Mom could keep an eye on them and work, too. And Mom can get supper started, or throw in a load of laundry whenever she gets a free minute. Of course, those minutes are awfully hard to come by, around income tax time."

Until Zach cut the motor, Kelly hadn't been aware that they'd pulled into a parking lot at a 24-hour food mart. "I used the last of the coffee this morning and need to pick up a couple of other things real quick. I hope you don't mind, but there wasn't time to do it earlier."

"That's okay. I know how it goes. I've been running my tail off for the past week, practically meeting myself coming and going," she told him.

He grinned at her again. "I hope not. I'm real partial to that cute little tail of yours." He unbuckled his seat belt. "Come on in with me. You can help me pick out a get-well card for Dad."

By the time they'd wound their way through the aisles, they checked out half a cart full of groceries, much of it munchies. "Three varieties of snack chips and two kinds of cookies?" Kelly observed, her brows rising. "My obstetrician would have a cow, or warn me that I'm going to."

"Yes, but we got ice cream to go with them, and that constitutes milk, doesn't it?" Zach countered. He picked up the plastic sacks and followed Kelly toward the exit.

Just inside the doors, he stopped, plucking at her sleeve to get her attention. "Look at this!" he exclaimed in delight. "Talk about one-stop shopping! We can even get your engagement ring, right here!"

Kelly looked at the vending machine, full of cheap plastic rings, and had to laugh. Zach had already set the grocery bags down and was fishing through his change for two quarters. With a crank of his wrist, the ring plopped into the dispenser.

Though Zach had a moment of trouble extracting it, he got it unwedged and tossed the bulbous plastic case at her. "Here you go, darling. You lucked out and got one with a pretty green stone to match your eyes."

She fumbled the catch, almost dropping it. "Golly, Zach, you shouldn't have. You're such an extravagant devil!"

"Open it up. Let's see if it fits."

Kelly chuckled. "Of course it will, you nut! These things have those spaced bands, open at the bottom, to give them more flexibility."

"So? Take it out and put it on. I want to see how it looks on your finger."

"You're a certified screwball, Zach Goldstein," she alleged. She eyed the ring through the clear plastic container. "Gee, you're right. It is rather pretty. Did you notice, it's even faceted to make it look more like a real emerald?"

She popped the clear plastic case in half, and the ring fell into her palm. That's when Kelly's eyes widened in disbelief. She hefted it, judging the weight. Then, as if afraid to believe her own senses, she picked it up by the band. Instead of gold-painted plastic, her fingers touched metal—smooth shiny gold, a solid, unbroken band of it. The oval gem winked at her, as did the heart-shaped jewels set into the band on either side of it. Her heart thundering, she held it up for closer inspection.

Her voice quavering, she declared softly, "Holy Moses, Zach! Am I hallucinating, or is this thing real? This looks like a genuine emerald, and I could swear the diamonds are, too.''

"They'd better be,'' Zach announced with a gruff laugh. "Uncle Saul charged me enough for them, though he did claim he gave me the usual family discount. Of course, it was a rush order, and he took particular care to make it look like the actual 'fake' article. See? He even made those little grooves in the band, and curved the bottom of it so it looks like two pieces butted together.''

Kelly turned to him with happy tears making her eyes sparkle brighter than the emerald. "Oh, Zach! This is so special! So wonderfully incredible!'' She handed the ring to him and held out her hand. "Put it on for me. Please.''

He slipped the ring onto her finger, his eyes glowing with adoration. "A perfect fit. A good omen.''

Kelly nodded. "How did you know my ring size? Or was it just a great guess?''

Zach laughed. "No, I cheated. I measured your finger with a piece of string one night while you were sleeping.''

Kelly gazed at the ring in awe. "I still can't believe it. You actually had this ring created expressly for me.''

"Do you like it?'' he asked hesitantly. "It was somewhat of a challenge to avoid that gaudy look you said you dislike and still get it to resemble a half-dollar vending machine ring.''

"I love it,'' she claimed. "I'd love it if it really was made of colored glass and plastic. But most of all, I love you, for all the special pains you took to have it made for me—and just because you're you, the most marvelous, caring, sensitive man in the world.''

There, blocking half the exit aisle, and standing in front of a huge window where half of Seattle could watch, they shared a passionate kiss that threatened to steam the ads off the plate-glass. "Let's go home, before we get arrested for indecent behavior," Zach rasped when he could finally tear his lips from hers.

As he picked up the grocery sacks, Kelly thought to ask, "Did we really need any of that stuff, including the coffee?"

"Not a single item," he admitted. "I just wanted to get you in here to that machine."

"And I suppose you had my ring tucked in your pocket all the while," she surmised. "So, where's the one the machine spit out?"

"Still in the dispenser, of course."

Kelly reached down, flipped the metal flap, and retrieved the plastic ring. "A memento," she explained. "I'm one of those sentimental females who keeps flowers pressed between book pages, and old high school programs. I even have the first tooth I lost, and a lock of my baby hair."

Zach shook his head in amazement. "Does that mean if I die before you do, you'll have me stuffed by some taxidermist and set me in a corner?"

She gave him a glorious, impish smile. "Now, there's a novel idea. Then, I'd have you with me always, but I suppose I'd have to dust you once in a while. I hope you're not allergic to Endust."

Chapter 30

It was a long, worrisome day. Kelly couldn't imagine hell could be worse than this—cooped up for hours in a drab, airless waiting room supplied with lumpy plastic furniture, praying for the best and anticipating the worst. The operation lasted for six hours, during which Zach paced back and forth until Kelly thought he'd wear a hole through the flooring. Sarah prayed, sighed, wept, and then went through the whole routine over and over again. Beth and Leah, worried stiff themselves, tried to comfort their mother, while Dave and Pete attempted to comfort them.

Though feeling like an intruder, Kelly stayed close, for approximately every fifth lap Zach cease pacing long enough to grab her hand for a quick squeeze, or to pat her shoulder, or just brush his fingers over the top of her head. This small contact, however fleeting, seemed to soothe him. Kelly noticed, even if Zach was unaware of it, that every time he stopped to touch her, Becky would glare at the two of them. Bored, but equally anxious about their grandfather, Becky, Myra, and Gabe were biding the time by playing cards in a corner of the room.

Finally, around eleven o'clock, Kelly offered to escort the kids down to the cafeteria and buy them some lunch. Even if they didn't need nourishment, she needed something in her stomach to counter the stale donuts, scalded coffee, and two cans of soda pop she'd consumed. Zach and the other adults declined her offer to bring sandwiches back. They were running on raw nerves and caffeine overload by now.

Gabe and Myra were quiet, but very polite, and thanked Kelly for buying them the meal. Becky was sullen throughout, and though she understood the girl's animosity, Kelly's patience was wearing thin. She had to bite her tongue to keep from giving the child a piece of her mind, frazzled as it was. Afterward, Kelly took the children into the gift shop and suggested they choose a get-well present for their grandfather, warning them that he probably wouldn't be allowed real flowers in his room for a couple of days. They selected a small ceramic duck, which would double as a paperweight for Ike's office desk. When Kelly asked if they would like to buy a couple of comic books for themselves, Beth's youngsters leapt at the chance.

Becky bridled. "I'm not in a funny mood," she sniped at Kelly. "I'm worried about Grandpa, even if you're not. Of course, you're not really part of our family, and you never will be, even if you do marry Dad."

Her cousins stood by silently, looking decidedly chagrined by Becky's rude behavior.

"Well, excuse me!" Kelly snapped back. "I merely thought it would give you something else to do to pass the time while we're waiting. Perhaps if you search the shelves, you can find something morbid to read, to match your mood."

"Get a crossword puzzle book, Beck," Myra suggested

timidly, trying to play peacemaker. "That's not funny, and Gabe and I can help you work them."

"If you want one, get it yourself," Becky retorted. "I don't want anything, especially if she's paying for it."

"You know, Becky," Kelly commented, softening her words with a strained smile. "For a cute kid, you certainly can be a snot. My advice to you would be to wise up real fast, pumpkin, and stop antagonizing the lady who is going to be your stepmother in a few short weeks. I'm not your enemy, but we're not going to be friends either, until you get that chip off your shoulder."

It was two hours more before the surgeon finally arrived to say, "The surgery went well. Ike is in the recovery room now, and should be transferred to intensive care in another couple of hours. You can see him then, one at a time, and only for a total of ten minutes every hour, however you want to divide the time between you. In a day or so, he'll be moved to a private room, and you can visit for longer periods, but right now he needs his rest."

"Is he going to be all right?" Sarah worried.

"He'll be up and better than new before you know it," the doctor assured her. "But he's going to have to take better care of himself from here on out. That means getting out of the office for some exercise each day, revising his diet, and losing those few extra pounds he's been carrying. See he does that, and you'll have him around for another twenty or thirty years, running circles around you."

They stayed until Zach and Becky both got a turn to see Ike. Then, knowing Sarah would want more time with him, and that they wouldn't have another opportunity until morning, Zach proposed that they leave. He kissed his mother, who had arranged to stay through the night, told her to call if there was any change in Ike's condition or if she just needed to talk, and ushered Becky and Kelly out

"What do you say about getting a pizza on the way home?" Zach suggested.

When the other two agreed, he asked Kelly, "What do you like on yours?"

"Just about anything but anchovies."

"Pepperoni? Olives? Green peppers? Mushrooms?"

Kelly nodded. "Sounds fine to me."

"I don't like mushrooms," Becky piped up petulantly from the back seat. "Neither do you, Dad."

Kelly was too tired to argue. "Leave the mushrooms off, Zach."

"No. If you want them, that's what we'll get. Becky and I can pick them off and give our share to you."

"I don't want olives either," Becky said, just to make things more difficult. "Or green peppers."

Zach pulled to the side of the street, stopping the car in a No Parking zone. He turned in his seat to face his daughter, noting the smirk on her face.

"Look, little lady. You've eaten your pizza that way since you were old enough to chew it, so don't give me any more guff, or I'm going to paddle your butt. It's pizza with olives and peppers, or you can make yourself a blasted peanut butter sandwich and a bowl of cereal for supper. It's your choice."

Later, Becky made a big production out of stripping the extras off of her pizza, but she didn't say anything more until it was time for her to go to bed. "Do I have to go to school tomorrow?" she whined. "I want to go back to the hospital and see Grandpa again."

"I'll take you after school," Zach told her. "You've missed enough class as it is, and your grades won't stand much more. Which reminds me, did you get your homework done?"

"Most of it."

"Then what were you doing watching television?" Zach

demanded, with an exasperated sigh. He consulted his watch. "I'll give you an extra half an hour to finish it. Bring it to me when it's done, and I'll check it for you."

"I don't know if I can get it done by then," Becky hedged. "It's English, and it's real hard. We're diagraming sentences, and I missed some of it while we were in Hawaii."

Zach grimaced. "I'd be happier if it was algebra. Then I could help explain it to you."

"I'd be glad to help you, Becky," Kelly offered, ignoring the little voice that told her to stay out of this. "English was my best subject."

Becky's nose tilted into the air, in as fair an imitation of Alita as Kelly had seen. "Never mind, I'd rather do it myself."

Kelly shrugged. "Okay, kiddo. It's no skin off my back, either way."

When Becky was finally in bed, Zach again apologized for his daughter's belligerence. "This is not the way I pictured it. I was hoping she'd be thrilled with the idea of having a mother again, and that we'd all be one happy family."

Kelly gave a rueful chuckle. "Dream on, Zach, and stop watching all those old reruns of 'Leave it to Beaver.' They're giving you delusions. The modern family doesn't operate that way, and if you're expecting June Cleaver's clone to greet you at the door every evening, you're in for a rather rude awakening, love."

"Boy, you really know how to burst a guy's bubble," he grumbled with a grin.

"You want bubbles?" she inquired with an arch look. She took his hand and pulled him off the couch. "You got 'em, sweetcheeks. I've been sitting here for the last ten minutes, yearning for a long soak in a tub overflowing with the stuff.''

"Sorry," Zach said with an apologetic shake of his head. "I'm fresh out of bubblebath."

"I'm not," she countered smugly, tugging him toward the master bathroom. "You should know by now that when I pack, I try to allow for every possibility. Come on, darling, we're going to pop a whole tub full of bubbles, and I can promise you won't regret the disappearance of a single one."

Kelly and Zach found time the following day to make a jaunt to Uncle Saul's jewelry store, where Kelly chose a wedding band to go with her engagement ring, and one to match for Zach. They also went to the courthouse and applied for their marriage license, after deciding it would be easier for Kelly and her family to go to Washington for the wedding than for Zach's whole tribe to head south. Additionally, Ike's operation and recuperation were determining factors in choosing the location. Naturally, the clerk specified that the license would be held in reserve until Kelly could produce documented proof that her divorce from Brad was finalized.

Kelly flew home to Phoenix the next morning. Both she and Zach, though apart, had much to do in the few weeks until the wedding, which was tentatively scheduled for mid-October. Zach would continue negotiations to buy the island, as well as conduct his usual business affairs. Kelly had to prepare for her wedding, pack for the move to Seattle, and resolve issues surrounding the reopening of the salons.

Zach surprised her by flying into Phoenix on the last Friday of September. He arrived bearing a huge bouquet of red roses.

"What in the world?" Kelly was stupefied.

Zach grinned at her over the top of the flowers. "Happy birthday, sweetheart!"

"Oh, my gosh! I'd all but forgotten about it!" she confessed. "Everything's been so hectic. How did you know?"

"I remembered you saying you'd turn twenty-eight in September, and I asked your mother the date. I was relieved to learn I hadn't missed it."

Sydney was tickled pink at seeing Zach again, and the feeling was mutual. That evening, Zach took them both out to dinner, where an octet of waiters and waitresses presented Kelly with a birthday cake and sang "Happy Birthday" to her before an entire restaurant crowded with diners, utterly embarrassing her.

"Darn you, Zach Goldstein! You just wait till your birthday rolls around! You're going to be in for it, then, buster," she promised.

Later, after Sydney had been tucked in for the night, Zach talked Kelly into modeling some the more exotic lingerie items she carried in her boutiques. He was particularly intrigued with one black teddy trimmed in white lace, with garters and fishnet hose. It was part of a set that included lace wrist-cuffs, a frilly choker collar, a little apron, and a perky maid's cap.

"Sweetheart," he told her, wearing an expression of awe and anticipation, "you are the answer to a man's most erotic dreams."

Kelly struck a provocative pose. "Are you ready to be served, sir?"

Zach glanced down at his jockey shorts, and the prominent bulge within. "That, and then some."

To his befuddlement, she turned to exit the bedroom. "Wait a minute. Where are you going?"

"To fetch the whipped cream, of course," she called back saucily. "No dessert is quite complete without it."

* * *

They were on their second round of love play, with Zach spritzing whipped cream over Kelly's mostly nude body and licking it off—she was still wearing the hose and accessories, though the teddy had long since hit the floor—when a tiny voice inquired from the side of the bed, "Whatcha doin'?"

Zach let out a startled yell and nearly leapt to the ceiling at the unexpected intrusion. Only Kelly's hands, clutching his shoulders, kept him from becoming airborne. "Uh, well . . . uh . . ." he stammered, while Kelly howled with laughter.

"We're playing, sweet pea," Kelly finally managed to say. "What are you doing out of bed? You're supposed to be sleeping."

"Gotta go potty," Syd informed them with childish nonchalance. "Can I play, too?" she asked innocently, propping her chin on edge of the mattress.

By now, Zach had snatched the sheet over himself and Kelly. "No, this is a grown-up game, dumplin'. Do you need some help, or can you go to the bathroom by yourself?"

"I go myself," the toddler said.

"And climb right back into your bed when you're done," Kelly instructed, her words vibrating with lingering amusement. She dabbed a dot of whipped cream on Sydney's nose, making her grin. "Go on now, before you wet your jammies."

Sydney trotted obediently out of the room, and Zach collapsed atop Kelly with a martyred moan. Kelly dissolved in riotous giggles, smothering the sound by pressing her face into Zach's neck.

"Oh! Oh, my goodness!" she gasped between chortles. "I thought we were going to peel you off the ceiling fan!"

"Before or after you revived me?" he queried wryly. "I

nearly went into shock!'' He chuckled, adding, "For as noisy as that child usually is, she can sure sneak up on you when you least expect it. I wonder how long she was watching us?''

"Not for long, I don't imagine, or she'd have had a lot more questions.''

"The ones she had were sufficient to deflate my ardor on the spot,'' Zach admitted ruefully.

Kelly laughed. "Yeah, I noticed that.'' She flung back the sheet, and climbed out of bed. "I guess this sort of thing is to be expected when you have children. The trick, they say, is to remain calm.'' She grabbed her terry robe off the back of the closet door. "Didn't Becky ever walk in on you and Rachel at an inappropriate moment?''

"No, thank God. As for remaining calm, I'm not sure that's possible, when they creep up on you from out of nowhere like that. And to prevent such an occurrence in the future, I'm going to install a lock on our bedroom door.''

Kelly headed out of the room, and Zach called after her, "Where are you off to now?''

"To make sure Sydney got back to bed all right and to take a quick shower.'' She popped her head back inside the bedroom and gave him a taunting grin. "Why? Were you hoping I'd return with some magic potion to restore your flagging . . . ego?''

Zach called from Seattle a few days later. "How is our little Peeping Sydney?''

"As inquisitive and ornery as ever,'' Kelly told him. "She's determined to unload all the boxes I've already packed. I finally had to go to the hardware and buy some heavy-duty duct tape.''

Zach laughed. "For her or the carton?''

"For the boxes, mostly, but thanks for the idea."

"I've dickered the price down a bit on the island, but it's still too much." He named a sum that made Kelly's eyebrows rise several inches. Even the down payment he quoted was staggering.

"What are you going to do?" she asked.

"Try to get them to lower the price, of course, but they're pretty firm about it, so they won't reduce it by much, if at all. On the bright side, they have agreed to include mineral rights, and give us a reduced tax rate for the first ten years, but I've still got to come up with some ready cash. I can't sell my business, or we won't have the equipment we'll need to build on the island or to do any mining, which is going to cost a pretty penny as it is, not to mention that I would no longer have a source of income."

"We'd have mine," she reminded him. "I've got the Australian club up and running again, and I'm close to doing the same with the other two."

Zach nixed that proposal. "I'm not going to sponge off my wife, like some damned gigolo," he stated adamantly.

"What if you sold your house and moved in with me?" she suggested.

"Your apartment only has two bedrooms," he pointed out. "What would we do with Becky?"

"The couch makes into a bed, or she could bunk in with Syd. It would be rough, but we could make do for a while. At least we wouldn't have to pay rent someplace, and we'd be down to one set of utilities."

"And Becky would have to change schools in the middle of the year. No, there's got to be another solution."

"Okay, you think about it, and so will I. In the meantime, keep the negotiations open," she said. Then, "I found my wedding dress. It's perfect. Very simple and just right for a second marriage."

"I can't wait to see you in it," he declared. "By the way,

everything's arranged on this end. Judge Simon is going to perform the ceremony, and we've rented the lodge at the lake. If the weather cooperates, we can exchange vows outdoors, under the gazebo, which would please Mom to no end. To her way of thinking, the gazebo would almost double for a *huppah*."

"A what?"

"The canopy that symbolizes the home in the traditional Jewish wedding," Zach explained. "She's determined that some of our rites and rituals will be included, even if it is basically a civil ceremony. She even wants us to break the wine glass at the end."

"Signifying what?" Kelly questioned.

"The destruction of Jerusalem and the dispersion of our people."

"In that case, I don't see why we can't," Kelly conceded. Then she admitted with some chagrin, "I always thought it symbolized the end of the bride's virginity, and we both know mine has been nonexistent for years—in which case breaking the glass would have been too sacrilegious for my peace of mind. It's enough that we've gone from a simple exchange in the judge's chambers to having bride's maids and a reception afterward."

"Is Alita still going to be able to stand up with you as your mind of honor?" Zach inquired. Gavin had already arranged leave in order to be Zach's best man.

"Yes, but Blair has sent her regrets and a gift. She's up to her ears trying to get her book written before the baby is born, plus trying to teach Anton the fundamentals of housekeeping and childcare. I told her we understood, and that we'd get together at a later date."

"Becky's still bucking the idea," Zach warned. "Her dress is ready, but she insists she doesn't want to take part in the wedding."

"Then we'll have to be satisfied with one flower girl

instead of two," Kelly replied with an inward sigh. "I only suggested it in the first place so she wouldn't feel excluded. We've still got Syd, and little Seth as ring bearer."

"I still say he's mighty young to be a ring bearer," Zach contended. "He only learned to walk a few months ago, and he'll probably fall half a dozen times before he gets to me. Which is why I intend to have Gavin keep your ring in his pocket, and let Seth carry a fake. I suggest you do likewise, or we may have to delay the ceremony to search for it under our guests' feet."

"It will all work out fine, Zach. You'll see. And those little tykes, all dolled up in fancy dress and tux, are going to steal the show. Which will take some of the heat off of us, thank heaven."

"Ah, now I see the method behind your madness. Getting the prewedding jitters, darling?"

"Not yet, but I intend to, big time."

Their wedding day dawned bright and clear, with no rain in the forecast, and a warm front predicted to send the autumn temperature into the mid-seventies by afternoon. It was a perfect fall day, made to order for an outdoor ceremony. Inside the lodge, Kelly was surrounded by a swarm of chattering women. Her mother kept fussing with Kelly's veil. Sydney had stepped on the hem of her dress, which Kathy was now hastily basting back into place. Leah was attempting to remove gum, which the little boy had found stuck to the underside of a chair, from Seth's bowtie. Alita and Beth were trying to get Becky into her dress, despite the girl's continued and loud protests to the contrary. Not even for Alita, her idol, would she relent. Altogether, in Kelly's estimation, they favored a disorganized band of circus performers—primarily clowns.

Alita's patience lasted far longer than Kelly would have

guessed, but they finally gave out with a predictable spate of Spanish curses. "You rotten little *mocosa!*" she exclaimed, throwing her hands in the air. "You stinking spoiled brat!" She shook a lacquered fingernail in Becky's face. "You are too stupid to know when you have it good. Here you are, feeling so sorry for yourself, when I would have given my right arm to have a mother like Kelly. But no, you have to pout and whine and make everyone else as miserable as you!"

Again, she tossed her hands out, as if to wave Becky away like a pesky fly. "Bah! Have you even tried to be friends with Kelly, for your father's sake? I think not. Well, let me tell you something, *chica*. She is my best friend in the whole world, and your dad loves her very much. They are going to be married today, with or without your cooperation, and they are going to be very happy together. The only one who is going to be sorry is you, all because you are too stubborn to see the truth.

"What did you think, Becky? That if you threw enough of a fit, your father would give her up? He'd have to be *loco* to do that. And I'll tell you another thing I'll bet you do not know. If not for Kelly, your father might not be here today. He'd be buried back on that island, with a bullet in him. Kelly is the one who threw herself at him, preventing him from getting himself shot. She put her own life, and that of the baby she carries, in danger to save your precious papa for you. So chew on that news, little girl. Think about it long and hard. Also think how lucky you are that your daddy is home again, and happy, and wanting to give this wonderful woman to you, so you can have a real mama again, a real family with brothers and sisters."

"Alita," Kelly interrupted. "That gun wasn't e—"

Alita pointed that fingernail-cum-dagger at Kelly. "You hush! I am speaking to Becky," she commanded sharply.

She turned back to Becky, who was staring up at her in mute stupification. "It seems to me you have two choices, *niña*. You can either go on being a brat, or you can make the best of things and be nice. Which do you think would make your papa most pleased with you?"

When Alita finally paused, Becky replied in a shaky whisper, "Being nice."

Alita nodded curtly. "That is correct. Now, if you truly want to make him happy, you will get your sweet tush into that dress, pull in that lip you are about to step on, and put a smile on your face. No more pouting, no more sniveling, no more nastiness. Let that be your wedding gift to your father and Kelly on this, their special day. It will be better than any present you could buy for them, especially if you keep being pleasant, and really try hard to put your jealousy aside. Not only that, it will make me, and all of us, very proud of you."

From that point, the wedding progressed smoothly. Becky was nominally pleasant, which was more than Zach had expected. Syd and Seth were everybody's darlings, even when Seth tripped halfway down the aisle and put up such a wail that his Gramma Sarah had to rescue him and hold him on her lap through the remainder of the ceremony. Kelly was a vision of loveliness, taking Zach's breath away as she approached him in her antique white gown, with her hair unbound and flowing down her back like a second veil.

The reception afterward was an odd blend of Jewish and Christian revelry, and everyone seemed to have a grand time. They toasted the bride and groom, stuffed themselves on a variety of delicious foods, and danced long into the night to the eclectic mix of music the band provided.

The newlyweds took their departure earlier in the evening, after the traditional tossing of the bridal bouquet and garter, seeking blessed solitude in a suite at a seaside hotel. As Zach rubbed Kelly's aching feet, she declared with a sigh, "It was lovely, but I never want to have to go through that again! I'm so tired, I feel as if I've been beat with a stick!"

Zach responded by sticking her toe into his mouth and suckling it, which immediately brought Kelly bolt upright, with a high-pitched squeal. "You devil!" she shrieked, laughing. "You know that always sets me off!"

"Like fireworks on the Fourth of July," he replied with a roguish grin. "Now that you've got your second wind, how about some fireworks of our own, Mrs. Goldstein?"

"Kelly Goldstein," she mused with a dreamy smile. "I do love the sound of my new name, not to mention the man who gave it to me."

"You'd better," he told her fervently, reaching for her hand and kissing the finger that now bore his ring. "It and I are going to be yours for a long, long time."

Epilogue

Two years later—Spice Island

Kelly closed the bedroom door, snapped the lock, and smiled at Zach, who was lying on the bed waiting for her. "That's it. The kids are in bed, and I'm all yours until morning."

Zach returned her smile, and patted the space next to him. "Then come here, sweetheart, and let's make every minute count. God knows, with four children running about underfoot, especially the twins, we deserve a little time to ourselves when we can steal it."

Sure enough, just as Kelly had warned, their "baby" turned out to be a pair of boys. Aaron and Adam were now a year and a half old, and into everything that wasn't tied down or hung out of their reach. But Becky really was good about helping to watch her baby brothers, when she wasn't busy with her schoolwork, which she did via a computer-linked classroom similar to the school of the air used by students in Australia. Then there was Sydney, now four years old and still full of mischief. Her only blood relative, her mother's sister, had entered a convent and therefore hadn't been able to take Sydney. Sister Agnes had heartily approved of Zach and Kelly adopting the little girl, and tried to visit the child every few months or so.

Kelly kicked off her shoes, and flopped onto the bed, fully clothed. Zach automatically leaned over and began undressing her, slowly revealing the delights that awaited him.

"The grand opening of the resort went well, don't you think?" Kelly commented lazily.

"Thanks to you and your idea of holding a memorial service for Frazer and the crash victims, we're booked solid," Zach said. "And inviting the President to be part of it was a stroke of genius." He swirled his tongue into her naval, and chuckled as she gave a wild lurch. "Ah, another ticklish spot to add to my repertoire. This just keeps getting better and better."

"Speaking of repertoires, Alita was in excellent form this evening. I've never heard her sing with so much feeling."

"Maybe seeing Gavin again inspired her," Zach suggested. "I can't believe he's already been married and divorced."

"I can't believe he's actually studying to become a lawyer!" Kelly exclaimed, her tone that of someone betrayed. "After Brad, I'm really sort of soured on them, but Gavin claims he's going to be one of the 'good guys.' I can only hope so."

"He will be, I'm sure. It's Blair and the transformation in her that has me in shock. Having a bestseller made into an Oscar-nominated movie has really given her a wealth of self-confidence. Poor Anton can barely hold his own with her now."

"Yes, the shoe certainly is on the other foot in that

household," Kelly agreed. "And high time, too. I hope the movie wins this year's Oscars. At least one for Blair and her film script, and another for Alita as best actress. And I'm not just saying that because they're our friends. It is an excellent film."

They'd been invited to the premiere, and had left Pete in charge of continued construction on the resort while they extended their trip to the U.S. mainland to visit both sets of relatives. Pete, Leah, and Seth were now permanent residents of Spice Island—so dubbed by Becky upon smelling the vanilla, ginger, and multitude of fragrant fruits and flowers growing in such abundance. The other family members had taken to reserving their vacations and holidays for extended visits to the island, and would probably do so more frequently now that the resort was open for business.

It had been a long time coming, and it wasn't entirely complete as yet. Zach still wanted to build several private bungalows to complement the main villa, and a group of industrious Polynesians had just begun work on an authentic thatch-hut community along one of the beaches. It promised to be a great tourist draw, with the villagers selling their handmade arts and crafts. The small landing strip along the west coast had been one of the first projects to be initiated, essential for bringing in goods and building materials. However, some items and guests still arrived the old way, by ferrying in on flat-bottomed rafts from ships docked beyond the reefs. The tourists from the cruise liners seemed to get a kick out of arriving in that fashion, claiming it added that special island flavor to their trip.

Fortunately, the geohydrological report Zach had ordered before beginning construction had sited a large underground freshwater spring, the hidden origin of the pool. Without this, or some other source sufficient to sustain a small community, they would have had to abandon the notion of creating a resort on the island. Nor would they have been able to do it if the mining project had proved unprofitable. They'd hit a large vein of rich ore, which extended out onto the ocean floor. And they wouldn't have been able to purchase the island at all, if Kelly hadn't sold her two U.S. salons and presented the proceeds to Zach in the form of a bridal dowry, to use as their down payment on the bank note.

Zach had, at first, been adamant against using her funds, but Kelly had been even more stubborn. "It's going to be my island, too, Zach, and I want to contribute my fair share," she argued. "And you can't reject my dowry, after all, without rejecting me as well."

In the end, he'd relented, and it had all gone splendidly. So well, in fact, that Gavin's share would allow him to start his own law firm immediately upon graduating and passing the bar exam. And Blair's portion, along with the royalties from the book and film, had ensured she would never have to clip coupons or shop for her children's clothes at garage sales again, unless she wanted to do so. As for Alita, if she never made another album or movie again—which she would, of course—she'd always be able to afford her caviar and champagne and those outrageously flamboyant costumes she so adored.

For Zach and Kelly, it meant the resort, combined with Kelly's newest health club/boutique, and raising their family on the island where they'd first fallen in love—far from the fast-paced, crime-ridden environment beyond their shores. This time they weren't totally isolated, as they had been before, and had the added convenience of indoor plumbing, which made their tropical paradise all the more pleasurable. After spending a fortune to tap into the undersea cables, they had electricity, telephone, and fax service, instant communication with the outside world—a world just a few hours away by plane, or a couple of days by boat, in case Kelly got the urge to immerse herself in a major shopping binge at an honest-to-goodness mall.

For now, however, they were perfectly content with their semi-isolation, and the only thing Kelly wanted to immerse herself in at the moment was her private whirlpool tub, built for two. "What do you say, Zach? Do you feel like romping in the spa with me?"

He grinned at her. "Sure, but no more of that wimpy mermaid/merman stuff. This time I want to be an octopus on the attack."

She chortled, tugging at the dark fur on his chest. "Aren't you always?" she joked. "From the beginning it's seemed to me you've had more than the normal quota of arms, not to mention Russian hands and Roman fingers."

"It's the only way I can combat that glib tongue of yours," he countered, scooping her off the bed and heading toward the spa. He bent his head to lap at her bare breast. "Ah, I have the twins to thank for these. They were nice before, but now they're spectacular. Lady, you really can fill out a sarong!"

Minutes later, they were submerged up to their necks in soothing, swirling water, letting the jets pulsate pleasantly against their bodies. Zach tugged Kelly onto his lap. "Put your arms around my neck," he instructed. "I want to try something. It's occurred to me that these jets are like liquid vibrators. I want to see if they have the same affect."

"Zach! You're incorrigible!" As he twisted her around, aiming for a more advantageous angle, she objected weakly, "Are you deliberately trying to drown me?" Followed by, "Holy Moses, Zach! I'm not double-jointed." Then, on a sharply indrawn hiss, "Oh, my! Oh, God! Oh, Zach!"

Things were just getting really interesting when the tub-side phone rang. "Let it ring," Zach murmured past the nipple now clasped lightly between his teeth.

Kelly was already fumbling for the connect button. "I can't. It might be something important."

It was, in an oblique sort of way. Alita's voice came over the speaker phone. "Gavin and I were just talking over old times, and I suddenly remembered something strange I forgot to tell you and Zach. Last month, when I was in L.A. promoting the movie, I saw a man who reminded me very strongly of Earl, but this guy had a beard. I only caught a quick glimpse of him through the limousine window, but it was enough to give me the willies."

"It couldn't have been him, Alita," Zach stated flatly. "He's dead."

"It was probably just someone who looked a lot like him," Kelly put in.

"Maybe, but one thing really struck me odd. He only had one arm. The other one was missing from the elbow down. Like maybe he'd lost it in an accident of some sort— or had it bitten off by a shark. Or perhaps even got it ripped off, like Earl might have, struggling to stay aboard the raft in that storm, or if those handcuffs got hung up on something."

Kelly's eyes widened, meeting Zach's in mutual query. After a moment of thought, Zach said, "Thanks for telling us, Alita, but even if it was Earl, which I seriously doubt, I don't think any of us have anything to worry about. He'd still be a fugitive from the law, and lying low. He'd avoid us, knowing we might recognize him. He certainly wouldn't want us to know he was still alive."

"Oh. I was afraid he might do just the opposite, and come after us because we could identify him," Alita explained. "It had me really worried."

"All for nothing, most likely," Gavin added, having appropriated Alita's phone. "I told her she was being silly, but I guess she needed to hear it from someone else, or she wasn't going to be satisfied. Sorry if we disturbed you folks. See you in the morning."

After Gavin had hung up, Kelly said with a shiver, "Lord! That's enough to give a person the heebie-jeebies, isn't it? A one-armed man who looks like Earl? Do you suppose it's remotely possible that it truly is him?"

"I think you and Alita are getting worked up over nothing. She's a very high-strung, emotional woman with an overactive imagination."

"I wouldn't criticize someone else's imagination after the trick you just pulled with those jets, fella," Kelly rebutted. "Only you, with your twisted, inventive mind, could come up with something that bizarre."

Zach shot her a satisfied, if slightly pompous look. "It worked, didn't it? Or were you just screaming to high heaven to exercise your vocal chords?" He pulled her close, and began nibbling on her ear lobe. "Now, where were we before we were so rudely interrupted?"

Kelly's hand delved below the water in search of him. "Right about here, if I recall correctly," she murmured.

A short while later, Zach was sheathed within her satin-smooth body, as they created tidal waves in the spa and each other. They'd just reached that rapturous peak, and had begun their tumbling descent, when the telephone rang again.

"Damn, Sam! Don't answer it," he grated though climax-clenched teeth.

The phone continued to ring, until Kelly could stand it no longer. This time, it was Blair, who blurted excitedly, "The Baldwin sisters!"

Kelly frowned in confusion. "Pardon me?"

Zach, whose moment of ecstasy had been cut short, was feeling much less polite. "What the devil are you blathering about, Blair?"

"Those two old women on 'The Waltons.' Remember

when we were trying to identify all the characters from the show, and couldn't think of what they were called? Well, I finally, just this minute, remembered their names. They're Miss Emily and Miss Mamie Baldwin," she announced proudly.

"I'm thrilled for you," Zach grumbled, as Kelly started to giggle. "We'll issue you an extra banana at breakfast, as an award. Now, if you don't mind terrible, I was in the middle of making love to my wife."

"Oops! Sorry!" Blair said in an apologetic tone, and promptly disconnected.

"Hell's bells!" Zach declared disgustedly, pulling the plug on the phone. "We finally got the kids trained not to come barging in on us, and now we've got a bunch of idiot adults bugging the heck out of us! Is there no end to it?"

From the tree outside the open window, a shrill voice called out, "Hell's bells! Damn Sam! Awk!"

Zach sank into the tub with a persecuted groan. "Blast you, Fricassee!"

Kelly, convulsed with gales of laughter, choked out, "I hear parrots can live to be a hundred years old. How long do you think Frick has got yet?"

"Only until I can catch his feathered butt and pop it into a stew pot," Zach proclaimed. "Then—maybe—with immense luck, we'll finally stand a chance of making love without anyone or anything intruding on our privacy at the most intimate and inopportune moments!"

"Don't bet the farm, or the island, on it," she advised him. "Now's probably not the best time to announce this, but I think I'm pregnant again—you virile, randy rascal."

SPINE TINGLING ROMANCE
FROM STELLA CAMERON!

ROMANCE FROM HANNAH HOWELL

MY VALIANT KNIGHT   (0-8217-5186-7, $5.50)

ONLY FOR YOU   (0-8217-4993-5, $4.99)

UNCONQUERED   (0-8217-5417-3, $5.99)

WILD ROSES   (0-8217-5677-X, $5.99)